IELTS雅思口說 最後9堂課

劍橋台北語文中心資深講師
Joshua Morgandale——著

留嘉伶——譯

眾文圖書股份有限公司

Author's Words

Language learning is like going on a long journey. Many people focus only on the goal of becoming completely fluent in their new language. However, just like going on a long trip, it is important to enjoy and learn from the experiences you will have on your way to your destination.

The best way to learn a language is to create an environment where you can use your language skills. Try every day to Read the news. Listen to TV programmes or movies. Speak to people using your new language. Write in a journal regularly in your new language about your experiences.

It is also important to have the correct view of making mistakes. No one can use a new language they are learning perfectly. Each time you make a mistake and someone corrects you, you will learn the right way to say or write something. Afterwards you will not forget it. So do not be afraid to make mistakes.

It is my hope that this book will help you on your journey of improving your English and achieving the IELTS score that you want.

作者的話

學習語言就像是場漫長之旅。許多人在學語言時，只專注在說出一口流利外語。不過就跟長途旅行一樣，我們學語言時應該要樂在其中，並在過程中吸取經驗。

學習一門語言的最佳方法，就是創造一個能夠運用語言技巧的環境。試著每天閱讀新聞、聆聽電視節目或電影、利用新語言和別人說話，或定期用新語言書寫日誌，記錄你的經驗。

我們也應該要以正確態度來面對失誤，因為沒有人能夠完美使用正在學習的新語言。每一次別人指正你的錯誤後，你都能夠從中學到正確的用法，之後便不會再忘記。所以不要害怕犯錯。

我希望，這本書能在你提升英文的旅途中派上用場，並且幫助你考到理想的雅思分數。

About the Author

Joshua holds a degree in education from the University of Saint Petersburg. He has worked as a language teacher for 20 years and has been teaching IELTS for 12 years. He has taught English and Chinese in the United States, South America, and several countries throughout Asia.

關於作者

Joshua 畢業於 University of Saint Petersburg，主修教育學，從事語言教學工作至今已有 20 年。過去 12 年，主要以教授 IELTS 課程為主，並在美國、南美洲及幾個亞洲國家教授過英文及中文。

How to Use this Book

如何使用本書

This book is designed for self-study and can also be used with a conversation partner. You and your partner can practice speaking about the topics and use the vocabulary and grammar patterns to make your speech more natural and fluent.

本書專為自學者所設計，也可以與對話搭檔一同使用。可以和搭檔練習書中各個主題，並且透過使用單字及句型結構，讓你的口說更加自然、流暢。

This book can be used by anyone who is preparing to take the IELTS exam. The book features detailed information regarding the most common mistakes that students make when taking the IELTS exam. In addition, the book explains the most common grammar-, vocabulary-, and logic-based errors made on the speaking exam and includes strategies and principles to overcome common obstacles that prevent students from obtaining high scores.

本書適用於所有準備參加雅思考試的人，內容集結了最常見的雅思考試錯誤。另外，也會說明考生在口說測驗中，最常犯下的文法、單字及邏輯錯誤，並且提供克服答題障礙所需的策略及原則，幫助考生取得理想的高分。

This book begins with a general overview of the speaking test and introduces some basic strategies that will be consistently employed throughout the rest of the book. The book features some of the most common topics that appear on the IELTS exam. There are sample answers for the three parts of the speaking test in each of the lessons, and strategies are provided to help you to give examples and reasons to make your answers sound more detailed and intellectual. In addition, the sample answers feature highlighted key vocabulary and fixed expressions to help you learn how to use them and improve your fluency.

本書在一開始提供了口說測驗的簡介以及答題策略，這些策略會運用於全書的範例答題上。書中收錄雅思口試最常見的各大主題。每堂課都包含口說測驗中三部分的答題示範，同時附上答題策略，幫助你提出例子和理由，使你的回答更加完整有深度。另外，答案中的關鍵單字及常見的英文用法也會以顏色標示，幫助你加強口說流利度。

Preparing for the IELTS exam can be challenging, but you can succeed! You are advised to schedule regular time slots for study instead of studying once a week for many hours. If you practise speaking several times a week, you will become more confident and get more used to using English logic and grammar. Eventually, you will be able to give well-organized answers that feature correct grammar and advanced vocabulary.

準備雅思考試是很有挑戰性的，但是你一定做得到！建議考生最好安排規律的讀書時間，而不是一週只選一天讀好幾個小時。如果一週能練習幾次口說，你就會變得愈來愈有自信，對英文的邏輯與文法也會愈來愈熟悉。最後，你就能使用恰當的文法和高階單字，說出有條有理的答案。

With the help of this book, you will get the score you want and achieve your goals!

有了這本書的幫助，你一定能取得理想分數，並且達成目標！

Speaking Test Basics 口說測驗簡介

Overview

Part 1

4-5 minutes. Most of the questions are about yourself, such as your work, education, hobbies, and background.

Part 2

You will be given a card with a topic, a pencil, and some paper. You will have 1 minute to prepare your answer and then speak about the topic for 1 to 2 minutes.

Part 3

4-5 minutes. You will be asked a wide range of questions that focus on your opinions, the pros and cons of certain issues, how a situation has changed over time, and how a situation may develop in the future.

概述

第一部分

四至五分鐘。此部分問題，大多是問與你自身有關的問題，例如你的職業、學歷、嗜好及家庭背景。

第二部分

你會拿到一張題目卡，還有鉛筆和紙張。你有一分鐘的時間可以準備答案，並且針對該題目進行一至兩分鐘的演說。

第三部分

四至五分鐘。考官會要求你針對各式各樣的議題提出看法；說明其優劣是否會隨著時間出現變化，或是未來將會如何發展等。

Grading Criteria

You will be graded in the following four areas. Here are some questions to ask yourself:

1. **Fluency and Coherence:** Are you able to speak at a natural pace without a lot of pausing and

評分標準

考官會根據以下四大項目來評分。可以問問自己下列問題：

流暢度及連貫性：你是否能用自然的語速說話，沒有太多的停頓

hesitation? Are your answers developed logically?

與猶豫？你的答案是否具有邏輯？

2. **Vocabulary:** Do you use a wide variety of academic words, or do you tend to repeat the same basic words for each topic that you are asked about? Do you use the most appropriate words for the topic that you are discussing?

單字：你是否會用各種比較進階的單字，且不會在回答每個問題時，一直重複使用一樣的基本單字？你是否能針對所談論的議題使用最適切的單字？

3. **Grammar:** Do you use both short sentence structures and longer, more complicated structures correctly? Do you always use the correct verb tenses?

文法：你是否能正確說出結構簡單的短句及複雜的長句？你是否會正確使用時態？

4. **Pronunciation:** Are you able to be understood? When you use proper nouns and technical terms, are they understood the first time you say them? Do you apply emphasis in all the appropriate places?

發音：考官能聽懂你說的話嗎？在說出專有名詞及術語時，考官能夠一聽就懂嗎？你的重音是否都落在了正確的位置？

Basic Strategies 答題基本策略

Part 1 第一部分

Do not give one-word answers or short one-sentence answers. Provide interesting details or reasons to support your answers.

不要只回答一個單字或是一個短句，而是針對你的答案提供一些有趣的細節或理由。

Example of a typical Part 1 Question

第一部分常見問題範例

Bad example

不好的回答

Examiner: Do you have any job experience?
Candidate: I am sales.

考官：你有任何工作經驗嗎？
考生：我是業務。

The candidate's answer is too short and grammatically incorrect.

考生的答案過短，句子文法也不正確。

Better example

較佳的回答

Examiner: Do you have any job experience?
Candidate: Yes. For the past 5 years, I have been working in the sales department of a technology company. I enjoy my job because I have a flexible schedule.

考官：你有任何工作經驗嗎？
考生：有。過去五年，我任職於一間科技公司的業務部門。我很熱愛這份工作，因為工作時間很有彈性。

The candidate uses correct vocabulary and grammar and gives details about their job and a reason that they enjoy their work.

考生使用了正確的單字及文法，並針對他的工作提供了細節，以及他熱愛這份工作的原因。

Part 2

第二部分

Think of this part as telling a story or sharing an experience with a friend. Use the minute that you have to prepare your answer wisely. DO NOT write out your answer in complete sentences. You do not have enough time to do this.

把這個部分當成是在說故事，或當成是在與朋友分享經驗。利用這一分鐘的時間，好好準備你的答案。切勿寫下完整答案，因為一定沒有足夠時間讓你寫出完整答案。

Make a brief outline using short phrases or key words to remind you of your main points. Put these words and phrases in a logical order. Finally, decide which of the points listed on the card you will spend the most time talking about and for which ones you will provide the most detail.

請利用短短幾個字或關鍵字，規畫簡短大綱，提醒自己在答案中需要提到的重點，並以符合邏輯的順序列出來。最後，針對題目卡上的要點，決定哪一點要花最多時間講述、提供最多細節。

Example of a typical Part 2 Topic Card

第二部分常見題目卡範例

Describe a memorable vacation you have been on.

You should say:
❶ where you went
❷ how you travelled there
❸ what you did there
❹ and explain why it was memorable.

描述一次令你難忘的度假。

應該提到：
❶ 你去了哪裡
❷ 怎麼去的
❸ 你做了些什麼
❹ 說明為什麼難忘。

Here is how a possible outline of your answer could be arranged:

可以按照如以下大綱來規畫答案：

❶ Krabi, Thailand—first trip abroad
❷ airplane, direct flight, 4 hours
❸ water sports—diving/snorkelling, clear water, a lot of fish and coral, shopping—cheap prices for

❶ 泰國喀比——首次出國
❷ 飛機、直飛、四個小時
❸ 水上活動——潛水／浮潛、乾淨海水、許多魚和珊瑚；購

clothes, great food—variety of restaurants

物——便宜服飾；美食——各式各樣的餐廳

❹ first time in another country, new experiences, very relaxing, good times with my friends

❹ 第一次出國、全新體驗、非常放鬆、跟朋友一起度過的美好時光

After using keywords for each of the four points on the card, the candidate will likely be able to speak for 2 minutes and give a very logical answer.

只要針對題目的四項要點，用以上關鍵字講述答案，考生就能說滿兩分鐘，給出合乎邏輯的答案。

Part 3

第三部分

Give your answer a clear direction. Many candidates make the mistake of talking too much and giving too many reasons or examples. The results are that your answer becomes difficult to understand and that you may speak off topic.

第三部分的答案要有明確方向。許多考生的常見錯誤就是說得太多，且提供了太多理由或例子，導致答案難以理解甚至離題。

Example of a Three-Step Answer

三步驟答題示範

1. Clearly and directly answer the question in your FIRST sentence.
2. Give a specific, detailed example to support your answer.
3. Briefly conclude your comment in just one sentence.

1. 在第一句話就清楚並直接了當回答問題。
2. 提供明確且詳細的例子來支持你的答案。
3. 用一個句子簡短總結你的論點。

These 3 steps can usually be completed in just under a minute.

使用這三個步驟答題，通常一分鐘以內可以講完。

Example of a typical Part 3 Question

第三部分常見問題範例

How has education changed in your country over the past few decades?

過去幾十年來，教育制度在你的國家有什麼改變？

A

❶ I think there are some very significant differences in education now compared with when my parents were in school.

❷ When my parents were young, education mainly emphasised manufacturing and agriculture because most people worked in these fields back then. However, over the last 20 to 30 years, developments in technology have greatly influenced how we are educated. Now, from a very young age, students learn how to use computers and access many different types of information. This type of education is geared towards helping young people find jobs using these skills.

❸ In summary, I truly feel that education is radically different today than how it was a few decades ago.

❶ 我認為現在的教育，跟我父母還在讀書時相比，有一些蠻大的差異。

❷ 在我父母年輕時，教育主要著重於製造業和農業，因為那是當年多數人從事的職業。不過，科技在過去 20、30 年來的發展，大幅影響了我們所受的教育。現在的學生，從很小開始就要學習使用電腦，並且接觸各式各樣的資訊，這樣的教育，都是為了幫助年輕人在未來能利用這些技巧求職。

❸ 總之，我真心認為現今的教育，跟幾十年前相比差異很大。

What should you do if you do not understand a question the examiner asks?

如果聽不懂考官的問題，該怎麼做？

Imagine you have been asked this question:

想像一下考官問了你以下這個問題：

Q **Do you think parents in different cultures have different ways of disciplining their children?**

你認為不同文化中的家長，管教小孩的方式會有不同嗎？

What do you do if you do not understand the word 'disciplining'?

如果聽不懂 disciplining（管教）這個字，該怎麼辦？

You could ask:

你可以這樣問：

'Could you **REPEAT** the question?'

「能否請你**重複**問題？」

However, if you do this, the examiner will likely ask the question again in the same way, using the same words. Therefore, if you did not understand the question the first time, you probably will not understand it the second time.

但要是這樣問，考官只會用同樣的句子重述問題。因此如果你第一次就聽不懂問題了，第二次可能依然還是不會明白。

Instead, try asking this question:

試試看這樣問：

'Could you **REPHRASE** the question?'

「能否請你**重述**這個問題？」

This time, the examiner is likely to use different words. For example, they might say:

這樣一來，考官可能會使用不同的字來問問題。例如他可能會這樣問：

Do you think parents in other countries use different methods to punish or educate their children?

你認為不同國家的家長，會以不同的方式來懲罰或教育他們的孩子嗎？

In this context, the words 'punish' and 'educate' are similar in meaning to 'discipline'.

在這個句子中，punish（懲罰）和 educate（教育）的意思就類似於 discipline（管教）。

Another strategy is to ask for the meaning of the word that you do not understand. For example, you could ask:

另一個策略是，直接詢問考官你聽不懂的單字意思。例如你可以這樣問：

'What do you mean by "disciplining"?'

「disciplining 是什麼意思？」

If you ask this question in this way, the examiner is likely to explain what this specific word means.

如果你這樣問，考官就可能會向你解釋這個單字的意思。

CONTENTS

目 錄

Additional Tips and Resources 補充技巧及資料

LESSON 1

Free Time

閒暇時間

LESSON 1

Free Time 閒暇時間

Part 1 Questions 第一部分 問題

🔊 1-01

Q01 What do you enjoy doing in your free time?

你閒暇時間喜歡做些什麼？

Strategy

Do not give a one word answer. Give some details regarding your favourite recreational activities to make your answer more complete.

策略

不要只回答一個單字。針對你最喜歡的娛樂活動提供一些細節，讓你的答案更加完整。

A Every Friday night, I enjoy watching a movie at home on Netflix. This activity helps me to unwind after a long week at work.

每週五晚上，我喜歡在家看 Netflix 上的電影。這有助於我在漫長的一週工作後放鬆身心。

🔊 1-02

Q02 What do you enjoy doing with your friends?

你喜歡跟朋友們做些什麼？

Strategy

Avoid common grammar mistakes such as 'I like to jogging'. Use 'go + V-ing' to describe an activity.

策略

避免出現常見的文法錯誤，例如 I like to jogging.。可用〈go + V-ing〉來說明所從事的活動。

A I like to go jogging with my friends *at the weekend. We are currently preparing to participate in a marathon. We usually start very early in the morning before the weather

我喜歡在週末跟朋友去慢跑，我們正準備要參加一場馬拉松。通常我們一大早就會出門，以免天氣變得太熱。

gets too hot.

* at the weekend ㊟ on the weekend ㊤

🔊 1-03

03 Do you think you have more free time now than you did in the past?

你覺得自己的休閒時間比從前多嗎？

Strategy

You could directly answer this question with either a 'yes' or a 'no' and then provide a reason for your answer.

策略

可以直接回答「是」或「否」，並針對你的答案提供理由。

A Definitely not. Since I started working, I have been so busy that I haven't been able to meet my friends like I was before. Now, I have time only at weekends.

絕對沒有。自從開始工作之後，我就一直很忙，不能像從前那樣跟朋友見面。我現在只有週末有空。

🔊 1-04

04 Do you play any sports?

你會什麼運動？

Strategy

A lot of sporting activities are accompanied by specific verbs and vocabulary that are used to describe them. Using these words will help to improve your vocabulary and grammar scores. The Sample Answer below uses basketball-related vocabulary.

策略

有許多運動都有專門的動詞及單字。使用這些字能幫你在單字及文法項目獲得加分。以下範例答案使用了與籃球相關的單字。

A I really enjoy playing basketball. That is, I like to shoot hoops with my friends. I can dribble really fast, and I take a lot of three-point shots. I can't slam dunk, though.

我非常喜歡打籃球，我喜歡跟朋友一起打。我運球的速度很快，也很會投三分球，不過我不會灌籃。

1-05

Q05 Do you enjoy using a computer in your spare time?

你喜歡在閒暇時間使用電腦嗎？

Strategy

As with the previous question, there is a lot of vocabulary specific to technology. Use computer- or internet-related vocabulary in your answer to improve your vocabulary score.

策略

跟上個問題一樣，科技領域也有不少專門用字。回答時使用電腦或網路的相關字，能提高單字項目的分數。

A I enjoy surfing the internet and looking up (searching for) information. In addition, I am a blogger; I blog about my daily experiences.

我很喜歡上網和查找資料。此外，我還是一名部落客，我會在部落格記錄我的每一天。

1-06

Q06 Do you enjoy doing art?

你喜歡從事藝術活動嗎？

Strategy

Art-related vocabulary can be challenging. Reading about different types of art will help you to learn such vocabularies. The Sample Answer below uses art-related vocabulary.

策略

藝術相關的單字可能會有點挑戰性。閱讀不同的藝術類文章能幫助你學習這類單字。本題範例答案使用了藝術相關的單字。

A I like to sketch people and landscapes. I sometimes go to the lake and take my brushes, canvas, and a lot of different pigments to paint the scenery.

我喜歡畫人像和風景素描。我有時候會帶著畫筆、畫布和各種顏料到湖邊畫風景畫。

1-07

Q07 Do you have any unusual hobbies?

你有什麼特殊嗜好嗎？

Strategy

For this type of question, you can describe any unique activity that you have engaged in before.

策略

面對這種問題，你可以描述過去做過的任一特殊活動。

A I once went deep sea fishing with my uncle, and I really enjoyed the experience. We went out into the ocean on a boat, and I learned how to use several types of bait to attract various types of fish.

我曾經和叔叔去深海釣魚，我非常享受那一次的經驗。我們乘著一艘船出海，我學到如何使用不同的魚餌來吸引不同的魚類。

1-08

Q08 Have your hobbies changed as you have gotten older?

隨著年齡增長，你的嗜好有改變嗎？

Strategy

Contrast your childhood hobbies with what you enjoy doing now. Remember to use appropriate verb tenses.

策略

將你童年和現在的嗜好進行比較，記得使用正確的時態。

A My interests have changed over the years. When I was young, I spent a lot of time at home, playing with toys or drawing. Now, I prefer outdoor activities, such as hiking and jogging.

我的興趣在這幾年來有所改變。小的時候，我花很多時間待在家玩玩具或畫畫，現在我更喜歡戶外活動，例如健行或慢跑。

1-09

Q09 How old were you when you learned how to ride a bike?

你在幾歲時學會騎腳踏車？

Strategy

Give your own personal experience, and provide details. Remember to use past tense verbs.

策略

詳述你的個人經驗，記得使用過去式。

A I think I was about 7 years old when I learned how to ride a bike. My dad took me to a park near the river because it was very flat there, so it would be easy for me to keep my balance. I still enjoy riding bikes even today.

我想我是在七歲時學會騎腳踏車的。我爸帶我到河邊的一座公園，因為那裡很平坦，比較能夠保持平衡。即使到現在，我還是很喜歡騎腳踏車。

🔈 1-10

Q10 Do you enjoy shopping in your free time?

你喜歡在閒暇時間逛街嗎？

Strategy

Describe your personal shopping habits. If you enjoy shopping, you can use words like 'often' or 'usually' + a present tense verb.

策略

描述你的購物習慣，如果你喜歡逛街，可以使用〈often（經常）/ usually（通常）+ 現在式動詞〉來回答。

A Shopping is one of my favourite activities. I often go shopping in the evenings with my friends. We usually buy clothes from department stores.

逛街是我最喜歡的消遣之一。我很常在晚上和朋友去逛街，我們通常會在百貨公司買衣服。

Part 2 Questions
第二部分 問題

As discussed in the 'Basic Strategies' section of this book, here are some reminders for answering the Part 2 Questions:

正如本書在「答題基本策略」部分所述，以下要點是針對第二部分問題的作答提點：

- Plan your answer;
- Decide which points you will answer briefly;
- Decide which points will require more details;
- Use specialised vocabulary; and
- Try to give specific examples or experiences in your answer.

- 規畫你的答案
- 決定哪些問題要簡短回答
- 決定哪些問題要提供細節
- 使用專門用字
- 盡量在答案中給予實際例子或引述經驗。

1-11

01 **Describe a popular sport in your country.**

描述一項在你國家的熱門運動。

You should say:

❶ what it is
❷ where it is played
❸ what equipment is used
❹ and explain why people enjoy this activity.

應該提到：

❶ 是什麼運動
❷ 在哪裡進行
❸ 會使用哪些設備
❹ 說明人們為何喜歡這項運動。

❶ Even though a lot of people haven't heard of it, squash is gaining popularity in this country.

❶ 雖然聽過壁球的人不多，但該運動在我的國家愈來愈受歡迎。

❷ This sport is originally from the UK. Recently, I have seen increasing numbers of sports centres in my local area including squash courts in their lists of facilities. Unlike tennis, squash is played on an indoor court.

❷ 這項運動起源於英國。最近我觀察到我住的這一帶有愈來愈多運動中心，在設施清單中加入了壁球場。壁球不像網球，它是在室內場地進行。

❸ Squash involves hitting a small, black rubber ball against four walls. The ball is smaller and harder than a tennis ball, and there is no net. All you need to play is a racket, a ball, and a good pair of shoes.

❸ 壁球是一種對著四面牆擊打一顆黑色橡膠小球的運動，球體比網球更小、更硬，而且沒有網子。只需要一個球拍、一顆球，及一雙好球鞋，就可以打壁球。

❹ Since squash is an indoor sport, it can be played year round and is not dependent on the weather. This is something that a lot of people like about the sport. In addition, it is fast-paced, so it is good cardio exercise. You really work up a sweat while playing. I usually play once a week with four friends. Because squash is becoming more popular, it is a good idea to reserve court time early before all the time slots fill up.

❹ 由於這是一項室內運動，一年四季都能進行，不必仰賴天氣，這是許多人喜歡這項運動的原因。此外，它的節奏也很快，所以是很好的有氧運動，真的會打到滿頭大汗。我通常一週會跟四個朋友一起打一次。因為壁球愈來愈受歡迎，得提早預約球場時間，否則所有時段都會被約滿。

Analysis

Specialised vocabulary for this hobby was used throughout the Sample Answer above. Because a lot of people may be unfamiliar with squash, contrasts to tennis are given in the second and third points. This contrasting technique is used to explain the basic concepts and rules of squash.

分析

以上範例答案使用了不少該項運動的專門用字。由於很多人可能不熟悉這項運動，因此答案在第二及第三點都將壁球與網球進行了比較，藉此解釋這項運動的基本觀念和規則。

1-12

Q02 Describe a popular game (e.g., an electronic game or a board game).

描述一項熱門遊戲（如電動、桌遊）。

You should say:

❶ what it is
❷ where it is played
❸ what is needed to play it
❹ and explain why it is so popular.

應該提到：

❶ 是什麼遊戲
❷ 在哪裡玩
❸ 玩時需要用到什麼
❹ 說明該遊戲為何受歡迎。

A

❶ When I was young, I was addicted to video games. Every day after school, I would play *Super Mario Brothers*. Even though that was more than 30 years ago, *Super Mario Brothers* is still a very popular game series today.

❶ 我年輕時非常沉迷於電動，每天放學後都會玩《超級瑪利歐兄弟》。雖然是 30 多年前的遊戲，該遊戲至今還是非常熱門的系列。

❷ I would play at home or at my friend's house. We would usually play before we started our homework. Then, after I finished my homework, I would continue playing. Sometimes, I would play until late at night.

❷ 我會在家或是去朋友家玩。我們通常會先玩一下再開始寫作業。我寫完作業後就會繼續玩，有時候還會玩到深夜。

❸ At that time, all a person needed was a television, a game console, a game cartridge, and a controller. Nowadays, the situation is very different. Now, people can play games any time or anywhere on their mobile devices.

❸ 當年的人需要一台電視、一台遊戲機、一個遊戲卡匣和遊戲手把才能玩電動。這跟現在的情況相去甚遠，現在的人隨時隨地都能在行動裝置上玩遊戲。

❹ I think the Mario games are so popular because they have a very simple premise. That is, the story is very simple: Your goal is to save the princess. In addition, each world you have to play through has different

❹ 我覺得「瑪利歐」遊戲之所以能大受歡迎，是因為遊戲的背景設定非常簡單；就是它的故事相當簡明，你的目標就是拯救公主。此外，在每個遊戲世

environments, and there are puzzles that you have to solve. My favourite game in this series is *Super Mario Brothers 3*. I remember playing it every day during my summer vacation. It was the first game to introduce new environments or 'worlds' in the series. For example, there was a water world and a desert world. All these games are a lot of fun to play. Therefore, I think people will still be playing Mario games for generations to come.

界裡都要通過不同關卡，還必須解開謎題。該系列遊戲中，我最喜歡的是《超級瑪利歐兄弟 3》，我還記得我暑假每天都在玩。那是整個系列當中第一款引入不同遊戲環境或「世界」的遊戲，像是水底世界和沙漠世界。所有遊戲玩起來都非常有趣，因此我認為未來世代的人也會繼續玩「瑪利歐」遊戲。

Analysis

The Sample Answer above contrasts how video games were played 30 years ago with how they are played now. In point 3, specific details are given about the types of electronic equipment needed to play games then and now. In your answer, you do not need to choose a game that is complicated or difficult to describe. The *Super Mario Brothers* games are games that most people have played before, so they are easy to describe.

分析

此範例答案對比了 30 年前和現在玩電動的方式，第三點詳細說明了過去和現在玩遊戲所需要的電子設備。考生不需要選太複雜或難以描述的遊戲，《超級瑪利歐兄弟》是多數人都曾玩過的遊戲，所以很容易描述。

🔊 1-13

Q03 Describe a popular shopping centre.

描述一處熱門的購物中心。

You should say:

❶ what it is
❷ where it is
❸ what can be bought there
❹ and explain why it is so popular.

應該提到：

❶ 是什麼樣的購物中心
❷ 該購物中心在哪裡
❸ 可以在那裡買到什麼
❹ 說明該中心為何受歡迎。

A

❶ Just a few miles away from downtown ❷ Pattaya is a traditional market that caters to international tourists.

❸ This market sells a variety of souvenirs that tourists can buy when they go to Thailand. There are small wood carvings of elephants and also toys for children. Handmade traditional clothing for men and women are available in a variety of colours and sizes. There are also food stalls that sell all manner of exotic cuisines for customers to sample. Finally, there is also a river that runs through the market, with boats that sell fruits and vegetables. This market is just like the traditional floating markets found in many places in Thailand.

❹ One of the reasons I think this market is so popular is its location. It is not too far from several vacation hot spots, and there are regular buses that go to and from it throughout every day. A bus ride to the market from downtown Pattaya takes about 20 minutes, so getting there is very easy and convenient. Another reason for its popularity is that it was designed to allow visitors to experience a very traditional atmosphere. It feels like an authentic Thailand market experience.

❶ 在距離芭達雅市中心的幾哩 ❷ 外，有一座傳統市場能滿足國際觀光客的需求。

❸ 這座市場販售了觀光客到泰國會想買的各種紀念品，舉凡小型的大象木雕，到其他供孩子玩的玩具，還有各式色彩、各種尺碼的手工傳統男女服飾。該市場還有小吃攤，販售各種異國小吃，供顧客品嘗。最後，還有一條河流貫穿這座市場，河裡有船隻在販售蔬果。這座市場就像是泰國許多地方能看見的傳統水上市場。

❹ 我覺得那裡之所以會大受歡迎，原因之一是地點。該處距離好幾個觀光熱點都不遠，而且一整天都固定有巴士往返。從芭達雅市中心搭乘巴士過去大約 20 分鐘，交通非常便利。另一個原因是，這座市場設立的初衷就是為了讓遊客沉浸在傳統氛圍中，感覺就像是在體驗正宗的泰國市場。

Analysis

- In the Sample Answer points 1 and 2 are answered together in just one sentence.
- More details are given in points 3 and 4, which describe the experience of going to the market.

分析

- 範例答案用一個句子回答了第一及第二點。
- 在第三及第四點提供了更多細節，描述到該市場的經驗。

When answering this question, it is best to describe a store or stores that you have been to. This method will help you to describe the things that you saw and experienced while shopping there.

在回答這題時，最好描述你曾親自去過的店家，有助於說明你在那裡購物時的所見所聞。

1-14

Q04 Describe a club or sports team that you have participated in.

描述一個你參與過的社團或運動團隊。

You should say:

❶ what type of club it was
❷ who the members were
❸ what activities were held
❹ and explain how you felt about participating in these activities.

應該提到：

❶ 是什麼社團
❷ 有哪些成員
❸ 該社團舉辦過什麼活動
❹ 說明你參與這些活動的感想。

A

❶ While in elementary school, I took violin ❷ lessons and later became part of the school's orchestra. Most members were students from grades three to six. We were generally students who did well in our academic classes and so were allowed to participate in this extracurricular activity. In total, I think there were about 50 students in the orchestra.

❶ 我小學的時候上過小提琴課，❷ 並在後來成為學校的管弦樂團成員。多數成員都是三至六年級的學生，通常我們在課業上的表現都很好，所以才能夠參與這項課外活動。我想管弦樂團總共有 50 名左右的學生。

❸ Aside from weekly practice sessions, we had two major concerts a year. The first was usually in the middle of December. Most of the songs we performed were winter themed, and there were a few holiday songs as well. The second annual concert was held in May, a few weeks before the end of

❸ 除了每週的練習時段，我們一年會有兩場大型音樂會。第一場通常舉辦在 12 月中旬，表演的曲目多半是以冬季為主題，還會有幾首節慶曲目。第二場年度演奏會舉辦在五月，在學年結束前的幾週。這場春

the school year. This springtime concert was sometimes connected to the graduation of the grade six class. It was their last concert before they would graduate and move on to junior high school the following year.

季音樂會有時候會結合六年級的畢業典禮，這是他們在小學畢業、於隔年上國中前的最後一場音樂會。

❹ I enjoyed being part of the orchestra. It was a good experience. I learned not only more about music but also how to cooperate with others. Each instrument played a different part in the songs, and it was rewarding to experience the benefits of cooperating with others. Finally, it was exciting to be on a stage, performing in front of our parents and fellow students.

❹ 我很享受在管弦樂團裡的日子，那是一段很美好的經驗。我不僅學到更多關於音樂的知識，也學會與他人合作。每一種樂器在不同曲子裡都扮演不同角色，如此能看到與他人合作所帶來的好處，令人很有成就感。最後，能站上舞台並在家長和同學面前表演，也很令人興奮。

Analysis

- In the Sample Answer points 1 and 2 are combined to describe the people involved in the club.
- Point 3 is the longest point and uses linking words to put the main ideas in chronological order.
- Point 4 uses expressions that describe feelings and emotions.

分析

- 範例答案將第一及第二點合併在一起回答，描述了參與該社團的人。
- 第三點的內容最多，且使用了轉折詞，按照時間順序說明重點。
- 第四點使用了表達感受的字彙來描述感覺和情緒。

The Sample Answer above gives details regarding the activities held by a school orchestra over the course of a school year. Although this question uses past tense verbs to indicate past experiences, if you are currently part of a club or sports team, you can describe your involvement using the present tense. Remember to use the correct verb tense.

以上範例答案詳述了學校管弦樂團在學年間所舉辦的活動。雖然問題使用了過去時態，暗示你可以描述過往發生過的經歷，不過如果你現在也有參加社團或運動團隊，當然也可以用現在式說明，記得使用正確的時態即可。

🔊 1-15

05 Describe a book, television series, or movie that you enjoyed.

描述你喜歡的一本書、一部電視影集或電影。

You should say:

❶ what the story was about
❷ what the setting was
❸ who the characters were
❹ and explain why you enjoyed it.

應該提到：

❶ 是什麼樣的故事
❷ 背景設定是什麼
❸ 有什麼角色
❹ 說明你喜歡的原因。

A

❶ I recently watched a documentary series ❷ about modern-day criminals. All the episodes are based on actual events that happened over the past few decades in places such as the US and European countries.

❶ 我最近看了一系列的當代犯罪 ❷ 紀錄片，每一集都是根據過去幾十年來的真實事件所改編，範圍遍及美國、歐洲各國。

❸ The stories focus on the criminals and investigators involved in each of the cases. In addition, details are given about the backgrounds of the criminals and the police who have been assigned to these cases. As I watched this documentary, this information helped me to understand the motives of why these people committed these crimes.

❸ 紀錄片重點在於每一樁案件的涉案罪犯和調查員，此外還詳細介紹了罪犯和辦案警察的背景。這些資訊讓我在看紀錄片時，幫助我了解這些人的犯案動機。

❹ I think the producers of this documentary did a very good job of making these complicated stories easy to follow. Each case followed a very logical progression. Also, I thought the camera angles, music, and lighting helped to create a suitable atmosphere for these types of stories, creating suspense and making me want to keep watching to see the conclusion of each case. I highly

❹ 我覺得這部紀錄片的製作人功不可沒，他們讓這些複雜的故事變得易於理解，每一樁案件都以非常合乎邏輯的方式呈現。此外，我也覺得鏡頭角度、配樂和光線，有助於呈現出這種紀錄片所適合的調性，使節目充滿懸疑感，也讓我想要看完每一樁案件的結論。我

recommend this documentary to others.

會大力向他人推薦這部紀錄片。

Analysis

- Often, when describing a book, television series, or movie, the where, when, and what of the story can be described together. That is why points 1 and 2 are answered together in the Sample Answer above.
- Points 3 and 4 use a lot of vocabulary that is specific to describing books and movies.

分析

- 在描述一本書、一部電視影集或電影時，常常會一起說明故事的發生地點、時間和劇情，以上的範例答案便是一併回答了第一及第二點。
- 針對第三及第四點，範例答案使用了大量專門描述書籍和電影的用字。

Try to use a variety of vocabulary in your answer to enhance your score. Examples of useful and academic vocabularies are given in the Note section on the following page along with sample sentences.

盡可能在答案中使用各種不同單字來提高分數。下頁的 Note 提供了有助益的學術性單字和例句。

Note: Vocabulary

Additional vocabulary for books, television series and movies:

以下是針對書籍、電視影集和電影的一些補充字彙：

- **story:** Synonyms include plot and storyline.
  - The plot of the movie is based on actual events.
    這部電影是根據真實事件改編。

- **故事**：同義字包括 plot（情節）、storyline（劇情）。

- **tone:** Words that can be used to describe the feeling of the movie/book: dark, depressing, light and happy, serious, warm.
  - The tone of this drama is very depressing.
    這部電視劇的調性非常壓抑。

- **調性**：用來描述一部電影或書籍所給人的感覺的字詞，相關字包括 dark（黑暗的）、depressing（壓抑的）、light and happy（輕鬆愉快的）、serious（嚴肅的）、warm（溫暖的）。

- **pace/pacing:** The speed at which the story progresses. Some stories have a lot of action, so the pace is very quick. Other stories, like dramas, tend to have a slower pace.
  - The pacing of many romantic movies is very slow.
    許多浪漫電影的步調都非常緩慢。

- **節奏 / 步調**：指故事進展的速度。有些故事有很多動作場面，因此節奏非常快。而有些故事的節奏緩慢，例如劇情片。

- **setting:** Where and when the story takes place.
  - The setting for this historical film is ancient China.
    這部歷史電影的背景設定在中國古代。

- **背景設定**：指故事發生的時間和地點。

- **characters:** The people in the story. You could describe how the characters look, including their body type, clothing style, and personality.

- **角色**：故事中的人物。可以描述角色外觀，包括他們的體型、穿衣風格和個性。

- The characters in this movie have very realistic personalities.
  這部電影角色的個性都非常寫實。

– **special effects:** Modern movies, especially action and science fiction (sci-fi) movies, tend to have a lot of explosions or computer generated images.

– 特效：當代電影有很多爆炸畫面或電腦合成影像，尤其是動作片和科幻片。

- The special effects in the movie were pretty good, but the movie didn't have a compelling story.
  這部電影的特效還不錯，但故事卻不夠吸引人。

Book/Movie *Genre 書籍／電影類型

action	動作	crime/detective	犯罪／偵查
adventure	冒險	horror	恐怖
comedy	喜劇	fantasy	奇幻
drama	劇情	romance	愛情
sci-fi	科幻	animation	動畫
romantic-comedy	浪漫喜劇	musical	音樂劇
historical	歷史	*western	西部片
documentary	紀錄片	*thriller	驚悚

***genre:** Synonyms include kind, type, and category.

類型：同義字包括 kind（種類）、type（類型）、category（類別）。

***western:** A western takes place in the American West about 100 years ago. They are also known as cowboy movies.

西部片：「西部片」的背景大約是一百年前的美國西部，又被稱為「牛仔電影」。

***thriller:** A thriller is a very suspenseful or scary movie. It is different from a horror movie because it generally does not contain monsters or other supernatural elements.

驚悚片：驚悚片指的是非常懸疑或駭人的電影。不同於恐怖片，驚悚片通常沒有怪物或超自然元素。

Part 3 Questions

第三部分 問題

As discussed in the 'Basic Strategies' section, remember our three-step process for giving a complete answer:

正如「答題基本策略」部分所述，記得按照以下三步驟給予完整回答：

❶ Give your opinion (directly answer the question)

❷ Provide a specific example to support your opinion

❸ Give a brief conclusion

❶ 說出你的觀點（直接回答問題）

❷ 提供一個實際範例來支持你的觀點

❸ 簡短扼要的結論

See how this strategy can be used to answer the Part 3 Questions.

接著來看看如何以這項策略回答第三部分的問題。

1-16

Q01 Why is it important to take time to relax?

為什麼花時間放鬆很重要？

Strategy

Give specific examples of how people are affected by stress.

策略

舉出人們受到壓力影響的實際例子。

❶ If someone is under constant stress, they start to develop a lot of physical and mental problems.

❷ A lot of serious illnesses are related to having a busy lifestyle, such as high blood pressure and depression. These health conditions can lead to even more serious problems, such as a stroke. Therefore, people need to be able to take time out from their busy schedules. People also need to find balance in their lives by pursuing

❶ 如果一個人長期處於壓力之下，就會開始產生許多生理和心理問題。

❷ 許多嚴重的疾病都與忙碌的生活方式有關，例如高血壓和憂鬱症。這些健康狀況可能會導致更嚴重的問題，例如中風。因此，人們需要從繁忙的日程中抽出空檔，並追求其他興趣，以從工作或其他責任中獲得短暫休息，藉此在生活中取

interests to give them momentary breaks from work or other responsibilities.

得平衡。

❸ This is why I think everyone should try to find a few minutes to relax every day.

❸ 因此我認為所有人每天都應該盡量花時間放鬆幾分鐘。

Analysis

Several specific health conditions are named to show the seriousness of this situation. Health-related vocabulary can be found in news articles and scientific journals.

分析

範例答案中舉出了具體的健康問題，用以強調這個情況的嚴重性。在新聞文章或科學期刊中，都能找到與健康議題相關的單字。

1-17

How have leisure activities changed over the past 20 years?

休閒娛樂在過去 20 年間有何改變？

Strategy

Give contrasts to show how people's choices of recreational activities have changed in recent decades.

策略

在答案中進行比較，說明人們近幾十年來在娛樂活動的選擇上有何改變。

A

❶ I think technology has caused the biggest changes in people's recreational choices in recent years.

❶ 我認為在近年來，科技對於人們在娛樂的選擇上，造成了最大的改變。

❷ I remember that when I was young, we would play outside almost every day after school. We would play sports or go exploring around our neighbourhood. Technology has given young people a lot more options to choose from, such as video games and social media. Unfortunately, kids today don't seem to be able to enjoy themselves if they don't have an electronic device in their hands.

❷ 我記得小時候我們幾乎每天放學都會在外面玩耍，我們會運動或是在家裡附近四處探索。科技讓年輕人有更多選擇，例如電玩和社群媒體。可惜現在的小孩要是沒有拿著電子設備，似乎就會玩得不盡興。

❸ Technology has definitely had the biggest effect on our choices of entertainment.

❸ 科技確實對我們的娛樂選擇造成了最大影響。

Analysis

Technology is given as the main reason for changes in people's choices of recreational activities in recent decades. As seen in the Sample Answer above, if you talk about a past action that was a habit or routine, you can use the following structure: 'would + present tense verb'.

- We would go to school at 7 a.m. every day.
- He would watch TV before going to bed.

分析

在此範例答案中，科技被視作改變人們娛樂活動選擇的主因。正如以上答案所示，如果要講述過去的一項習慣或例行日程，可使用〈would + 現在式動詞〉來表達。

- 我們以前每天早上七點就去上學。
- 他以前會在睡覺前看電視。

1-18

Q03 What are the pros and cons of legalised gambling?

賭博合法化有什麼優缺點？

Strategy

Discuss both sides of this issue in a balanced way. You can also give your personal opinion.

策略

對等討論此議題的正反兩面，也可以闡述個人觀點。

❶ This is definitely a controversial topic for many reasons.

❷ There are some economic benefits of legalised gambling, such as more job opportunities in the hospitality industry. Hotels and restaurants are often built around casinos, which can give more people jobs and increase tax revenue for the local area. However, there are also a lot of disadvantages that come with gambling. Crime, such as prostitution and *drink driving, may increase in the local area. Other undesirable consequences, such as drug or alcohol addiction and domestic

❶ 這絕對是個爭議性的話題，原因有很多。

❷ 合法化賭博，在經濟方面能帶來一些好處，例如餐旅業能有更多工作機會。飯店和餐廳經常蓋在賭場周圍，因此這能讓更多人找到工作，並且提高當地的稅收。然而賭博也伴隨著許多缺點，當地的犯罪率可能會上升，例如賣淫和酒駕。其他負面影響還包括毒品和酒精成癮，以及家暴情況通常也會增加。

violence, usually increase as well.

❸ These are the reasons why I am personally against legalising gambling.

* drink driving ㊕ drunk driving ㊡

❸ 基於以上原因，我個人反對賭博合法化。

Analysis

When discussing two sides of an issue, use a transition word to signal that you have begun talking about the opposite viewpoint. Use words such as 'however', 'on the other hand', 'by contrast', 'conversely', etc.

分析

在討論一個議題的正反面時，使用轉折詞可以表明你已經開始講述相反觀點。例如 however（然而）、on the other hand（另一方面）、by contrast（相較之下）、conversely（相反地）等。

🔊 1-19

Q04 Do older people and younger people like the same types of movies?

年紀大的人和年輕人喜歡的電影類型一樣嗎？

Strategy

Use specific examples to show the differences between these two age groups and the types of movies they prefer to watch.

策略

提供實際例子，說明這兩個年齡層及兩者偏好的電影類型差異。

A

❶ I think there is a big difference in the movie preferences of people the same age as my parents and those of young people such as myself.

❶ 我認為跟我父母同齡的人，和我這種年輕人有很不一樣的電影偏好。

❷ Older people seem to like movies that have a slower pace and more depth to their stories. For example, they usually prefer dramas or historical movies. These movies' storylines tend to have more of an emotional impact. By contrast, most young people today would probably choose to watch an action or sci-fi movie. Movies such as these

❷ 年紀大的人似乎喜歡節奏更慢、更有深度的電影，他們通常偏好劇情片或歷史電影。這些電影的故事線會有更多的情緒渲染力。相較之下，現今多數的年輕人可能會選擇看動作片或科幻片，這種電影的節奏往往較快，而且通常都有大量

tend to have a faster pace and usually include a lot of cutting-edge special effects.

前衛的特效。

❸ I definitely think there is a huge difference in the types of movies that appeal to older and younger audiences.

❸ 我強烈認為，吸引年長觀眾和年輕觀眾的電影類型相去甚遠。

Analysis

Specific movie-related vocabulary is used throughout this answer. The phrase 'By contrast' is used to introduce the preferences of the second age group.

分析

此範例答案使用了電影相關的專門用語，並運用 By contrast（相較之下）這個片語來帶出第二個年齡層的偏好。

1-20

05 In your opinion, which is more important: a movie's storyline or special effects?

你認為一部電影的故事線和特效哪個更重要？

Strategy

It is best to choose which of these two options you support to give your answer a clear direction.

策略

最好從這兩個選項中挑出你支持的一方，這能讓你的答案有明確方向。

❶ I feel that the plot is the most important part of any movie.

❶ 我覺得任何電影最重要的元素都是劇情。

❷ Nowadays, too many movies rely on special effects to sell movie tickets. However, most of the time, such movies have bland, two-dimensional characters without any personality, and the storyline is usually very dull and predictable. A really engaging movie should have a story with twists, or things that you don't see coming, and the characters should have personalities that are very realistic.

❷ 現在有太多電影都靠特效來賣票，但這些電影多數時候都很無趣，且角色塑造平板又缺乏個性，故事劇情通常還相當乏味，而且非常好預測。一部真正引人入勝的電影，應該要有曲折的故事、讓人料想不到的情節，角色個性的塑造也應該要寫實。

❸ I feel that a really good movie doesn't even

❸ 我覺得一部真正好的電影甚至

need to have special effects as long as it has an intriguing plot and well-developed characters.

不需要特效，只要有耐人尋味的劇情，及發展良好的角色即可。

Analysis

In the Sample Answer above, contrasts are given to show the speaker's personal opinion that many modern movies rely too heavily on special effects to attract viewers and that as a result, more important things, such as realistic characters and an interesting story, are missing.

分析

以上範例答案給予了明確比較，以表明個人觀點，指出許多現代電影過度依賴特效來吸引觀衆，結果喪失了更重要的元素，例如寫實的角色和有趣的故事。

1-21

Q06 Should young children be allowed to watch violent movies?

該不該讓兒童看暴力電影？

Strategy

A question such as this asks for your opinion. You can describe how strongly you feel about this issue.

策略

這類問題是在徵詢你的意見，可以描述自己對這個議題有多強烈的看法。

A

❶ Absolutely not!

❷ If a child is exposed to violence in any form, it can seriously affect their development in many ways. Violent images can warp a child's view of proper and improper behaviour. After watching violent movies, children may begin to feel that violence is a normal way to express one's emotions or a normal way to handle disagreements. Research has shown that after watching TV shows or movies with a lot of fighting or cursing, children start to imitate these types of behaviour.

❶ 絕對不行！

❷ 如果讓兒童接觸任何形式的暴力，會嚴重影響他們在許多方面的發展。暴力畫面可能會扭曲兒童對正當和非正當行為的看法。看完暴力電影後，兒童有可能會開始覺得，這是表達情緒或處理紛爭的正常方式。研究顯示，看過含有大量打架或咒罵內容的電視節目或電影後，兒童會開始模仿這種行為。

❸ I feel very strongly that parents should know what their children are being exposed to and take action to prevent them from seeing acts of violence.

❸ 我堅決認為家長應該要知道他們的孩子在接觸什麼內容，並採取行動來避免他們看見暴力行為。

Analysis

A short sentence is given at the beginning of this answer to show how strongly the speaker feels about this issue. Throughout the answer, key words are used. For example, note the use of the following word forms: violent: adjective; violence: noun.

分析

範例答案在開頭以一個短句來表明自己對此議題的強烈看法。整段答案使用了多個關鍵字來表達意見。舉例來說，請注意下述字彙的使用：violent（暴力的）是形容詞，violence（暴力）是名詞。

1-22

Q07 In the future, will people still go to theatres to watch the latest movies, or will theatres be replaced by online streaming services?

未來人們還會繼續進電影院觀賞最新電影嗎？還是會被線上串流服務給取代？

Strategy

When answering this question, you have to guess or speculate about what changes will occur in the future. Use future tense verbs or phrases that describe possible future scenarios in your answer.

策略

回答這個問題時，必須推測或猜測未來會發生哪些改變。回答時要使用未來式描述未來可能發生的情況。

A

❶ I think that in the distant future, people will no longer go to the cinema. However, I believe that in the short term, movie theatres will still be around for a little while longer.

❶ 我認為在遙遠的未來，人們不會再進電影院。不過，我認為短期而言，電影院還是會繼續存在一段時間。

❷ The cinema still plays an important role in our culture. Everyone has fond memories of going to a theatre to see a long-anticipated

❷ 電影院在我們的文化中仍然扮演了重要角色。進電影院觀賞期待已久的電影是人人都有過

movie. For example, some people's first date with their spouse took place at a movie theatre. Nevertheless, I think that eventually, cinemas will lose their popularity because of new technology. Streaming platforms allow people to watch the latest movies in the comfort of their own home.

的美好回憶。舉例而言，有些人跟伴侶的初次約會就是在電影院裡。然而，我認為電影院最終還是會因為新科技而退流行，串流平台讓人們能夠舒服地在自家觀賞最新電影。

❸ My opinion is that probably 50 years from now, there will no longer be cinemas because new technologies will come along and replace them.

❸ 我的看法是約莫 50 年後就不會再有電影院了，因為新科技會出現並取而代之。

Analysis

The answer above talks about the importance of the cinema now and then gives a prediction for the future. Even though the two periods of the present and the future are discussed, the opinion is very clear because it is mentioned in point 1 and then repeated in point 3. Repeating your opinion will prevent your answer from becoming confusing.

分析

上述答案提到電影院之於現在的重要性，接著預測了未來。雖然範例答案談論了現在和未來這兩個時間段，但意見還是相當清楚，因為答題者在第一及第三段都重複強調自己的意見。重申你的意見能避免不明不白的答案。

1-23

08 How often do you go shopping for new clothes?

你多久買一次衣服？

Strategy

This question asks 'How often...' There are various ways to discuss time and personal habits that you can use to answer this question. The following Sample Answer uses several different key words and phrases to related to time and frequency.

策略

這個問題問了 How often...（多常…），有許多表達時間和個人習慣的說法能用來回答此問題。以下範例答案使用了好幾個和時間、頻率有關的關鍵字和片語。

A

❶ I am a bit of a shopaholic, so I go shopping all the time.

❶ 我算是個購物狂，所以我一天到晚逛街。

❷ Where I work is near a very popular shopping district, and so every night on my way home from work, I go window shopping, looking at the display windows of the department stores that I pass. Sometimes, I can't help myself, and I just go into a store if I see something really cute to wear. I have a wardrobe for each season, so I am constantly updating my outfits, especially if I see an advertisement for a clearance sale.

❷ 我工作的地方離一個流行商圈很近，所以每天晚上下班回家經過百貨公司，我都會看看櫥窗裡展示了什麼商品。如果看見很可愛的衣服，我有時候會無法克制自己走進店裡。我為每個季節都準備了一整個系列的衣服，所以我總是經常在更新我的治裝，尤其是看見清倉大拍賣廣告的時候。

❸ I would say that I buy new clothes on a weekly basis.

❸ 我想我每週都會買新衣服。

Analysis

As seen in this Sample Answer, after describing your personal habits, you can use your conclusion to summarise your comments. This is done in point 3 of the answer above.

分析

正如範例答案所示，描述完個人習慣行為後，你可以做個總結，例如此處的第三點。

1-24

09 Is buying brand name items important to you?

買名牌對你來說重要嗎？

Strategy

Brand name items are made by companies that are known all over the world. Use a specific example in your answer.

策略

名牌產品是由全球知名公司所製造，可在你的答案中舉一個實際例子。

A

❶ Even though a lot of people are swayed by brand names, they are not the most important factor I consider when making a purchase.

❶ 雖然有很多人會對名牌心動，但這卻不是我在消費時最重要的考量。

❷ For me, the practicality and usefulness of an item is the most important thing. Take sports shoes as an example: A pair of Nike shoes

❷ 對我來說，一項產品的實用性和效用才是重點。以運動鞋為例，某些人可能會因為品牌認

might be very attractive to some people because of brand recognition. However, I feel that a generic brand of shoes is basically the same and is usually about half the price.

同，而受到 Nike 球鞋的吸引，但我覺得普通品牌的鞋子基本上也一樣，而且價格通常還少一半。

❸ For me, determining whether I need the item or not and considering the price is more important than buying from a well-known brand.

❸ 在我看來，決定我是否需要這項產品並考量價格，會比考量品牌的知名度更加重要。

Analysis

The example of Nike shoes was used in this answer as an example of a brand name. A contrast was also given to compare Nike shoes to shoes made by lesser-known companies.

分析

範例答案舉出 Nike 球鞋作為名牌的例子，並將 Nike 球鞋和較不知名的鞋互相比較。

🔊 1-25

Q10 When you make a purchase, which is more important, an item's price or its quality?

你在消費時，比較重視物品的價錢還是品質？

Strategy

For this type of question, choose a side: either the price of an item or its quality. Then, use an example to support your opinion.

策略

碰到這種問題時要選邊站，也就是必須在價格或品質間擇一，接著舉例來支持你的看法。

❶ I think it depends on the item I am buying.

❷ If I was going to buy a high-ticket item such as a new mobile phone, I would consider the reputation of the manufacturer because that usually affects the quality of the phone. Take for instance the Apple iPhone, which is more expensive than most other brands but also generally very well made. I had an

❶ 我想這要視我買的東西而定。

❷ 如果我要買像手機這樣的高昂產品，我會考慮製造商的名聲，因為那通常攸關手機的品質。舉例來說，一支 Apple 的 iPhone 通常比其他多數品牌來得貴，但一般來說品質非常好。我有一支用了五年以上的

iPhone that I used for more than five years, and I never experienced any problems with it. During the same five-year period, my friend who used another brand of phone purchased three different phones. In the end, he ended up spending more money on those three phones than I did on my iPhone.

iPhone，從來沒有出過任何問題。在這五年期間，我有個使用它牌手機的朋友已經換了三支手機，結果跟我買 iPhone 所花的錢相比，他反倒花了更多錢。

❸ My viewpoint is that even though some items might cost a little more, they tend to have higher quality and a longer life. Therefore, in the long run, you could actually save money by buying a more expensive item.

❸ 我的觀點是，有些東西雖然可能稍嫌昂貴，卻有更好的品質及更長的壽命。所以長遠而言，購買價格高昂的產品，其實是在省錢。

Analysis

The example of the iPhone was used in this answer to compare and contrast price with quality. Specific examples such as this will help to enhance your overall speaking score.

分析

範例答案舉了 iPhone 為實例，比較產品價格和品質的差異。像這種實際例子有助於提高你的整體口說分數。

Note: Synonym

Oftentimes, when asked to describe two sides of an issue, test candidates have trouble understanding the question they are being asked. Here are some terms and synonyms that you may hear in these types of questions:

被問到一個議題的正反面時，考生經常會難以理解問題的意思。以下這些同義字都可能出現在這種問題當中：

pros（優點）	cons（缺點）
positive points/aspects/sides	negative points/aspects/sides
advantages	disadvantages
benefits	drawbacks

Additional Tips and Resources 補充技巧及資料

How to Introduce Your Topic 如何切入你的主題

Many candidates make the mistake of repeating the words on the Topic Card in the first few sentences of an answer. OR They talk as though they are giving a speech and unnecessarily reintroduce the topic. Let's look at an example:

很多考生在回答第二部分的題目卡時，常常會在答案開頭重複題目卡上的問題，或有如在發表正式演說般，把題目卡上的小主題又重複一次。讓我們看以下例子：

Describe a book you read as a child.

描述一本你小時候讀過的書。

You should say:

1. what the book was
2. what the book was about
3. who the characters were
4. and explain why you enjoyed the book.

應該提到：

1. 是什麼書
2. 那本書在講什麼
3. 有什麼角色
4. 說明你喜歡這本書的原因。

Common Mistakes 常見錯誤

A

1. Today, I am going to talk to you about a book I read as a child. What the book was: The book was called *The Three Little Pigs*.
2. What the book was about: The book was about three pigs that built their houses out of different things...

1. 我要來講一本我小時候看過的書。是什麼書呢？這本書叫做《三隻小豬》。
2. 這本書是在講什麼？這本書是在講三隻豬用不同的建材蓋房子……

What's the problem? 問題出在哪裡？

You and the examiner already know the topic you are

你和考官都已經知道要說的主題

going to talk about. Therefore, you do not need to introduce the topic by reading from the card.

了，因此不需要為了扣題而將題目卡上的問題唸出來。

A Better Introduction

較好的開頭

A When I was young, I read a story that I can recall to this day. It was titled *The Three Little Pigs*. In this story, there are three brother pigs who decide to build their own houses. Each one chooses a different material, such as...

我小時候看過一個故事，到現在都還記得。那本書叫做《三隻小豬》，故事講述小豬三兄弟決定要建造他們自己的房子，每一隻都選擇了不同的建材，像是……

LESSON 2

Work

工作

LESSON 2

Work 工作

Part 1 Questions 第一部分 問題

◀)) 2-01

01 What do you do for work?

你從事什麼工作？

Strategy

Give details, such as the company you work for, the department you work in, and your role. Also, give details about your daily routine at work and the things you are responsible for.

策略

可提供細節，例如你就職的公司、你工作的部門和職位，並且詳細說明你工作的日常流程，以及你的職責。

A I am currently working in the accounting department of a technology company. I am responsible for handling the employee payroll and paperwork related to taxes. Because the company has about 500 employees, there are a lot of forms and reports that I need to deal with on a daily basis.

我目前任職於一間科技公司的會計部門，負責處理員工薪資和稅務相關的文書工作。由於敝公司大約有五百名員工，所以我每天都要經手許多表格和報告。

◀)) 2-02

02 Do you have any job/work experience?

你有任何工作經驗嗎？

Strategy

If an action started in the past and has continued until now, use these verb tenses (present perfect tense and present perfect progressive tense):

策略

如果要描述的動作始於過去，且持續至今，請使用「現在完成式」或「現在完成進行式」：

- I have worked in a coffee shop for the past 2 years.
- I have been working in a coffee shop for the past 2 years.

- 過去兩年，我都在咖啡廳工作。
- 我從兩年前一直到現在，都在咖啡廳工作。

A I have been working in a coffee shop for the past 2 years. I take customer orders, make drinks, and work the cash register. I have learned a lot of new skills since I started working here. Also, I get to meet a lot of interesting people, and I like that my work hours are very flexible.

我過去兩年都在一間咖啡廳工作。我要為顧客點餐、調製飲品及結帳。自從在這裡工作後，我學到了很多新技能。我還得以認識許多有趣的人，也喜歡相當彈性的工時。

2-03

Q03 Do you enjoy your job? What do you like or dislike about your job?

你喜歡你的工作嗎？你喜歡或討厭這份工作的什麼地方？

Strategy

Avoid common grammar mistakes such as 'My work is very tired'. Instead, you should say 'My work is very tiring' OR 'My work makes me tired'.

策略

避免出現常見的文法錯誤，例如 My work is very tired.，正確說法應該是 My work is very tiring. 或 My work makes me tired.（我的工作令我疲憊。）

A I work in sales, so I am on the road a lot, travelling to different companies. Even though it can be a little tiring, I enjoy this job because I like interacting with customers.

我在業務部門工作，所以經常要奔波於不同的公司。雖然這可能有點累人，但我很享受做這份工作，因為我喜歡跟客戶互動。

2-04

Q04 What would your dream job be in the future?

你未來的夢想工作是什麼？

Strategy

Give some reasons to explain why this type of job would make you satisfied. When describing possible situations, use 'would'.

- I would like to open my own store.
- If I had $1 million I would...

策略

講述一些理由來說明這個職業為何讓你感到滿足。在描述「可能發生」的情況時，要使用助動詞 would（將會）。

- 我會想要自己開店。
- 如果我有一百萬，我就會……

A I would love to open my own boutique where I could sell shoes and handmade accessories. I would enjoy bringing my designs to life and the flexibility of being my own boss. This would be my dream job.

我會想要開一間自己的精品店，販售鞋子和手工飾品。我喜歡看到自己的設計變成真正的實品，並享受自己當老闆的彈性，這會是我的夢想工作。

2-05

Q05 What types of work would you find interesting?

你會對哪種工作產生興趣？

Strategy

You could give a contrast with a type of job that you would not want to do. This would help to explain the strengths of your ideal job.

策略

可以利用不想從事的工作來進行比較，這樣有助於說明你理想工作的優勢。

A I would not like a job where I would have to sit in front of a computer all day. Instead, I would like a job where I could go out to different locations, see the world, and have new experiences. That is why I think I want to be a nature photographer. This job would be interesting and satisfying.

我不想做必須整天坐在電腦前的工作，我喜歡做有機會能夠前往不同地點的工作，見見世面，獲得新的歷練。因此我想要成為一名自然風景攝影師，這工作會很有意思，也會令人很有成就感。

2-06

Q06 Is there any type of job you would not want to do?

有任何工作是你不想從事的嗎？

Strategy

For this question, you could describe an experience that you or someone else has had working a less than ideal job.

策略

回答這類問題時，可以描述自己或他人曾做過的工作，且這份工作經驗不甚理想。

A While in high school, I had a part-time job working in a convenience store, and I hated every minute of it. I had to work nights and weekends, so I had no social life. Also, the customers I had to deal with were very rude and complained a lot. Finally, the pay was very low. I would never want to do that type of job again.

我高中時曾經在便利商店打工，我痛恨在那裡上班的每分每秒。我必須輪夜班和假日班，所以毫無社交生活可言。還有，我要應付的顧客都相當無禮又愛抱怨，最後，工作薪資也低到不行。我絕對不會想要再做那種工作。

2-07

Q07 Is it difficult to find work in your country?

在你的國家求職很難嗎？

Strategy

Comment on current trends in your country that you have observed, such as things you have read about in the news.

策略

說明你在國內觀察到的當前趨勢，例如你在新聞中看到的消息。

A If a person wants to have a job with flexible hours and decent pay, it can be very challenging to find such a job. Most jobs that are available are office or manufacturing jobs that have the standard Monday-through-Friday, nine-to-five schedule with mandatory overtime and weekend hours. If a person wants to get more out of life than just work, it can be very hard to find a job in my country.

想找到一份工時彈性、薪資像樣的工作，可能會非常有難度。多數職缺主要是辦公室或製造業工作，上班時間是標準的週一至週五、朝九晚五，還要強制加班，週末也必須出勤。在我的國家，如果想過不被工作綁架的生活，那可能會很難找到工作。

2-08

How far is your commute to work?

你上班通勤的距離有多遠？

Strategy

Describe how you travel to work by stating your means of transport and the amount of time it takes.

策略

描述你上班的交通方式及所耗費的時間。

A My daily commute isn't too bad. In my city, most people don't need to own a car because there are a lot of options when it comes to public transport. I live next to a bus stop, so I take the bus a few stops to a subway station. After transferring to the subway, it is only a ride of a few minutes to my office. In total, it takes only about 25 minutes for me to get to work.

我每天的通勤狀況還可以。在我住的城市，多數人都沒有開車的必要，因為有許多大眾運輸能夠選擇。我家旁邊就有一個公車站牌，所以我會先搭公車搭個幾站到地鐵，轉乘地鐵後，只要再幾分鐘車程就能抵達我的辦公室。我去上班大概只花 25 分鐘。

2-09

Do you get on well with your co-workers?

你跟同事相處得好嗎？

Strategy

Describe the relationships that you have with your co-workers by giving specific examples.

策略

提供明確的例子，描述你與同事之間的關係。

A I think I have good relationships with most of my workmates. Most people in my department are very friendly, and a lot of us have common interests. Several times a year, some of us go hiking and camping together. I think that doing this has made us feel like a team, and as a result, we work well together.

我認為我和多數工作夥伴的關係都不錯。我們部門的同仁大多都很友善，許多人也都有共同愛好。我們有幾個人每年都會相約一起去健行和露營個幾次。我覺得這樣讓我們感覺就像一個團隊，也因此能好好一起共事。

2-10

Q10 What was your first day at work like?

你第一天上班的狀況如何？

Strategy

Describe your personal experience. You should describe what you did and how you felt at that time.

策略

描述你的個人經驗，講講自己做了什麼，還有當時的感覺。

A I was so nervous on my first day of work. I was so afraid that I would make a lot of mistakes and that none of my co-workers would like me. I remember, however, that after I had my orientation meeting and met everyone in my department, I started to calm down. It still took me a few more weeks until I started to feel confident about what I was doing. Nevertheless, that first day was very memorable.

我第一天上班那天非常緊張。我很擔心自己會犯下很多錯誤、同事都不會喜歡我。但我記得在迎新會見過部門的所有人之後，我開始冷靜下來。我還是過了幾週後才開始對工作感到自信，儘管如此，第一天實在是令人難忘。

Part 2 Questions 第二部分 問題

🔊 2-11

Q01 Describe a well-known company.

描述一間知名的公司。

You should say:

❶ what it is
❷ what it makes or what services it provides
❸ how you feel about the company
❹ and explain how the company became well-known.

應該提到：

❶ 是什麼公司
❷ 該公司製造什麼或提供什麼服務
❸ 你對這間公司的感覺
❹ 說明該公司為何知名。

A

❶ I think everyone has heard of the Apple company. This technology company's products have become a part of daily life.

❷ Almost everyone today owns a smartphone or tablet, which were both pioneered by Apple. This company has also expanded its products to include services to download music and movies. Also, now, we can even link our credit card or bank account to our mobile devices and use Apple Pay to make purchases.

❸ I think it has gotten to the point where modern society cannot function without the technology and services provided by this company. I personally feel that Apple's products are of very high quality and are an indispensable part of my daily life.

❶ 我想大家都聽過 Apple 公司，這間科技公司的產品已經成為我們日常生活的一部分了。

❷ 現在幾乎人人都有智慧型手機或平板電腦，而 Apple 公司是製造這兩種產品的先驅。這間公司也將其產品類型，拓展至包括串流音樂和影劇的服務。還有，我們現在甚至能夠將信用卡或銀行帳戶綁定在行動裝置上，使用 Apple Pay 來進行消費。

❸ 我想現代社會已經離不開這間公司所提供的科技與服務了。我個人認為 Apple 公司的產品品質非常好，是我日常生活中不可或缺的一部分。

❹ However, I remember not too long ago when Apple wasn't as respected as it is today. About 15 years ago, IBM and software like Windows were viewed as the most advanced and reliable companies in the technology field. But after the iPhone became so mainstream, Apple surpassed these other companies. Now it is one of the most valued companies in the world.

❹ 不過我記得不久之前，Apple 公司還不像現在一樣備受重視。大約 15 年前，IBM 和微軟公司還被視作科技業中最先進、最可靠的品牌，但在 iPhone 成為主流之後，Apple 公司便超越了其他品牌，如今成為了世上最有價值的公司之一。

Analysis

For this type of topic, choose a company that is easy to talk about, such as McDonald's or Starbucks. Describe the products or services of this company along with general information about how this company became well-known.

分析

針對這類主題，請選擇一間易於講述的公司，例如麥當勞或星巴克，並描述該公司所提供的產品或服務，提及該公司為何聞名的事蹟。

2-12

02 Describe the type of employer you would like to have.

描述你心目中理想的雇主。

You should say:

❶ what qualities they would have
❷ how they would treat you
❸ how you would interact with them
❹ and explain why you feel they would be a good employer.

應該提到：

❶ 對方會有什麼特質
❷ 對方會如何對待你
❸ 你會如何與對方互動
❹ 說明為何你認為這樣會是好雇主。

❶ In my opinion, an ideal boss has reasonable expectations for their employees. They are also approachable and open to new ideas. Finally, they are a good communicator.

❷ Everyone, regardless of their social status, wants to be treated with respect. I think

❶ 在我看來，理想的雇主會對員工抱持合理的期待，且平易近人，願意接受新點子。然後這種雇主也善於與人溝通。

❷ 無論社會地位的高低，所有人都想要得到尊重。我想一名雇

an employer should always treat those working under them in this way. I once had a manager who thought that they knew the best way to handle every situation and would never take the time to hear others' ideas. This was very frustrating for everyone who worked in the department. Unfortunately, I think this was the main reason that so many of my co-workers either quit or transferred to other departments.

主應該要時刻以這種方式來對待下屬。我曾碰過一位經理，他認為自己最懂得如何處理所有情況，永遠不花時間聽聽他人的想法，這讓部門裡的所有同仁都非常挫折。很遺憾，我想這正是我有那麼多同事辭職或轉調到其他部門的主因。

❸ If my supervisor was reasonable and approachable, I would not hesitate to communicate with them regularly and offer my input regarding work-related situations.

❸ 如果我的上司通情達理又平易近人，我就會常常找他們討論，並且針對不同的工作情況提供個人見解。

❹ An employer like this would promote a positive and constructive work environment where everyone would look forward to going to work. Each employee would feel very confident in trusting this type of employer. Therefore, I think these are the traits of a really good leader.

❹ 這樣的雇主能營造一個正面又積極的工作環境，所有人都會很期待去上班，每一位員工都能有信心去信任這樣的雇主。因此，我認為這些特點就是一名優秀領導者所具備的特質。

Analysis

- Point 1 directly states the qualities that would make someone a good employer.
- In point 2, an experience is described to show the results of a boss with an undesirable personality.
- Points 3 and 4 show the good results that would likely come from an employer with the positive traits mentioned in point 1.

分析

- 第一點直接闡述一位好雇主會有的特質。
- 第二點分享了一個經歷，表明討人厭的雇主會導致什麼結果。
- 第三點和第四點指出，雇主若具備第一點所提到的正面特質，會帶來哪些好結果。

The Sample Answer above gives a personal experience of working with a manager who had a difficult personality. This experience is

以上範例答案提供了個人經驗，說明與一名難相處的經理一起共事的經歷，此經歷能與第一點形

described to give a contrast and to highlight the benefits of the positive traits that are mentioned in point 1.

成對比，凸顯第一點提及的正面特質。

2-13

Q 03 Describe a project you have completed at work.

描述一件你在工作上執行過的專案。

You should say:

❶ what it was

❷ how you finished it

❸ how much time you spent on it

❹ and explain how you felt about working on it.

應該提到：

❶ 是什麼專案

❷ 你如何完成的

❸ 耗費了多少時間

❹ 說明你執行這項專案時的感覺。

A

❶ When I first started working in my current job as a secretary, I noticed that the filing system we were using was very outdated and that it was therefore difficult to find information regarding previous clients and cases the company had handled. So, I volunteered to overhaul this system.

❶ 我最開始從事目前這份祕書工作時，發現歸檔系統非常過時，也很難查找過往客戶的資料及公司經手過的案件。於是我便自願改造這個系統。

❷ It was a very big undertaking that took about ❸ 3 months to complete. I required the help of many of my co-workers who were already familiar with the system that we were using. I found the experience and suggestions from my workmates to be invaluable in finishing this project. In the first phase, we took all of the paper files and digitised them. Then, we had to organise them by date and category. The categories we used were based on the types of companies to which our clients

❷ 這是一項重大任務，耗時三個 ❸ 月才完成。我向許多同事徵求協助，因為他們早已經熟悉原本所使用的這個系統。我覺得同事們的經驗與建議都非常寶貴，讓我得以完成這項專案。在最初階段，我們得將所有紙本文件數位化，接著按照日期及文件類型分類整理。我們以客戶所屬的公司類型來分類這些文件，這讓查找客戶的歷史

belonged. This method made it much easier to look up client histories and to know their specific needs.

資料更加容易，也能了解他們的特殊需求。

❹ Even though this project was very tedious and monotonous, finishing it gave me a great sense of accomplishment. It was very satisfying to use the new filing system after it was completed. I received a lot of commendation from my manager and even the company owner. Everyone who now uses the updated filing system has said that it is very efficient and easy to use.

❹ 儘管這項專案相當乏味又單調，但完成後卻讓我有莫大的成就感。新的歸檔系統完成後，使用起來令人備感滿意。我的經理大力表揚我，甚至連公司老闆都讚不絕口。所有使用過這個新歸檔系統的人，都說這個系統不僅效率高又容易使用。

Analysis

- Background information about the project and the company's needs is given in point 1.
- Points 2 and 3 are combined because the factors of time and how the project was completed are closely connected.
- Point 4 contains several adjectives that describe feelings about work.

分析

- 第一點闡述了這項專案，和公司需求的背景資訊。
- 一併說明第二及第三點，因為時間和完成專案的方式環環相扣。
- 第四點使用了好幾個形容詞來描述對這項工作的感覺。

This question requires you to relate a personal experience. In the Sample Answer above, after the introduction to the job position that the speaker held, the major steps of the project are outlined. The assistance that others contributed to the project is also mentioned along with how others felt about the project after it was completed.

這個問題要你說明一個親身經歷。答題者在此範例答案中先提到自己的職務，接著說明執行專案的主要步驟。而同仁對這項專案的協助，以及對專案完成後的感想，也在答案中一併提及。

2-14

Q 04 Describe an entrepreneur.

描述一名企業家。

You should say:

❶ who the person is

❷ what business they started

❸ why they decided to start their own business

❹ and explain how successful their business has become.

應該提到：

❶ 這個人是誰

❷ 這個人創立了何種事業

❸ 這個人為何決定自行創業

❹ 說明這個人的事業有多成功。

A

❶ My uncle runs his own financial consultancy ❷ firm. He works with companies both large and small and helps them to save money and increase their earnings. He has a very small office with just one employee, who is his secretary.

❶ 我叔叔自己開了一間金融顧問 ❷ 公司。他與各種不同規模的公司合作，指導他們如何開源節流。他有一間很小的辦公室，只有一名員工，就是他的祕書。

❸ My uncle worked in a lot of different companies over the years, such as manufacturing and technology companies. As a result, he gained a lot of experience related to a business's day-to-day operations, product manufacturing processes, and human resources policies. He also worked in international sales, so he got used to travelling. After several years of maintaining an exhausting schedule, he decided it was time to slow down and use his experience in a practical way. Thus, he decided to start his own consultancy firm.

❸ 我叔叔多年來待過各式各樣的公司，例如製造和科技公司。他因此獲得許多與企業日常營運、產品製造及人力資源政策的相關經驗。他也做過國際線業務員，所以很習慣四處旅行。在經歷了長年來的勞累日程後，他覺得是時候放慢腳步、實際發揮自身經驗了，所以才因此決定經營自己的顧問公司。

❹ Because of his good reputation, thorough understanding of business operations, and very charming personality, my uncle has become very successful. He now only has

❹ 由於我叔叔聲譽優良，非常了解企業經營之道，而且充滿個人魅力，所以他的事業很成功。他現在每週只需要工作幾

to work a few hours a week and thus has a lot more time to spend with his family. He lives a very comfortable life. He has a nice home and a new car and isn't under a lot of stress like he used to be. I really admire him for what he has accomplished.

個小時，因此有更多時間陪伴家人，過著舒服愜意的生活。他現在有一棟漂亮的房子、一輛新車，生活不像從前那樣充滿壓力。我非常佩服他的成就。

Analysis

- Points 1 and 2 are answered together because they would be very awkward to separate and answer independently.
- Point 3 gives the background and experience of the person being described.
- Personal opinions and observations of this person are given in point 4.

分析

- 一併回答第一及第二點，因為分開講述這兩個要點會很奇怪。
- 針對第三點提供此人的背景及經歷。
- 在第四點提到對此人的想法與觀察。

As seen in the Sample Answer above, it is a good idea to choose to speak about a person with whom you are familiar so that you can give details about this person's background.

正如範例答案所示，選擇你所熟悉的人來講述會是較好的策略，如此才能提供有關此人的背景細節。

2-15

05 Describe your ideal working environment.

描述你理想中的工作環境。

You should say:

❶ where it would be
❷ what it would look like
❸ who you would work with
❹ and explain why it would be a satisfying environment.

應該提到：

❶ 會在哪裡
❷ 會是什麼樣子
❸ 你會跟誰共事
❹ 說明此環境之所以理想的原因。

❶ Since I am a designer, I need to work in a place with a lot of positive energy where

❶ 由於我是設計師，我必須在充滿正能量的地方工作，才能獲

I can get inspiration. I don't want to be in a confined space in an office building. I would want to be in a studio surrounded by nature.

得靈感。我不想要在辦公大樓裡的狹窄空間內工作，我會想要待在被自然景物所包圍的工作室。

❷ This studio would have large windows with a great view of the natural surroundings. I also need large tables to work on my designs. In addition, the interior needs to have some colour because I don't want to stare at white walls all day. I would also like to have a lot of indoor plants, like my own personal garden. Years ago, I had to work in a small cubicle surrounded by about 20 other people. I found it so depressing, and it made my work feel very dull and uninspiring.

❷ 這個工作室會有好幾片大窗戶，能看見周圍的自然美景。我需要大桌子來進行設計工作，還有，室內必須要有一些色彩，因為我不想要整天都盯著白牆。我還希望室內能有許多植栽，這樣就很像我的個人花園。許多年以前，我曾和其他 20 多人擠在辦公室小隔間裡一起工作，我覺得那樣非常壓抑，也讓工作相當乏味沉悶。

❸ I am not opposed to working alone. In fact, I have found that when I am alone with my thoughts, I tend to be more creative. However, if I were to work with others, I would want to be surrounded by positive and creative people. I think that we could collaborate with one another on a variety of projects and help one another to come up with new ideas.

❸ 我並不反對獨自工作，我覺得獨處時，我會更有創意。但若是跟他人一起工作，我希望身邊是充滿正面又有創造力的人。我覺得我們可以彼此合作各式各樣的專案，並與他們互相激發新點子。

❹ I think it would be very satisfying to have my own personal studio because I would really look forward to going there every day. I think that type of environment would be very stimulating and would enable me to continue to improve my skills.

❹ 能有個人工作室，我一定會很心滿意足，因為這樣我每天都會很期待到工作室去。我覺得這種環境更能夠激發靈感，也能持續精進自己的技能。

Analysis

- Information about the type of job the person has is given in point 1.

分析

- 針對第一點提供了自己的職業資訊。

- Point 2 gives a description of the work environment and provides a contrast with a not so desirable place to work.
- Working alone versus working with others is discussed in point 3.
- Point 4 gives reasons why this environment would be ideal to work in.

- 針對第二點描述理想工作環境的樣子，並對比令人反感的工作環境。
- 第三點談到了獨自工作和與人共事的差異。
- 第四點說明這個工作環境之所以理想的原因。

The speaker of the Sample Answer above uses a personal experience of a place where they worked before that they did not like. This example helps to illustrate and emphasise the elements that make up their ideal working environment. In the same way, contrasts between ideal and undesirable work environments can be given to extend your answer.

以上範例答案提供了個人經驗，講述自己曾經待過但不喜歡的工作環境，這有助於描繪並強調理想工作環境的樣子。像這樣提供理想及反感環境之間的對比，可以增加答案長度。

Part 3 Questions

第三部分 問題

🔊 2-16

01 What factors influence when a person decides to retire?

哪些因素會影響一個人決定要退休？

Strategy

When listing several reasons for something, use signalling words to show where a new point begins (e.g., 'The first', 'Secondly', 'Lastly'). Also, explain or give an example for each of your reasons.

策略

針對問題列出多個原因時，使用轉折指示詞作為新要點的開端（如 The first〔首先〕、Secondly〔其次〕、Lastly〔最後〕），並針對每個原因提供實例，或予以解釋。

❶ I think there are three primary factors that affect how a person would make this decision.

❶ 我認為有三個主要因素會影響一個人做此決定。

❷ The first is the person's financial situation. They should have some money saved, and they need to figure out how much money they need for their monthly expenses. Secondly, a person needs to consider their health. Specifically, they should retire when they are still healthy enough to enjoy their retirement and should not wait until they have developed major health problems that would prevent them from enjoying retirement. Lastly, a person should consider their family responsibilities. If they have children who are still in school or if they have to take care of their aging parents, this will have a major effect on the age at which they choose to retire.

❷ 首先是要考量一個人的經濟狀況，他應該要有積蓄，並且要釐清每個月需要多少開銷。其次要考量到自身健康，尤其應該要在身體還健康時退休，才能享受退休生活，而不是等到健康出現嚴重問題才退休，屆時已經無法享清福了。最後，一個人應該要考慮到家庭責任，如果有還在就學的子女，或者是要照顧年邁的雙親，這都會對退休的年齡造成重大影響。

❸ These are the things that I think likely to have the most major influence on people's retirement decisions.

❸ 我想這些是影響一個人是否退休的主要因素。

Analysis

The factors of a person's financial situation, health, and family responsibilities are explained in this answer. Sequence words (i.e., 'The first', 'Secondly', 'Lastly') are used to introduce these three factors.

分析

範例答案提到了一個人的經濟狀況、健康和家庭責任，都是會影響退休的因素，並使用轉折指示詞（如 The first〔首先〕、Secondly〔其次〕、Lastly〔最後〕）來分別說明這三個要點。

2-17

02 In your opinion, what is more important: having an enjoyable job or having a high-paying job?

在你看來，是有趣的工作重要，還是高薪的工作重要？

Strategy

For the sake of logic and clarity, choose one of these options. If you try to give reasons and examples in defence of both of these options, your answer may become very confusing.

策略

為了使答案邏輯清晰，請從問題中的立場挑一個回答。如果同時針對兩個立場都提供理由和實例，你的答案可能會變得非常模稜兩可。

A

❶ I think both options have their advantages, but in my opinion, having a job you like is more important.

❶ 我覺得兩種觀點都有其優勢，但我個人認為從事喜歡的工作更重要。

❷ If someone doesn't enjoy their job, they will dread going to work every day and will likely have very low productivity. Even if someone is paid well for what they do, if they are unhappy, it could result in depression. Since a large part of adult life is spent working, we should look forward to going to work. I know a lot of people that make a lot of money but

❷ 如果不喜歡自己的工作，每天都會害怕去上班，產能可能也會很低。即使工作的薪水優渥，但不快樂的情緒可能會導致憂鬱症。既然成年生活有很大一部分會耗在工作上，我們應該要期待上班才對。我認識很多人收入雖豐厚，但他們總

are always in a bad mood because of work-related issues.

是因為工作上的事而心情低落。

❸ No amount of money can make up for being unhappy.

❸ 再多的薪資都彌補不了低落的心情。

Analysis

Having an enjoyable job is the option chosen for this answer. The word 'if' is used several times to describe possible situations and to acknowledge the opposing viewpoint. Specific examples similar to the ones in this Sample Answer will make your answer very logical and easy to understand.

策略

範例答案選擇了有趣的工作比較重要，來作為答題立場，並使用好幾個 if 來闡述幾種可能的情況，以及帶出對立觀點。採用這種方式提供例子，能讓你的答案邏輯清晰且易於了解。

2-18

Q03 Do you think it is necessary to have a college degree to find a high-paying job?

你認為大學文憑對於尋找高薪工作是必要的嗎？

Strategy

Sometimes, you may have a viewpoint that is very different from the values that society usually promotes. If you feel strongly about an issue such as education, you can freely express your opinion. This type of question asks you to give your personal feelings, so there is no standard right or wrong answer.

策略

有時候你所抱持的觀點，可能會與普世價值觀相左。若你對於一項議題有強烈看法，例如教育議題，可以盡情抒發己見。這類問題就是要你提供個人想法，所以答案的對錯並沒有標準。

A

❶ I think a lot of people will disagree with me, but my answer is no, it is not necessary to be a college graduate to find a job that pays well.

❶ 很多人可能不會認同，但我的答案是「否」，大學畢業並不是擁有高薪工作的必要條件。

❷ I personally know a lot of people who have college degrees that seem worthless. People study subjects like philosophy

❷ 我認識很多人雖然有大學學歷，但感覺沒什麼用。有些人讀的哲學或藝術史等科系，能

and art history, which have very limited application in the real world. More practical skills, like plumbing and carpentry, are in higher demand, and as a result, workers with such skills can earn a high wage even though they do not have a college degree.

應用在現實世界的地方非常有限。而管線工作、木工等實用技能的需求量更大，因此即使沒有大學學歷，具備這些技術的工人，也能夠有豐厚收入。

❸ Therefore, I think that getting a college education isn't the only way to make a comfortable living.

❸ 所以我認為，接受大學教育並不是過上優渥生活的唯一方式。

Analysis

The first sentence of this Sample Answer indicates that the speaker has an opinion that may be different from that of most people. Next, university degrees with limited real-world application are mentioned to contrast with practical skills, which are in high demand today, to emphasise the speaker's personal opinion.

策略

範例答案的第一句話指出自己的意見可能與多數人相左，接著提及哪些大學文憑在現實世界的實用性有限，並與如今需求量大的實用技能互相比較，藉此強調個人看法。

2-19

Q04 Which do you think is more practical: going to college immediately after high school or first gaining some work experience?

你認為高中畢業後立刻去上大學比較實際，還是先取得工作經驗比較實際？

Strategy

For this type of question, you should choose which option you support. You can also use an experience you have had or a hypothetical situation to explain your answer.

策略

面對這類問題，應該要選擇自己支持的立場。也可以透過親身經歷或假設性情況，說明自己的答案。

A

❶ I think that life experience is more important than having a degree.

❶ 我認為生活經驗比擁有學位更加重要。

❷ If I was an employer looking at several job applicants' resumes, I would choose an applicant with work experience over a new college graduate with zero experience. Someone who has worked before has learned basic things such as how to be punctual, how to be responsible, how to handle money, and communication skills. I think these are skills that can't be learned by sitting in a classroom.

❷ 如果我是雇主，在查看眾多求職者的履歷時，比起毫無經驗的大學畢業生，我會選擇有工作經驗的人。工作過的人已經具備守時、負責任、處理財務和溝通等基本技能，我認為，坐在教室裡是無法學會這些技能的。

❸ So, my personal opinion is that I think everyone should work before going to college.

❸ 因此我的想法是，所有人都應該先去工作再讀大學。

Analysis

The hypothetical situation of an employer looking at job applicants' resumes is given to develop the opinion stated in the opening sentence. The personal opinion is stated again with different vocabulary in the concluding sentence.

策略

範例答案以雇主瀏覽求職者履歷的假設情境，在第一句話就闡述了自己的立場，並在總結句中使用不同說法重申了個人看法。

2-20

Q05 How do you feel about teenagers having part-time jobs?

你對於青少年打工有什麼看法？

Strategy

When asked 'How do you feel about...' you can use words such as 'absolutely' and 'definitely' to show how strongly you feel about the subject.

策略

被問到 How do you feel about...（你有什麼看法）時，可以利用 absolutely（絕對）和 definitely（肯定）等字來表達自己對於某議題的強烈觀點。

❶ I think every teenager absolutely should have a part-time job while they are still in high school.

❶ 我認為所有青少年都有必要在高中期間就去打工。

❷ No matter what type of job they have, it will teach them about being independent, the value of hard work, and the importance of being responsible. Service industry jobs will teach them how to communicate with customers. Manual labour jobs will teach them other valuable skills. I feel that putting a lot of emphasis on test scores puts an unhealthy amount of pressure on young people. Also, taking tests can't prepare you for real life.

❷ 無論是哪一種工作，都能教導他們獨立、努力工作的價值觀，還有負責任的重要性。服務業的工作會教導他們與顧客溝通的方式，勞力工作會教導他們其他重要技能。我認為過度強調考試成績讓年輕人承受了太多不健康的壓力，而且考試無法讓你做好面對現實生活的準備。

❸ I definitely feel that everyone should gain some job experience before they graduate from high school.

❸ 我強烈認為所有人都應該在高中畢業之前，去累積一些工作經驗。

Analysis

In this Sample Answer above, specific industry jobs are mentioned along with the skills young people will gain by having these jobs. Also, a contrast is given between taking tests in school and gaining real-life experience.

分析

以上範例答案提及了特定產業的工作，還有年輕人從事這些工作能習得的技能，並比較了在學校考試，及取得真實生活經驗兩邊的差異。

2-21

06 Do you think celebrities are paid too much for what they do?

你覺得名人是否領取過高報酬？

Strategy

'Celebrity' is a very broad category. It includes movie stars, athletes, singers, and other performers. You can choose to talk about the type of celebrity or work that you are most familiar with.

策略

celebrity（名人）是非常廣泛的人物類別，包含電影明星、運動員、歌手和其他演藝人員。你可以從中選擇談論你最熟悉的一種產業。

❶ Yes, without a doubt, celebrities are paid too much.

❶ 沒錯，他們的收入無疑過高。

❷ Some people will argue that athletes have only a few short years in their career and that the time they spend earning money is therefore shorter than it is for most other professionals. However, the average NBA player makes more money in 1 year than most people make in a lifetime. I once read that one NBA player in his first year made around $7 million, and then every year after that, his salary increased exponentially. Sports stars also make money from advertising and endorsements with companies like Nike. Finally, they only work for a few months out of the year, and they get paid to engage in their hobby.

❷ 有些人會說運動員只有短短幾年的職業壽命，所以他們能夠賺錢的時間比多數職業更短。然而一名普通 NBA 球員的年收入，卻超出多數人一輩子的收入。我讀過一篇文章，一名球員在生涯第一年大約能賺進七百萬美元，之後的薪水會逐年大幅增長。運動明星也能靠廣告和代言 Nike 等公司的產品來賺錢。還有，他們每年只需要工作幾個月，而且還是靠興趣賺錢。

❸ Therefore, yes, I think celebrities are overpaid.

❸ 因此，是的，我認為名人的收入過高。

Analysis

This Sample Answer contains some statistics about the salary of an athlete. When giving this type of information, you do not have to name the specific source where it came from, nor do you have to give exact figures. A general summary of information is enough.

分析

範例答案中包含了一些運動員收入的數據。在提供這種資訊時，不需要說出明確的資料來源，也不需要提供準確數字，大致總結一些資料就夠了。

LESSON 2 Work

2-22

Q07 Who do you think should be paid more: celebrities or teachers?

你認為誰應該拿更多薪水，名人或是教師？

Strategy

As stated before, with this type of question, make a clear case as to which side you support, in favour of either celebrities or teachers. Then, be specific in your examples.

策略

正如先前所述，遇到這類問題時，要明確表示你支持的立場：是名人或教師，並舉出清楚例子說明。

A

❶ I really feel that educators today are severely undervalued, especially when it comes to their salaries.

❷ Teachers should be paid more because of the positive contribution they make to society. They are responsible for shaping young lives in very important ways. However, some school teachers make barely enough money to survive, and so they have to work two jobs. By contrast, a movie star works for just a few weeks filming a movie and gets paid millions of dollars. Furthermore, actors often live very scandalous and immoral lives and thus can have a negative effect on young people.

❸ I really think the difference in the salaries of these two professions is very unfair. Teachers should be paid more, and actors should be paid less.

❶ 我真心認為現今教育工作者的重要性被嚴重低估，尤其他們的薪資更是低廉。

❷ 教師的薪資應該要更高，因為他們為社會帶來正面貢獻。他們肩負重任以形塑年輕人的一生。然而，有些學校教師的薪資少到難以生存，導致他們必須做兩份工作。相較之下，電影明星拍攝一部電影只需要幾週的時間，卻能賺進數百萬美元。此外，演員還常常過著傷風敗俗的生活，這可能會對年輕人造成負面影響。

❸ 我真的認為這兩種職業的薪資差異很不公平，教師的報酬應該要更高，而演員的報酬應該更低。

Analysis

An explanation of the importance of teachers' role in society along with their low salary is given. This is followed by a contrast describing movie stars' salaries and their impact on society. This contrast is provided to form a convincing and clear answer.

分析

範例答案解釋了教師這個角色在社會上的重要性，並提到他們的薪資低廉。接著描述了電影明星的收入及其對社會的影響，以與教師的例子進行對比。這樣的比較，能組織出一個令人信服且立場清楚的答案。

2-23

Q08 What jobs do young people in your country NOT want to do?

你國家的年輕人不想從事哪些工作？

Strategy

Comment on the trends you see in modern society. Describe the different views people have towards different types of jobs.

策略

根據你在現代社會所觀察到的局勢發表評論，描述人們對不同工作的看法差異。

A

❶ I think any type of job where you have to get your hands dirty would be considered undesirable by most young people today.

❷ Nowadays, most people want to have a desk job where they can sit in front of a computer in a climate-controlled office. Gone are the days when young people wanted to work in a factory or in agriculture. Today, very few young people want to work outside or work with their hands; such jobs are considered to be those done by the uneducated. However, those jobs actually pay very well, and in some countries, people can make a comfortable living from them.

❸ I think any type of manual labour job is likely to be avoided by most young people today.

❶ 我認為現在年輕人大多認為，任何會弄髒雙手的工作都不算理想。

❷ 當今多數人會想要從事辦公室工作，坐在有溫控的辦公室裡，面對著電腦。年輕人會想要待在工廠或從事農業的日子已經過去了，現在很少有年輕人會想要在戶外工作，或是靠雙手勞動，這些都被視為沒讀書的人才會做的工作。然而這些工作的報酬其實很高，部分國家的人還能因此過上優渥生活。

❸ 我認為現在多數的年輕人可能都會避開任何勞力工作。

Analysis

The choices made by the majority of young people and their attitudes toward certain types of work are commented on in this Sample Answer. Specific examples of undesirable jobs, such as manual labour jobs, are given.

分析

範例答案闡述了多數年輕人偏好的職業，以及他們針對特定職業所持的態度，並舉出非理想工作的明確例子，例如勞力工作。

2-24

Q09 How have jobs in your country changed over the past few decades?

過去幾十年來，工作型態在你的國家產生何種改變？

Strategy

Describe trends you have seen in how jobs have changed. If you have years of work experience, comment on changes you have experienced personally. You could also comment on changes that have occurred in the jobs your parents or relatives have had over the years.

策略

針對工作型態，描述你觀察到的改變。若你已經有數年的工作經驗，可以說說自己的親身經歷。也可以講述在這些年來，你的父母或親戚遇到的工作型態變化。

A

❶ Just a few decades ago, the majority of people in my country had manufacturing or farming jobs.

❶ 在短短幾十年前，我國家的多數人還在從事製造業或農業。

❷ My grandparents had their own farm, where they grew mostly fruit trees. After that, my parents worked in factories, assembling electronics. They thought that this was a great improvement over doing farmwork. Nowadays, most people my age work in technology-related or service industry jobs. I personally do website design. I would never want to have the types of jobs that previous generations had.

❷ 我的爺爺奶奶有自己的農場，主要都是種植果樹。後來我父母在工廠組裝電子零件，他們都認為這比起農業已經是一大進步。如今我多數的同齡人都從事科技相關或服務業的工作。我個人在做網頁設計，我絕對不會想要從事上一輩的那種工作。

❸ I think advancements in technology really affect the jobs that people have; these two things are very closely related.

❸ 我認為科技的進步確實大大影響了人們的職業，這兩者有密切關聯。

Analysis

This Sample Answer gives a logical progression regarding changes in jobs over three generations of the same family. The concluding

分析

範例答案以合乎邏輯的順序，講述一家三代人的職業變化。結尾的發言總結了這些改變的可能原

statement summarises the most likely reason for these changes, namely advancements in technology.

因，也就是科技的進步。

2-25

Q10 How do you think jobs will change over the next 20 years?

你認為工作型態在未來 20 年會有什麼改變？

Strategy

This question requires you to use your imagination to come up with an answer. Changes you have noted in the types of jobs available in your country will help you to predict how things may progress in the future.

策略

這個問題要求你發揮想像力來回答。從你所觀察到的國內職缺類型變化，有助於你想像未來可能會有的演變。

A

❶ I think that 20 years from now, most manufacturing and food production jobs will have moved to neighbouring developing nations. I also think that tourism will really take off in my country.

❶ 我想 20 年以後，多數製造業和食品生產業會轉移到鄰近的開發中國家。我也覺得我國的觀光業可能會變得很發達。

❷ Over the past few years, a lot of foreign tourists have been coming to my country, and a lot of resorts and restaurants have been opening. Therefore, I think that almost everyone will be working in service industry jobs in the future. In addition, working in hotels or restaurants or being a tour guide will be very popular. Furthermore, because there are tourists coming from many different countries, another job that will be in demand will be language instructors. I have already seen many hotel and restaurant staff taking language classes so that they can communicate better with overseas visitors.

❷ 過去幾年，來了許多外國觀光客，還有很多度假村和餐廳陸續開張。因此，我認為在未來，多數人都會去從事服務業。此外，飯店業、餐廳或是導遊等工作都會相當熱門。還有，由於有許多來自不同國家的觀光客，因此另一種備受需要的工作是語言教師。我注意到已經有許多飯店及餐廳員工在上語言課程，以便跟海外旅客溝通得更順暢。

❸ These are the main job trends that I have observed over the past few years, and I think these trends will become more significant in the future.

❸ 這些是我在過去幾年，所主要觀察到的工作型態變化，我認為這樣的趨勢在未來會變得更明顯。

Analysis

This Sample Answer describes trends that are seen in a lot of countries today. It describes the transition from an agricultural and manufacturing-based economy to one that is more dependent on tourism. Specific examples of tourism and service-industry-related jobs are given.

分析

範例答案描述了現今在許多國家都能看見的趨勢，並說明了國家經濟一開始以農業和製造業為基礎，過渡成為現在比較依賴觀光業的經濟型態，並舉出觀光業和服務業等相關工作的實例。

Additional Tips and Resources 補充技巧及資料

Sentence Build-Ups 延長句子

After you have learned a new grammar pattern, add new words and phrases to sentences you already know; doing this will enhance your grammar score.

在你本來就會的句子結構裡加入新的字詞，可以幫助你延長答案，以提高文法的得分。

1. I had lunch. 我吃了午餐。

+ time 加上時間	**Yesterday** I had lunch. 我**昨天**吃了午餐。
+ location 加上地點	Yesterday I had lunch **at the café**. 我昨天**在咖啡廳**吃了午餐。
+ person 加上人物	Yesterday I had lunch **with my friend** at the café. Yesterday I had lunch at the café **with my friend**. 我昨天**跟朋友**在咖啡廳吃了午餐。
+ food item 加上食物品項	Yesterday I had **a sandwich** for lunch at the café with my friend. 我昨天跟朋友在咖啡廳吃了**三明治**當午餐。
+ adjective 加上形容詞	Yesterday I had a **delicious** sandwich for lunch at the café with my friend. 我昨天跟朋友在咖啡廳吃了一份**好吃的**三明治當午餐。
+ future tense 加上未來時態	**Tomorrow I will** have a delicious sandwich for lunch at the café with my friend. **明天**我要跟朋友在咖啡廳吃好吃的三明治當午餐。

2. The boy ran. 那男孩在跑步。

+ adverb 加上副詞	The boy ran **quickly**. 那男孩跑得**飛快**。
+ location 加上地點	The boy ran quickly **down the street**. 那男孩**在街上**跑得飛快。
+ a detail 加上細節	The boy ran quickly down the street **in the rain**. 那男孩在**下了雨**的街上跑得飛快。
+ a reason 加上理由	The boy ran quickly down the street in the rain **to get away from the dog**. 那男孩在下了雨的街上跑得飛快，**以逃離那隻狗**。

LESSON 3

Education

教育

LESSON 3

Education 教育

Part 1 Questions | 第一部分 問題

3-01

01 What is/was your major? How did you choose this major?

你現在／之前主修什麼？為何選擇這門主修？

Strategy

Give details about the types of things you study or have studied, any projects you have done in school, and whether or not you like or liked your major.

策略

針對你正在研讀，或曾經讀過的科系提供細節，可提及你在學校做過的任何專題，以及你是否喜歡這門主修。

A While at university, I majored in political science. I really was not interested in this course, but it was the only major that my test scores allowed me to qualify for. We had to do a lot of reading about politics, which I found very boring.

我大學時主修的是政治，我對政治課程真的不感興趣，但是我的考試成績只能讀這個科系。我們要讀很多政治相關的文獻，我覺得非常無聊。

3-02

02 How long have you been studying English?

你學英文多久了？

Strategy

Remember to use the present perfect tense or present perfect progressive tense discussed in the previous chapter for an action that began in the past, has continued until the present, and will probably continue into the future.

策略

記得使用先前章節提過的「現在完成式」或「現在完成進行式」來描述起始於過去、持續進行到現在、且有可能延續到未來的動作。

A I have been studying English for the past 15 years since I was in kindergarten. I really like English and enjoy reading news from the US and the UK. I think this activity has really helped my English improve.

我從幼稚園開始學英文，已經學了 15 年。我真的很喜歡英文，也樂於閱讀美國和英國的新聞，我想這件事確實有助於加強我的英文能力。

3-03

Q03 Why do you think it is important to study English?

你覺得學英文為什麼重要？

Strategy

Reasons that show how English has become an international language and a tool for global communication could be given to help develop your answer.

策略

可以在答案中說明理由，講述英文已經成為一門國際語言，也是全球的溝通工具，如此可以幫助你擴展答案。

A English has become a modern-day lingua franca. It is the most widely spoken language in the world today and has become the main language used in fields such as business, technology, and medicine. Therefore, I think it is essential for everyone to learn at least some English.

英文已經成為現代世界的通用語了，它是目前世界上最為廣泛使用的語言，也已經成為商業、科技和醫療領域人士所使用的主要語言。因此，我認為所有人都有必要至少學一點英文。

3-04

04 What is the most challenging aspect of studying English for you?

對你來說，學英文最大的困難是什麼？

Strategy

Discuss your personal experience of learning English.

策略

談談你學習英文時的親身經歷。

A I think the most difficult area to improve in is speaking. In my country, very few people

我認為最大的困難在於加強口說。我的國家沒什麼人會說英

speak English, so it is very hard to find someone to practice speaking it with. For this reason, when I do get to speak English with others, I find that I speak too slowly and that it is hard to think of the right words to use.

文，所以很難找到對象來練習說英文。正因如此，我在跟別人說英文時，我發現自己的語速很慢，也很難想到能用什麼精準的字詞。

🔊 3-05

05 How do you plan to use English in the future?

在未來，你打算如何使用英文？

Strategy

Describe your future plans for study or work and explain how you will use English in these areas.

策略

描述你未來的求學或工作計畫，並解釋你會如何在這些計畫中用到英文。

A I plan to study in Canada and then find a job there. All the classes I will take will be in English, and then after I start working, all of my co-workers will also speak English. So, I plan to use English every day. It will become a big part of my life after I move abroad.

我打算到加拿大讀書，然後在那裡求職。我要上的所有課程都是全英語授課，在我開始就業之後，所有同事也都是說英文，所以我預計每天都會用到英文。我出國之後，英文會成為我生活的一大部分。

🔊 3-06

06 Do you participate in any clubs or extracurricular activities?

你參加過任何社團或課外活動嗎？

Strategy

Many students have difficulty understanding this question and often speak off topic. The word 'curriculum' means regular school classes and their content, whereas 'extracurricular' refers to any activity at school that occurs in addition to regular classes, including activities like sports, music, and student associations.

策略

許多學生聽不懂這個問題，在回答時經常會離題。curriculum 的意思是「（學校）全部課程」，而 extracurricular 指的是「課外的」，也就是任何基本課程之外的校內活動，包括體育活動、音樂表演或學生會等。

A I joined my high school dance team. At first, I wasn't really interested in dance; I joined because I thought it would be a good way to make new friends. However, later, I found out that I was really good at dancing. We took part in some competitions with other schools and eventually won first place.

我高中參加了學校舞蹈隊。起初我對跳舞沒什麼興趣，我會參加是因為我覺得這是個交新朋友的好方法，但我後來發現自己很擅長跳舞。我們參加了一些校際比賽，最後還得了第一名。

3-07

Q07 What was your favourite subject while in school?

你在求學期間最喜歡什麼科目？

Strategy

Discuss your personal experience. You can describe how you felt about studying this subject.

策略

談談你的親身經歷，描述研讀這門科目所帶給你的感受。

A I really loved art class. I found this class to be very relaxing because we were not under any pressure to get a high score. We were allowed to be creative and express ourselves. I enjoyed working with various materials such as clay, wood, and paint to make things.

我真的很愛美術課，我覺得這堂課很輕鬆，因為我們不必追求高分，所以沒有壓力。我們可以盡情發揮創意、表達自我。我喜歡使用各式各樣的材料來創作，例如黏土、木材和顏料。

3-08

Q08 Did you have a favourite teacher while in school?

你在求學期間有最喜歡的老師嗎？

Strategy

Describe the personality of this teacher. You could also give a brief account of something this teacher said or did.

策略

描述這位老師的個性，也可以簡單舉例這位老師說過的話或做過的事。

A My favourite teacher was my eighth-grade history teacher, Mr. Smith. In his class, we always had a lot of fun. He wasn't a strict

我最喜歡的老師，是八年級的歷史老師——史密斯老師。我們上他的課總是很開心。他不是位嚴

teacher. He let us ask questions and allowed us to work on group projects together. I learned a lot about history, and I think this was because of his relaxed teaching style. Every day, we all looked forward to his class.

格的老師，他會讓我們問問題，也會讓我們跟同學一起做小組專題。我學到很多歷史知識，我想這都是因為他的教學風格很輕鬆。我們每天都很期待上他的課。

3-09

Q09 Did you have a lot of friends when you were in school?

你在求學期間朋友多嗎？

Strategy

You can choose to talk about your interactions with your classmates in elementary school, middle school, high school, or university.

策略

可以講述自己跟小學、國中、高中或大學同學的互動。

A When I was in elementary school, I was very quiet and shy, so I did not have many friends. The summer before high school, my family moved to a new town, so I knew I would be going to a new school with new classmates who didn't know me. I decided that this was a new beginning for me and that I needed to become more outgoing. Even though this wasn't easy for me to do at first, the result was that I made a lot of new friends in high school, some of whom I still keep in touch with even today.

我小學時非常安靜、害羞，所以我沒有什麼朋友。在上高中前的那個夏天，我們家搬到了新的城鎮，因此我知道自己得到新學校和新同學一起念書了，而那些新同學都不認識我。所以我決定把這當作是自己的新起點，我必須外向一點。雖然一開始這對我來說並不容易，但最後我在高中交到很多新朋友，我們至今也都還保持聯絡。

3-10

10 How do you feel about taking tests?

你對考試有什麼看法？

Strategy

Improve your Vocabulary score by using academic synonyms for common words. Then,

策略

使用學術性同義字來取代一般單字，可以提高你的字彙分數。並

use their different forms in different grammatical structures. Look at the vocabulary choices below:

針對不同的文法架構，使用字彙的不同詞性。例如：

Band Score 分數等級	5	6	7
adjective 形容詞	nervous 緊張的	anxious 焦慮的	apprehensive 憂心的
noun 名詞	nervousness 緊張	anxiety 焦慮	apprehension 憂慮

A Preparing for a test makes me very apprehensive, and I always experience a lot of anxiety the night before a test. Even though I do all my homework so that I always understand the material well, I'm just not good at taking tests. I think this is what makes me so nervous about taking tests.

準備考試讓我非常憂心，我在考試前一晚總是會非常焦慮。就算我做完所有作業，充分理解了課程內容，我還是不擅長考試。我想這就是考試讓我如此緊張的原因。

Part 2 Questions | 第二部分 問題

3-11

Q01 Describe a useful skill.

描述一項實用技能。

You should say:

❶ what it is

❷ where it can be learned

❸ what is needed to learn this skill

❹ and explain why this skill is useful.

應該提到：

❶ 是什麼技能

❷ 可以在哪裡習得

❸ 要學會這項技能需要什麼

❹ 說明這項技能的實用之處。

A

❶ I feel that problem solving is a skill that is seriously neglected in many educational systems today. Problem solving is related to logic and reasoning, common sense, and the ability to make conclusions based on evidence.

❶ 我覺得解決問題的技能，是現今許多教育系統都嚴重忽略的能力。解決問題與邏輯推理、常識，以及根據證據做出結論的能力有關。

❷ Everyone can acquire problem-solving skills ❸ in everyday life by making observations and by interacting with people. Education systems today, especially in places like Asia, focus only on memorising facts and preparing students for written tests. However, 5 minutes after the test is over, all the facts that have been memorised are forgotten.

❷ 只要在日常生活中觀察並與人❸ 互動，大家都可以習得解決問題的這項技能。現今在亞洲等地方的教育系統只重視背誦知識，讓學生針對考試做好準備。然而，在考試結束五分鐘後，學生就會把背過的所有知識都忘光。

❹ The facts and information that people memorise in school often can't be used in real life. Most people will never use things like complicated math formulas and statistical information after they graduate

❹ 人們在學校背誦的知識與資訊無法應用在現實生活中。多數人在畢業後，永遠用不到像是複雜的數學公式和統計資料這種東西。正因為有這種教育系

from school. Because of this type of school system, people might be intelligent in an academic way but unaware how to make decisions or communicate with others in the real world. I think this issue is related to a lot of problems seen in families and society as a whole.

統，人們在學術課業上可能很厲害，卻不懂得如何做決定或與人溝通。我想這個議題和許多家庭以及整體社會的眾多問題相關。

Analysis

Contrasting examples of memorising facts to pass a test and the real-world application of knowledge are used in several places in the Sample Answer above. Such examples are used to emphasise the value of the main skill being discussed, namely problem solving in this case.

分析

以上範例答案多處比較了利用背誦而來的知識通過考試，和知識應用在現實生活中的例子。透過這些實例可用來強調答案中所探討的主要技能有多重要，也就是解決問題的技能。

3-12

Q02 Describe a project you did at school.

描述你在學校做過的一項專題。

You should say:

❶ what it was
❷ how long you worked on it
❸ who worked on it with you
❹ and explain how you felt about the project.

應該提到：

❶ 是什麼專題
❷ 你花了多少時間
❸ 誰跟你一起進行
❹ 說明你對這項專題的感想。

A

❶ When I was in third grade we made a 3D model of the solar system. This was a very memorable project for me.
❷ Our teacher instructed us to work in groups ❸ of four, and we spent almost a month working on the project. The reason that it took so long to complete was because we

❶ 我三年級的時候，和同學做了一個太陽系的 3D 立體模型，這個專題作業令我相當難忘。
❷ 我們老師指派我們四人一組進❸ 行專題，我們花了將近一個月的時間製作。之所以花這麼多時間才完成，是因為我們想要

wanted to make our model as accurate as possible. We divided the workload, and each of us worked on two or three planets individually. We really paid attention to getting the details of each planet right. For example, we made each planet to scale so that its size was accurate, and then we spent a lot of time getting the colours of each one right, too. The teacher supplied us with Styrofoam balls of various sizes and other art supplies that we could use for the planets. I remember that I wanted to make my planets look extra special, so I went to a number of art supply stores and bought extra paints and colours to enhance the look of the planets I was working on. Therefore, some of the planets took me more than a week to complete.

盡可能呈現準確的作品。我們分配了工作，每人獨自負責兩、三顆星球。我們非常仔細還原每一顆星球的細節，像是我們按比例來製作每一顆星球，這樣大小才正確，接著又耗費許多時間調整各個星球的顏色。老師提供我們不同尺寸的保麗龍球，和其他美勞用品，讓我們製作星球。我記得我想讓我的星球看起來格外特別，所以我跑去不同的美術用品店，買了額外的塗料和染料來加強我負責製作的星球。因此有些星球花了我一週以上的時間才完成。

❹ I really enjoyed this project. I learned so much about the solar system. I still remember facts and details about the planets I worked on even today. In other words, the project had a lasting impression on me. As a result, today, I still enjoy reading about planets and other space-related discoveries. In addition, I really enjoyed working with my classmates. Since this was in elementary school, it was the first time I got to work on a group project. In summary, this was a very memorable project.

❹ 我非常喜歡這項專題，從中學到許多太陽系知識，即使到了現在，我都還記得我負責製作的星球有哪些特徵和細節，也就是說這個經驗讓我印象深刻。所以到了現在，我還是很喜歡閱讀星球文章，並探索其他與太空相關的知識。此外，我也很喜歡跟同學合作。由於這是小學的事，所以這是我第一次做小組專題。總之，這是非常難忘的小組專題作業。

Analysis

- The project is briefly introduced in point 1.
- Points 2 and 3 are discussed together

分析

- 第一點簡短介紹了這項專題。
- 一併詳述第二及第三點，因為

because these ideas are referred to several times throughout this portion of the answer.

– Point 4 discusses the lasting impression made by working on this project.

這兩點在回答時經常放在一起講。

– 第四點講述製作這項專題時所留下的印象。

Although the topic of the solar system may sound very complicated, notice how the names of the planets are not mentioned in this Sample Answer. If you do not know any scientific or technical words in English, you can still discuss the question topic in general terms, as seen above.

雖然太陽系的話題聽起來可能很複雜，但範例答案中並沒有提及星球名稱。如果你不知道該怎麼用英文表達科學名詞或術語也無妨，還是可以使用如以上範例答案中這些較籠統的字詞，來談論這類主題。

🔊 3-13

03 Describe a subject you have studied before.

描述一門你曾經學過的科目。

You should say:

❶ what it was
❷ how long you studied it
❸ why you studied it
❹ and explain whether it was useful.

應該提到：

❶ 是什麼科目
❷ 你學了多久
❸ 你為何學習該科目
❹ 說明該科目是否有用。

A

❶ I went to a vocational high school, which offered classes that were very different from conventional academic classes. In vocational classes, students can learn specialised skills while they are still in high school. I chose to study auto mechanics because I knew that this was a skill that was in demand.

❶ 我就讀職業高中。職業高中所提供的課程跟一般學術課程相去甚遠。在這些職業課程裡，學生在高中就能學到專業技能。我選擇學習汽車維修，因為我知道這項技能的需求量很大。

❷ This was a 4-year course. For the first 3 years, we studied in the classroom and in the workshop at the school. Then, in my

❷ 這是四年制的課程，我們前三年要在教室和學校工作坊學習。高四的時候，我在校外有

senior year, I did an internship, where I went out and worked at an auto repair shop for about 4 hours a day. I got a lot of hands-on experience this way, and I learned a lot from the mechanics I worked with. They had been working in this field for more than 20 years, so they knew how to handle all different types of vehicles and the best ways to repair them.

一份實習工作，每天要到一間汽車維修廠工作四小時左右。這讓我得到許多實際經驗，也從共事的技師身上學到很多。他們已經在這個領域從業 20 多年了，所以懂得如何處理各式各樣的汽車，還有最佳的維修方式。

❸ I chose to study auto mechanics because I ❹ knew it would be a very valuable skill for me to have. Unlike other jobs that go through drastic changes due to developments in technology, being an auto mechanic is a job that will always be in demand. Everyone drives a car, and every car needs maintenance. Therefore, I knew that I would be able to find a job immediately after graduation, and I was able to do just that. I have been working as a mechanic for the past 5 years now. I have always had steady work, and the pay is very good. I have no regrets with regard to my choice to take this course while I was in high school.

❸ 我選擇學習汽車維修，是因為 ❹ 我知道這對我來說會是一項寶貴的技能。不像其他工作會因為科技發展而產生劇烈變化，汽車維修這份工作永遠都會有需求。每個人都會開車，而每一輛車都需要保養。因此我知道我一畢業就能立刻找到工作，而事實也正是如此。我已經當了五年的汽車維修技師，我的工作量始終很穩定，酬勞也相當優渥。我完全不後悔在高中時選擇了這門科目。

Analysis

After background information about the local education system is given, the speaker describes in chronological order the highlights of the auto mechanics programme. The benefits of this skill are explained in the final part of this Sample Answer.

分析

範例答案先是提及了當地教育系統的背景資訊，接著按照時間順序描述了這門汽車維修課的重點事項，並在最後一部分解釋了這項技能的優點。

3-14

Q 04 Describe your school.

描述你的學校。

You should say:

❶ your impression of the school
❷ what it looks like from the outside
❸ its location
❹ and introduce any special facilities it has.

應該提到：

❶ 你對學校的印象
❷ 學校外觀看起來如何
❸ 學校的地點
❹ 介紹學校有的特殊設施。

A

❶ I remember that I was one of the first students that went to our newly built middle school. This school was much bigger and more modern than my elementary school. I recall walking through the main doors on my first day and being amazed at how broad and spacious the hallways were.

❶ 我記得我是第一批就讀新成立中學的學生，這所學校比我的小學大很多，也更加現代化。我還記得第一天走進校門的時候，寬大又開闊的走廊讓我驚豔不已。

❷ From the outside, the building appeared massive. It was two storeys high and grey in colour with red highlights on the corners of the outside walls.

❷ 學校外觀看起來相當巨大，有兩層樓高，外牆是灰色的，角落則用了紅色作為點綴。

❸ I lived in a very rural area, so the school was in a picturesque location. It was surrounded by trees and big fields that were used for playing sports. In the distance, you could see mountains. I thought it was a very peaceful setting and very conducive for studying.

❸ 我住在非常鄉下的地方，所以學校所在地的景色如詩如畫。學校周圍都是樹木和運動用的遼闊場地，還能看見遠方的山脈。我認為這個環境非常平靜，非常有利於學習。

❹ There were many modern facilities that other schools in the area did not have. We had a computer lab where we took basic computer classes, which was something very new to me at the time. There was a cosy library that had a real working fireplace.

❹ 我的學校有許多其他附近的學校所沒有的現代化設施。我們有一間電腦教室能上基本電腦課程，這在當時對我而言可說是非常前衛。還有一間舒適的圖書館，裡面有一座真的能運

The gymnasium was huge and had different areas for different sports. Also, each of the classrooms had air conditioning, which was something very unique for the time. The place where I lived had a cool climate, so most schools in that area did not have air conditioning. I have very fond memories of going to this school.

作的壁爐。體育館非常大，每種運動在體育館內都有各自的獨立區域。每間教室還都裝有空調，這在當時非常特殊；因為我住的地方氣候涼爽，所以大部分學校並沒有空調。在這所學校就讀，是非常美好的回憶。

Analysis

This answer uses a lot of phrases to describe feelings, size, and dimensions. Such vocabulary can be used in any answer where you have to describe a building, a place, or an object. Use past tense verbs if you have already graduated from school or present tense verbs if you are still enrolled in the school.

分析

範例答案中有各種用來描述感受、尺寸及空間的用字。在描述建築物、地點或物品時，都可以使用這一類字彙。如果已經從該所學校畢業了，要使用過去式；如果還在校就讀，就使用現在式。

3-15

05 Describe a school event you have participated in before.

描述一場你參加過的學校活動。

You should say:

❶ what the event was
❷ what activities were involved
❸ how you felt about this event
❹ and explain whether you thought the event had educational value.

應該提到：

❶ 是什麼活動
❷ 包含什麼項目
❸ 你對這場活動的感想
❹ 說明你認為該活動是否具有教育意義。

❶ Every year, in my elementary school, every class got to participate in Field Day, when we would spend the entire day outside participating in sports competitions.

❶ 每一年，我小學的所有班級都要參加「運動會」。我們一整天都會在戶外參加體育競賽。

❷ These competitions included relay races, long distance running, and team sports like soccer and baseball. Also, every year, some of the teachers would come up with some other creative sports just to add some variety.

❷ 這些競賽包含大隊接力、長跑，還有團隊運動，例如足球和棒球。而且每年都會有老師想出一些另類的創意競賽，以增加活動多樣性。

❸ My classmates and I really enjoyed Field Day, and we looked forward to it all year. I think it was good for us to get out of the classroom and get some fresh air and exercise. The only problem was that the weather was sometimes really hot, so we had to drink a lot of water and be careful not to get sunburnt.

❸ 我和同學都非常喜歡運動會，我們一整年都很期待這一天。我覺得能夠走出教室、呼吸新鮮空氣並運動對我們是一件好事。唯一的問題在於，有時候天氣會非常熱，所以我們得多喝水，也要小心不要曬傷。

❹ Although some parents might have thought that this event was a waste of time, I thought it had real educational value. We learned to cooperate with our classmates and work as a team. We also learned about one another's strengths and weaknesses, such as who was the quickest in short sprints and who had more endurance so that they could do the long-distance run. At the end of the day, we all had a sense of belonging and a feeling of camaraderie. I wish that more schools today would hold these types of sports events. Kids really need to get out of the classroom and burn off some energy sometimes.

❹ 儘管有些家長可能會認為這種活動是在浪費時間，但我覺得這項活動非常具教育意義。我們能夠學習與同學互助合作，團結一致，也可以藉此了解彼此的強項與弱點，例如誰的短跑速度最快，或是誰的耐力更強，能夠負責長跑。一天結束後，大家都能獲得歸屬感和同胞情誼。我希望現今能有更多學校舉辦這種體育賽事，有時候孩子真的需要走出教室，燃燒一些精力。

Analysis

As seen in this Sample Answer, for questions such as this, you can relate a story about your school life. A contrast is given in point 4, which

分析

正如範例答案所示，面對這種問題時，你可以講述自己的校園生活故事。第四點做了比較，先說

first expresses the opposing viewpoint that many parents might have regarding this type of activity, before the personal opinion of the speaker is clearly stated in the remainder of the answer.

明有許多家長對這種活動抱有負面看法，接著在後半段清楚表明答題者自己的個人觀點。

Part 3 Questions

第三部分 問題

🔊 3-16

Q01 How has education changed in your country over the past few decades?

過去幾十年來，教育系統在你的國家有什麼改變？

Strategy

Make a contrast between what you learned in school and things your parents might have learned when they were in school.

策略

比較你和你父母過去在學校所學到的知識。

A

❶ Years ago, many countries' economies were based on agriculture and manufacturing. Most people worked on farms or in factories, and so the education system at that time emphasised agricultural and manufacturing skills.

❷ However, nowadays, most jobs are technology or service industry related. This change has resulted in more computer-based classes. There used to be a factory near my house, and my father says that most of our neighbours were employed there, so it is clear why education was geared toward factory work back then. However, that factory went out of business a few years ago. I think that given the choice, most young people today would rather work in an office than in a factory, and I think that this is why the focus of education has shifted over the past few decades.

❶ 許多年前，很多國家的經濟基礎都建立在農業和製造業之上。多數人都在農場或工廠工作，因此當時的教育系統比較著重在教授農業及製造業的技能。

❷ 然而，現今多數工作都與科技業或服務業有關，也因此出現更多以電腦為基礎的課程。我家附近以前有一座工廠，我父親說鄰居大多都是那裡的員工，所以很顯然當時比較著重於以工廠為導向的教育。不過那座工廠已經在幾年前倒閉了。我想如果能夠選擇的話，現今多數年輕人會寧願在辦公室而不是在工廠工作。這可能就是為什麼教育在這幾十年間發生了轉變。

❸ I believe these are the biggest changes in education in recent times.

❸ 我覺得這些就是近年來教育系統最大的改變。

Analysis

The beginning of the Sample Answer above discusses trends in employment decades ago. In point 2, comparisons are used to describe how these trends have changed and how these changes have affected not only people's job choices but also the focus of modern education.

分析

以上範例答案開頭談到了數十年前的就業趨勢，並在第二點透過比較來說明這些趨勢的改變，及其對於人們選擇工作與現今教育系統的影響。

🔊 3-17

What skills do you think should be taught in schools nowadays to help young people find employment?

你認為現在的學校應該要教授什麼技能，才能幫助年輕人求職？

Strategy

If you have a job, think about the skills that are needed in your job. If you are still a student, consider the skills you may need in the future.

策略

如果你有工作，想想這項工作需具備何種技能。如果你還是學生，請思考看看未來可能會需要哪些技能。

A

❶ I think that computer literacy and communication skills should be given priority in our education system.

❶ 我們的教育系統應該優先考量電腦素養和溝通技巧。

❷ Most jobs today use computer systems, and so a basic knowledge of computers is essential. Whether people work in an office or a restaurant, they all need to use some type of computerised system. Being an effective communicator is equally important. We all need to talk with others, send emails, and collaborate with colleagues in everyday

❷ 現今大多數工作都會用到電腦系統，所以基本的電腦知識必不可少。無論是在辦公室或是餐廳工作，都會需要用到某種電腦化系統。而具備與人有效溝通的能力也同樣重要，因為我們每天都要與他人交談、寄送電子郵件，還要跟同事合

life. Some people may be good with computers but not know how to interact with others. This can cause a lot of problems in the workplace.

作。有些人可能擅長使用電腦，卻不懂得如何與他人互動，這在職場上可能會造成許多問題。

❸ This is why computer literacy and communication skills are the most important things that people should be taught in school.

❸ 這就是為什麼電腦素養及溝通技巧，是人們在學校最應該習得的重要技能。

Analysis

In point 2 of the Sample Answer above, examples are given regarding the most common jobs that people have today, and the skills that are required to succeed in these jobs are mentioned. Specifically, computer skills and communication skills are universally important regardless of the job a person has.

分析

以上範例答案在第二點舉例說明現今常見的工作，並點出做好這些工作所需的技能：也就是無論一個人的工作為何，電腦知識和溝通技巧通常都是很重要的技能。

3-18

03 What are the pros and cons of school uniforms?

學校制服有什麼優缺點？

Strategy

With this type of question, give a balanced answer by talking about both sides of the issue. Try to give at least one specific example for both the positive and negative aspects of wearing school uniforms.

策略

面對這類問題，請對等說明該議題的正反面。盡量針對穿學校制服的優點和缺點，至少各提供一個實例。

❶ I think there are a lot of varying opinions for and against school uniforms.

❶ 對於學校制服的議題，看法眾說紛紜。

❷ As for the advantages, I think uniforms can eliminate a lot of distractions. Students often like to compare what their classmates are wearing. If a student comes from a

❷ 就好處而言，我認為制服能排除許多使學生分心的因子。學生常常都會和同學互相比較衣著，如果有學生的家庭背景較

poor background and therefore can't buy expensive clothing, they may be teased by their classmates. This type of behaviour might distract students from their studies. With regard to the disadvantages of uniforms, I have heard many people say that they think a dress code stifles self-expression. Specifically, some students feel that they can't express themselves if they are dressed just like everyone else.

為貧困，買不起昂貴的衣服，可能會遭到同學嘲笑，如此行為有可能使學生無法專心在課業上。至於穿制服的缺點，我聽過許多人認為規定學生衣著會扼殺自我表達的能力。也就是說有些學生覺得，所有人都穿得一模一樣會使他們無法展現自己。

❸ Personally, I think both sides have valid points when it comes to this issue.

❸ 就我個人而言，我認為這個議題正反雙方的看法都有道理。

Analysis

Brief examples are given for both sides of the issue. Eliminating distractions is the reason given in support of uniforms, while the loss of freedom of expression is the reason given to oppose uniforms. A personal opinion is very briefly given at the end of the answer.

分析

範例答案針對該議題的正反兩面舉了簡單例子。支持制服者的理由是因其能排除分心因子，而反對制服者的理由則是制服會讓人喪失自由表達的能力。答案的結尾簡潔有力地闡述了個人觀點。

3-19

Q04 Do you think children learn better in a co-ed or single-sex environment?

你覺得讓兒童在男女混合的環境中學習較好，還是在單一性別的環境中學習較好？

Strategy

If you do not understand a question such as this, use context to help you to understand unfamiliar vocabulary. In the question above, the word 'co-ed' is used with the word 'or'. The word 'or' is often used to present a contrast between two choices. You probably know what 'single-sex' means (an all-boys or all-girls

策略

如果你聽不懂這個問題，可以透過觀察上下文幫助自己理解不熟悉的字詞。在上述問題中，co-ed 與 or 這個字同時出現，or 一字經常用來連接兩個對立的選項。你可能知道 single sex（純男校或純女校）的意思，因此可根據該詞

school). Based on this knowledge, you can probably guess that 'co-ed' means boys and girls together in the same school or class.

推測 co-ed 應是「男生和女生在同一所學校或班級上課」的意思。

A

❶ I think it is possible for students who attend a single-sex school to do well academically. However, I do not believe that this type of school is good for their social development.

❷ Going to school isn't only about getting good test scores; it also involves learning how to be a productive member of society. After graduating from an all-boys or all-girls school, many young people find it hard to adjust to a work environment where they have to interact with the opposite sex. Young men may not respect certain boundaries when interacting with women because of how they are used to interacting with other boys, and young women may feel awkward or intimidated when interacting with men because they are not used to doing so.

❸ This is why I feel that studying at a co-ed school is better than studying at a single-sex school.

❶ 我想就讀單一性別學校的學生可能會有更好的課業表現，但我不認為這樣的學校有益於他們社會化。

❷ 上學並不只是為了得到好成績，也是要學習成為社會上有生產力的一分子。從男校或女校畢業後，許多年輕人在和異性一起工作的環境裡，會感到難以適應。年輕男性在和女性互動時，可能會不懂得拿捏分寸，因為他們已經習慣那樣跟其他男性互動了。而年輕女性在和男性互動時，則可能會感到尷尬或畏縮，因為她們不習慣這樣的行為。

❸ 所以我認為就讀男女混合的學校，會比就讀單一性別的學校更好。

Analysis

Academics versus social development are the main themes of this Sample Answer. A long-term view of children's development is taken into consideration in the examples given, and a personal opinion is stated at the beginning and end of the answer.

分析

範例答案的主旨著重在比較學生在課業上及社會上的發展。答案考量到了孩童的長期發展，並在開頭及結尾皆表達了個人觀點。

🔊 3-20

What should children learn at home from their parents?

孩童在家中應該向家長學習什麼？

Strategy

Give examples of what you think parents should teach their children. You could draw on your own experience with regard to what your parents taught you when you were young.

策略

舉例說明你認為家長應該要教導孩子什麼事。你可以引用自身經歷，講述你爸媽在你小時候教過你什麼。

A

❶ Parents are responsible for teaching their children moral values and the difference between right and wrong.

❷ The main way parents can do this is through examples from personal experiences. Parents should not lie, steal, or discriminate against others because of their ethnic background. As children observe their parents behaviours, these behaviours leave a lasting impression on a child's perspective. Additionally, parents should tell their children the reasons that behaviour such as lying is unacceptable. If a parent notices that their child has a tendency to lie or to be selfish, they should immediately address this problem.

❸ Both through examples and by taking specific action, parents can instil moral values in their children.

❶ 家長要負責教導子女道德觀念，和分辨是非對錯。

❷ 家長可以做的主要就是以身作則。家長不應該說謊、偷竊或歧視他人的種族背景。孩子在觀察家長的行為時，會讓他們留下深刻印象。除此之外，家長應該告訴孩子為什麼說謊是不能容忍的行為。如果家長發現自己的孩子有說謊傾向，或是行為自私，應該要立刻處理這些問題。

❸ 透過身教和採取特定教導行為，家長就能灌輸孩童正確價值觀。

Analysis

The main examples in this Sample Answer are related to moral values. Because morality is a very broad topic, specific examples of immoral behaviours are mentioned. Also,

分析

範例答案以「價值觀」作為主旨。因為價值觀是很廣泛的主題，答案中便舉出實例說明何謂不道德的行為。整段答案都強調

the importance of parents' own behaviour is emphasised throughout the answer.

了家長自身行為的重要性。

3-21

06 How long do you think school holidays should last?

你認為學校假期應該要多長？

Strategy

You can use your own experience regarding school holidays or comment on any recent changes you may have noted in school policies related to holidays.

策略

可以講述自己在學校時的經驗，或是針對現今學校的假期政策，說明你觀察到的任何改變。

❶ I think summer vacation should be at least 3 months long.

❷ I remember that when I was young, our summer break ran from the beginning of June until the first or second week of September. This gave everyone enough time to go travelling with their family, take up a new hobby, and just decompress from the stress of the school year. Now, some school vacations don't start until July, and then the kids are back in school by late August. Also, during these few weeks, the kids have a lot of assignments or homework that they still have to complete. I think this is really unfair.

❸ Summer vacation should be a time for rest and relaxation, and this is why I think it should be as long as possible.

❶ 我覺得暑假應該至少要長達三個月。

❷ 我記得我小的時候，暑假是從六月初開始，一直放到九月的第一或第二週。這樣所有人都有足夠的時間能和家人一同去旅遊、培養新嗜好，或是單純擺脫上學的壓力。現在有些學校的假期會拖到七月才開始，然後八月底就要學生返校。而且在這短短幾週內，孩子們還有很多任務或作業要完成，我覺得這很不公平。

❸ 暑假應該是休息和放鬆的時間，所以我認為應該要愈長愈好。

Analysis

Contrasts including specific dates are given to show the difference between the lengths of summer breaks years ago and those of

分析

範例答案提供了明確時間點，比較了以前和現在暑假的長度差異。另外也提到了孩童能在暑假

LESSON 3 Education

summer breaks today. Activities that children can engage in during summer vacation are also mentioned.

從事的休閒活動。

3-22

07 What do you think is the role of a teacher?

你認為教師扮演了什麼樣的角色？

Strategy

You can draw on your own experience to answer this question. For example, you could refer to the qualities of a teacher you had who you thought was an excellent teacher.

策略

你可以從自身經驗來回答這個問題，例如可以談論自己過去遇過的教師有哪些出色的特質。

❶ I think the primary role of a teacher is to be a guide.

❷ As a guide, a teacher should introduce knowledge and new possibilities to their students. They also should allow their students to understand how these things can be used in life. I think the majority of teachers today do not do this. Most teachers focus too much on preparing their students for written tests and reading from textbooks. I also think teachers talk too much and do not allow their students to ask questions or express themselves enough.

❸ If a teacher functions as a guide, a lot more responsibility is placed on the students, which allows them to grow into responsible adults.

❶ 我認為教師的主要角色是引導者。

❷ 身為引導者，教師應該要向學生介紹新知識和新的可能性。他們也應該要讓學生了解新知識如何應用在生活上。我認為現在多數教師都沒有做到這一點。大多數老師都過度專注在如何讓學生準備好應付考試，且讓學生只吸取教科書上的內容。我也覺得老師在課堂上說得太多，都不讓學生發問或是充分表達自我。

❸ 如果老師做好引導工作，學生就能學會負起更多責任，成為負責任的大人。

Analysis

The concept of a teacher acting as a guide is defined and explained. Contrasts with less

分析

範例答案認為教師的角色為引導者，並給予定義及解釋，同時以

effective teachers are made to further explain how a teacher can serve as a guide for their students.

效率較低的教師作為對比，進一步說明教師可以如何引導學生。

3-23

Q08 Do you think there is a difference between how adults learn and how children learn?

你認為成人和兒童在學習行為上有何差異？

Strategy

To answer this question, it would be useful to discuss what you have observed regarding teaching methods used on children and adults. Contrasts can be given to discuss both groups of people.

策略

回答這個問題時，可以從教導兒童和教導成人的不同教育方式切入，並進行比較。

A

❶ Although many people today feel that there is a big difference between the way children and adults learn, I believe that fundamentally, they are the same.

❷ Take learning another language as an example. Children may naturally learn a language faster than adults because they are usually taught the new language through many media. For example, children may sing songs, play games, and engage in physical activities all while using a targeted language. By contrast, many adults learn a foreign language by sitting at a desk and memorising long lists of vocabulary and grammar. As a result, their progress can be quite slow. I think that if adults were to immerse themselves in the study of a language by playing games and singing songs, they would learn more quickly.

❶ 雖然現在有許多人認為，兒童和成人在學習行為上有很大的差異，但我覺得本質上是一樣的。

❷ 用學習新語言為例，兒童或許能比成人更快學會一門語言，因為教師通常會利用許多教學媒介來教學。例如兒童會用目標語言來唱歌、玩遊戲，還有參與實體活動。相較之下，許多成年人學習外語的方式，就是坐在書桌前背誦一長串單字和文法，因此成人的學習進度會有些緩慢。我覺得，成人若能以玩遊戲或唱歌等沉浸式學習方法來習得新語言，會學得更快速。

❸ Even though an adult might feel silly using the same methods to learn as a child does, I think they would progress at a faster pace if they did so.

❸ 即使成年人可能覺得，用跟兒童一樣的方式學習有點傻，但我覺得以如此方式，他們反而會進步得更快。

Analysis

A generally accepted view is stated first, followed by the opinion of the speaker. This is done to add emphasis to the personal opinion. The example of studying a foreign language is used as the primary example in this answer. Specific ways that children and adults learn languages are contrasted throughout this answer.

分析

範例答案先是說明了一個普世觀點，接著提出答題者自己的看法，這樣的方式能強調個人意見。此答案舉出學習外語做為主要範例，並比較了兒童和成人學習語言的方式。

3-24

09 Do you think computers will one day replace teachers?

你認為電腦會有取代老師的一天嗎？

Strategy

This is an opinion question, so there is no standard right or wrong answer. Examples for and against teachers being replaced by computers should be clearly developed.

策略

這是一個詢問意見的問題，所以答案沒有標準對錯。應該要清楚闡述自己認同或不認同老師會被電腦取代，並舉出例子。

❶ No, definitely not.

❷ No matter how advanced AI may become in the future, I do not think it could ever replace teachers. Teachers do more than dispense knowledge and facts; they also interact with their students and guide them in their learning. In particular, when it comes to correcting children's behaviour, I don't think a computer will ever have the capacity to manage a classroom full of students each

❶ 絕對不會。

❷ 無論人工智慧的技術在未來變得多麼先進，我都不認為它可以取代老師。老師並不只是在傳授知識和真相，他們還要與學生互動，並且引導他們學習。尤其是還要糾正孩童的行為；我不認為電腦會有能力管理一整班的學生，況且每個孩子都有自己的獨特需求。此

with their unique needs. Also, I don't believe any parent would want their child to be taught by a computer because there would not be any authentic interaction between the computer and the child.

外，我也不相信會有家長希望由一台電腦來教育自己的孩子，電腦和孩子之間並不會有任何實際互動。

❸ I firmly believe that regardless of any advancements in technology, teachers will always be flesh and blood humans who play an active role in their students' development.

❸ 我堅信無論科技有多麼進步，老師永遠都會是有血有肉的人類，在學生的人生發展中，扮演著積極正面的角色。

Analysis

A clear and definitive opinion is stated at the beginning of this Sample Answer. The role of teachers and their interactions with their students is the primary reason given for why teachers can never be replaced by computers. An additional example of the viewpoint of parents is also briefly mentioned.

分析

範例答案的開頭表明了清楚且堅決的立場。老師的角色和他們與學生間的互動，正是老師無法被電腦取代的主因。另外也簡短提到家長的觀點作為額外的例子。

3-25

Q10 What makes a good student?

怎樣算是一名好學生？

Strategy

Although this question deals with an abstract concept, you do not need to make your answer overly complicated or philosophical.

策略

雖然這個問題的概念很抽象，但也不需要回答得太過複雜或是太有哲理。

A

❶ I think that being curious and the desire to expand one's knowledge are the main qualities of a good student.

❶ 我認為擁有好奇心和拓展知識的慾望，是一名好學生所具備的主要特質。

❷ Whether we are still in school or graduated a long time ago, I think we can possess these qualities and be good students. We should never stop learning. We all have things that interest us, such as nature,

❷ 無論我們還在學校或是早已畢業了，我想我們還是能保有這些特質，並且當個好學生。我們永遠不應該停止學習。我們都有感興趣的事物，例如大自

history, or art, and we should continue to expand our knowledge of these things. A lot of people believe that after someone graduates from school, they stop being a student, but I believe that even after we grow old, we are all still students of life. In other words, there will always be something new for us to learn.

然、歷史或藝術，應該持續拓展自己對這些事物的知識。很多人認為從學校畢業後，就不必再像學生般學習。但我認為即便長大了，我們仍是一輩子的學生；也就是說，總是會有新事物能讓我們學習。

❸ In summary, I feel that if a person remains curious and continues to expand their knowledge, they can always be considered a good student.

❸ 總之，如果一個人保有好奇心，並持續拓展知識，就算是一名好學生。

Analysis

The opening section of this answer states some qualities that every good student should have. The answer also argues that learning should not be limited to when a person is in school; a person can be a student of life even after they have grown old.

分析

範例答案的開頭說明了所有好學生都應該具備的一些特質，並表明學習不該只侷限在校內，即便長大了也仍可以一輩子繼續學習。

Additional Tips and Resources 補充技巧及資料

Cause and Effect 因果關係

Giving reasons in your answers will make them more logical. Here are some different ways to do this:

為你的答案提供理由，會讓答案顯得更具邏輯性。以下提供幾個能用來闡述理由的句型：

♦ 'because' emphasises the cause
- I had to walk to work because my car had broken down.
- Because my car had broken down, I had to walk to work.
- We didn't go to the park because it was raining.
- Because of the rain, we didn't go to the park.

用 because 強調原因
- 我必須用走的去上班，因為我的車拋錨了。
- 因為我的車拋錨了，所以我必須用走的去上班。
- 我們沒有去公園，因為下雨了。
- 因為下雨了，所以我們沒去公園。

♦ 'so' emphasises the result
- I didn't prepare for the test, so I got a bad score.
- I was very tired, so I slept all day.

用 so 強調結果
- 我沒準備考試，所以考得很差。
- 我非常疲憊，所以睡了一整天。

♦ 'so' and 'that' emphasise the result
- There were so many people in line that I had to wait for an hour.
- We had so much free time that we got bored.
- There was not enough food, and we were so hungry that we ate again later.

用 so 和 that 強調結果
- 太多人在排隊了，所以我得等上一個小時。
- 自由時間太多了，所以我們很無聊。
- 食物不夠多，我們又太餓，所以後來又吃了東西。

♦ 'too' shows degree and emphasises the cause
- It's too cold to go to the beach today.

用 too 來展現程度及強調原因
- 今天太冷了，不適合去海邊。

- I have too much work to do.
- 我要做的工作太多了。

♦ 'enough' shows amount and emphasises the cause

用 enough 來表示數量及強調原因

- There were not enough people to play the game.
- I did not have enough money to buy lunch.
- She is not old enough to drive.

- 人數不夠，所以遊戲玩不成。
- 我錢不夠，所以買不了午餐。
- 她年紀不夠大，所以不能開車。

LESSON 4

Culture

文化

LESSON 4

Culture 文化

Part 1 Questions 第一部分 問題

4-01

Q01 What is your culture known for?

你國家的文化以什麼聞名？

Strategy

Choose something that is positive about your culture or an aspect of it that is widely known to people from other countries.

策略

從你國家的文化中，選擇廣受其他國家熟知的正面事物或其中一個層面講述。

A When most people think of my culture, the first thing that probably comes to their minds is that we are very social. In my culture, we like to make new friends, so it is very common to invite people over to our homes for big meals. Cooking our traditional foods and entertaining guests are big parts of life in my country.

說到我國的文化，多數人最先想到的可能會是，我們非常善於社交。在我國的文化中，人們喜歡交新朋友，所以常會邀請客人到家中款待他們。以料理傳統食物的方式招待賓客，是我國文化中很重要的一部分。

4-02

Q02 Are people from other countries familiar with your culture or traditions?

其他國家的人熟悉你國家的文化或傳統嗎？

Strategy

To answer this question, you could use an example regarding something that has appeared in the news, a local food, or a traditional holiday. These are things about your

策略

回答這個問題時，可以舉出新聞曾報導過的事物作為例子，如當地食物或傳統節日，其他國家的人可能會熟悉你國家文化中的這

culture that individuals from other countries might be familiar with.

些面向。

A I think that most people are familiar with various aspects of my culture. An example is that most people have heard of Chinese New Year. This is our biggest holiday, and it is celebrated by Chinese communities all over the world. For example, many big cities in the US with a Chinatown celebrate this holiday.

我想多數人都熟知我國文化的許多層面。舉例來說，大部分的人都聽說過農曆新年，這是我們最重大的節日，世界各地的華人社群都會慶祝，像是美國有中國城的許多大城市，都會慶祝這個節日。

4-03

Is there anything you would change about your culture?

你國家的文化當中，有任何部分是你想改變的嗎？

Strategy

There will always be something we wish we could change about our own culture. When answering this question, try not to sound like you are complaining or extremely dissatisfied with your culture.

策略

我們總會希望能改變自身文化的某些部分。在回答這個問題時，盡量別聽起來像在抱怨，或像是極度不滿自己的文化。

A I think the pace of life in my country is too fast and that most people don't take time to enjoy their lives. Although most people have a very good work ethic, I think we need to slow down and spend more time enjoying life instead of always working. This is probably the first thing I would change about my culture.

我覺得我國家的生活步調太快了，多數人都沒有花時間享受人生。雖然大部分的人都有良好的職業道德，但我覺得我們還是應該放慢腳步，花更多時間來享受人生，而非總是在工作。這可能是我國文化當中，我最想改變的部分。

🔊 4-04

Q04 Do you practice any traditions from your country?

你會遵循任何你國家的傳統嗎？

Strategy

This is a very broad topic. Comment on an aspect of your culture that affects your life in some way.

策略

這是一個很廣泛的主題。可以講述你國家文化的某個層面，及其如何影響你的生活。

A My culture is known for respecting the elderly, which is deeply rooted in our traditions. Therefore, I visit my grandparents regularly and always take gifts to them. I think this is a tradition that other cultures should also develop. Not a lot of cultures respect elderly people in the same way that my culture does.

我國的文化以尊重長輩聞名，這一點深植於我們的傳統當中。因此我會定期去拜訪爺爺奶奶，也總是會帶上伴手禮。我認為其他文化也應該要發展這項傳統，許多其他文化，不太會像我們這樣尊重長者。

🔊 4-05

Q05 What is your favourite holiday?

你最喜歡什麼節日？

Strategy

A holiday can be religious, political, or related to a special cultural, historical, or traditional event. Choose one holiday that you are familiar with to describe.

策略

此節日可以是與宗教、政治或是與特殊文化、歷史、傳統相關的節日，選擇一個你熟悉的節日來描述。

A In my country, the final weekend in May is regarded as the start of summer. Originally, it was designated as a memorial day for the date that a war had ended. However, it is no longer considered a sombre occasion. It is now a holiday on which people go to the beach or have picnics with their families. I have fond memories of this holiday, and that is why it has become my favourite.

在我的國家，五月的最後一個週末，算是邁入夏季的開端。原本那一天被定為某場戰爭結束的紀念日，不過現在該節日已經不再被視作是悲傷的日子了。如今這天已成為人們與家人到海邊，或是外出野餐的節日。這個節日帶給我許多美好回憶，這就是為何這天是我最愛的節日。

🔈 4-06

Q06 What other culture have you learned about?

你是否曾了解過其他文化？

Strategy

Be specific about an aspect of a foreign culture that you have studied. You could mention something about this culture that you admire or find interesting.

策略

明確講述你研究過的外國文化的某個面向。可以提到這個文化令你崇拜或是覺得有趣的一面。

A After going on a trip to Japan I became very interested in learning more about its culture. Japan has a very ancient culture that can still be seen in the architecture of the buildings and in people's behaviour. I really like how Japanese people are polite and efficient. And everything is so clean and orderly there.

去過一趟日本後，我就對了解日本文化感到非常有興趣。日本的文化歷史非常悠久，從建築和人們的習慣都能看出這一點。我很喜歡日本人的有禮及效率，而且日本的一切看起來都很整潔又有秩序。

🔈 4-07

Q07 What countries have you travelled to?

你曾去過哪些國家？

Strategy

Do not just give a list of places that you have travelled to. Instead, you can mention some notable aspects of some of the places you have been to.

策略

切勿單純列出你曾去過的地方，可以談談曾經去過的這些地方有哪些獨特之處。

A I have travelled extensively throughout Asia. I have been to Japan, Korea, and about ten different regions of China. Of all the places I have been to, I would say Myanmar is my favourite. The scenery there is breathtaking. The country is very mountainous, and there are a lot of waterfalls, but I think the real

我曾周遊亞洲各國，我去過日本、韓國等地，還有中國的十多個地區。在我去過的所有地方之中，我覺得我最喜歡緬甸。那裡的景色美到令人屏息，整個國家滿佈山巒，還有許多瀑布。但我認為旅途真正的亮點在於我遇見

highlight of my trip was the people I met. The locals are very friendly and hospitable.

的人，當地人都非常友善且好客。

4-08

What are the benefits of travel?

旅行的好處是什麼？

Strategy

Discuss the positive effects that being exposed to other cultures can have on a person. You could refer to how you personally have benefitted from travel.

策略

談談接觸其他文化能帶給一個人什麼樣的正面影響，例如你從旅行中獲得的收穫。

A I think that witnessing other lifestyles and cultures can help people to be more tolerant and accepting of others. Before I started travelling, I was very limited in my perspective, but after I was exposed to other cultures, I began to see that there are a lot of different values and lifestyles around the world. Travel really broadened my viewpoint about life.

我認為觀察不同的生活方式與文化，能讓人變得更加寬容，也更容易接納他人。在我開始旅行以前，我的眼界非常狹隘。但是接觸過其他文化後，我開始明白世界上還有許多不同的價值觀與生活方式。旅行確實拓展了我對人生的看法。

4-09

Do you like to try food from other cultures?

你喜歡嘗試其他文化的食物嗎？

Strategy

To answer this question, you could talk about experiences you have had of trying a variety of different foods.

策略

回答這個問題時，可以談談自己過去曾品嚐過各種食物的經驗。

A I am a foodie, so I love trying exotic cuisines. Food in my country is sometimes very bland, so I love food that has a variety of flavours. I particularly enjoy Thai food; I love its combination of spicy and sweet flavours,

我是個饕客，所以我熱愛品嚐異國料理。在我的國家，食物有時候非常淡而無味，所以我喜歡風味十足的菜餚。我尤其喜歡泰式料理，那些結合辣味及甜味的料

which are used in many of its dishes.

理讓我著迷。

4-10

Q10 Describe a traditional food from your country.

描述一種你國家的傳統食物。

Strategy

There may not be English words available to describe certain foods. You can use the following steps to describe a food:

❶ Describe how it is cooked or prepared.

❷ List the ingredients.

❸ Say when it is eaten, such as at what time of day, at which meal, or on which holiday or special occasion.

策略

在描述某種特殊食物時，可能沒有相對應的英文說法。可利用以下方法來描述食物：

❶ 描述該食物的烹調或製作過程。

❷ 列出食材。

❸ 說明吃該食物的時機，例如會是在一天當中的何時、哪一餐，或是在什麼節日、在什麼特定場合吃這種食物。

A A lot of people have probably heard of stinky tofu. This is deep fried tofu that has been fermented. We usually eat this for a snack. It is found in many night markets. A lot of foreign visitors don't like it the first time they try it. I think it does take some getting used to, but I love it.

很多人可能聽過臭豆腐。這是一種油炸的發酵豆腐，我們通常當作點心來吃，在許多夜市都看得到臭豆腐這種食物。很多外國遊客第一次吃時並不喜歡，我覺得確實需要適應一下，但我很愛吃。

Note: Vocabulary & Grammar

Vocabulary

Cooking Method 料理方法	Ingredients 食材	Meal/Occasion 餐／時機
sautéed/pan-fried/stir-fried 煎炒／油煎／快炒的	meat/fish/protein 肉／魚／蛋白質	breakfast/lunch/dinner 早餐／午餐／晚餐
deep-fried 油炸的	vegetable/fruit 蔬菜／水果	snack 點心
boiled/stewed 水煮／燉煮的	starch/carbohydrate 澱粉／碳水化合物	dessert 甜點
baked/roasted/barbecued 烤（麵包）／烤（肉、咖啡）／燒烤	rice/bread/noodle 米飯／麵包／麵條	holiday/festival 節日／節慶
steamed/raw 蒸煮／生的	natural/artificial 天然／人工的	entrée/main course 前菜／主餐

Grammar

When describing how food is prepared, use the adjectival form of the cooking method shown in the chart above (add '-ed' to the end of the word).

在描述食物的料理方式時，可使用上方表格中的形容詞。

- I like the flavour of pan-fried fish.
- Boiled meat does not have a good flavour.

- 我喜歡煎魚的滋味。
- 水煮肉的味道並不好。

Part 2 Questions | 第二部分 問題

4-11

Q01 Describe an important event in your country's history.

描述你國家的一個重要歷史事件。

You should say:

❶ what it is
❷ when it is observed
❸ why it is observed
❹ and explain what is involved in this event.

應該提到：

❶ 是什麼事件
❷ 是在何時紀念
❸ 人們紀念該事件的原因
❹ 說明這個事件的相關活動。

A

❶ Most people are familiar with America's Independence Day.
❷ It is commemorated every year on July 4th.

❶ 多數人都知道美國的獨立紀念日。
❷ 我們在每年的 7 月 4 日紀念這一天。

❸ This holiday is to memorialise the day when America declared its independence from Britain. Prior to this day, America was made up of 13 colonies that belonged to England. On July 4th, 1776, the leaders of these colonies met and signed a document stating that America was no longer a part of England and that it was an independent country. This event took place during the Revolutionary War, also known as the American War of independence.

❸ 這個節日是為了紀念美國宣告從英國獨立。在這天以前，美國是由英格蘭殖民的 13 個領地所組成，但在 1776 年 7 月 4 日，這些殖民地的領導人會面並簽署了一份文件，聲明美國不再是英格蘭的一部分，而是獨立國家。這件事發生在獨立戰爭期間，也就是所謂的美國獨立戰爭。

❹ On July 4th, the weather is usually hot in most places in the US, so there are a lot of outdoor activities. People have the day off from work and have picnics and barbeques.

❹ 每年的 7 月 4 日，美國多數地區通常都很熱，所以會有許多戶外活動。人們不用上班，所以會去野餐和舉辦烤肉活動。

Some people like to go to the beach, play baseball, or go swimming. A lot of places also have annual fireworks displays for people to go to in the evening. More patriotic people usually attend a parade or political event that is designed to make people feel proud to be American.

有些人喜歡去海邊、打籃球或是去游泳。很多地方還會舉辦年度煙火大會，人們會在傍晚前去觀賞。如果是更愛國的人，通常會去參加遊行或政治活動，這些活動會讓人以身為美國人為傲。

Analysis

The speaker is very familiar with an event in their nation's history. They explain the background of the holiday in depth in point 3. In point 4, activities associated with the holiday are discussed.

分析

答題者非常熟悉其國家歷史中的該事件，並在第三點解釋了這個節日的背景故事，在第四點則說明了與這個節日有關的活動。

4-12

Q02 Describe something you have learned from another culture.

描述你在另一個文化裡所學到的風俗。

You should say:

❶ what it is
❷ what you know about this custom
❸ how this custom affects you
❹ and explain why you think it is interesting or important.

應該提到：

❶ 是什麼風俗
❷ 你對這項風俗有什麼了解
❸ 你受到什麼影響
❹ 說明為何你覺得這件事很有趣或很重要。

A

❶ I think there is a lot of variety among the education systems of different countries. From my exposure to people from Western countries, I have learned the importance of the ability to think and reason before making a decision.

❶ 我認為不同國家的教育系統有很大的差異。在與西方人接觸的過程中，我學到了在做決定之前，先思考及推論的重要性。

❷ In most Asian countries, emphasis is put on memorisation. For example, to prepare for written tests, we memorise many facts or vocabularies. Then, a few minutes after taking a test, we forget all the things that we memorised. We don't learn about how to use these things in the real world.

❷ 多數亞洲國家比較強調背誦能力，例如為了準備考試，我們要記誦許多知識和字詞。但考完試的幾分鐘後，我們就會把背過的一切都忘光光。我們並沒有學到如何在現實世界中運用這些知識。

❸ After observing the behaviour of people from Western countries, I understand how a lot of trouble can be avoided by first learning the facts of a situation and then considering the various consequences that could result from a decision. Therefore, recently, I have started doing this: When I am faced with a decision, I don't act on impulse; I pause and consider my options, and I think about the possible repercussions of my decision.

❸ 但在觀察了西方人的行為後，我了解到先釐清事情的真相，並思考不同的決擇會導致什麼後果，能避開許多麻煩，於是我最近也開始這樣做。面臨抉擇時，我不會衝動行事，我會停下腳步並思考各個選擇，也考慮我的決定可能帶來什麼後果。

❹ I have really benefited from doing this. I have found that my relationships with people have improved and that I feel less regret about the decisions I make. I think that if everyone learned this skill, they would avoid a lot of trouble in their lives.

❹ 這樣做確實為我帶來許多好處。我發現我的人際關係變好了，做完決定後也比較不會感到後悔。我想如果大家都學著這樣做，就能避開生活中的諸多麻煩。

Analysis

First, a comparison is made regarding the different focuses of Asian and Western education systems. The positive way a person's decision-making is affected is elaborated on as a major benefit of exposure to another culture.

分析

範例答案首先比較了亞洲和西方教育系統的不同核心，接著闡述接觸其他文化所得到的最大好處，也就是一個人的決策方式獲得了正面影響。

🔊 4-13

Q03 Describe an interesting aspect of your culture.

描述你國家的文化中有趣的一面。

You should say:

❶ what it is
❷ how it began
❸ how it affects the lives of people
❹ and explain why it is interesting.

應該提到：

❶ 是什麼文化
❷ 起源是什麼
❸ 如何影響人們的生活
❹ 說明為何有趣。

A

❶ I think that many people would be surprised to know how superstitious my culture is even in this modern age of technology. We have numerous customs associated with a fear of death.

❶ 我想多數人會對即便身處現代這個科技時代中，我國文化還深深迷信的情況感到訝異。我們有許多習俗，都跟害怕死亡有關。

❷ No one is really sure where or when these traditions started. They have been passed down from generation to generation over thousands of years.

❷ 沒有人能夠真正確定這些傳統始於何時何地，這些習俗已經代代相傳了數千年。

❸ Customs and rituals associated with the veneration of ancestors affect people's everyday lives. In most homes, there is an altar where incense is burned or where fruit is offered to the dead on a daily basis. The superstition that our deceased ancestors can affect our daily lives is also reflected in other customs. For example, there are numerous temples that have spirit mediums and fortune tellers who claim to have the ability to communicate with the dead. My parents and grandparents regularly go to the neighbourhood temple to consult with these mediums. Many people do not make

❸ 與崇敬祖先有關的習俗和儀式，影響了人們的日常生活。多數人家中都有一張神桌，每天都會焚香或供奉水果給亡者。逝去的祖先能夠影響我們的日常生活，這個迷信也反映在其他習俗當中，像是我們有很多寺廟，廟裡有靈媒或算命師，他們自稱有與亡者溝通的能力。我的父母和祖父母會定期到家裡附近的寺廟去找靈媒諮詢。有很多人也都要先到寺廟去，和算命師討論一番後，才有辦法做出人生的重大決定。

any big decisions in life without first going to a temple and discussing the matter with a fortune teller.

❹ I think this is a very interesting aspect of my culture because by most appearances, it seems as though my culture is very modern and progressive. Everyone has a smartphone, and most people work for large corporations. However, these superstitions are a big part of life. I think a lot of people would be surprised to learn this.

❹ 我認為這是我國的文化中很有趣的一面。因為我國的文化表面上似乎非常現代化及進步，人人都有智慧型手機，而且多數人都在大企業工作，但是這些迷信深深影響著我們的生活。我想很多人若知道這件事會感到驚訝。

Analysis

An understanding of your own culture is required to answer this question. You could choose something from your culture that is widely known by people from other countries. The Sample Answer above describes customs and superstitions regarding dead ancestors. Specific vocabulary for these rituals are used throughout the answer.

分析

你必須了解自己國家的文化才能回答這個問題。可以從自身文化當中，選擇外國人所熟知的事物來描述。以上範例答案描述了關於過世祖先的習俗與迷信，並使用了相關專門用語。

4-14

Q04 Describe a place you have travelled to.

描述一處你曾去旅遊的地方。

You should say:

❶ where it was
❷ what the culture is like there
❸ how the people are there
❹ and explain how this place is different from your home.

應該提到：

❶ 是什麼地方
❷ 那裡的文化如何
❸ 那裡的人如何
❹ 說明這個地方跟你的家鄉有何差異。

A

❶ Several years ago, I went on a hiking trip in a jungle in Borneo with two friends. After we had been hiking for about 3 days, we realised that we were lost and that our supplies were running out. We had no phone signal or GPS. We were very worried. ❷ By accident, we came upon a local village ❸ of Indigenous people. Their lives were very basic; they had no modern conveniences, and they lived completely off the land. Even though we didn't speak each other's languages, they could tell that we needed help. They were so kind and helpful. They allowed us to stay with them for a few days so that we could rest and recover. They cooked for us and gave us homemade ointment for the insect bites that we had gotten on our trek. We wanted to repay their kindness, so we spent a day working in their fields with them. Eventually, when it was time to go, two of them accompanied us part of the way to where we could find a main road that would take us back to civilisation. ❹ I don't think my own culture would receive strangers so kindly. In my country, we tend to be very suspicious of strangers and don't go out of our way to be helpful. I learned a lot about basic human kindness from this experience.

❶ 多年前，我曾經跟兩個朋友一起到婆羅洲的叢林去健行。走了大約三天後，我們發現自己迷路了，補給品也消耗殆盡。我們手機沒有訊號，也沒有GPS，所以非常焦慮。❷ 我們意外來到一座當地原住民 ❸ 村落，他們的生活很簡單，沒有便利的現代化設施，而是完全依靠土地來生活。儘管我們雙方的語言並不相通，他們仍能看出我們需要幫忙，非常友好且樂於助人。他們讓我們留下來待了幾天，以便休息和恢復體力。這些居民還做飯給我們吃，並給我們自製藥膏，用來治療我們因長途跋涉所致的蚊蟲咬傷。我們想要回報他們的好意，於是花了一天跟他們一起到田裡工作。最後，到了該離開的時候，他們有兩個人陪我們走了一段路，帶我們找到重返文明的主要道路。❹ 我不認為自己的文化會如此友善地接待陌生人。在我的國家，我們通常對陌生人充滿戒心，也不會想辦法去幫助有困難的人。這段經歷讓我對人性本善的說法多有體會。

Analysis

- Point 1 provides the setting and background information for this experience.

分析

- 第一點提供了這段經歷的地點和背景資訊。

- Points 2 and 3 are answered together because they describe the local people and their culture.
- Comparisons and lessons learned from this experience are discussed in point 4.

- 一併講述第二及第三點，描述當地居民和他們的文化。
- 第四點提供了比較，和這段經驗的見聞。

This question requires you to share an experience. As seen in the Sample Answer above, it is usually best to give your account in chronological order so that it is clearly understood.

這一題要求你分享一段經歷。正如以上範例答案所示，最好是按照時間順序講述，這樣才能說得清楚。

4-15

Q05 Describe a traditional wedding in your country.

描述你國家的傳統婚禮。

You should say:

❶ who attends
❷ what type of clothing people wear
❸ where it is held
❹ and explain what customs and food are involved.

應該提到：

❶ 有誰參與
❷ 人們會穿哪一種服裝
❸ 在哪裡舉辦
❹ 講述婚禮當中的習俗和食物。

A

❶ In my culture, a wedding is regarded as a major event in a person's life, and so weddings are attended by a lot of people. Immediate family and extended family members attend as well as the friends and workmates of the bride and groom.

❶ 在我國的文化中，婚禮被視為一個人的人生大事，所以會有許多人參加；除了直系親屬和其他親友，還有新郎、新娘的朋友及同事會參加。

❷ The bride wears a beautiful, white gown that is usually very expensive. The groom wears a very formal suit or a tuxedo. The bridesmaids wear matching dresses that are

❷ 新娘會穿上美麗的白紗禮服，通常價格不斐，新郎則會穿著非常正式的西裝。伴娘會穿與新娘禮服相襯的洋裝，而且通

usually the favourite colour of the bride. The suits that the groomsmen wear are decided upon by the groom.

常是新娘最喜歡的顏色，伴郎穿的西裝則由新郎來決定。

❸ There are usually two venues used in a ❹ wedding. The first is usually a church, which is where the actual wedding ceremony takes place. A religious leader gives a speech about marriage, and then the bride and groom exchange wedding vows. The second location is where the wedding reception is held. The reception is a big dinner for all the invited guests. The food at most weddings is of very high quality and delicious. Oftentimes, guests can choose between dishes such as steak, fish, and chicken. Then, there are usually dancing and games that the guests can take part in. Finally, family members and close friends give short speeches about the bride and groom.

❸ 一場婚禮通常會用到兩個不同 ❹ 的場地。第一個場地通常是教堂，真正的婚禮儀式就在這裡舉行。宗教領袖會發表一段婚姻主題的演說，接著由新娘和新郎交換婚禮誓言。第二個場地則用於舉辦婚宴，會是一場盛大的晚宴，宴請所有受邀賓客。多數婚禮的食物都非常高檔美味，賓客通常能自己選擇吃牛排、魚肉或雞肉。接著，通常會有舞蹈時間和遊戲供賓客參與。最後，家庭成員和好友會發表和新郎、新娘有關的致詞。

Analysis

- Point 1 introduces the significance of weddings in this particular culture and explains who typically attends a wedding.
- Point 2 outlines the various participants at a wedding and their clothing.
- Points 3 and 4 are answered together because there are different customs that take place at the different locations involved in a wedding.

分析

- 第一點描述了婚禮在該文化中的重要性，並說明通常會有誰參加婚禮。
- 第二點列出婚禮中的各種參與者及其服飾。
- 答案一併講述了第三及第四點，因為該婚禮涉及了不同地點及相關的婚禮習俗。

This answer uses very specific vocabulary related to the wedding customs seen in most

範例答案用了和婚禮相關的專門用字，多數西方文化都有這些婚

Western cultures. If you do not know the specific words for certain wedding traditions, you can use more general vocabulary to describe these activities.

禮習俗。如果你不知道某些傳統婚禮的專門用字，可以使用較一般的字彙來描述這些活動。

Part 3 Questions | 第三部分 問題

4-16

Q01 How is globalisation affecting cultures today? Is it a positive development?

全球化如何影響現今的文化？是正面影響嗎？

Strategy

This question has two parts that you must answer. Specific examples should be given for both the effects of globalisation and your personal opinion.

策略

針對這個問題，必須講述兩個重點，包括全球化所帶來的影響，及自己的個人觀點，並提供明確例子。

A

❶ I think that globalisation is having a detrimental effect on a lot of cultures. The result is that many cultures today are slowly fading away.

❶ 我想全球化對許多文化造成了負面衝擊，導致現今的許多文化正在逐漸消逝。

❷ For example, many traditional values and customs, such as families spending time together, are being replaced with forms of entertainment found in the media of many countries. In most homes today, family members prefer to use their mobile devices instead of talking with one another. Also, local nutritious foods are being traded for fast food, which negatively affects people's health.

❷ 舉例來說，很多傳統價值觀及習俗，如家人相聚時光，在許多國家都被娛樂媒體所取代。如今多數家庭的成員寧願玩手機，也不想跟彼此交談。此外，道地的營養食物也被速食給取代，對人們健康造成不良影響。

❸ On balance, globalisation does have positive effects, such as access to information and medical resources; however, we must work to preserve our local customs before they disappear completely.

❸ 整體而言，全球化確實帶來了正面影響，例如人們較容易取得資訊和醫療資源，但在本土習俗徹底消失之前，我們得趁早將其保存下來。

Analysis

Points 1 and 2 explain the negative effects that globalisation has on many cultures. In point 3, some benefits of globalisation are mentioned along with the importance of preserving local customs.

分析

第一及第二點解釋了全球化對諸多在地文化的負面影響。第三點提到全球化的部分好處，以及保存在地習俗的重要性。

4-17

02 Is your culture greatly affected by the climate of your country?

你國家的氣候是否大幅影響了文化？

Strategy

The topic of the climate and geography of your country can provide you with a lot of examples to talk about. Aspects such as seasonal changes can be discussed.

策略

你國家的氣候和地理條件是回答這題的好素材，例如可以談談季節變化等內容。

❶ Yes, I definitely think the weather has a huge impact on our daily life.

❷ I live in a tropical country, so temperatures do not vary much year round. Hot and humid weather affects our daily routine. For example, people start their working day early, and markets usually open early in the morning so that people can get things done before the heat of the day kicks in. There are also markets that open in the evening so that people can go there after work. Also, food spoils quickly, so a lot of care and attention are given to the preparation and storage of food.

❸ The climate is one of the biggest factors that has shaped the development of my culture.

❶ 對，我認為氣候絕對大幅影響了我們的日常生活。

❷ 我住在熱帶國家，所以一年四季的溫度變化並不大。炎熱潮濕的天氣影響著我們的日常生活。像是人們一大早就會出門工作，市場通常很早就會開張，我們可以趁天氣變熱之前做完該做的事。傍晚也會有市場，所以人們下班後也可以去採買。另外，食物也壞得很快，所以在準備和儲存食物時，要非常細心注意。

❸ 氣候是造就我國文化的最大要素之一。

Analysis

This answer discusses the impact that a hot tropical climate has on daily life. Aspects such as food and people's habits are used as examples. Examples such as these can be used when discussing any type of climate.

分析

範例答案探討到高溫熱帶氣候對日常生活的影響，並舉出食物和人們的習慣作為例子。在談論任何氣候時，都可以列舉類似例子。

4-18

03 Does music play an important role in your culture?

音樂在你國家的文化中是否扮演著重要角色？

Strategy

An understanding of different types of music, such as types that are usually played at special events or a form of music that may have originated in your country, can be commented on in this answer.

策略

可以在答案中談論各種音樂，例如通常在特殊場合會播放的音樂，或可能是起源自你國家的獨特音樂形式。

❶ Classical music plays an important place in the cultural identity of people from my country.

❷ From a very young age, most children receive some basic training regarding how to play an instrument such as the piano, violin, or flute. If a child has a natural ability for playing an instrument, they are usually enrolled in a special music academy. In these institutes, students' time is divided equally between studying academic subjects and practicing their instrument. After graduation, those who can play their instrument to a very high level have a promising career in music ahead of them because their skills will be in high demand.

❶ 古典音樂在我國國民的文化認同中占有重要地位。

❷ 從很小的時候開始，幾乎所有孩童都會接受演奏樂器的基礎訓練，例如學習鋼琴、小提琴或長笛。如果一個孩子有演奏樂器的天分，他們通常會去讀特殊的音樂學院。在這些學院中，學生的時間會被平均分配在學習學術科目，及練習樂器上。畢業之後，善於演奏樂器的人會有很大的機會在音樂界發光發熱，因為社會對他們的技能有很高的需求。

❸ As a result of this emphasis on classical music, this type of music can be heard everywhere in my culture.

❸ 由於我國的文化如此重視古典音樂，因此走到哪都能夠聽見這類音樂。

Analysis

This Sample Answer focuses on classical music and reveals its importance in educational and career opportunities. This example illustrates the prominent role that music plays in this particular culture.

分析

範例答案著重在講述古典樂上，並表明古典音樂對教育和工作機會方面的重要性。這個例子清楚說明了音樂在該文化中扮演了重要角色。

4-19

04 Are people from your country very patriotic?

你國家的人很愛國嗎？

Strategy

The term 'patriotic' refers to people being very proud and supportive of their country, government, or national identity. There may be certain behaviours or customs that people engage in that can be used as examples to describe whether or not people in your country are patriotic.

策略

patriotic（愛國的）一字，是指人們對自己的國家、政府或對國家認同非常引以為傲且強烈支持。或許能舉出一些特定行為或習俗為例子，來表達你國家的人是否愛國。

❶ Yes, I think people in my country really love our nation and the values it stands for.

❷ This feeling of patriotism starts very early in schools, where we regularly have patriotic ceremonies, such as the flag salute. Also, before every sporting event, the audience first stands and sings the national anthem. This makes everyone feel united. Finally, many homes display our nation's flag outside because it is a symbol of personal freedom and the ability to determine your own future.

❶ 是的，我認為我國的人非常愛國，也熱愛國家所代表的價值。

❷ 這種愛國主義情操從每個人剛入學時就開始培養，我們會定期舉辦升旗等愛國儀式。此外，所有體育賽事開始前，觀眾都要先起立並唱國歌，這能讓所有人感到團結。最後，許多住家都會掛上國旗，因為這象徵著個人自由，還有決定自我未來的能力。

❸ I have noticed that the citizens of other countries don't seem to be as proud of their national heritage as those from my country are. Therefore, I think that patriotism is a very unique part of my culture.

❸ 我注意到別國國民，似乎並沒有像我國家的人這樣，如此以國家文化為傲。因此，我認為愛國主義是我國文化中很特別的一部分。

Analysis

This Sample Answer uses examples from everyday life to show to what degree patriotism is expressed in this culture. Ceremonies such as the flag salute in schools and the singing of the national anthem at sporting events are used as examples to show the prevalence of patriotism in this country.

分析

範例答案講述日常生活中的例子，表達該國文化展現出愛國主義情操的程度。學校的升旗典禮和在體育賽事上唱國歌等儀式，都展現了這種情操在該國的普遍性。

4-20

Are the origins of traditional celebrations widely known in your culture?

傳統節慶的起源，在你國家的文化中廣為人知嗎？

Strategy

Traditional celebrations can include holidays that are related to religion or that predate the founding of your country. Oftentimes, the origins of these celebrations are found in old stories or have been forgotten with time.

策略

傳統節慶可以是和宗教相關的節日，或是在你的國家建國前就存在的節日。這些節慶的起源經常會出現在老故事當中，或是隨著時間被人淡忘。

A

❶ I think that years ago, people were more aware of the origins of traditional holidays, and grandparents would share the origin stories of festivals with their grandchildren.

❶ 我想多年前的人們比較了解傳統節日的由來，祖父母會跟子孫分享這些節慶的起源故事。

❷ Nowadays, however, I think most people just enjoy having a day off from work or school. Take the Mid-Autumn Festival as an example: Most people view this holiday

❷ 不過現在，我想多數人只單純享受能放假一天，不必上班或上課。以中秋節為例，大部分人只將這個節日視為和親朋好

simply as a chance to get together with their family and friends and have a barbeque. I think that if you were to ask the average person about the significance of this festival or the story behind it, they would not be able to give you a clear answer.

友團聚烤肉的機會。我覺得如果去問一般人這個節日的重要性或背後的起源，他們說不出清楚答案。

❸ I also think this is probably true of most holiday celebrations.

❸ 我想多數節慶可能也都是這樣的狀況。

Analysis

The beginning of this Sample Answer presents a contrast between the older generation and people nowadays to show a shift in perspective regarding holidays. The Mid-Autumn Festival is then used as an example to illustrate how most people today view traditional holidays.

分析

範例答案在開頭比較了以前和現代的人，展現出雙方對於節日觀點的變化。此處舉出中秋節作為例子，說明現代多數人如何看待傳統節日。

4-21

Q06 Does local culture affect family size in your country?

在地文化是否影響了你國家的家庭規模？

Strategy

Recent trends in society or your own family size can be used to answer this question.

策略

可以在答案中說明現代的社會趨勢，或你自己家庭的規模。

❶ I think that in recent years, the economy has played the biggest role in determining the sizes of most families.

❶ 我想近幾年來，經濟狀況對多數家庭規模，都造成了最關鍵的影響。

❷ Years ago, this was not the case. When my parents were young, every family had at least four children. However, over the past few decades, because of the rising cost of living and resulting economic pressure, most couples now are actually afraid to have children. They believe that they will

❷ 以前並不是這樣的。在我父母還年輕的那個年代，每個家庭至少都有四個孩子。不過最近幾十年來，由於生活成本上升，及其帶來的經濟壓力，導致現在多數夫妻不敢生小孩。他們認為自己無法充分滿足孩

not be able to provide adequately for their children's education and other basic needs. As a result, family sizes are much smaller than they were 20 or 30 years ago.

子的教育及其他基本需求。因此，家庭規模比 20、30 年前要小了許多。

❸ In summary, I would say that the economy is the main factor that has shaped family size in recent years.

❸ 簡言之，我認為，經濟狀況是形塑近年來家庭規模的主要因素。

Analysis

After drawing a contrast between societal norms several decades ago and those now, the economy is cited as the biggest influence determining the number of children in modern families. Terms such as 'rising cost of living' are used to explain the concerns that most parents have regarding family size nowadays.

分析

範例答案先將幾十年前的社會常態與現今進行對比，表示經濟狀況是決定現代家庭子女數量的最主要因素，並使用 rising cost of living（生活成本上升）等說法，表示現今多數家長在考量到家庭規模時，其為最主要的顧慮。

4-22

07 Do most people in your country live in one area, or is the population spread out?

你國家的多數人是住在同個地區，還是分散開來？

Strategy

A basic knowledge of the geography of your country can help you to answer this question. In many countries, mountainous areas usually have lower populations. In addition, most large cities are located near coasts, rivers, valleys, plateaus, or other flat areas.

策略

具備對你國家的基本地理知識能幫助你回答這個問題。許多國家的多山地區，人口通常較少。此外，多數大城市都是坐落在海邊、河邊、山谷、高原或其他平坦地區。

A

❶ In my country, most major population centres are concentrated in the southern half of the country.

❶ 在我的國家，大部分的主要人口中心聚集在我國的南半部。

❷ The northern portion has a very cold and inhospitable climate. That is where most

❷ 北部的氣候非常寒冷又不宜居，大部分的高山都位在那

of the high mountains are located. In that region, the winters are very long, and the growing season is extremely short. As a result, that half of the country is mostly uninhabited. By contrast, the southern region has a very mild climate with plenty of sunshine and adequate rainfall, which are ideal conditions for growing food. Also, that area is very flat, so it is where all our major cities are located. These cities also have all the job opportunities that people are looking for.

裡。該地區的冬天相當漫長，生長季則極短，因此全國有一半的地區幾乎無法住人。反之，南部的氣候宜人、陽光普照，還有充足的降雨量，種植糧食的條件良好。此外，該區域相當平坦，所以我們的主要城市都位在這個地方，人們所尋覓的就業機會也都在這些城市裡。

❸ If given the choice, I don't think anyone would want to live in the north. Everyone would prefer to live in the south.

❸ 如果能夠選擇，我不認為會有人想要住在北部，大家應該都會比較想住在南部。

Analysis

General comparisons between the climate and geography of the northern and southern parts of a country are explained. Notice that the vocabulary describing these natural features is not overly complicated.

分析

範例答案大致比較了該國北部及南部的氣候與地理，可以注意到，不用使用很難的字也可以清楚描述這些自然環境現象。

4-23

Q08 How do parents choose names for their children in your culture?

在你國家的文化中，父母如何為孩子命名？

Strategy

In order to answer this question, a general understanding of this aspect in your own culture is required. In some cultures, children are named after relatives. In other cultures, parents like the way a name sounds or choose a child's name based on its meaning in a particular language.

策略

要回答這個問題，必須對自己國家文化中的命名習慣有一定了解。有些文化喜歡以親戚的名字來為孩子命名，有些父母則是根據唸起來的感覺，或是根據名字在特定語言中的含意來為孩子命名。

A

❶ In my culture, most people's names are chosen because of their meaning in the local language.

❷ Many parents do a lot of research to find a name that reflects the expectations they have for their child. For instance, in school, many of my classmates' names were synonymous with traits such as intelligence or virtue. Some parents will find archaic words that have the same meanings as these characteristics but are not widely used today. They may feel that the more obscure the spelling of a name is, the more unique their child's personality will be.

❸ I think it is true in most cultures that the name a parent gives a child reflects the hopes and expectations that the parent has for the child.

❶ 在我國的文化裡，人們的名字，大多是根據其在當地語言裡所代表的含意來選擇。

❷ 許多父母會做很多研究，來找到一個反映他們對子女期待的名字。舉例來說，在學校裡，我有很多同學的名字都是聰明或美德等特質的同義字。而有些父母會找一些同樣代表這些特質，但現在較少使用的古字來為孩子命名。他們認為名字的拼法愈少見，子女的性格就會愈獨特。

❸ 我認為在多數文化中，家長為小孩的命名，都反映了他們對子女的希望與期待。

Analysis

This answer uses the example of the meanings of the speaker's classmates' names and then discusses another basic concept, namely the hopes and expectations that parents have for their children. Using examples such as these from your own experience will be helpful in answering questions that deal with abstract concepts such as the meaning of a name.

分析

答題者以同學名字的含意作為範例，進而談到另一個命名基礎，也就是父母在取名時，都抱持對子女的希望與期待。取材自這種親身經歷，有助於你回答抽象概念（例如名字的含意）的問題。

4-24

Q09 Do you think that learning another language can help you learn about other cultures?

你認為學另一門語言，有助於學習其他文化嗎？

Strategy

You can draw on your own experience of learning English or another foreign language to answer this question.

策略

可以想想自己學習英文或其他外語的經驗，以回答此問題。

A

❶ I believe that language and culture are inseparable. You can't learn a language without understanding its culture.

❷ I first noticed this when I was studying Korean. Early on, I noticed that the Korean language has a lot of different titles for people and that which title you use depends on whether the person you are speaking to is older or younger than you. I was confused by this for a long time, but then when I went to Korea, I saw the way people interacted with one another, and I heard these titles being used in real life. After that, I really understood their culture and the reasons why they have so many titles. Koreans show a lot of respect for older people, and this is seen in their culture and language.

❸ I definitely feel that learning a foreign language can help you to understand a culture better.

❶ 我認為語言和文化是密不可分的，不了解該文化就無法學會一門語言。

❷ 最早注意到這一點，是在我學韓文的時候。我一開始就發現韓文有許多不同稱謂，使用稱謂時，要注意跟你對話的人是比你年長或年幼。這讓我困惑了很長一段時間。但我後來去了韓國，觀察人們互動的方式，並聽見這些稱謂實際應用在現實生活中。在那之後，我才真正了解他們的文化，以及為何有這麼多稱謂的原因。韓國人非常尊重長輩，這一點體現在他們的文化及語言之中。

❸ 我強烈認為學習一門外語絕對能更了解該國的文化。

Analysis

The experience of learning the Korean language and then seeing interactions between Korean people shows the connection between culture and language. Points 1 and 3 emphasise the strong connection between language and culture.

分析

學習韓文和觀察韓國人互動的例子，展現出文化及語言的關聯。範例答案在第一及第三點都強調了語言和文化的密切關係。

4-25

Do you think it is easier to learn about other cultures now than it was in the past?

你認為現在要學習其他文化是否比過去更容易？

Strategy

Give comparisons regarding people's understanding of other cultures years ago and nowadays. Cultural misunderstandings that you have observed could be included in your answer.

策略

試著比較過去和現在的人對其他文化的理解，也可以加入自己觀察到的文化誤解。

❶ Thanks to the internet, we can learn about any culture nowadays. This, unfortunately, was not the case years ago.

❶ 多虧了網路，我們現在可以學習任何文化，可惜在過去並非如此。

❷ Even 20 years ago, there were a lot of places that many people had never heard of before. For instance, some people thought Thailand and Taiwan were the same place because their names sound similar. As a result, there were a lot of misconceptions about different cultures and customs. Today, by contrast, we can use search engines and online encyclopaedias to find not only articles but also pictures and videos about every culture on earth. This type of globalisation has brought about a lot of positive trends, such as tolerance and greater understanding of other cultures.

❷ 即便只是在 20 年前，也有許多地方是人們聞所未聞的。舉例來說，有些人以為泰國和台灣是同一個地方，因為這兩個國名聽起來很像，所以造成許多不同文化和習俗的誤解。反之，我們現在可以透過搜尋引擎和網路百科找到各種文章，還能找到地球上任一文化的相關照片及影片。這種全球化帶來許多正向趨勢，例如對不同文化的包容及理解。

❸ Technology really is the main reason for these positive developments.

❸ 科技正是造就這些正面發展的主因。

Analysis

A contrast between 20 years ago, when the internet was still maturing, and the situation

分析

答案以 20 年前網路仍不發達的情況，對比今日現況作為例子，表

nowadays is cited as the major reason for improvements in cultural understanding. A humorous example (that of Thailand and Taiwan) is given to illustrate the type of cultural misunderstandings that occurred in the past.

示這是人們在文化理解上進步的主因，並也提供了一個幽默的例子（泰國和台灣），來說明過去人們所產生過的文化誤解。

Additional Tips and Resources 補充技巧及資料

Phrasal Verbs 動詞片語

Phrasal verbs are used with prepositions. They can make your speaking sound more natural. Practice using them until they become a habit. Look up the meaning of any phrases you do not understand.

動詞片語是指動詞加上介系詞的組合。使用動詞片語，能讓你在說話時聽起來較自然。請持續練習，習慣使用這些動詞片語。碰到任何看不懂的片語就要查閱。

♦ **cut**

- Cut up the paper with the scissors. 用剪刀剪那張紙。
- The politician cut through the regulations to get the project done sooner. 那名政治人物為了要盡快完成計畫而沒有嚴守規定。
- All the trees in the forest were cut down. 森林裡的每一棵樹都被砍倒了。
- Our power was cut off after the storm. 暴風雨過後，電力被切斷。
- The rude person cut in line in front of me. 那個無禮的人插隊到我前面。
- Cut it out! You are so annoying! Stop doing that! 夠了！你好煩！別再這樣了！

♦ **come**

- He said he is going to come out this evening and tell us his big secret. 他說他今晚要吐露心聲，跟我們說他的大祕密。
- 'Come in and have a seat,' said the old woman to the man outside her home. 「請進來坐。」老太太對她家外頭的男子說道。
- I don't know how this new idea will come across to others. What is your opinion? 我不知道其他人會覺得這個新點子如何。你有什麼看法？
- The book will come apart if it gets wet; it is very fragile. 如果這本書弄濕了，會變得四分五裂。它非常脆弱。
- I am going to come down the stairs to meet you on the ground floor. 我會下樓，在一樓跟你會合。

♦ **get**

- 'Get back, or I will shoot!' yelled the policeman.
- 「退後，否則我開槍了！」警察喊道。
- I have to get back to the office before the boss realises that I'm gone.
- 我得趕快回去辦公室，免得老闆發現我不見了。
- She needs to get away to the beach for the weekend.
- 她週末需要去一下海邊，逃離現狀。
- How will we get across the river? There is no bridge.
- 我們要怎麼過河？那裡可沒有橋。
- I need to get off the bus at the next stop.
- 我要在下一站下車。
- It took her a long time to get over her boyfriend after they broke up.
- 他們分手後，她花了很長一段時間才放下前男友。
- You need to forget the past and get on with your life.
- 你必須忘掉過去，繼續過你的人生。

♦ **give**

- Apple is going to give away a new iPhone to the winner of the contest.
- Apple 要送出新的 iPhone 給比賽贏家。
- I'm too tired to keep running. I give up!
- 我累到跑不動了，我放棄！
- Don't give up on the student just because he got a low grade on his test.
- 不要因為那名學生的考試成績不好就放棄他。
- He made a bad choice when he decided to give in to the demands of the people.
- 他決定向他人的要求妥協，這不是個好抉擇。
- He wants to give back to society by making a large donation to the charity.
- 他想要回饋社會，所以向慈善機構捐了大筆善款。

♦ **hold**

- 'Hold on one moment while I direct your call', said the receptionist.
- 「請稍等一下，我為你轉接。」接線生說道。

- The thieves planned to hold up the bank and steal $1 million.
- 那些竊賊打算打劫銀行並盜走一百萬美元。
- My boss is holding me back. He won't give me more responsibility.
- 我的老闆在阻礙我的發展。他不願讓我負擔更多責任。
- Hold down the dog while I give him the injection; don't let him move.
- 壓住狗讓我為牠打針，別讓牠動來動去。
- All the landlords agreed to sell their land except for one who held out and refused.
- 所有地主都同意出售土地，只有一人堅決不退讓。

♦ **keep**

- I have so much work to do. I can't keep up.
- 我的工作太多了，趕不上進度。
- Every good student wants to keep on making progress every day.
- 所有好學生都想要每天持續進步。
- The sign said keep off the grass, so don't walk on the grass.
- 那塊牌子上寫著遠離草坪，所以別走到草坪上。
- We should keep chemicals out of reach of children.
- 我們得讓孩童遠離化學藥劑。

♦ **turn**

- I forgot my wallet, so I had to turn back and go home to get it.
- 我忘了帶錢包，所以還得掉頭回家去拿。
- She turned around to look at the person walking behind her.
- 她轉身看向那個走在她身後的人。
- The teacher wants us to turn in our report before Friday.
- 老師要我們在週五前交報告。
- A caterpillar will turn into a butterfly.
- 毛毛蟲會蛻變成蝴蝶。
- Turn down the music before the neighbours start to complain.
- 在鄰居還沒開始抱怨以前，把音樂聲調小。
- Turn off the air conditioner when you leave the house.
- 你出門時要關掉冷氣。
- I can't find the switch to turn on the lamp.
- 我找不到開檯燈的開關。

- We are hoping that at least 500 people turn out for the concert tonight.
- 今晚的演唱會，我們希望至少能有五百位觀衆出席。

♦ **do**

- The teacher didn't like my report, so I have to do it over.
- 老師不喜歡我的報告，所以我得重寫。
- After my father lost his job, we had to do without a lot of luxuries.
- 我父親失業後，我們不得不將就，過著沒有奢侈品用的日子。
- The villain in the movie did away with the hero by shooting him.
- 電影的反派為了擺脫英雄，便朝他開了槍。
- The company wants to do away with our lunch break. We can't let them do that!
- 公司想要廢除午休時間，不能讓他們這樣做！

LESSON 5

Technology

科技

LESSON 5

Technology 科技

Part 1 Questions 第一部分 問題

5-01

01 Which of your mobile devices do you find the most useful?

你認為你的哪一個行動裝置最有用？

Strategy

Describe your personal preferences regarding the technological devices that you own. The term 'mobile device' can refer to a mobile phone, a device that plays music, or an electronic tablet.

策略

根據自己所擁有的科技產品，講述個人偏好。「行動裝置」一詞可以指涉手機、音樂播放裝置或平板電腦。

A My mobile phone is the most versatile device that I own. It's not bulky like a laptop or tablet; it's very portable. It fits in my pocket and has all the functions that I need to use on a daily basis. I can check my messages, surf the internet, and make phone calls.

手機在我所有的裝置中有最多功能，它不像筆電或平板電腦那樣笨重；手機方便攜帶，能放進我的口袋，還能滿足我日常所需的所有功能；可以查看訊息、上網，甚至是打電話。

5-02

02 How old were you when you first started to use a computer?

你第一次開始用電腦是幾歲？

Strategy

Discuss your own personal history with regard to computer use. Your earliest memories of learning to use a computer can be described.

策略

談談你個人的電腦使用史，可以描述你最早學習使用電腦的記憶。

A When I was in elementary school, we had computer literacy classes. These classes were designed to introduce us to the basic functions of a computer. We learned how to type, use a mouse, and surf the internet. I was in first grade at the time, so I would say I was about 7 years old.

我在上小學時，我們有電腦素養課，這些課程是為了讓我們認識電腦基本功能。我們學到如何打字、使用滑鼠，還有上網。我當時就讀一年級，所以大概是七歲。

5-03

Q03 What do you use the internet for?

你都用網路做什麼？

Strategy

Pay careful attention to word form when discussing your use of the internet. 'The' is placed in front of 'internet' when you use it as a noun. For example, 'The internet is very popular'. If you use the word 'internet' as an adjective, you do not need to use 'the'. For example, 'Internet sites are easy to use'.

策略

在談論使用網路的話題時，請特別留意用字的詞性。internet 當名詞使用時，要在前面加上 the，例如 The internet is very popular.（網路非常受歡迎。）而 internet 若當形容詞使用，則不需要加上 the，例如 Internet sites are easy to use.（網站用起來很容易。）

A I use the internet for both work and relaxation. I work for an international trading company, so I would not be able to do my job without access to websites where I can buy and sell goods. In the evenings, I like to watch YouTube videos to relax after a long day at work. The internet is really a big part of my life.

在工作和放鬆休息時，我都會用到網路。我任職於一間國際貿易公司，所以要能夠連線到網站上買賣商品，我才有辦法工作。到了傍晚，我喜歡在漫長的工作結束後看 YouTube 影片來放鬆。網路真的占了我的生活很大部分。

🔊 5-04

What types of websites do you visit the most?

你最常造訪什麼網站？

Strategy

Describe your own personal habits with regard to internet use.

策略

講述你個人使用網路的習慣。

A I like to know what is going on in the world, so I frequent a lot of news websites. For international news, I usually check BBC News a few times a day. As for national news, there is a website that is updated several times a day that gives local news stories and weather reports. I visit these sites about three times a day on average.

我喜歡了解世界發生什麼事，所以我常常瀏覽許多新聞網站。我每天通常會瀏覽幾次 BBC 新聞網站，看看國際新聞。至於國內新聞，有一個網站每天會更新幾次地方新聞和天氣預報。我一天平均會造訪這些網站三次。

🔊 5-05

Do you use the internet for work or school assignments?

你會用網路工作，或是寫學校作業嗎？

Strategy

To answer this question, you can cite an example of a work or school project that required you to find information online.

策略

回答這個問題時，可以舉出一個需要上網查資料，才能完成的工作或學校作業。

A I have a lot of reports to write for my classes, and my teachers require these reports to contain a lot of facts and references. The internet is extremely helpful for finding information. My teacher says that I am not allowed to quote information directly from Wikipedia. Thankfully, there are a lot of more reliable online encyclopaedias that I can use to find the information that I need.

我有很多課堂報告要寫，我的老師要求這些報告得要包含大量事實，且要有參考資料。而在查找資訊時，網路真的起了很大的作用。我的老師說，不可以直接引用維基百科的資料，幸好還有許多可靠的網路百科能用來搜尋我需要的資訊。

5-06

Q06 How often do you send text messages?

你多久傳一次訊息？

Strategy

Describe your personal habits regarding texting.

策略

描述你個人發送訊息的習慣。

A Some days, I send text messages every few minutes. If there is something important happening with my friends or at work, I text others to keep up with what is going on. Texting has become my primary way of communicating with others.

我有時候每隔幾分鐘就會傳一次訊息。如果我朋友或工作上發生什麼重要的事，我就會傳訊息給他們，以了解最新狀況。傳訊息已經成為我與他人溝通的主要方式了。

5-07

Q07 Which messaging apps are popular in your country?

在你的國家，流行哪種通訊軟體？

Strategy

Discuss the reasons why certain messaging apps may be preferred over others. These reasons could include the popularity of an app or the functions that it features in addition to sending messages.

策略

談談某些通訊軟體較受歡迎的原因，可以提到該應用程式的熱門度，或是傳送訊息以外的其他功能。

A The most widely used app in my country is called WETEXT. Everybody uses it. It's more than just an app for sending texts; our credit cards, bank accounts, and social media accounts are also tied to this app. Therefore, we can make purchases, order food, or post photos simply by pushing a few buttons. I think it is the convenience that this app offers that has made it the most popular app in my country.

我國最普遍的應用程式叫做WETEXT，每個人都在用。它不只是傳訊息的應用程式，我們的信用卡、銀行帳戶和社群平台都綁定在這個應用程式當中。因此我們只要按幾個按鈕，就能夠消費、訂購食物和張貼照片。我想便利性正是這個應用程式在我國大受歡迎的原因。

5-08

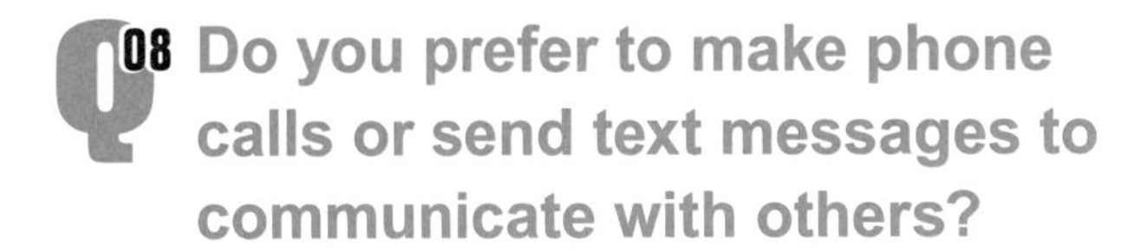

Q08 Do you prefer to make phone calls or send text messages to communicate with others?

你比較喜歡打電話，還是傳訊息與他人溝通？

Strategy

Recent developments in social norms and personal preferences can be elaborated on in this comment.

策略

可以談談整個社會的趨勢或個人的使用習慣。

A Making a phone call without texting first is now actually considered to be rude by many people. In order to talk to someone on the phone, they have to be available and not busy doing something else. That's why I love texting. I can send a short message or a long and detailed one to someone, and they can respond when they are ready.

其實現在有很多人都認為，不先傳訊息說一聲就打電話很失禮。打電話給對方時，對方得要有空，沒在忙其他事情才能接聽。所以我更喜歡傳訊息，我可以傳短訊息，或是資訊詳細的長篇訊息給對方，而對方可以等有空時再回覆我。

5-09

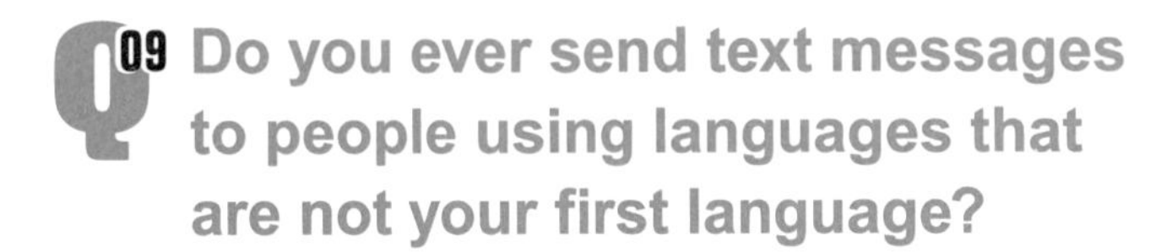

Q09 Do you ever send text messages to people using languages that are not your first language?

你曾經用非母語的語言傳訊息給別人嗎？

Strategy

You could share a brief personal experience when answering this question.

策略

回答這個問題時，可以簡單分享一段親身經歷。

A I studied Spanish for a few months, and once, I tried to send a Spanish text message to a Mexican friend of mine. It took me an hour! I had to look up each word in a dictionary, and wasn't sure if my grammar was correct. So, after that, I decided just to send English texts to him.

我學了幾個月的西班牙文，所以我曾試過用西班牙文傳訊息給我的墨西哥朋友，這花了我一個小時！每個字我都得查字典，而且也不確定文法是否正確，所以在那之後，我決定用英文傳訊息給他就好。

5-10

Could you do your job without a computer?

你的工作可以不用電腦嗎？

Strategy

Describe how essential the use of a computer is in what you do for work. Comment on how often you use this type of technology when carrying out your daily tasks or assignments.

策略

講述電腦對你的工作而言有多重要，並說明你的每日日程或工作有多常用到此科技。

A I work as a waiter in a restaurant, and the computer system we use for placing orders and communicating the orders to the kitchen staff and printing customer receipts is very useful. However, this job could be done without a computer. Once, our computer system broke down, so we had to write out every customer order and receipt by hand. It added a few steps to what we had to do, but it also showed that we could still run the restaurant without a computer.

我在一間餐廳擔任服務生。我們有一個電腦系統，用來點餐、與廚房工作人員溝通、列印收據都非常好用，不過這些工作不用電腦也能夠辦到。有一次我們的電腦系統壞了，所以我們得以手寫方式將每個顧客所點的餐點記錄下來，收據也得手寫。這比我們原本的流程多出了幾個步驟，但這也表示即便沒有電腦，餐廳還是能繼續營業。

Part 2 Questions | 第二部分 問題

🔊 5-11

01 Describe a time when technology helped you solve a problem.

講述科技曾幫助你解決困難的一次經驗。

You should say:

❶ what situation you faced
❷ the type of technology you used
❸ how you used this technology
❹ and explain why it was helpful to you.

應該提到：

❶ 你面對的情況
❷ 你使用到的科技
❸ 你如何使用這項科技
❹ 說明該科技為何有幫助。

A

❶ Once, about 5 years ago, I got lost while on a business trip in Chile. I don't speak Spanish, and I had never been to that city before. It was getting dark, and I was in an area that didn't seem very safe.

❷ Thankfully, I had a full battery on my phone and an internet connection, so I was able to use Google Maps and a Spanish-to-English translation app.

❸ First, I was able to see on the map how to get to a bus station. The roads on the map were very accurate and easy to follow. After walking for about 10 minutes, I was able to find my way to the bus station. After I arrived there, I was able to use the translation app to communicate with the woman at the ticket counter, so I was able to buy the right ticket to my destination. Also, while at the station, the app helped

❶ 大約五年前，我在智利出差的時候迷路了。我不會說西班牙文，也從來沒有去過那個城市。天色愈來愈暗，而且我在一個看起來不太安全的地區。

❷ 幸虧我的手機電量滿格，還有網路訊號，所以我可以用 Google 地圖和翻譯應用程式，將西班牙文翻成英文。

❸ 首先，我看了地圖，知道要如何前往巴士站，地圖上的道路非常精準，也很容易照著走。走了十分鐘左右後，我就知道怎麼走去巴士站了。抵達之後，我使用翻譯應用程式跟售票亭的女子溝通，順利買到前往目的地的車票。此外，在車站的時候，我也借助於那個應用程式，在附近一間餐廳買了

me to order some food at a restaurant nearby. I then rode on the bus for about 5 long hours. After I reached my destination, I was also able to get a hotel room for the night by using the translate function on my phone. I was then finally able to get a good night's sleep.

食物。接著，我搭上巴士，搭了大概五個小時的車程。抵達目的地之後，我用手機上的翻譯功能訂到一個飯店房間，然後終於可以好好睡上一晚。

❹ I don't know what I would have done if I hadn't had my phone. I think that having access to modern technology has become a matter of life and death. I feel that my phone literally saved my life on that trip!

❹ 如果沒有帶手機，我不知道我該如何是好。我想是否擁有現代科技已經成為生死攸關的問題了。我覺得在那趟旅途中，我的手機救了我一命！

Analysis

When you see a Part 2 Question that says 'Describe a time when...', this is your chance to tell a story. You are being asked to give a personal experience, so imagine that you are telling a friend a story about something that happened to you. The Sample Answer above includes descriptions of how things looked from the speaker's perspective as well as their feelings at the time. Linking expressions such as 'First', 'After', 'Also', 'then', and 'finally' are found throughout point 3. These words introduce different locations or important events in the experience.

分析

如果你拿到的第二部分題目卡是以 Describe a time when...（講述一段…經歷）開頭，那麼這就是你講故事的機會。你要提供一段親身經歷，所以可以想像你在跟一名朋友講述一件曾發生在你身上的事。以上範例答案透過答題者的視角，說明事件的經過以及其當下的感受。另外，在第三點中，答案使用了 First（首先）、After（之後）、Also（接著）、then（然後）和 finally（終於）等字，用以串聯該段經驗中的各個地點和不同事件。

🔊 5-12

Q02 Describe your favourite website.

描述你最喜歡的網站。

You should say:

❶ what it is
❷ what information it contains
❸ how you found out about it
❹ and explain what you use it for.

應該提到：

❶ 是什麼網站
❷ 網站上有什麼資訊
❸ 你如何得知該網站
❹ 說明你用該網站做什麼。

A

❶ Every day, I check a news website called XinWen several times throughout the day.

❷ This website features local and international news as well as breaking news. The site is updated every few minutes, so if there is a breaking or developing story, I can stay updated. It also has several different sections, including sports, finance, weather, and culture. Every Friday, there is a special feature that describes activities happening in my city that weekend. This helps me decide what I can do for fun on my days off.

❸ A friend first recommended this website to me a few years ago. After that, I became a regular viewer.

❹ In addition to the regular news stories it features, there is also a special 'Language' feature, where each news story has been translated into multiple languages. This feature has helped me to improve my English. Every day, I read a short article on a different subject, and this helps me to expand my vocabulary. I choose to read

❶ 我每天都會瀏覽一個叫做 XinWen 的網站好幾次。

❷ 那個網站上面有本地和國際新聞，以及頭條新聞。網站每隔幾分鐘就會更新一次，因此如果有突發新聞或發展中的事件，我就能得知最新狀況。網站上有好幾個版面，諸如體育、財經、天氣和文化。每週五都有一篇特輯，介紹我所在的城市週末有什麼樣的活動，這能讓我決定放假時要去哪裡玩。

❸ 起初是一位朋友在幾年前介紹我這個網站，後來我就變成固定讀者了。

❹ 除了一般的新聞報導之外，網站上還有另一個特別的「語言」功能，每一則新聞都翻譯成多種語言，這幫助我提升了英文能力。我每天都會讀一篇不同主題的短文章，這有助於增加我的字彙量。我選擇閱讀一些具有挑戰性的文章，像是

articles that are challenging for me, such as topics like politics, law, and crime, which usually describe situations that I am not very familiar with. After reading articles like these every day for a few weeks, I noticed that my reading comprehension had improved a lot. In summary, I view this website as not only a way to get news but also a valuable resource to help me learn English.

政治、法律和犯罪等主題，這些文章描述的都是我不太熟悉的內容情境。連續幾週每天閱讀這些文章後，我發現自己的閱讀理解能力進步許多。簡言之，我不僅將這個網站視為新聞來源，更視為是幫助我學習英文的寶貴資源。

Analysis

This Sample Answer uses vocabulary specific to news in the second point. The practical value of this website is elaborated on in the final section. The benefits of reading the news are explained as more than just enabling a reader to stay well informed; improved language skills are also noted as an additional benefit.

分析

範例答案在第二點使用了新聞領域的專門用字。最後一段詳述這個網站的實用價值，說明閱讀新聞的好處不只是讓讀者吸收資訊，增強語言能力也被視為額外的好處。

5-13

Q03 Describe your mobile device.

描述一台你的行動裝置。

You should say:

❶ what it is
❷ what it looks like
❸ what functions it has
❹ and explain what you use it for.

應該提到：

❶ 是什麼裝置
❷ 外觀怎麼樣
❸ 有什麼功能
❹ 說明你用該裝置來做什麼。

A

❶ My iPhone's exterior looks like that of a ❷ typical smartphone. The phone is very compact and portable; it fits in my pocket. It's rectangular in shape and has a touch screen. It is thinner than the previous model that I owned.

❶ 我的 iPhone 外觀看起來就像 ❷ 典型的智慧型手機，非常小巧、便於攜帶，能放入我的口袋。機身形狀是長方形，配備觸控式螢幕，比我先前拿的機型更薄。

❸ It has all the functions that you would expect from a modern mobile device. It is internet capable and has GPS. The latest camera technology has been integrated into it; it has four different lenses and takes amazing pictures, far better than any pictures I've ever taken with a standard camera. It also has some practical functions, such as a flashlight and a calculator. As with all smartphones these days, I can add new functions to my phone each time by downloading new apps. In short, the phone's functions seem almost limitless.

❸ 你所想得到的現代行動裝置該有的功能它都有。它可以上網，也具備 GPS，並附有最先進的相機技術，擁有四顆不同鏡頭，得以拍出精美的照片，照片畫質遠比我用標準相機拍出來的更好。我的這支手機還有一些實用功能，例如手電筒和計算機。正如現在所有的智慧型手機一樣，我每次下載新的應用程式，就等於為手機增添了不同的功能。簡言之，手機的功能幾乎可謂無窮無盡。

❹ It has now gotten to the point where I could not live without my phone. I am very dependent on it. For example, I use it a lot for work; all of my appointments are kept in my calendar app. I have to attend a lot of meetings, so I use Google Meet for that. A lot of work documents—such as proposals, Word documents, and even PPT's—I can make or edit on my phone. I would say that I use my phone a lot for recreation also. I can listen to music and watch videos whether I am at home, on a beach, or even commuting. I think that for most of us nowadays, modern smart devices have become an integral part of our daily lives.

❹ 我現在已經到了沒有手機就活不下去的程度，我非常依賴它。舉例來說，我在工作上經常使用手機，我的所有預定日程，都記在日曆應用程式裡。我有很多會議要參加，所以我會用到 Google Meet 功能。我可以用手機製作或是編輯許多工作上的文件，例如提案報告、Word 文件，甚至是 PPT 簡報。我也用手機進行很多娛樂活動，我在家、在海邊，甚至是在通勤時都可以聽音樂和看影片。我想對現代的多數人而言，當代的智慧型裝置已經成為日常生活中，密不可分的一部分了。

Analysis

Terms used to describe shape, size, and

分析

第一及第二點使用了描述形狀、

dimensions appear in points 1 and 2. Comparisons appear throughout the answer, such as those between the current phone owned by the speaker and their previous phone model and standard cameras. In the final section, the two main ideas are how this person uses their phone for (1) work and (2) recreation. Both of these points show how the person cannot live without their phone.

大小和尺寸的字詞。整段答案進行許多比較，例如答題者將自己目前的手機，對比其先前所持的機型和相機。最後一段提出兩個重點，說明手機用於「工作」和「娛樂」上，清楚表達出答題者離不開手機的情況。

5-14

Q04 Describe an important invention.

描述一項重要發明。

You should say:

❶ what it is

❷ how it was invented

❸ what functions it has

❹ and explain why you think it is important.

應該提到：

❶ 是什麼發明

❷ 如何發明的

❸ 有什麼功能

❹ 說明你為何認為該發明很重要。

A

❶ I think the automobile, or car, is one of the greatest inventions in human history. It has really affected the lives of everyone who has lived in the last 100 years.

❶ 我認為汽車是人類史上最偉大的發明。汽車在過去一百年間，確實影響了所有人的生活。

❷ A little more than a century ago, a lot of inventors were trying to engineer something they called the 'horseless carriage'. This was basically the technology that would become today's car.

❷ 在一個世紀多以前，許多發明家都嘗試打造所謂的「無馬馬車」，而這基本上就是現代汽車的科技源頭。

❸ We all know that the car is primarily used for transportation. It transports not only people but also the goods that we buy, and in many places in the world, it has

❸ 我們都知道汽車主要的用途是運輸，不僅用於載運人類以及其所購買的物品，在世上許多地方，車輛更用以乘載資訊及

been used to transport information and for cultural exchange. In addition, today, the type of car a person drives can indicate their social status. Some automobiles are big enough for people to live in, so we even have homes that people can drive from place to place.

交換文化。此外，在現今，一個人能憑藉其所開的車來展現社會地位。有些車輛大到能住在裡面，所以我們甚至能擁有可開往各處的移動住家。

❹ As mentioned earlier, the invention of the automobile has really shaped our personal lives and even human history. Before there were cars, societies and cultures were very limited. People's movements were restricted to just a small area, and so the ideas they were exposed to, the jobs they could have, the things they could buy, and the health care they had access to were all confined to the local area where they lived. After the car was invented, all of these aspects of life were no longer so limited. People, ideas, technology, and possibilities could then travel farther than anyone had previously imagined.

❹ 就像我剛剛說的，汽車的發明確實塑造了我們的生活，甚至是全人類的歷史。在有汽車以前，社會和文化的傳播非常受限，人們僅能於一個小區域內移動，因此他們接觸到的思想、能從事的工作、能購買的物品，以及能夠接受的健康照護，全都限制在他們居住的地區。而汽車發明後，這些都不再如此受限，人群、思想、技術和可能性都得以傳播到遠方，超乎先前所有人的想像。

Analysis

The Sample Answer above links the opening comment of the car affecting the lives of every person with the conclusion in point 4. The phrase, 'As mentioned earlier' is used to connect these two portions of the comment. The significance of the car is also described in points 3 and 4, where both physical objects and intangible things (e.g., ideas and possibilities) are mentioned as things that are transported.

分析

範例答案第四點的總結呼應了開頭的第一點，表示汽車影響了所有人的生活，並使用 As mentioned earlier（稍早說過）來串聯這兩點的發言。第三及第四點都提到了汽車的重要性，表示實體物件和無形事物（思想和可能性）都可透過汽車運輸。

5-15

Q05 Describe a type of technology you would like to learn to use.

描述一種你會想要學習使用的技術。

You should say:

❶ what it is
❷ what its functions are
❸ how you would like to learn about it
❹ and explain how you would like to use it.

應該提到：

❶ 是什麼技術
❷ 有什麼功能
❸ 你想要如何學習
❹ 說明你打算如何使用這項技術。

❶ I would really like to learn how to operate a drone.

❶ 我真的很想學怎麼操控無人機。

❷ Nowadays, I see more and more photographers and video makers utilise drones in their work. Whenever I go to a beach or another scenic spot, I also see amateurs using drones. The recent increase in the popularity of drones is due to how easy it has become to operate one. Each drone is equipped with cameras that can record videos or take still photographs. The controller that the operator holds enables them to adjust the altitude, speed, and direction of the drone. Camera angles and other functions are also operated by the controller.

❷ 我觀察到現今愈來愈多攝影師、影片拍攝者，會在工作中使用無人機。無論是去海邊或其他風景區，我也都會看到業餘人士在操控無人機。最近無人機愈來愈受歡迎，因為它很好操控。每一架無人機都配有攝影機，能夠拍攝影片或是靜態照片。操作員手中的遙控器能夠調整無人機的高度、速度和飛行方向。而攝影機的角度和其他功能，也都能用遙控器控制。

❸ Since drones are very expensive and can break easily, I would want to receive some training before purchasing my own. Online, I have seen advertisements for group classes for drone operators and those interested in learning how to use them.

❸ 由於無人機非常昂貴，又很容易損壞，所以我希望在購買無人機之前，先接受一些訓練。我在網路上看過一些相關的團體課程廣告，開設給無人機操作員或有興趣學習的人參加。

Professional drone operators share their experiences with those in the group and show how to use various functions and how to avoid accidents.

專業無人機操作員會在這些團體課上分享自身經驗，並示範如何使用各種功能，以及如何避免意外。

❹ I am really keen on travel, so I am considering making travel vlogs in the future. I think a drone would really help me out in doing this. I could obtain aerial views of the places I go to and would be able to share with my viewers how it feels to be in these locations. Also, I think that if I got really good at using a drone, I could use it to make commercial advertisements for companies, which might even become my full-time job in the future.

❹ 我非常熱衷旅行，因此我考慮之後要拍攝旅遊影像日誌，我想無人機能夠幫上大忙。我可以從空中拍下所到之處的風景，並跟我的觀眾分享我當下的感受。要是我變得很擅長操作無人機，我也可以用無人機來為各大公司拍攝廣告，甚至有可能在未來成為我的全職工作。

Analysis

This question requires you to talk about something that you have not yet done. Whenever you discuss a possible action in the future or a hypothetical situation, you can use phrases such as 'I would + verb' and 'I could + verb' to describe possible situations. These grammar structures appear several times throughout the Sample Answer above.

分析

這一題是要你談談自己沒試過的事情。凡是在講述未來行動或是假設情況，都可以使用〈I would + V〉和〈I could + V〉等句型來描述表示可能性的狀況。以上範例答案就用了好幾次這種文法架構。

Part 3 Questions

第三部分 問題

🔊 5-16

Q01 What are the pros and cons of modern technology?

現代科技的優缺點為何？

Strategy

Both sides of this issue must be addressed with examples to explain the pros and cons. Linking terms that introduce the opposing side can be used when beginning to discuss your next point.

策略

務必談到此議題的正反兩面，並提供實例說明優缺點。要開始談議題的另一面時，可以使用轉折指示詞來帶入相反的觀點。

A

❶ Smartphone technology gives us access to more information now than anyone ever thought possible previously. However, this technology has not improved our relationships with others.

❷ I needed to write a report about the economy of the African country of Namibia. I had never heard of this country before. However, I looked it up online, and I easily found all the information I needed to finish my report. I would say this is the biggest advantage of modern technology. On the other hand, even though everyone owns a smartphone nowadays, I have noticed that families don't communicate like they did in the past. I have seen that when a family goes out to dinner, they might all be sitting together in a restaurant, but they are all busy on their phones and are not talking to each other.

❶ 現在的智慧型手機科技，讓我們能夠獲得更多資訊，這超出了先前所有人的想像。不過這項科技並沒有改善我們與他人之間的人際關係。

❷ 我之前要寫一篇關於非洲國家納米比亞經濟的報告。我過去從未聽過這個國家，但我上網查了之後，輕鬆找到了完成報告所需的一切資料。我認為這是現代科技的最大優勢。另一方面，儘管現在人人都有智慧型手機，我發現家人之間不再像過去那樣交流了。例如一家人外出用餐時，雖然大家在餐廳裡坐在一起，每個人卻都忙著滑手機，而不跟彼此交談。

❸ These are the biggest benefits and drawbacks of smartphone technology that I have seen.

❸ 對於智慧型手機，這些是我觀察到的最大益處和壞處。

Analysis

Access to information is the main benefit discussed, whereas the negative effect on human interaction is the primary example of a disadvantage of this type of technology. The linking terms 'However' and 'On the other hand' are used to signal a transition from discussing an advantage to explaining a disadvantage, or vice versa.

分析

範例答案提到獲得資訊是現代科技的主要好處，而影響到人類社交，則為現代科技的缺點。答案使用了轉折詞 However（然而，不過）和 On the other hand（另一方面），這類詞用來提示接下來要從討論優勢切換到討論劣勢，反之亦然。

🔊 5-17

02 How has technology changed over the past few decades?

科技在過去這幾十年間有何改變？

Strategy

Using contrasts between technology today and technology from the past to answer this question. You can draw on trends or developments in technology that you have observed.

策略

回答這個問題時，可以比較現今和過去的科技。你可以提出自己觀察到的科技趨勢或發展。

A

❶ I think that technology nowadays is designed to make our lives more comfortable and to make more options available to us.

❷ Take cars as an example. I remember years ago, when I was considering buying a new car, the most important thing that I wanted to know about was how fuel efficient the car I was thinking about buying was. Aspects like engine size and how many kilometres per litre of fuel the car could do were things

❶ 我認為現代科技，是為了讓我們生活得更加舒適，並提供我們更多選擇。

❷ 以汽車為例，還記得多年前我在考慮要買新車，我最在乎的重點是，我想買的那輛車有多省油。引擎大小和每公升燃料能開幾公里，都是我的考量層面。不過我最近開了一輛全新的車，車子的設計各方面考量

that I researched. However, I recently rode in a brand new car, and I was so surprised by how it was designed to offer the driver a variety of comforts. For instance, there was a display console that enabled the driver and passenger to control things like the temperature, music, and GPS route and even watch videos. It was as if all the functions of a smartphone had been integrated into the car.

駕駛的舒適性，讓我很驚艷。像是車上有一個中控台，能讓駕駛和乘客掌控溫度、選擇音樂及設定不同的 GPS 路線，甚至還能看影片，簡直就像將智慧型手機的所有功能都導入這輛汽車。

❸ In summary, I would say that this is the biggest change: There has been a noticeable shift from technology improving efficiency to technology now focusing on the personal comfort of individuals.

❸ 簡言之，我認為這是最大的改變；科技本是用來提升效率，如今更重視帶給人的舒適感受，這樣的變化相當明顯。

Analysis

Comparisons of cars years ago with a brand-new car today are used to illustrate changes in technology. Details are given to show how technology has changed from focusing on efficiency to now focusing on comfort and giving users unlimited options.

分析

範例答案比較了過去汽車和現今全新汽車的設計，來闡述科技的改變，並提供細節說明科技如何從專注在效率上，轉變成如今專注在舒適度及提供使用者無限選擇上。

5-18

03 Should young children be allowed to use the internet unsupervised by their parents?

幼童能否在沒有父母監督的情況下使用網路？

Strategy

This question deals with the safety of children. The term ‘unsupervised’ can mean ‘alone’ or ‘without rules or guidance’. The situation mentioned in this question is often discussed by government officials and in the news.

策略

這個問題攸關兒童的安全，unsupervised（無人監督的）一字隱含著「獨自一人」或是「沒有限制或引導」之意。這個問題也常見於政府官員所關切的議題和新聞報導中。

A

❶ I feel very strongly that young children should not use the internet alone because in today's world, there are too many dangers online.

❷ Unfortunately, in online chat rooms and games designed for children, there are often deviants who are looking to exploit children. Parents need to educate their children about these dangers and what to do if they encounter such individuals. Basic skills such as how to reject invitations to meet people in person should be taught from a very young age.

❸ In conclusion, parents should be with their very young children when these children go online to provide them with appropriate guidance.

❶ 我堅決認為幼童不應該獨自使用網路，因為現今的網路世界有太多危險。

❷ 很遺憾，有些專為兒童所設計的聊天室和遊戲，其實背後都有想要利用兒童的怪人。父母必須教育孩子認識這些危險，以及如果接觸到這些人的時候該怎麼應對。如何拒絕見面邀約，這種基本常識應該要從小就開始教起。

❸ 總之，幼童在上網時，父母應該要在一旁陪同，提供適當指引。

Analysis

Although many people like to think that children can use the internet safely, this, unfortunately, is not the case today. The Sample Answer above discusses some very real dangers that children may encounter when using the internet. Vocabularies such as 'deviant' and 'exploit' are used to emphasise the seriousness of this problem. Practical suggestions for how parents can protect their children are given.

分析

儘管大家普遍認為兒童能夠安全上網，但現實情況並非如此。以上範例答案談到了兒童使用網路時，可能會遭遇的真實危險，並使用 deviant（怪異的人）和 exploit（利用）等字來強調這個問題的嚴重性，另外也提供了父母可如何保護兒童的實質建議。

5-19

Could there be any negative social effects if a child receives a smartphone at a very early age?

兒童若太早開始使用智慧型手機，是否會對其社會化發展造成負面影響？

Strategy

This question includes the word 'age'. This word indicates how to answer the question. You can give your opinion as to what age is too young for a child to have their own phone with internet capabilities and also describes the negative effects that could result.

策略

問題中出現的 age（年齡）一字，給了如何回答此題的暗示。可以講述你認為幾歲讓兒童擁有能夠上網的手機算是太早，並且說明此舉會帶來什麼負面結果。

❶ If a child under the age of 12 starts to use a smartphone unsupervised, it could result in delayed social development.

❶ 12 以下歲的兒童，若在無人監督的情況下開始使用智慧型手機，可能會導致其社會化發展遲緩。

❷ I know young people who are addicted to their phones. This addiction has resulted in them often being in their own world, isolated from other people. They are not able to communicate with others, and they become agitated when they are not allowed to use their phone.

❷ 我認識一些沉迷於手機的年輕人，這種成癮現象使他們永遠活在自己的世界裡，與他人隔絕。他們無法與他人溝通，如果被禁止使用手機，還會變得易怒。

❸ Parents need to set guidelines appropriate to the age of the child regarding the amount of time they let their kids use their phone.

❸ 家長必須要按照兒童的年齡來設立規範，訂定他們允許孩子使用手機的時間長度。

Analysis

In point 2, 'addicted to' and 'addiction' appear. These words are sometimes used incorrectly. Please note that 'addiction' is a noun. 'addicted to + V-ing' is used as a set phrase.

- He has a drug addiction.
- I am addicted to gambling.

分析

答案在第二點使用了 addiction 和 addicted to，這兩者有時會出現誤用情況。請注意 addiction 是名詞，而 addicted to 則必須使用〈addicted to + V-ing〉的固定用法。

- 他有毒癮。
- 我沉迷於賭博。

🔊 5-20

05 How do you feel about using apps to order food?

對於使用應用程式叫外送，你有什麼想法？

Strategy

You are being asked to give your opinion about this fairly new type of technology. Your personal use of this technology can be cited as an example. You can also mention other trends that you have noticed regarding how it is utilised by others.

策略

此問題要求你針對這項新興科技發表意見。你可以舉例說明自己使用這項科技的經驗，也可以談談他人在使用這項科技時，你所觀察到的情況。

❶ As with any type of technology, I think food ordering platforms should be used in moderation.

❷ This method of ordering food is relatively new, but it has become extremely popular because of the ongoing pandemic. I personally have used these services a few times, and I think they offer a lot of convenience. Nevertheless, I have seen them overused in a lot of cases. For example, my neighbour uses these apps to order all three of his meals every day. His wife used to cook, but now, she refuses to because she feels that ordering food is more convenient than cooking.

❸ I don't think that dependence on technology in this way is a positive development. If a person ends up losing a basic skill because of technology, this shows that the technology is being abused.

❶ 就跟其他任何科技一樣，我覺得使用食物外送平台應該要適可而止。

❷ 這種訂餐方式還算很新穎，但持續不斷的疫情卻使其變得極度熱門。我個人使用過幾次這種服務，我覺得非常方便。然而，我也見過不少這種方便性被過度濫用的例子。像我鄰居每天都用這種應用程式來訂三餐。他的太太之前會下廚，現在卻拒絕做飯，因為她認為叫外送比自己煮方便多了。

❸ 我覺得這樣依賴科技並不是正向發展。如果一個人因為科技而最終失去基本生活技能，就代表這項科技被濫用了。

Analysis

The Sample Answer above includes the phrase

分析

範例答案中使用了 used in

'used in moderation'. This phrase offers a way of expressing a neutral opinion and expresses that there are pros and cons to the issue being discussed. These pros and cons are then elaborated on to discuss both the convenience and the possibility of overdependence on this technology.

moderation（適度使用）這個用法，這個用法除了可以用來表達中立立場，也暗示答題者對該議題有正反兩面的看法。答題者接著就講到該科技的優缺點，也就是該科技帶來的便利性以及造成過度依賴的可能性。

5-21

06 How popular has internet shopping become in your country?

網路購物在你的國家有多受歡迎？

Strategy

Comment on recent developments regarding online shopping that you have observed. Also, notice the verb tense in the question ('has... become'); the present perfect tense indicates that these developments are still ongoing.

策略

針對你近期觀察到的網購發展趨勢發表看法，也請注意問題中所使用的時態 (has ... become)，現在完成式代表這些發展會持續進行。

❶ Especially over the past 2 years, in part because of government restrictions, online shopping has really taken off.

❷ People's habits have changed; people are going out a lot less, so now there are a lot more internet sites where you can buy things. Shopping platforms seem to offer everything now. Some of the larger sites have all the same categories as a department store: They have clothes, groceries, electronics, makeup, etc. In addition, these sites are becoming easier to navigate, so you can always find the items you are looking for. Finally, they have also

❶ 部分基於政府禁令的原因，網購在過去兩年來的確蓬勃發展。

❷ 人們的習慣有所改變；大家出門的時間少了很多，所以現在出現了更多能夠買東西的網站。現今的購物平台似乎什麼都賣，有些大型網站涵蓋了百貨公司所有類型的產品，包括服飾、雜貨、電子產品、化妝品等。此外，這些網站也變得更好操作，能輕易找到想要的商品。另外，他們也增加了付款的方式。

expanded the range of payment methods they accept.

❸ I would say that nowadays, most people do the majority of their shopping online.

❸ 我認為現今多數人都是在網路上進行大部分的購物。

Analysis

The Sample Answer above mentions a cause, namely 'government restrictions', which are COVID-19 related. One of the results has been changes in people's shopping habits and improvements to online shopping services. In addition, the answer uses the present perfect tense in several places, such as 'has really taken off' and 'have changed'. This tense indicates that these actions began in the past and are currently still taking place.

分析

範例答案點出與新冠疫情有關的 government restrictions（政府禁令），就是導致人們的購物習慣改變的主因，也因此帶動了網路購物的成長。答案中多處使用了現在完成式，例如 has really taken off 和 have changed，代表這些動作始於過去，且目前仍在進行中。

🔊 5-22

07 **Are there any disadvantages to buying things online?**

網路購物有任何缺點嗎？

Strategy

This question is not asking for a balanced answer discussing the pros and cons of online shopping. Rather, it is steering your comment in the direction of mentioning some negative aspects to this phenomenon, so you should answer accordingly.

策略

此問題並非要你針對網路購物的優缺點對等談論，而是要引導你談論這個現象的負面層面。

❶ I think that buying clothing on the internet presents some major drawbacks.

❷ Trying on clothes, in my opinion, is essential when purchasing clothing, but you can't do this through a website. A lot of customers have been disappointed when they receive

❶ 我認為在網路上買衣服，有幾個主要缺點。

❷ 在我看來，試穿是買衣服時的必要之舉，但是在網站上無法做到這一點。許多消費者收到下訂的衣服後，都會感到失

their orders to find that the clothing doesn't fit or the colour of the item doesn't look the same as it did online. Also, clothing seen on websites is often tailored to match the figure of the model you see online. Therefore, it is often difficult for a customer to gauge the right size for themselves.

望，因為衣服不合身，或是商品顏色跟網路上的看起來不一樣。此外，網站上的服飾，往往是為你在線上看到的模特兒所量身打造，所以消費者很難判斷適合自己的正確尺寸。

❸ Although using websites to buy clothes offers a lot of convenience, I feel that it also carries the risk of choosing the wrong size.

❸ 雖然使用網站購買衣服非常方便，但我認為其中也隱含了選錯尺寸的風險。

Analysis

Purchasing clothes without being able to try them on is the disadvantage that is given in this answer. This example was chosen because it is simple, it happens quite often, and everyone can agree that it is a big disadvantage of online shopping.

分析

買衣服不能試穿是範例答案提出的缺點，會選用此作為範例是因為很簡單，而且人們經常在網路上購物，所有人都會認同這是網路購物的一大缺點。

5-23

08 Do you think online shopping will one day eliminate the need for shopping malls?

你認為網路購物總有一天會淘汰掉購物中心的需求嗎？

Strategy

This question asks you to comment on a hypothetical future scenario. For your answer, you could comment on trends in technology or on more basic reasons that people leave their homes to buy things.

策略

這個問題要你談談假設性的未來情境。你可以從科技趨勢切入，或是談談人們為何要出門購物的基本原因。

❶ Definitely not. I think physical brick-and-mortar stores will always be a part of our society.

❶ 絕對不會，我認為實體店面永遠都會是我們社會的一部分。

❷ Online shopping saves time and can offer us a lot of choices, but shopping is about more than just efficiently purchasing goods. For many, shopping is a social activity that they enjoy with their friends. For others, it is the main way that they connect with their community. For others still, it is their primary means of exercise. For whatever reason people go shopping, it is clear that we enjoy this activity and enjoy connecting with others through it.

❷ 線上購物能節省時間，還提供我們許多選擇，但是購物並不只是為了能高效率購買商品。對許多人而言，購物是一種能跟朋友一起享受的社交活動；對另一些人來說，這是他們與其群體交流的主要方式；還有一些人把這視為主要的運動方式。無論人們出於什麼原因而去購物，我們顯然很享受這項活動，也很享受透過這個方式與他人聯繫感情。

❸ No matter how advanced technology becomes in the future, I think that physical shopping malls and markets will always be a part of our lives.

❸ 無論科技在未來變得多麼發達，我想實體購物中心和商場都永遠會是我們生活中的一部分。

Analysis

This Sample Answer focuses on reasons other than buying things that motivate people to go shopping in physical stores. The social aspects of shopping are highlighted in several examples.

分析

此範例答案說明除了單純買東西，還有其他理由促使人們出門到實體店購物。答案中以多個例子強調了購物這項活動的社會功能層面。

5-24

How popular are computer games in your country?

電玩遊戲在你的國家有多受歡迎？

Strategy

To answer this question, you could comment on the habits of people in your community. In many countries, playing computer games is very prevalent and is considered a favourite recreational activity of many.

策略

回答這個問題時，你可以從你周遭的人的習性切入。在許多國家，玩電玩遊戲是非常普遍的行為，並且被許多人視作最喜愛的娛樂活動。

❶ Everywhere I go, people are playing games on their mobile phones.

❶ 無論我到哪裡，人們都在用手機玩遊戲。

❷ I take the subway to commute to work, and everyone around me is glued to their phones. I have seen people miss their stop or get off at the wrong stop because they are so engrossed in their games. Gaming companies know how much people love their games. As a result, nowadays, there are many huge billboards and posters in shopping malls and transportation hubs advertising the latest games.

❷ 我會搭地鐵通勤上班，身邊的每個乘客都緊盯著自己的手機。我曾看過有人太過沉迷在遊戲中，導致坐過站或是下錯車站。遊戲公司也知道人們有多愛玩遊戲，所以現今的購物中心和交通轉運站，都設有許多巨幅廣告看板以及海報，用來宣傳最新的遊戲。

❸ In my opinion, calling video games 'popular' is an understatement. I think they are becoming a serious addiction for many.

❸ 在我看來，說電玩「受歡迎」都算是輕描淡寫，我想對許多人來說，這已經成為一種嚴重的成癮症了。

Analysis

The prevalence of mobile phone games is presented in a negative light in this answer. The example of situations that happen on the subway and the phrases 'glued to' and 'engrossed in' are used to show how individuals' attention is often focused too much on playing games instead of more important things.

分析

範例答案以負面角度評論玩手機遊戲的普遍現象，並舉例在地鐵上發生的情況，使用 glued to...（緊盯著…）、engrossed in...（沉迷於…）等片語，以強調人們常常將注意力過度集中在遊戲裡，而非更重要的事情上。

🔊 5-25

10 Why do you think some parents are opposed to their children playing video games?

你認為為何有些家長反對孩子打電動？

Strategy

As noted previously, this type of question is steering your comment toward discussing

策略

正如第七題所提到的，這種問題是要引導你談論此議題可能有的

possible drawbacks of an issue.

缺點。

A

❶ Many parents are concerned about the negative effects that playing video games can have on their children's physical health and social development.

❶ 多數家長都很擔心，玩電玩會對兒童的生理健康及社會化發展造成負面影響。

❷ Playing computer games is a sedentary activity. Prolonged hours of sitting in front of a screen while eating junk food can result in obesity and cardiovascular problems. Also, with regard to social development, kids who play a lot of games tend to isolate themselves from others. This in turn leads to them not being able to interact well with others or to express their own emotions appropriately.

❷ 玩電玩遊戲是一項久坐活動，長時間坐在螢幕前面，同時又吃垃圾食物，都會導致肥胖及心血管問題。至於社會化方面的發展，長時間打電動的兒童往往讓自己疏離他人，這導致他們無法與他人有良好互動，或難以適當表達自己的情緒。

❸ Parents have a right to be concerned about their children's gaming habits, and they also have a right to place restrictions on the amount of time and the types of games their children play.

❸ 家長有權利擔心孩子玩遊戲的習慣，也有權利限制孩子玩遊戲的時間及遊戲種類。

Analysis

The two primary negative effects related to playing video games mentioned in this answer are those on physical health and those on social development. These effects are both elaborated on in point 2. The conclusion of this answer gives suggestions for what parents can do to reduce the harm that excessive gaming can have on their children.

分析

範例答案提及兩種與玩電玩有關的主要負面影響，分別是對生理健康和社會化發展的影響，並在第二點針對這些影響給予詳細說明。最後在結論還建議父母可以怎麼做，以減少過度玩遊戲對兒童造成的危害。

Additional Tips and Resources 補充技巧及資料

Commonly Misused Words 常見誤用字

This section reviews common mistakes that are made with word form. These mistakes can have a negative effect on your grammar score.

以下收錄的單字，是考生常誤用詞性的字，這些錯誤可能會影響你的文法得分。

1 boring/bored

形（人事物）令人無聊的／（某人）感到無聊的

- The boring teacher made me feel bored.
- 這個無趣的老師讓我感到好無聊。

2 success

名 成功

- The success of the product made the company a lot of money.
- 該產品的成功讓那間公司賺了很多錢。

successful

形 成功的

- The successful product made the company a lot of money.
- 那個成功的產品讓該公司賺了很錢。

successfully

副 成功地

- The successfully advertised product made the company a lot of money.
- 那個宣傳有方的產品讓該公司賺了很多錢。

succeed

動 成功

- The new product helped the company to succeed.
- 新產品使那間公司大獲成功。

3 danger

名 危險

- Fighting in a war can put your life in danger.
- 參加戰爭可能會讓你陷入生命危險。

dangerous 形 危險的
- Fighting in a war is very dangerous.
- 參加戰爭是非常危險的。

4 **discussion** 名 討論
- I had a discussion with my teacher about my grades.
- 我跟老師針對我的成績進行了討論。

discuss 動 討論
- I discussed my grades with my teacher.
- 我跟老師討論了我的成績。

5 **health** 名 健康
- The doctor told me to protect my health.
- 醫生叫我注意自己的健康。

healthy 形 健康的
- The doctor told me to eat more healthy food.
- 醫生叫我要多吃健康的食物。

6 **patience** 名 耐心
- A good parent has a lot of patience.
- 一位好的家長有很多耐心。

patient 形 耐心的
- A good parent is very patient.
- 一位好的家長要很有耐心。

7 **relaxation** 名 消遣
- After working hard, I need some relaxation.
- 辛苦工作過後，我需要一些消遣。

relaxing 形 放鬆的
- After working hard, I like to enjoy a relaxing activity.
- 辛苦工作過後，我喜歡做一些放鬆的活動。

relax

動 放鬆

- After working hard, I like to relax at home.
- 辛苦工作過後，我喜歡在家放鬆。

8 **stress**

名 壓力

- Studying for a test gives me a lot of stress.
- 準備考試讓我倍感壓力。

stressful

形 有壓力的

- Studying for a test is very stressful.
- 準備考試是很有壓力的事。

stress sb. out

動 令（人）緊張

- Studying for this test is really stressing me out!
- 準備這個考試真是讓我壓力爆表！

LESSON 6

The Natural World

自然環境

LESSON 6

The Natural World 自然環境

Part 1 Questions　第一部分 問題

🔊 6-01

Q01 What is your favourite animal? Why do you like this animal?

你最喜歡什麼動物？為何喜歡這種動物？

Strategy

For this question, you could give details about an animal, such as its appearance, colour, size, personality, and other characteristics. If you have ever had an experience with this animal, this can also be commented on.

策略

面對這種問題，你可以詳述某種動物，例如牠的外貌、顏色、體型、性格及其他特徵。如果你曾經接觸過該動物，也可以提出來。

A I love dogs. Since I was very young, my family has always kept at least one dog as a pet. I have trained my dogs to perform a lot of different behaviours, and I have a lot of fun with them. Most importantly though, dogs are extremely loyal animals. They are always by your side, and they are willing to go anywhere with you.

我愛狗，從我很小的時候，我們家都至少有一隻寵物狗。我訓練我的狗做各式各樣的動作，總是跟牠們玩得很愉快。不過最重要的是，狗是極其忠誠的動物，牠們總是陪在你身邊，而且願意跟你一起走遍天涯海角。

🔊 6-02

Q02 Do you enjoy going to the zoo? What types of animals do you enjoy seeing there?

你喜歡去動物園嗎？你喜歡在動物園裡看什麼動物？

Strategy

For these two questions, you can first give your opinion of zoos and then discuss any animals you like to see at zoos.

策略

針對這兩個問題，你可以先提出自己對動物園的看法，接著談談你去動物園喜歡看什麼動物。

I think a day spent at the zoo can be very relaxing. Most modern zoos are designed to enable their guests to enjoy a comfortable natural environment. I really look forward to seeing monkeys at the zoo. They are usually some of the most active animals that can be seen there. I enjoy watching them swing through the trees and their interactions with one another.

我認為在動物園待上一天非常放鬆身心，多數現代動物園都經過特別設計，以讓遊客置身於舒適且自然的環境中。我非常期待在動物園裡看見猴子，牠們通常是動物園最活躍的動物之一。我喜歡看著牠們盪過樹林之間，還有牠們跟彼此的互動。

6-03

03 What types of plants or animals is your country well-known for?

你的國家以什麼動植物聞名？

Strategy

Some countries are known for having certain types of animals, especially rare or endangered species. You could describe the status of an animal in your culture, such as whether it is employed for farmwork or whether it plays a role in legends or holiday celebrations.

策略

有些國家以擁有特有動物而聞名，尤其是稀有或瀕危的物種。你可以描述該動物在你國家文化中的地位，例如該動物是否是在農場工作的動物，或是否在傳說或節慶當中扮演要角。

The elephant is the national symbol of my country; it even appears on our nation's flag. Elephants used to live in every part of the country, but now, they can be found only in a few national parks. The keepers of elephants are well respected and hold a very high position in my culture.

大象是我國的國家象徵，牠甚至出現在我們的國旗上。大象曾經棲息在全國各地，但現在只能在幾座國家公園裡看見牠們。大象保育員非常受到敬重，在我國的文化中具有崇高地位。

🔊 6-04

04 Do you often go hiking or for walks in the park?

你經常去健行或是到公園散步嗎？

Strategy

Discuss your personal habits with regard to going on hikes or going to parks.

策略

談談你自己健行或是到公園散步的習慣。

I am in a hiking club, so at least twice a month, I go on a long hike. The area where I live is surrounded by mountains that vary in altitude, so there are a lot of trails to choose from. A few times a year, we organise longer trips where we camp out in the mountains for a night or two. I really look forward to these excursions.

我加入了一個健行社，所以每個月至少會參加兩次長途健行。我住的地方被不同海拔的群山所環繞，所以有很多山間小徑能夠選擇。我們一年會安排幾次長途旅行，在山上露營一、兩晚。我都非常期待這些遠足活動。

🔊 6-05

05 Do you enjoy nature?

你熱愛大自然嗎？

Strategy

Give your opinion of nature, and provide reasons to support your opinion.

策略

提供你對大自然的看法，並講述理由以支持你的意見。

Even though I live in a large metropolitan area surrounded by buildings and roads, I love nature. In fact, I can't get enough of it. Every chance I get, I go hiking, to the beach, or on long bike rides beside the river. I have found that if I go too long without being out in nature, I start to get depressed. I believe that everyone needs to have regular contact with beautiful, natural places. I think if everyone were to get out of the city regularly, we would all have a lot less stress in our lives.

雖然我住在大都會區，被許多建築和道路包圍，但我熱愛大自然，實在是非常熱愛。只要有機會，我就會去健行、去海邊，或是去河邊騎一陣子的腳踏車。我發現如果太久沒有接觸大自然，我會開始變得憂鬱。我認為所有人都需要常常到美麗的大自然中走走。我想如果大家都能定期走出城市，我們的生活壓力一定能減少許多。

6-06

Q06 Are there any famous national parks in your country?

你的國家是否有任何知名的國家公園？

Strategy

Describe a famous park or natural landmark in your country. It can be a place that is internationally known or somewhere that is popular with local people.

策略

描述你國家的一座知名公園或自然地標，可以是聞名國際的地點，或是受到當地人歡迎的地方。

A Because I come from a very large country, we have hundreds of national parks. I imagine that everyone has probably heard of Yellowstone National Park, which is one of the most famous parks in the world. Yellowstone has hundreds of miles of undeveloped land where many species of animals such as bears and deer can move around freely. It is a very peaceful and beautiful place.

我的國家國土很大，所以有上百座國家公園。我想大家可能都聽過黃石國家公園，這可能是全世界最著名的公園之一。黃石公園擁有數百哩未開發的土地，許多種動物都可以到處自由移動，例如熊和鹿。這是一個非常祥和、美麗的地方。

6-07

Q07 What environmental issues are you concerned about?

你有關心哪些環境議題嗎？

Strategy

You could comment on an issue you have read about that is affecting the whole world, or you could discuss one that has affected you personally.

策略

可以講述自己曾經讀過的，影響全世界的議題，也可以談談對你個人造成影響的議題。

A I am very worried about climate change. I recently watched a documentary on this subject. The film showed how arctic ice near the North Pole has been melting in recent years. It also showed how polar bears are

我非常擔心氣候變遷。我最近看了一部關於這個議題的紀錄片，片中記錄了近年來北極附近的冰層一直在融化，還記錄了北極熊難以獲取足夠食物，因而餓死的

unable to get enough food and so are starving to death. It was really heartbreaking. We need to do something about this problem before it gets any worse.

現象。這畫面真的讓人非常痛心，我們必須在這個問題惡化以前採取行動。

6-08

Q08 Is pollution a big problem in your hometown?

在你的家鄉，汙染是個大問題嗎？

Strategy

Describe any environmental problem that is affecting the lives of local people such as your neighbours or your own family members.

策略

可以描述任何影響到當地人的環境問題，例如你鄰居或是你家人碰到的問題。

A The small city that I live in is extremely industrialised. There are many factories that make metal parts and chemicals. The river that runs through the downtown area is black with pollution, and the air quality is also very poor. Every day is very smoggy, and it is extremely rare that we see a clear blue sky. It may be an inexpensive place to live, but I think that if people live there for too long, their health will be seriously affected.

我居住的地方是一個高度工業化的小城市，有許多工廠在製造金屬零件和化學製品。流經市中心的河流因為汙染而變黑，空氣品質也非常糟糕。每天都有非常嚴重的霧霾，我們幾乎看不見澄澈的藍天。生活在這個地方雖然不貴，但我想如果在那裡住太久，會嚴重影響到健康。

6-09

Q09 Do you use any green energy or technology?

你是否有使用任何綠色能源或科技？

Strategy

'Green energy' and 'green technology' refer to environmentally friendly technologies, which include things like solar and wind power and electric vehicles.

策略

green energy/technology（綠色能源／科技）指的是友善環境的科技，包含太陽能和風力發電，或是電動車等產品。

A I recently bought an electric motorbike, and I really like it. It is very fuel efficient, and its operating costs are very low compared with those of the gas-powered bike I used to ride. There is a charging station just a few blocks from my house, so a few times a week, I go there and get a fully charged battery. I think that this method of transportation is cheap, convenient, and good for the environment.

我最近買了一台電動機車，我非常喜歡。它非常節能，而且跟我之前騎的燃油機車相比，交通成本非常實惠。距離我家幾條街區之外，就有一座充電站，所以我每週會過去幾次，換一顆充飽電的電池。我覺得這種交通方式很便宜又方便，而且對環境有益。

6-10

Do you recycle?

你是否會做回收？

Strategy

Describe your personal habits with regard to recycling. Things such as the reasons that you recycle or the items that you recycle can be discussed.

策略

描述你個人的回收習慣，也可以提到為何會做回收，或是你會回收的物品。

A The local government of the area where I live is obsessed with recycling. Specifically, recycling is mandatory for all households, so if things like plastic and glass get mixed in with non-recyclable trash, you can get fined. In addition, all items that intend to recycle have to be thoroughly cleaned first; otherwise, the recycling centre will not accept them. They are really strict.

我居住的地方，當地政府非常重視回收活動，家家戶戶都必須做回收。所以如果塑膠、玻璃等物品混入不可回收的垃圾當中，就可能會被罰錢。此外，所有要回收的物品都要先徹底沖洗乾淨，否則回收中心會拒收，他們可是非常嚴格的。

Note: Vocabulary

plastic 塑膠	paper/cardboard 紙張 / 紙板	metal 金屬	glass 玻璃
drink bottle 飲料瓶	box 箱子	tin 錫	jar 罐子
food container 食物容器	book/magazine 書本 / 雜誌	aluminium 鋁	bottle 瓶子
bag 袋子	newspaper 報紙	steel 鋼	can 罐頭

Part 2 Questions | 第二部分 問題

🔊 6-11

01 Describe an environmental problem in your country.

描述你國家的一個環境問題。

You should say:

❶ what it is

❷ what is affected by it

❸ why it is a problem

❹ and explain how it could be solved.

應該提到：

❶ 是什麼問題

❷ 會影響到什麼

❸ 為何這是問題

❹ 說明解決辦法。

A

❶ My country has a lot of low-lying coastal ❷ cities, so in recent years, rising sea levels have begun to cause serious flooding in these areas.

❸ These cities are a key indicator that the environment is undergoing serious changes. These cities were built hundreds of years ago, and they have always been below sea level. For centuries, they have been unaffected by flooding. However, that all began to change about 20 years ago. Now, every year, whenever there is heavy rain or a hurricane passes by, these cities become inundated with floodwater. At first, it seemed like an isolated phenomenon, but it has kept happening. In fact, last year alone, one city flooded 12 times. The result is that people are now leaving these cities. They are selling their houses and moving farther inland.

❶ 在我國有相當多低窪濱海城 ❷ 市，因此近年來海平面上升，開始在這些地區造成嚴重的水患問題。

❸ 這些城市是很關鍵的指標，能看出環境正在經歷重大改變。這些於數百年前建立的都市，一直都低於海平面。幾世紀以來，這些城市都沒有受到洪水影響。然而一切都在 20 多年前開始改變，現在每年只要下大雨或是有颶風行經，這些城市就會被洪水淹沒。起初這似乎只是零星事件，但現在卻不斷發生。其實光是去年，就有座城市歷經了 12 次水患。這導致人們正逐漸搬離這些城市，他們賣掉房子，並往內陸搬遷。

❹ I don't know if this situation can be reversed. One city has built walls and dams around it in an attempt to minimise the effects of flooding. Unfortunately, so far, these measures have been ineffective. The flooding has been so heavy that the water flows right over the walls. I am afraid that if this problem cannot be solved in the near future, the city will become an uninhabited ghost town.

❹ 我不知道這個情況是否可以扭轉。有一座城市，周圍都築了高牆和水壩，試圖將洪水的影響降到最低。可惜到目前為止一點用都沒有，洪水大到能夠直接淹過圍牆。我擔心這個問題若無法在短期內解決，該城市就會變成杳無人煙的鬼城。

Analysis

- Points 1 and 2 are answered together because they show how geography and the environmental problem are related.
- Point 3 is the longest point and gives a lot of detail regarding how certain areas are affected.
- Point 4 gives a realistic assessment of the problem and the difficulty of finding a solution.

分析

- 一併回答第一及第二點，因為地理及環境問題息息相關。
- 第三點提供了最多細節，講述該地區如何受到影響。
- 第四點針對此問題及尋找解方的困境，提供實際評估。

This Sample Answer discusses flooding as a result of climate change. Terms such as 'floodwater' and 'inundated' are used to emphasise the severity of this problem. Geographical terms are also used to describe the physical area. These terms include 'low-lying coastal cities' and 'below sea level'. The answer ends on a realistic note, namely that there appears to be no short-term solution to this problem.

範例答案提到了洪水是氣候變遷下的結果，並使用 floodwater（洪水）和 inundated（淹沒的）等字來強調這個問題的嚴重性。也使用了地理名詞具體描述實際地區，包括 low-lying coastal cities（低窪濱海城市）和 below sea level（低於海平面）。答案結尾實在地表示了顯然短期內沒有辦法能夠解決這個問題。

6-12

Q02 Describe a scenic place in your country.

描述你國家的一處風景區。

You should say:

❶ where it is
❷ what it looks like
❸ what you can do there
❹ and explain why people enjoy going there.

應該提到：

❶ 風景區在何處
❷ 看起來如何
❸ 可以在那裡做什麼
❹ 說明人們為何喜歡去那裡。

A

❶ The most idyllic place I have ever been to is on the east coast of Taiwan, in Hualien County. Deep in the mountains, very far from civilisation, is an area that is protected by the government. Only a certain number of people are allowed into this area each day, and those who intend to enter must apply months in advance.

❶ 我去過最具田園風光的地方位在台灣東岸的花蓮縣，那個地區位於深山、遠離文明，受到政府的保護。每天只允許一定數量的人進入，而且想去的人必須提前幾個月就先申請。

❷ It is like the Garden of Eden, a true paradise on Earth. It is located in a small valley that is surrounded by mountains on each side. A river of turquoise blue flows through the valley. There are deep pools of water and small waterfalls along the course of the river. Each day, at sunrise, the light from the sun is reflected on the surface of the water, creating breathtaking scenery. Wildlife is rarely seen in this protected area; however, there have been sightings of various types of deer and even black bears.

❷ 那裡就像伊甸園，是真正的人間仙境。該地位於一座小山谷中，四周被群山環繞，還有一條土耳其藍的河川流經山谷。河川沿岸有幾個很深的水池和小瀑布。每天日出時，陽光都會照映在水面上，形成令人屏息的景色。在這個保護區很少見到野生動物出沒，但人們曾在此地看過不同種類的鹿，甚至是黑熊。

❸ You can spend the whole day there, swimming in the cool waters. You can also

❸ 你可以在那個地方待上一整天，泡在冰涼的水裡游泳；也

go hiking up one of the mountain trails and take in the views or go exploring in one of the nearby caves. If you are a true nature lover, the activities that you can do there are limitless.

可以在其中一條山間小徑健行，飽覽美景；還可以到附近的其中一個洞穴探險。如果是真正的大自然愛好者，那麼該地還有無數活動可以進行。

❹ It is such a quiet and relaxing place, miles away from the nearest town. It is a place where you can enjoy unspoiled nature and relax in the calm and quiet atmosphere. I highly recommend taking a trip there to anyone who enjoys nature and outdoor activities. You will not regret it.

❹ 那裡真的是個相當靜謐且令人放鬆的地方，距離最近的城鎮有好幾哩。你可以在這個地方享受未經破壞的大自然，並且沉浸在寧靜的氛圍中放鬆。我大力推薦任何熱愛大自然和戶外活動的人到那裡走走，絕對不會後悔。

Analysis

This answer uses various terms to convey the beauty of the place being described. 'Idyllic' is a term used to describe incredible natural beauty. To further emphasise the beauty of the area, the term 'Garden of Eden' is also used; then, to further explain the meaning of this term, the answer continues by saying 'a true paradise on Earth'. Terms such as these are commonly used in English to describe places of outstanding natural beauty.

分析

範例答案使用了不同字詞，表達出該地點有多美。idyllic（田園風光的）一字，可用於描述無與倫比的自然之美，為了進一步強調該地點的美，還使用了 the Garden of Eden（伊甸園）一詞，接著為了深入解釋該片語的意思，繼續說道 a true paradise on Earth（真正的人間仙境）。像這樣的說法在英文中很常見，經常用於描述非比尋常的自然之美。

🔊 6-13

Q03 Describe a natural disaster that you have heard about.

描述一起你知道的天災。

You should say:

❶ what type of disaster it was

❷ where it occurred

❸ what damage was caused

❹ and explain how people were helped afterwards.

應該提到：

❶ 是什麼天災

❷ 發生在哪裡

❸ 造成什麼損害

❹ 說明人們在事後如何取得幫助。

❶ Several years ago, a massive earthquake ❷ caused a tsunami in the Indian Ocean off the coast of Indonesia.

❸ This earthquake was one of the largest ever recorded in history. It caused many buildings to crack and collapse. The tsunami, however, caused even more extensive damage. The large waves washed away entire towns that were located in coastal areas. The places affected included not only islands of Indonesia but also beach resorts in Thailand and even places in Africa thousands of miles away. Unfortunately, the death toll was enormous. The actual number of people who lost their lives is still unknown, but estimates put the number of fatalities in the hundreds of thousands.

❹ The rescue and recovery efforts lasted for several months, and volunteers came from multiple countries to assist. Now, some areas have been completely rebuilt, and

❶ 好幾年前，一場規模極大的地❷ 震，導致印度洋在印尼沿海引發了海嘯。

❸ 那是有史以來最大的地震之一，造成許多建築崩裂與坍塌，然而海嘯所造成的傷害更是劇烈。巨浪沖刷了沿岸地區的整座城鎮，不僅是印尼的島嶼遭受影響，泰國的海灘度假村也受到波及，甚至連遠在數千哩之外的非洲地區也遭殃。很遺憾，死亡人數極高，至今仍不知道喪命者的確切人數，推估死亡人數達數十萬人。

❹ 救援與修復行動持續了數個月，有許多來自其他國家的志工前往協助。現在有些地區已經重建完成，當地經濟也已復

their local economies have recovered. In many of these areas, you would not be able to tell that this disaster took place. For example, the tourist industry is once again thriving in these places, and most hotels and restaurants have been rebuilt. Unfortunately, however, in other coastal areas, damage still remains; many homes and businesses were never rebuilt, and some people are still displaced.

甦。在很多地區，可能看不出來該地曾受過這場災難重創，例如很多地區的觀光業都再度興盛起來，多數飯店和餐廳也都已經重建。然而很遺憾，其他海岸地區的傷害猶在；很多住家與商店從未進行重建，還有許多人流離失所。

Analysis

- Points 1 and 2 are answered together given that the place, time, and type of the disaster are included in the first sentence.
- Points 3 and 4 are longer because they first describe the damage that was caused and then explain how things were repaired or restored.

分析

- 一併回答第一及第二點，第一句話涵蓋了災難的地點、時間和類型。
- 針對第三及第四點的回答比較長，因為要先描述天災所造成的損害，接著再說明重建工作。

You do not always need to use exact numbers and figures in your answers. The Sample Answer above contains many phrases that show the massive scale of the disaster without giving specific numbers. Terms and phrases that are used to help indicate approximate amounts include 'several', 'thousands', 'unknown', 'estimates', 'multiple', and 'most'.

回答此題時不需要講出確切的數字和數據。以上範例答案就沒有提到明確數字，但成功傳達出了災難的巨大規模。以下這些字可以用來表達大概的數量：several（幾個）、thousands（數千）、unknown（未知的）、estimates（推估值）、multiple（多個的）、most（最〔大、多〕）。

6-14

Q04 Describe someone who has been involved in protecting animals or the environment.

描述一個曾經參與過動物保育或環境保護的人。

You should say:

❶ who the person is
❷ what they have done
❸ what the effects of their work have been
❹ and explain why you think their work is important.

應該提到：

❶ 這個人是誰
❷ 這個人做了什麼事
❸ 這個人帶來什麼影響
❹ 說明你為何認為這件事很重要。

❶ I remember reading about a scientist named Jane Goodall in high school. She studied many animals, but she became most famous for her work with chimpanzees in Africa.

❷ She wanted to understand these animals better, so she went to an African jungle to live with them for a while. This was a very revolutionary approach to studying animals. Back then, scientists usually studied animals for extended periods but only from a distance. Goodall, however, actually lived with chimpanzees. In doing so, she was able to interact with them and experience their life. Over time, she became accepted by these animals and was actually treated as a member of their community.

❸ She learned things about these animals' ❹ behaviour and social structure that no scientist had ever learned before. Subsequently, research was published,

❶ 我記得在高中時，曾在書裡看過一位名叫珍古德的科學家。她研究過許多動物，但以在非洲研究黑猩猩的工作最為著名。

❷ 她想要更加了解這些動物，於是她前往非洲叢林，並在那裡和牠們同住了一段時間。這種研究動物的方式非常革新。在當時，科學家通常會長時間研究動物，但是會保持距離。然而珍古德卻真的跟黑猩猩生活在一起。她藉此得以和牠們互動，並且體驗牠們的生活。一段時間後，她便受到猩猩群的接納，且真正被視作其群體的一分子。

❸ 她了解到這些動物的行為與社 ❹ 會結構，這些都是過去的科學家從來沒發現過的。接著她發表了研究，並成為所有靈長類

and this research set a new standard for all research regarding primates. Even now, despite her advanced age, Goodall still continues to lecture at universities. She has made many video documentaries about her experiences and findings, and she still does television interviews. Her work has really changed the way we view chimpanzees and other primates.

研究的新標竿。儘管到了現在，她年事已高，也仍持續在大學講課。她將自身經驗和研究發現拍攝成許多紀錄片，也還會接受電視節目的採訪。她的研究，真的改變了大家看待黑猩猩及其他靈長類的方式。

Analysis

- Point 1 recounts how the speaker first heard of this person.
- Point 2 outlines the work that this person has done.
- Points 3 and 4 are grouped together because the effects and importance of this person's work are interconnected.

分析

- 第一點簡單說明最初是如何得知這個人。
- 第二點列出這個人做過的事情。
- 由於此人所做的事有何影響及其重要性息息相關，因此一併講述第三及第四點。

To answer this question, you could describe a well-known scientist or host of a nature show or documentary. The Sample Answer above describes a scientist who is world renowned for their work with a certain type of animal. The answer briefly outlines what is known about this person and the importance of their work.

回答這類問題，你可以描述一位知名科學家，或一名大自然類型節目、記錄片等的主持人。以上範例答案，描述了一位因研究動物而聲名大噪的科學家，內容簡短陳述該人物的知名事蹟，以及其研究的重要性。

6-15

Q05 Describe something you can do that is good for the environment.

描述你能做的有益環境的事。

You should say:

❶ what it is
❷ who can do it
❸ how it can be done
❹ and explain why it is good for the environment.

應該提到：

❶ 是什麼事
❷ 誰能夠執行
❸ 可以如何執行
❹ 說明這件事為何有益環境。

❶ I think a beach cleanup is a great way to help the environment. This activity can be organised by a local community and held several times a year.

❶ 我認為淨灘是維護環境的一個好方法，可以由當地社群來組織這個活動，一年可舉辦個幾次。

❷ The beach cleanups I have participated in have been attended by young and old people alike. Anybody who lives nearby should be welcome to come and help out. I don't think that participants should need to belong to a special club or even need to live near the beach; anyone who has the desire to clean up the environment should be allowed to join.

❷ 我過去參加過的淨灘活動不分老少。這種活動應該要歡迎任何住在附近的人來參加。我不認為參加者必須要屬於某個特定社團，或甚至要住在海灘附近，任何有心清理環境的人都應該可參加。

❸ There does need to be some organisation and oversight for this activity. For example, tools and equipment such as trash bags, gloves, and masks should be prepared ahead of time. Also, arrangements should be made with local garbage disposal or recycling agencies so that waste taken from the beach can be disposed of properly.

❸ 這項活動確實需要組織監督，像是垃圾袋、手套和口罩等工具應該要事先準備好。也應該要跟當地的垃圾處理場或回收機構偕同，做好安排，這樣從海灘上收集的垃圾才能夠得到適當處理。

❹ Every year, at locations where beach

❹ 每年，從各處舉辦的淨灘活動

cleanups are held, tons of trash are collected in single days. This effort really helps local animals that otherwise might ingest bags or other plastic items. Also, this type of event raises awareness regarding important environmental issues, and it educates people about how and why they should dispose of waste properly. In particular, I think this activity can help children understand the role they can have in protecting the environment.

中，光是一天就能收集到成噸的垃圾。這對於可能會吃到袋子或其他塑膠的當地動物來說，真的大有助益。這種活動也可以提升大眾對重要環境議題的意識，教育人們如何以及為何要正確處理垃圾。我認為，這種活動尤其能幫助孩童了解他們在環境保育中所扮演的角色。

Analysis

Governments, environmental organisations, and local communities can organise activities that benefit the natural environment. The Sample Answer above discusses a beach cleanup, which has become a common activity in many areas. The logistics of holding such an activity and the value it can bring to both the local community and future generations are elaborated on in the second half of this answer.

分析

政府、環境組織或當地社群都能組織有益自然環境的活動。以上範例答案談到了在很多地方都相當常見的淨灘活動。答案的後半段闡述了籌辦這種活動的後勤工作，以及對社區和未來世代所帶來的價值。

Part 3 Questions | 第三部分 問題

🔊 6-16

What do you do to protect the environment?

你做了哪些事來保護環境？

Strategy

Your environmentally friendly (or 'green') habits can be described in your answer. You could also mention things that you learned in school about how individual efforts can help to protect the environment.

策略

可以在答案中描述你友善環境 (green) 的習慣。也可以提及在學校學到的，如何透過個人努力幫助保護環境。

❶ I contribute in whatever small way I can to helping the environment.

❷ For example, I have reduced the amounts of electricity and water I use every day by having very conservative habits. Also, I reuse items like plastic bags and plastic containers that I get from stores and restaurants. I also recycle old cans, bottles, and newspapers.

❸ I think that if everyone made such efforts, we would produce less waste and conserve a lot of natural resources.

❶ 我以各種小貢獻來幫忙保護環境。

❷ 舉例來說，我有很多嚴格的節約習慣，可減少每天的水電用量。還有，像是在商店和餐廳拿到的塑膠袋、塑膠容器，我都會重複再利用。我也會回收舊罐子、瓶子和報紙。

❸ 我想如果每個人都努力這樣做，我們會就能減少浪費，保存許多自然資源。

Analysis

This Sample Answer gives examples of putting the '3Rs'—Reduce, Reuse and Recycle—into practice. The 3Rs are often taught in schools as ways that each of us can protect the environment through individual efforts.

分析

範例答案講述了自己執行了「3R」的實例，「3R」也就是減量 (Reduce)、重複利用 (Reuse) 及回收 (Recycle)。學校經常會教這些，教育我們透過個人習慣保護環境。

🔊 6-17

02 Who do you think has the greater responsibility to protect the environment, the government or individuals?

對於保護環境的行動，你認為誰的責任更大，政府還是個人？

Strategy

For this type of question, you can choose a side and then elaborate on the responsibilities of that group. Another option is to discuss both governments and individuals as having equal responsibility.

策略

面對這種問題，你可以擇一立場回答，並闡述該群體的責任。另一個策略是，說明政府和個人在這個議題上有同等責任。

❶ I think that both sides should share this responsibility equally.

❷ Government regulations regarding aspects like factory emissions and the issuing of fines to violators of these regulations can help to reduce a lot of damage to the environment. However, individuals can also make a big difference. For instance, people can reduce their use of things like plastic bags and water. They can also conserve electricity by not running their air conditioners when they are not at home.

❸ I think that if both sides do their part, the environment will become a lot cleaner.

❶ 我認為雙方應該平等分擔這個責任。

❷ 政府的規範有助於大量減少對環境的傷害，例如規定工廠排放量，及對違規者的罰款。但是個人也能提供大貢獻；像是人們可以減少塑膠袋和水的用量，不在家的時候也可以關掉冷氣，藉此省電。

❸ 我想兩邊如果都各司其職，環境會變得乾淨許多。

Analysis

This Sample Answer describes how governments and individuals share equal responsibility to protect the environment. Specific actions that both sides can take are given in the answer.

分析

針對環境保護議題，範例答案講述了政府及個人有同等責任。答案也提供了雙方能保護環境的具體執行方式。

🔊 6-18

Q03 Which do you think is more important: raising people's standard of living or protecting the natural environment?

你認為提高人民的生活水準重要，還是保護自然環境重要？

Strategy

As with the previous question, you can either choose which side of this issue you support or adopt a neutral stance and develop reasons and examples in support of both sides.

策略

與上一題一樣，你可以選擇自己支持的立場回答此問題，也可以選擇持中立態度，並且針對兩邊立場提供支持的理由和例子。

A

❶ I think that it is more important for governments to take action to lift people out of poverty.

❶ 我想政府採取行動讓人民脫貧更為重要。

❷ It is true that measures to provide people with adequate housing, job opportunities, and decent transportation options may have some minor harmful effects on the environment in the short term; however, such infrastructure is crucial for improving people's lives.

❷ 提供人民足夠的住宅、工作機會和良好的交通運輸設施，這些政策在短期內可能確實會對環境造成少量危害。然而，像這些用來提升人民生活的基礎建設，是很必要的。

❸ Improving the lives of the citizens of a country is more important than protecting the environment for the long-term development of a country.

❸ 長遠而言，改善國民的生活，對國家發展更好，更勝環境保護。

Analysis

This answer supports the idea of governments working to improve people's quality of life. This may seem like a controversial stance, so to lessen the degree of offense that this opinion may cause, the term such as 'minor harmful effects' is used, and a description of balancing

分析

此答案支持政府應努力改善人民的生活品質。這個立場可能較有爭議，為了盡可能不冒犯到他人，答案中使用了 minor harmful effects（少量危害）一詞，也比較了長期的好處與短期的危害。

long-term benefits with short-term harm is given.

6-19

04 How does urbanisation affect the environment?

都市化如何影響環境？

Strategy

Urbanisation is the process of large numbers of people leaving rural (countryside) areas to move to cities (urban areas). Many metropolitan areas in Asia have experienced this urbanisation and could be used as an example.

策略

都市化指的是大量人口離開郊區（鄉村），搬往市區（城市）的過程。亞洲有許多大都會區都經歷過都市化，可以用來作為舉例。

❶ The rapid growth and development of cities has a detrimental effect on the environment.
❷ I witnessed this problem firsthand on a recent trip to Jakarta. In recent times, too many people have moved to this metropolis in too short a period, and as a consequence, the city's infrastructure has failed to keep pace with the population growth. This has resulted in groundwater being extracted at such a rapid rate that the city is now actually sinking. Another problem in Jakarta is that the air pollution from daily traffic jams is now so thick that you can see it.
❸ Most cities are not designed to accommodate such a large influx of people, and so the natural environment can suffer a lot because of such activity.

❶ 城市的急速成長與發展，對環境造成了有害的影響。
❷ 這是我最近去雅加達旅行時的親眼所見。在近幾年，有太多人在短時間內遷移到這座大都市，結果就是，城市的公共設施跟不上這樣的人口成長。這導致地下水被快速抽取，如今城市正在下陷。另一個問題是，每天因交通壅塞所造成的空氣汙染，嚴重到肉眼都可看見。
❸ 多數城市的設計都無法承受大量人口的湧入，而自然環境也因此受到很大的負面危害。

Analysis

Jakarta is used as a prime example of a city that has experienced rapid urbanisation. Terms

分析

範例答案舉了雅加達作為急速都市化的主要實例。rapid growth

such as 'rapid growth and development' and 'large influx of people' are closely associated with urbanisation.

and development（急速成長與發展）和 large influx of people（大量湧入人口）都與 urbanisation（都市化）緊密相關。

6-20

05 How does urbanisation affect people's lives?

都市化如何影響人們的生活？

Strategy

Examples of how many people living in a small area (overcrowding) can affect people's lives can be given. You can mention aspects such as health impairment, stress levels, lack of jobs, rising house (real estate) prices, and transportation problems.

策略

可以舉例說明許多人住在一個狹小地區（過度擁擠），會如何影響到人們的生活。可以提及健康危害、壓力程度、缺乏工作機會、房屋（房地產）價格上揚和交通問題等面向。

❶ The inhabitants of the Greater Manila metropolitan area are a prime example of how people can be affected by urbanisation. ❷ In recent decades, millions of people have flocked to this city in search of better wages, education, and health care, and the overcrowding in some areas is shocking. Multiple people may share one room for their accommodation, and public transportation is also operating beyond capacity. So many people confined to a small area and competing for space can have a negative impact on people's mental health. ❸ In summary, I think that stress is the primary effect that urbanisation has on people's lives.

❶ 人們如何受到都市化所影響，馬尼拉大都會區的居民，就是典型範例。❷ 近幾十年來，數百萬人湧入這座城市，尋求更好的薪資、教育及醫療保健。部分地區摩肩接踵的程度令人震驚。人們可能得好幾個人共享一間房間作為住所，大眾交通工具的運作也超出可負荷程度。這麼多人被限制在一個狹小的區域內競爭空間，可能會對人們的心理健康造成負面影響。❸ 簡言之，我認為都市化對人們生活造成的主要影響是壓力。

Analysis

Stress and poor mental health as a result of overcrowding are the main negative effects of urbanisation described in this answer. Manila is used as an example to illustrate how urbanisation can affect people negatively.

分析

範例答案闡述了過度擁擠所導致的壓力和心理健康問題，都是都市化的主要負面影響，並舉了馬尼拉作為例子，說明都市化對人們如何產生了負面影響。

6-21

06 What causes urbanisation?

是什麼造成了都市化？

Strategy

Give an example of something that may not be available in rural areas but is likely more prevalent in large cities. This example could be access to health care or education, well-paying jobs, or reliable transportation, for instance.

策略

可提出比較，對照鄉村地區沒有、大城市卻相對普遍的事物，例如醫療保健和教育資源、高薪工作和可靠的交通工具等。

❶ In many nations, especially developing countries, there is a huge disparity between the facilities available in big cities and those found in rural areas.

❶ 在許多國家，尤其是開發中國家，大城市和鄉村地區所具備設施數量，有著極大差距。

❷ Oftentimes, basic necessities such as stable electricity and comprehensive health care are greatly lacking in the countryside. Additionally, lower-salary jobs, such as those in agriculture and manufacturing, are often all that are available in small rural villages. It is no wonder that such inequality is causing millions of people each year to move to big cities.

❷ 鄉村往往嚴重缺乏基礎必要設施，例如穩定的電力和全面的醫療保健。此外，小農村就只有薪資較低的工作，例如農業及製造業。就是因為這種不平等的狀況，難怪每年都導致數百萬人搬遷到大城市。

❸ It is the hope of such migrants that a better life and better opportunities, which seem unobtainable in the countryside, can be found in large urban areas.

❸ 這些遷移者，希望能在大都會地區獲得更好的生活與機會，這是許多人認為在鄉村地區無法取得的。

Analysis

Various terms are used throughout this answer to describe the social imbalance of life in cities and that in rural areas. These terms include 'disparity', 'greatly lacking', 'inequality', and 'unobtainable'.

分析

答案中使用了不同措詞，描述城市與鄉村地區的社會不平等，包括 disparity（差距）、greatly lacking（嚴重缺乏）、inequality（不平等）和 unobtainable（無法取得的）等字詞。

6-22

07 To what extent do you think that climate change affects our daily lives?

你認為，氣候變遷會影響我們的日常生活到何種程度？

Strategy

When asked 'To what extent...', you should explain how much or to what degree you are affected by something. There are many views about what climate change actually is, but the most basic definition is something like 'changes in global weather patterns', such as temperature, precipitation (e.g., rainfall, snowfall), and the number and intensity of storms.

策略

面對像是 To what extent...（到什麼程度）這種問題時，應該解釋某事對你造成多少影響，或是影響程度有多大。氣候變遷的定義有許多看法，最基本的解釋是：「全球氣候模式的改變」，例如溫度、降水量（如雨、雪）和風暴的數量及強度的改變。

❶ I think that in recent years, we have all become more aware of changes in the weather and environment.

❶ 我認為近年來，大家都更加清楚意識到了氣候和環境的改變。

❷ Even though these changes began as gradual processes, climate change is now having a major impact on everyone's lives. Increasing occurrence of natural disasters such as fires and floods have made the price of food rise dramatically. Also, extreme weather has affected almost everyone;

❷ 儘管氣候變遷是循序漸進的過程，卻無疑對所有人的當前生活帶來極大影響。火災和洪水等不斷的天災，讓糧食價格遽增，此外，極端天氣也幾乎影響到了每一個人。在一年之中，可能隨時會有強烈風暴侵

powerful storms can happen at any time of year, and usually, there is little time to prepare for them. Some people I know live in constant fear of such events.

襲，而人們通常也沒有足夠時間能準備因應，我認識的一些人就常常生活在這種恐懼當中。

❸ Therefore, I believe that climate change is having a profound effect on everyone both financially and emotionally.

❸ 因此，我認為在財務及心理層面，氣候變遷都正在對所有人造成深刻影響。

Analysis

In recent years, news stories have regularly reported on natural disasters and their after-effects. The Sample Answer above draws on such events to describe how people are affected both financially and emotionally by climate change.

分析

近年來，新聞經常會報導自然災害及其後續影響。以上範例答案舉出這些事件，說明氣候變遷如何影響人們的財務狀況及心理層面。

6-23

08 What can be done to address climate change?

應該如何因應氣候變遷？

Strategy

Years ago, a term more widely used than 'climate change' was 'global warming'. However, this term merely describes hotter temperatures, whereas climate change includes both extremely hot and extremely cold temperatures, as well as extreme precipitation levels. You can discuss the scope of climate change when answering a question such as this.

策略

多年前，比「氣候變遷」更加受到廣泛使用的詞是「全球暖化」，不過這個名詞只用於描述升高的溫度，而氣候變遷包括極端高溫、極端低溫和極端降雨。在回答這類問題時，可以提及氣候變遷的規模。

A

❶ The United Nations has stated that the greatest emergency facing mankind now is climate change and that to reverse the effects of climate change, all nations must

❶ 聯合國已經聲明，人類目前所面臨的最大危機，就是氣候變遷。扭轉其影響的唯一辦法，是各國要學會共同合作。

learn to work together.

❷ Flooding, droughts, wildfires, and rising sea levels are just a few of the climate emergencies that have resulted from our mismanagement of the Earth. If every country continues to have their own standards for waste disposal and CO2 emissions, climate change will continue to worsen. Thus, all countries must reach agreements on new policies to radically reduce pollution. Then, they each must work to strictly enforce these policies.

❷ 洪水、乾旱、野火和上升的海平面，只是我們不當對待地球所導致的其中幾個氣候危機。如果各國都繼續遵循自己訂定的廢棄物處理和二氧化碳排放標準，氣候變遷只會持續惡化。因此，所有國家應該針對新政策達成共識，徹底減少汙染，並必須努力嚴格執行這些政策。

❸ I feel that this is the only way to address this problem; however, I fear that time may be running out. Therefore, every government must take swift and immediate action.

❸ 我認為這是解決此問題的唯一辦法，但時間恐怕不夠了，因此所有政府必須迅速且立即行動。

Analysis

Cooperation of all nations in adopting new standards and policies is the solution given for the problem of climate change in this answer. The opening sentence and the statements in point 3 show how serious this problem has become.

分析

此範例答案表示針對氣候變遷的解決之道，就是所有國家要通力合作採用新標準及政策。第一及第三點，都表達出了氣候變遷這個問題變得多麼嚴重。

6-24

How concerned are you about the future of animals?

對於動物的未來，你有多擔心？

Strategy

'How concerned...' is somewhat similar in meaning to 'To what extent...' In this answer, you should explain how much or to what degree you are concerned about the health

策略

How concerned...（有多擔心）這類問句，就類似於 To what extent...（到什麼程度），回答時，必須在答案中說明你有多擔

and safety of animals. You could discuss a specific species that you are familiar with and the dangers facing it.

心動物的健康與安危。可以談論自己熟悉的特定物種，還有牠們所面臨的困境。

A

❶ I am deeply concerned about Australian animals, especially koalas.

❷ The increasing prevalence of bushfires is destroying the natural habitat of koalas. As many people know, koalas eat just one type of food: eucalyptus leaves. They live in forests of eucalyptus trees. However, in recent years, many of these forests have been devastated first by droughts and then by subsequent fires. Recently, I saw on the news that millions of acres of these trees have been completely burned to the ground. If this trend continues, there will not be enough places for koalas to live in the wild.

❸ Koalas are just one example of many species that are threatened by climate change. I am so concerned about animals that I recently joined an organisation whose main purpose is saving animals.

❶ 我非常擔心澳洲的動物，尤其是無尾熊。

❷ 愈來愈普遍的森林大火正在摧毀無尾熊的自然棲息地。正如許多人所知，無尾熊只吃一種食物，那就是尤加利葉，牠們生活在尤加利樹的森林裡。然而近年來，這些森林先是被乾旱所摧殘，然後火災又接踵而來。我最近在新聞上看見，數百萬英畝的尤加利樹已經被徹底燒毀。這個情況若持續下去，無尾熊在野外的棲地就會不夠。

❸ 無尾熊只是受氣候變遷威脅的諸多物種之一。我非常關心動物福祉，最近還加入了一個組織，宗旨是拯救動物。

Analysis

The phrases 'deeply concerned' and 'so concerned' show the extent to which the speaker feels affected by this issue. Recent news events regarding wildfires in Australia and their effects on koalas are cited as the primary example in this answer.

分析

以上範例答案使用了 deeply concerned（非常擔心）和 so concerned（很擔心）傳達出答題者對此議題的憂心程度。答案中引述了近期的澳洲野火新聞事件作為主要實例，並說明其對無尾熊所造成的影響。

6-25

Q10 Do you think that stores should give customers plastic bags or that customers should take their own bags?

你認為店家應該提供塑膠袋給顧客，還是人們應該自備袋子？

Strategy

Plastic bag use has become a controversial environmental issue in recent years. If your local government has policies regarding their use and disposal, these could be discussed in your answer.

策略

塑膠袋在近年來已成為具爭議的環境議題。如果你住的地方，政府針對塑膠袋使用及處理制定了政策，就可以運用在你的回答中。

A

❶ I think that ideally, everyone should take their own reusable bags when they go shopping.

❷ Bags made from recycled or natural materials should be made freely available for purchase at all stores. In addition, I think that stores should gradually phase out plastic bags and offer alternative bags at affordable prices. I think that over time, people will get used to using such bags and also will get into the habit of taking these bags with them whenever they go out. I think it is reasonable for a country to set a goal to become plastic free by a certain date. A small number of countries have already achieved this goal, and this change has yielded some very positive results; some of these countries' environments are now free of plastic pollution, and the resulting positive effects on wildlife and the natural environment are very obvious.

❶ 理想上，我認為所有人去購物時，都應該自備可重複使用的袋子。

❷ 所有店家都應該提供回收或天然素材製成的袋子，供人自由購買。此外，我認為商店應該逐步淘汰塑膠袋，並提供價格平易近人的替代袋子。隨著時間一長，我想人們會習慣使用這種袋子，並且培養出隨時攜帶這些袋子外出的習慣。我認為，國家訂定目標在特定日期之前實現無塑化是很合理的。少部分國家已經達成這個目標了，且成果良好。在這其中的一些國家，環境沒有了塑膠汙染，且對野生生物和自然環境也產生相當顯著的正面影響。

❸ I think that the only way to achieve the goal of eliminating plastic pollution is for stores to stop providing plastic bags altogether. I know this will take time, but it is a worthwhile goal.

❸ 我認為根除塑膠汙染的唯一辦法，就是要讓店家停止提供塑膠袋。我知道這需要時間，但這個目標很值得。

Analysis

In the Sample Answer above, a plan for discontinuing the use of plastic bags is outlined. Basic steps and potential benefits of implementing this plan are discussed throughout the answer.

分析

以上範例答案提出了停止使用塑膠袋的計畫，也談論了執行此計畫的基本步驟與潛在好處。

LESSON 7

People and Relationships

人際關係

LESSON 7

People and Relationships 人際關係

Part 1 Questions 第一部分 問題

7-01

Q01 How many people are in your family?

你的家庭有多少人？

Strategy

To introduce more variety into your vocabulary, you can replace the word 'people' with 'members'. Also, 'siblings' is an academic way of saying 'brothers and sisters'. In English, there are no specific words for older or younger brothers and sisters, so you need to specify if they are older or younger than you.

策略

為了讓字彙更加多變，可以用 members（成員）一字來取代 people（人）。此外，siblings（手足）是 brothers and sisters（兄弟姊妹）的學術用字。在英文裡，區分兄弟姊妹長幼時沒有特別的用字，會以 older 或 younger 說明對方比你年長還是年幼。

I come from a very large family with seven children. I have three older brothers, one younger brother, and two younger sisters, so I am the middle child. I get along quite well with my siblings; I consider them to be my best friends.

我來自一個非常大的家庭，共有七個小孩。我是排在中間的孩子，我有三個哥哥、一個弟弟和兩個妹妹。我和我所有手足都處得很好，我把他們視為我最好的朋友。

7-02

Q02 Do people in your country tend to live with their immediate family or with extended family members?

在你的國家，一般家庭的組成比較傾向小家庭還是大家庭？

Strategy

'Immediate family' refers to your parents and siblings, whereas 'extended family' can refer to multiple generations of a family, such as grandparents, aunts, uncles, and cousins.

策略

immediate family 指的是由父母和小孩所組成的家庭，類似中文說的「小家庭」。extended family 則代表家族裡住著不同世代的親戚，例如祖父母、阿姨、叔叔、表親，類似中文說的「大家庭」。

A In my culture, it is quite common for three generations of a family to live together in one home. For example, I live with my parents, grandparents, and uncle. Our home is rather big, so everyone has their own bedroom. Every day, we all eat at least one meal together, and everyone helps out with preparing this meal or cleaning up after we have finished eating.

在我的文化當中，三代家族同住在一棟屋子裡是很常見的事情。舉例來說，我跟父母、祖父母還有叔叔同住，我們家蠻大的，所以大家都有自己的房間。我們每天都會至少一起吃一餐，所有人都會一起幫忙準備這頓飯，吃飽後也會一起幫忙收拾。

7-03

03 How well do you know your neighbours?

你跟鄰居有多熟？

Strategy

You can describe your interactions with the people who live next door to you or those who live on the same street or block.

策略

可以描述自己與隔壁鄰居的互動，或是與住在同一條街道、區域的人有什麼交流。

A Unfortunately, I don't know much about my neighbours. In the building that I live in, there are four apartments on each floor. I

很可惜，我對我的鄰居不甚了解。在我住的那棟大樓裡，每層樓都有四戶公寓。這些鄰居下班

see the people who live in these apartments when they come home from work, and we sometimes take the elevator together; however, I can't tell you their names or what they do for work. Years ago, everyone knew who their neighbours were, and neighbours were usually very friendly with one another, but it seems as though society is very different now.

回家時，我們會打照面，或是有時候我們會一起搭電梯，但我說不出他們的名字，或是他們的職業。多年前，所有人都認識自己的鄰居，通常關係也都非常友好，不過現在的社會似乎很不一樣。

7-04

Q04 Are people from your country generally very social?

一般而言，你國家的人善於社交嗎？

Strategy

Describe behaviours that you have observed in your culture. 'Social' means people being very outgoing and friendly; social people like to talk to others, and they make friends easily. They are usually not afraid to talk to strangers.

策略

描述你在自己的文化中觀察到的人群行為。social（善社交的）一般指的是很外向、友善的人；這種人喜歡跟他人說話，能夠輕鬆結交朋友。他們往往不害怕與陌生人交談。

A In my culture, chatting with others is a very big part of daily life. No matter where you are, whether in a park or at a market or restaurant, people are always having lively conversations with others. We like to chat with our friends and neighbours but also with people we are not very familiar with, and even complete strangers.

在我的文化中，與他人聊天是日常生活的一大部分。無論身在公園、市場或是餐廳，人們總是能爽快地與他人交談。我們喜歡跟朋友及鄰居聊天，也會跟不太熟的人說話，甚至是完全陌生的人。

🔊 7-05

Q05 Are people in your country known for being hospitable?

你國家的人是否以好客聞名？

Strategy

You can describe local customs in your country. In many cultures, being hospitable, or showing hospitality, involves having guests stay overnight in your home, cooking meals for friends or guests, and being helpful to strangers.

策略

可以描述自己國家的在地習俗。在許多文化中，好客或是展現友好的行為，包括了請客人留下來過夜、為朋友或賓客下廚，還有幫助陌生人等。

A Entertaining guests is a very important part of my culture. Food is also important to us. I remember that while I was growing up, every weekend, my parents were always inviting people over to our house. These guests included relatives, old school friends, and sometimes friends of our friends that we did not know very well. My parents still love to invite people to their house to treat them to a home-cooked meal.

招待客人在我的文化中非常重要。食物對我們來說也很重要。我記得從小到大，我父母每個週末都會邀請人來家中。這些客人包括親戚、老朋友，偶爾還會有我們朋友的共同朋友，是我們不太熟悉的友人。我父母到現在還是喜歡邀請人到他們家，親自下廚招待客人。

🔊 7-06

Q06 Do you have a lot of friends?

你有很多朋友嗎？

Strategy

When answering this question, you do not necessarily need to count how many friends you actually have. You could describe the type of friends you have, such as your close friends.

策略

回答這題時，不一定要細數自己到底有多少朋友。可以描述自己有哪種朋友，例如好朋友或是摯友。

A I don't consider myself to be very popular or to have a very outgoing personality. However, I have quite a few friends that I consider

我不認為自己很受歡迎或是非常外向，不過我有幾個我覺得相當親密的朋友。即使我們有一陣子

to be very close friends. Even if we have not seen each other in person for a while, whenever we get together, it is as though no time has passed. I think that the quality of the friendships a person has is more important than the number of friends they have.

沒見面了，但只要我們聚在一起，就彷彿時間從未流逝過。我認為人所擁有的朋友，品質比數量更加重要。

7-07

07 Are most of your friends people you know from school or work?

你的朋友大多是在學校認識，還是在職場上認識的？

Strategy

When answering this question, you could discuss people you currently spend a lot of time with and consider to be your friends.

策略

回答這題時，你可以談談那些自己目前花最多時間相處的友人。

A

It has been quite a few years since I left school, so I don't really do a lot of things with my old classmates. I would say that in my adult years, the majority of people who have become my friends have been work colleagues. Even though I have changed jobs several times, I am still in regular contact with a lot of my former workmates. Many of these people have similar goals to myself, and we have mutual respect for one another.

我離開學校已經不少年了，所以我不太會跟老同學一起出去玩。我認為在成年後，我的朋友大多都是同事，雖然我換過好幾次工作，但我還是跟許多前同事保持聯絡。這些人之中，不少人跟我有相近的目標，也都相互欣賞與尊重。

7-08

08 Do you still keep in touch with people from high school?

你跟高中同學是否還保持聯絡？

Strategy

The role that social media plays in keeping people connected could be commented on here if it is a method that you use to keep in

策略

如果你是透過社群媒體跟以前的同學保持聯絡，就可以提到在維繫人際關係上，社群媒體所扮演

contact with former classmates.

的角色。

After my classmates and I graduated from high school, we all started to go our separate ways. However, a few years later, I became curious about some of them, so I decided to look them up on Facebook. I was able to message them, and we arranged several meetups. We now have our own Facebook page, and we have class reunions at least once a year.

我和同學高中畢業就都各奔東西了。但幾年後，我對一些人感到好奇，因此決定到臉書上搜尋他們。我傳了訊息給他們，還安排了幾次見面。我們現在有自己的臉書粉專，至少一年會舉辦一次同學會。

7-09

09 What do you enjoy doing with your friends and family?

你喜歡跟朋友和家人做些什麼？

Strategy

The activities you enjoy with these two groups of people may be quite different, so you can comment on them separately.

策略

跟朋友和家人喜歡一起從事的活動可能很不一樣，可以分開談論。

I generally spend my evenings at home with my parents. We have dinner together most nights during the week, and we sometimes watch a movie at home. My weekends, however, are mostly spent going out with my friends. We like to plan a lot of activities for weekends, such as going shopping and eating out at restaurants.

我晚上通常都跟父母待在家中。平日大部分晚上，我們會一起吃晚餐，有時候還會在家裡看電影。不過我週末幾乎都會跟朋友外出，我們喜歡在週末規畫很多活動，例如逛街、去餐廳吃飯。

7-10

10 Are after-work social activities with workmates common in your culture?

在你的文化中，下班後是否經常會與同事進行社交活動？

Strategy

Comment on what are considered to be common expectations of your boss or co-workers in your country's work culture.

策略

談談你國家的職場文化中，老闆或同事通常會有什麼期待。

A My boss says that because the company I work for is a large company in a very competitive industry, we are like a big family. He tries to promote this idea by arranging weekly dinners for our department. It is mandatory that we attend these events. We always go to an expensive restaurant and stay out very late. Sometimes, it is hard to get up the next morning to go back to work. Such activities are very common in the corporate world in my country.

我在一間大公司工作，由於這個行業極為競爭，我的上司說我們就像是一個大家庭。他試著推廣這個理念，所以每週都會安排部門晚餐，而且強制我們參加。我們老是去一些昂貴的餐廳待到很晚，有時候隔天早上很難起床上班。這種情況在我國的職場中相當普遍。

Part 2 Questions

第二部分 問題

7-11

Q01 Describe a famous person whom you admire.

描述一位你崇拜的名人。

You should say:

1. who they are
2. what they are famous for
3. what you know about their background
4. and explain why you admire them.

應該提到：

1. 這個人是誰
2. 這個人以什麼而聞名
3. 你對這個人的背景了解多少
4. 說明你崇拜此人的原因。

A

❶ A very admirable historical figure whom a ❷ lot of people may not be very familiar with is Jean-Pierre Micard. Not only was he a ship captain and explorer, but he also gained a reputation for being an accomplished diplomat.

❶ 有一名值得敬重的歷史人物，❷ 可能很多人都不太熟悉，那就是尚 - 皮耶爾．米卡。他不僅是船長兼探險家，也以身為出色的外交官而為人所知。

❸ Micard was born and raised in France on his family's vineyard. His parents were very conservative and wanted him to inherit the family vineyard to follow in their footsteps. Micard, however, set a personal goal to leave his hometown at an early age, so at the first chance he got, he signed up to join a naval expedition.

❸ 米卡出生於法國，並在自家的葡萄園農區長大。他的父母都非常保守，希望他能遵循他們的腳步，繼承家族的葡萄園。然而米卡卻在很年輕的時候，便下定決心要離開家鄉，因此他一抓到機會便簽約加入了海軍的海上探險。

❹ Micard's outstanding qualities are what I admire the most. Thanks to his diligence, he rose through the ranks and eventually became a ship captain. He made first contact with many new cultures and proved

❹ 我最敬佩的是米卡卓越的特質，他的勤奮讓他官階節節高升，最後成為了一名船長。即便他首次接觸許多新文化，他也都相當有包容力，能夠理解

to be very tolerant and understanding of values and ways of life different from those he had been brought up with. In addition, he was always willing to make personal sacrifices for the good of his crew. He also had many personal interests that he cultivated, such as music, literature, and archaeology. Finally, he had a well-rounded personality and was very reasonable in his expectations of other people.

不同於自己文化的價值觀與生活方式。此外，他還總是願意為了船員而犧牲小我。他也培養了許多個人興趣，像是音樂、文學和考古學。最後，他還是個非常多才多藝的人，而且對待他人也很通情達理。

Analysis

- Points 1 and 2 are answered together because they introduce the person.
- Point 3 discusses the person's early life and family background.
- The accomplishments and qualities of the person are described in point 4.

分析

- 一併講述第一及第二點，介紹這位名人。
- 第三點談論此人的早年生活及家庭背景。
- 第四點描述此人的成就與特質。

In the Sample Answer above, several characteristics or personal qualities are mentioned, including diligence (i.e., being hardworking), self-sacrifice (i.e., a willingness to make personal sacrifices), and reason (i.e., not having unrealistic expectations). Using adjectives and phrases such as these and their synonyms can improve your overall vocabulary score.

以上範例答案提到好幾個人物特質或個性，包括 diligence（勤勞）、self-sacrifice（犧牲小我）及 reason（通情達理）等，使用這些形容詞及其同義字，能提高你的整體字彙分數。

🔊 7-12

Q02 Describe your best friend.

描述你最要好的朋友。

You should say:

❶ who the person is
❷ how you met them
❸ what they look like
❹ and explain why they are your best friend.

應該提到：

❶ 這個人是誰
❷ 你們是如何認識的
❸ 這個人的外表
❹ 說明你們為何是最要好的朋友。

A

❶ My best friend would have to be my former ❷ classmate Bob. We met on our very first day of kindergarten, and we went all the way through elementary school, high school, and even college together. He has been there throughout every phase of my life.

❶ 我最要好的朋友是我以前的同 ❷ 學鮑伯，我們從上幼稚園第一天就認識了，之後我們一路從小學、高中，甚至到大學都在一起，他陪我度過了人生的每一個階段。

❸ Physically speaking, Bob's appearance is fairly standard. He is about medium height and medium build, so I wouldn't describe him as very tall, and he's not overweight. However, one striking thing about his appearance that everyone comments on is his smile. He has a very genuine smile that a lot of people think is very charming.

❸ 從外貌上來看，鮑伯長得並不出眾。他的身高和身材都算中等，所以我不會說他很高，他也沒有過重。但他有一項人人稱讚的外表特色，就是他的笑容。他的笑容非常真誠，很多人都認為非常有魅力。

❹ As I said, I have known Bob for almost my entire life, and something about his personality that I really admire is his honesty. He is not afraid to tell the truth or to give a friend advice that they need to hear. I will give you an example: In high school, there was a classmate that I thought was very annoying, so I was

❹ 正如我所說的，我和鮑伯認識了幾乎一輩子了，我特別敬佩他的一項人格特質就是誠實。他不怕說實話，或是向朋友提出他們應該聽到的建議。讓我來舉個例子，高中的時候，我覺得有一位同學相當煩人，我總是在戲弄他。而有一天，鮑

always making fun of him. One day, Bob found out that this classmate's parents had recently gotten divorced and that the divorce had had a very negative effect on this classmate. One day in class, I started to make fun of this classmate, but Bob, in front of the entire class, told me that what I was doing was wrong. At the time, I felt betrayed. Later, however, I realised that Bob had been right and that I needed to change my behaviour. This quality of honesty has made my friendship with Bob even stronger over the years.

伯發現那位同學的父母那陣子剛離婚，對那位同學造成了非常負面的影響。有一天上課時，我又開始嘲笑這名同學，但鮑伯卻當著全班的面對我說，我這樣做是不對的。當下我覺得自己被背叛了，不過後來我意識到鮑伯是對的，我必須要改變自己的行為。鮑伯的這些誠實特質，讓我們的友誼在這些年來變得更加堅固。

Analysis

- Points 1 and 2 are answered together because they give background information regarding the friend and how the friendship started.
- A physical description of what the person looks like is given in point 3.
- Point 4 is the longest because here, an experience is given to describe why the person is considered the speaker's best friend.

分析

- 一併講述第一及第二點，說明這段友誼是如何開始。
- 第三點描述了這個人的外貌。
- 第四點的內容最多，描述這個人為何被答題者視為最好的朋友。

In point 3, the terms 'medium height' and 'medium build' are used to describe the physical appearance of this person. These phrases mean that the person would be considered not tall or short but in the middle. His build, or body type, is also described as average, so he would not be viewed as thin or overweight.

第三點用了 medium height（中等身高）及 medium build（中等身材）等說法來描述這個人的外表。這兩種說法代表此人不算太高或太矮，而是介於中間值；而體格 (build) 也同樣是平均值，所以不算是瘦或過重。

7-13

Q03 Describe one of your parents.

描述你父母的其中一位。

You should say:

❶ what they look like
❷ what they do for work
❸ what their personality is like
❹ how they have influenced you.

應該提到：

❶ 他／她的外貌
❷ 他／她的職業
❸ 他／她的個性
❹ 說明他／她如何影響到你。

A

❶ My father, when he was younger, was very tall. He was almost 2 meters in height and had a very athletic build. He really liked sports, and playing sports helped him keep in shape throughout his life.

❶ 我父親年輕時非常高，他的身高將近兩百公分，而且體格非常健壯。他很喜歡運動，這有助於他始終都保持好身材。

❷ My father had a very long and diverse work resume. When he was in high school, he worked as a chef in a neighbourhood diner for a few years. Then, when he turned 19, he enlisted in the military. At first, he was in the army, and then later, he joined the marines. He remained in the armed forces for more than 20 years. After coming out of the military, he started his own painting business, which had several employees.

❷ 我父親一生工作了很長的時間，也做過很多種工作。他讀高中時，在一間社區餐館打工，當了幾年的廚師。然後在19 歲那年，他加入了軍隊，起初他待在陸軍，隨後加入了海軍陸戰隊。他在軍隊裡待了 20 年以上。離開軍隊之後，他做起了油漆生意，底下有好幾名員工。

❸ I think that my father's time in the marines had the most profound effect on his personality. His life, even after being in the military, was highly regimented. He would get up at 5 a.m. every day, even on his days off, and he would eat his meals at the same time each day. The way he scheduled his time and ran his business was very organised, and he did not tolerate

❸ 我認為待在海軍陸戰隊的那段日子，對父親的性格造成最深的影響。即便離開軍隊後，他的生活依舊非常有紀律。他每天都在早上五點起床，即便休假也不例外，每天也都在同樣的時間用餐。他安排時間和經營事業的方式非常有條理，他也無法忍受常常遲到或是怠惰

employees who were often late or lazy.

❹ I think that I have a lot of the same qualities as my father. I am also a very self-disciplined person. I have a routine when it comes to things such as getting up in the morning, going to bed at night, and exercise, and I am very good at organising my time and responsibilities. Additionally, I am also very punctual and can't stand laziness. My father passed away several years ago, but I believe that his example has had a profound effect on the type of person I am.

的員工。

❹ 我認為自己有許多和父親一樣的特質。我也是個非常自律的人，無論是在起床、睡覺時間，或是運動等方面，我都有自己的一套規律。我非常善於規畫自己的時間和責任。除此之外，我也非常守時，無法忍受懶惰行為。我父親在好幾年前過世了，但我相信他所樹立的榜樣，深深影響了我，使我成為現在的樣子。

Analysis

This answer discusses several aspects of a parent's personality. Points 3 and 4 complement each other, as they both describe characteristics that the father had and how these are reflected by the child. Synonyms are used to avoid the repetition of vocabulary. For example: 'regimented' = 'self-disciplined'; 'scheduled his time' = 'organising my time'; 'did not tolerate' = 'can't stand'.

分析

範例答案談到了該位家長性格上的諸多面向。第三及第四點互相襯托，因為在這裡提到了父親的個性，以及這些個性如何影響了答題者。答案使用了許多同義字詞，以避免重複用字，例如 regimented（有紀律的）和 self-disciplined（自律的）、scheduled his time（規畫他的時間）和 organising my time（安排我的時間）、did not tolerate（無法忍受）和 can't stand（受不了）。

7-14

Q04 Describe someone who has had a significant influence on you.

描述一個對你有重要影響的人。

You should say:

❶ who this person is
❷ what your relationship with this person is
❸ what qualities they have
❹ and explain how they have influenced you.

應該提到：

❶ 此人是誰
❷ 你跟此人是什麼關係
❸ 此人有什麼特質
❹ 說明此人帶給你何種影響。

A

❶ When I was growing up, Mr. Smith, who ❷ was a friend of my parents, had a very profound effect on me. He was an elderly gentleman, and he and his family lived in our neighbourhood. Almost every weekend, we would go over to his home, or he would come over to ours. At first, he was my parents' friend, but I now consider him to be one of my close personal friends as well.

❶ 在成長的過程中，我父母的朋 ❷ 友史密斯先生對我的影響深遠。他是一名老紳士，跟家人同住在我們的社區。幾乎每個週末，我們都會去他家作客，不然就是他來我們家。他一開始是我父母的朋友，但我現在也將他視為自己的個人摯友之一。

❸ Mr. Smith is now 95 years old. He is a very wise person who is able to teach people a lot of life lessons by sharing experiences from his own life. Also, he is a very honest person, and so in many of the stories that he shares, he admits his own mistakes. I think he does this because he hopes that others will be able to learn how to avoid making similar mistakes in their lives.

❸ 史密斯先生現在已經 95 歲了，他是個非常有智慧的人，藉由分享自己的人生經驗，他教會人們許多人生課題。他也是個很誠實的人，所以在他分享的故事中，他會承認自己的錯誤。我想他之所以這樣做，是希望他人能了解，如何在自己的人生中，避免犯下類似錯誤。

❹ I always listen carefully to Mr. Smith's stories, and over the years, I have come to realise how important the lessons he has

❹ 我總是仔細聆聽史密斯先生的故事，這些年來，我意識到他想要教我的課題有多麼重要。

tried to teach me are. I think that because of the wisdom he has shared with me, I have been able to avoid a lot of foolish mistakes. Now that Mr. Smith is very elderly, there are a lot of things that he can't do for himself anymore. Therefore, I regularly go to his house and help him with tasks like cleaning and cooking. I think that this shows another lesson I have learned from him: the importance of expressing gratitude through not only our words but also our actions.

我認為多虧有他與我分享智慧，一直以來我才能避開許多愚蠢的錯誤。現在史密斯先生年事已高，有很多事情他無法靠自己完成，因此我會定期去他家，幫他打掃、做飯等等。我想這展現出我從他身上學到的另一項課題，那就是表達感謝不只可透過語言，也可以透過實際行動。

Analysis

This Sample Answer describes a relationship that has spanned several decades. There is not enough time in a Speaking Test Part 2 answer to give an extremely long and detailed story about this type of relationship. Therefore, in points 3 and 4, the overall messages of the stories shared by this elderly individual and the value of these messages are discussed in general terms.

分析

範例答案描述一段持續了長達數十年的關係。在口說測驗第二部分，並沒有足夠時間能鉅細靡遺地講述這段友誼故事。因此，答題者在第三及第四點使用比較概括性的陳述，談論這位長者分享的故事所傳遞的訊息，以及這些訊息的價值。

7-15

05 Describe someone who is considered a good person.

描述一位社會公認的好人。

You should say:

1. who this person is
2. what you know about their background
3. what things they have done
4. and explain why they are a good person.

應該提到：

1. 此人是誰
2. 你對此人的背景有何了解
3. 此人做過什麼事
4. 說明此人為何是好人。

A

❶ The famous leader Gandhi is considered by many to have been a good person. I think that most people alive today have heard of him.

❷ I remember learning in school that Gandhi ❸ was from India and that he came from a very poor background. The period when he was alive was a very chaotic time in India. At that time, India was still a colony of Britain, and there were a lot of unfair things happening to the Indian people. For example, there were many forms of inequality such as that in education and that in work opportunities. Also, many people lacked access to basic necessities, such as food and medical care. After World War II ended, the Indian people wanted to become independent of British rule. As a result, there were a lot of violent clashes between the Indian people and the British authorities. However, Gandhi became a political leader who used non-violent ways to help the Indian people establish their own independent country. This goal took several years to accomplish, but it was eventually achieved. Gandhi showed a lot of determination and dedication to accomplish this goal.

❹ Even though Gandhi was assassinated many years ago, he is still admired by many people today. His teachings are still used to show how people from different backgrounds can be tolerant of one another

❶ 知名領袖甘地，被許多人視為好人，我認為現今世上多數人都聽說過他。

❷ 我記得在學校時學過，甘地來❸ 自印度，背景非常困苦。他在世的那段期間，印度時局非常動盪，當時的印度仍然是英國的殖民地，所以那時候有許多不公不義的事情發生在印度人身上。例如教育和工作機會的不平等；另外，很多人也缺乏基本生活物資，像是食物和醫療照護。第二次世界大戰結束後，印度人想要脫離英國的統治，結果導致了當時的印度人和英國當局之間，發生許多暴力衝突。然而，甘地成為了一名政治領袖，並透過非暴力的方式幫助印度人獨立建國。這個目標花了好幾年的時間才達成，但最後仍然成真了。甘地展現出堅毅與奉獻精神來實現此目標。

❹ 儘管甘地在後來遭人暗殺，他至今仍然受到眾人景仰。他的教誨仍為人所用，展現出不同背景的人，如何包容彼此，而且我們無需動用暴力也能成大

and that we don't need to use violence to accomplish important goals. This is why he is remembered as a good person.

事。這就是為什麼他是社會公認的好人，且受到緬懷的原因。

Analysis

- Point 1 briefly introduces a well-known figure from modern history.
- Points 2 and 3 are discussed together because it would be difficult to separate Gandhi's background from his accomplishments.
- Point 4 gives reasons why Gandhi is admired today.

分析

- 在第一點簡短介紹了近代史中的一位知名人物。
- 一併談論第二及第三點，因為甘地的背景與成就難以分開講述。
- 第四點解釋了甘地至今為何受人崇拜。

It may be challenging to think of a person to describe who is considered 'good'. The Sample Answer above discusses a well-known person from history, namely Gandhi. The events surrounding Gandhi's life and what he did are quite complicated, so in the answer above, general facts about his background and accomplishments are described.

要想出一個公認的「好人」來描述可能會很困難，以上範例答案提到了一個知名歷史人物，也就是甘地。伴隨著甘地一生的事件，和他的所作所為相當複雜，所以以上答案只敘述了他的大致背景及成就。

Part 3 Questions | 第三部分 問題

🔊 7-16

How has technology affected the way we communicate with our families? Is this a positive or negative development?

科技如何影響我們與家人的溝通方式？這是正面還是負面的發展？

Strategy

There are several ways to answer this question. First, you could speak generally about ways families use technology to communicate, and then you could give your opinion.

策略

有許多答法可回答這題。首先可以大致說明你的家人如何使用科技溝通，接著提供自己的看法。

❶ In most modern families, every member has their own mobile device. These devices enable them to connect with one another through text messages or phone calls.

❷ I feel this can be a positive thing because in an emergency, family members can reach one another immediately. On the other hand, I have noticed that this type of technology has many drawbacks. For example, in some families, in the evenings, although all the members are together at home, they are all busy playing with their phones, so they rarely interact with one another.

❸ In summary, modern technology has both advantages and disadvantages when it comes to communication within a family.

❶ 在多數現代家庭中，所有家庭成員都有自己的行動裝置，這讓所有人都能透過訊息或電話相互聯繫。

❷ 我覺得這是有好處的，因為在緊急情況下，家庭成員能夠立刻聯絡到彼此。另一方面，我也注意到這種科技有許多缺點。舉例來說，在有些家庭中，晚上的時候，雖然家中所有人都在，但每個人都忙著滑手機，所以也很少跟彼此互動。

❸ 簡言之，說到與家人溝通談話的議題，現代科技有好處也有壞處。

Analysis

This Sample Answer gives a balanced view

分析

科技在溝通方面可能產生的正反

of the positive and negative effects that technology can have on communication. The phrase 'On the other hand' signals a transition from discussing the pros of the issue to discussing its cons.

影響，範例答案對此提供了對等看法。On the other hand（另一方面）這個片語，是用於暗示現在議題要從談論優點轉為談論缺點。

7-17

02 Do you think that parents in other countries discipline their children in the same way as parents in your country do?

你認為，其他國家管教兒童的方式，跟你的國家一樣嗎？

Strategy

'Discipline' can refer to educating or training children. It can also refer to punishment given to children. You could compare and contrast cultural norms in your country with those you have observed in other countries.

策略

discipline（管教）指的是教育或訓練兒童，也可以指對兒童的懲罰。可以拿自己國家文化的常態，跟你觀察到的其他國家文化進行比較和對比。

❶ I think that there is a highly noticeable difference between discipline in Asian and Western cultures.

❶ 我想，亞洲和西方文化在管教孩童方面，有很顯著的差異。

❷ Asian parents are very passive when it comes to training their children. In many Asian countries, when children are taken to public areas such as stores, parks, and even sidewalks, they run around and are allowed to touch anything they want. They behave as though they are in their living room at home. By contrast, in Western countries, children are trained to stay at their parents' side and are not allowed to touch anything without first asking permission.

❷ 亞洲家長在教育孩童行為方面，表現得非常消極。在許多亞洲國家，孩子被帶至商店、公園甚至是人行道等公共場所時，他們會四處亂跑，還會隨意碰觸任何東西，表現得彷彿是在自家客廳。相較之下，在西方國家，孩童會被訓練要待在父母身邊，而且若無徵求許可就不許觸碰任何東西。

❸ A lot of Westerners are shocked by the unruly behaviours of children in public

❸ 許多西方人在亞洲國家的公共場所時，會被兒童不守規矩的

places in Asian countries, and this suggests that Asian parents need to take a more active role in training and disciplining their children.

行為給嚇到。這代表亞洲父母必須要更加積極訓練他們的孩童。

Analysis

Comparisons between the behaviours of Asian and Western children are given in this Sample Answer. Behaviours seen in daily life reflect the types of discipline or training that children receive from their parents.

分析

範例答案比較了亞洲和西方兒童的行為。兒童日常生活中的行為，能反映家長對孩童的管教或訓練。

7-18

03 What do you think teenagers and their parents argue about the most?

你認為青少年最常為了什麼和家長起爭執？

Strategy

While speaking in general terms about teenagers' interactions with their parents, you could also talk about your own experience regarding what you and your parents disagreed over when you were a teenager.

策略

在談論青少年與家長之間的互動時，可以引用自身經驗，講述自己還是青少年時，會在什麼事情上跟父母產生歧異。

A

❶ Many teenagers want to have more freedom, and this is often a source of conflict between them and their parents.

❶ 青少年總是渴望更多自由，這常是他們與家長間的衝突來源。

❷ Young people want to be able to manage their time themselves and decide when to go to bed, hang out with their friends, and do school work. However, many parents don't think that their children are mature enough to make such decisions themselves, and so this is often a source of conflict.

❷ 年輕人想要能夠自己管理時間；像是自己決定何時上床睡覺、何時跟朋友出去玩及何時寫作業。但家長通常都認為自己的孩子不夠成熟，不能做這些決定，所以這常常是紛爭的來源。

❸ I think that if you were to ask the average

❸ 我想如果去問一般青少年這個

teenager about this, they would agree that independence is what they and their parents disagree over the most.

問題，他們都會同意最常跟父母產生歧見的，就是獨立自主的議題。

Analysis

More personal freedom is used as the primary example in this answer. Specific details regarding time management and social activities are then given to support this idea.

分析

範例答案以青少年渴望更多個人自由作為主要範例，接著列舉時間管理及社交活動等的實際例子，以支持該看法。

7-19

04 Are teenagers in your country very independent?

你國家的青少年很獨立嗎？

Strategy

Trends you have observed in society or your own experience can be used when answering this question.

策略

回答此問題時，可以講述自己在社會上觀察到的趨勢，或是個人經驗。

A

❶ Not at all. Parents in my country are too overprotective of their children, and as a result, young people depend on their parents for everything.

❶ 完全不獨立。在我的國家，父母過度保護他們的孩子，導致年輕人一切都要依賴父母。

❷ The term 'helicopter parent' is used to describe this type of behaviour, which, unfortunately, can continue to affect children after they reach adulthood. I have seen married adults in their 30s and 40s who are unable to make even minor decisions for themselves without first consulting their parents.

❷「直升機父母」一詞正是用來描述這種行為。很遺憾，這種行為會持續到孩子長大成人。我曾見過已婚的成年人，都已經 30、40 歲了還無法自己做決定，他們都要先諮詢過父母才能決定很小的事情。

❸ This is a very sad situation that makes me wonder how this cycle can be broken so that everyone can grow up to be emotionally stable adults.

❸ 這種情況非常悲哀，不禁讓人好奇該如何打破這個循環，所有人才能成長為情緒穩定的成年人。

Analysis

A specific behaviour of parents, alongside its short-term effects and long-term consequences, is used in this Sample Answer to show that the trend being described can yield many negative effects.

分析

範例答案講述了父母的某項特定行為，在短期內所造成的影響，及長遠後果，來體現這種情形會帶來的許多負面影響。

7-20

05 What do you look for in a friend?

你希望朋友能有什麼特質？

Strategy

You could describe the qualities or characteristics that you think are important for a friend to have.

策略

可描述你認為作為一位朋友，應該要有的重要特質或性格。

❶ For me, the most important quality that a friend needs to show is loyalty.

❷ I think that betrayal is probably the number one reason behind friendships ending. A loyal friend will not say bad things about you behind your back, and they will always be honest with you. Also, a loyal friend will not be afraid to tell you what you need to hear, even if it might make you upset for a while.

❸ I think that everyone should work on cultivating loyalty. If they do this, then they can be a true friend to others.

❶ 對我來說，作為朋友最重要的特質就是忠誠。

❷ 我認為背叛行為可能是一段友情告終的首要原因。一位忠誠的朋友，不會在背後說你的閒話，他們會永遠赤誠。一位忠誠的朋友，即使要讓你難過一陣子，也不會害怕對你實話實說。

❸ 我想每個人都應該要努力培養忠誠特質，如果能做到，那就能成為別人的真心朋友。

Analysis

Loyalty is given as the most important personality trait that a true friend should have. Loyalty is then contrasted with betrayal to emphasise its importance.

分析

在此答案中，首先提出忠誠是真朋友應該展現的首要特質。接著將忠誠與背叛行為進行對比，藉此強調忠誠的重要性。

🔊 7-21

Is the way we meet friends different nowadays from in your parents' day?

我們現在結交朋友的方式，跟父母那一代有差異嗎？

Strategy

This question refers to the ways in which we meet people for the first time rather than when we get together with friends we already have.

策略

問題中的 meet friends 在此指的是我們初次「認識朋友」，而不是指我們跟朋友「碰面」。

A

❶ I think that nowadays, technology plays a very prominent role in how young people make new friends.

❷ There are so many apps and websites that are designed to help individuals meet new people. Also, on social media, there are special interest groups that people can join for activities like hiking and diving. These groups organise events where members can meet in person. Also, there are a lot of dating apps these days; I even know some people who have married someone they met on one of these apps. Back in my parents' day, such technology did not exist, so people usually made friends through work, at school, or through mutual acquaintances.

❸ In summary, technology now enables people to greatly expand their social circles.

❶ 說到現今年輕人如何結交新朋友，我想科技扮演了很重要的角色。

❷ 有許多應用程式和網站，專門設計來讓人認識新朋友。社群媒體上也有健行、潛水等特殊興趣社團，供人們加入。這些社團會組織活動，讓成員可以見面。現在也有很多約會性質的應用程式，我知道甚至有些人會跟在這種應用程式上認識的對象結婚。在我父母的那個年代，這種科技並不存在，所以人們通常在職場、學校或透過共同朋友來結識新朋友。

❸ 簡言之，如今的科技，讓人們能夠大幅拓展社交圈。

Analysis

New technology is described to explain how young people today make new friends. These trends are then contrasted with more traditional ways that people made friends decades ago.

分析

範例答案講述了現今年輕人如何用新科技結交新朋友，接著將這種趨勢，與數十年前較傳統的交友方式做比較。

🔊 7-22

07 Have you ever volunteered?

你曾擔任過志工嗎？

Strategy

Volunteering usually involves unpaid humanitarian or educational work. If you have any volunteering experience, you can elaborate on what you did and how you felt about doing it.

策略

擔任志工通常是指從事無償的人道主義或教育工作。如果你有這樣的經驗，可以詳細說明你所做的事情，以及從事這些工作的感受。

A

❶ Several years ago, my university offered a special programme for volunteers to go to Cambodia and teach English at a school there over summer vacation.

❷ I thought this was a great opportunity, so I signed up right away. I spent 8 weeks in a rural village in Cambodia that had no air conditioning or other modern conveniences. My English students came from very poor backgrounds. Despite all the challenges that I faced, I really enjoyed this experience. I was able to help my students by giving them an opportunity that their parents had never had. I still keep in touch with most of these students.

❸ This experience was very rewarding. I think that everyone should do some form of volunteer work at least once in their lives.

❶ 好幾年前，我所就讀的大學開設了一個特別計畫，並招募了一些志工，在暑假期間前往柬埔寨的一所學校教授英語。

❷ 我覺得這是很棒的機會，所以我立刻報名參加。我在柬埔寨的一個農村度過了八週，那裡沒有冷氣或其他現代化的便利設施。那些學生背景貧困。雖然過程中面臨了很多挑戰，但我真的很享受這次體驗。我得以幫助我的學生，給他們一個他們父母從未享有的機會。到了現在，我仍與大部分的學生保持聯繫。

❸ 這次體驗收穫十足。我認為每個人一生都應該至少當一次志工。

Analysis

The background details of an experience are provided in this answer. In addition, the speaker describes the ways that they personally benefited from participating in the programme.

分析

範例答案提供了該次體驗的背景細節，此外，答題者描述了自己參與該項計畫所得到的益處。

7-23

08 Is volunteering the best way to help people in need, or are there other good ways?

想幫助需要幫助的人，最佳方式是當志工嗎？還是有其他好辦法？

Strategy

The importance of volunteering can be discussed along with other methods of assisting people.

策略

可以談論擔任志工的重要性，以及用於幫助他人的其他方法。

❶ I think that volunteering is an invaluable way to help individuals. In order to help society as a whole, however, governments need to play a more active role.

❷ When I was a volunteer in Africa, I was able to help a few families access clean water and medical care. I felt very good about helping these people. However, I came to realise that there were millions more people just like the families I helped that were also in need of assistance. Governments need to care more about their citizens by implementing policies that give everyone access to basic necessities.

❸ Volunteering is beneficial, but government action is also needed to yield long-term change.

❶ 我認為擔任志工幫助他人是無價的。然而為了幫助整體社會，政府所扮演的角色必須更加積極。

❷ 我在非洲當志工時，幫助一些家庭取得乾淨的水資源，以及醫療照護。能夠幫助這些人讓我感覺很好。然而，我意識到，有數百萬人也像我所幫助的這些家庭一樣需要援助。政府需要更關心他們的公民，透過執行必要的政策，讓每個人都能獲得基本生活物資。

❸ 擔任志工是有益的，但也得仰賴政府行動才能實現這種長期變革。

Analysis

An experience is given to describe not only the benefits of volunteering but also the need for governments to take action. Short-term benefits for individuals achieved through volunteering are contrasted with long-term benefits achieved through assistance by governments, which is

分析

範例答案舉了一段經驗，講述當志工的好處，但也強調政府同樣需要採取行動。接著比較了當志工為個人帶來的短期好處，以及政府若能提供幫助所能帶來的長期好處，以讓大量人口受惠。

needed to benefit large populations of people.

7-24

09 How important is it for parents to spend time with their children?

家長花時間陪伴孩子有多重要？

Strategy

Your personal opinion or observations that you have made regarding recent trends in society can be commented on when answering this question.

策略

在回答此問題時，可以提出你的個人觀點或觀察到的近期社會趨勢。

❶ I feel it is absolutely vital that parents spend time with their children.

❷ I think that many of the emotional and developmental problems that children have today are a result of parental neglect. In many families, because parents are working such long hours, the children live with their grandparents. Only when they are at school age do they go and live with their parents. This situation can be traumatic for a lot of children because their parents are almost like strangers. Children go to school all week while their parents are at work, and they see each other only on weekends.

❸ Parent-child relationships are extremely important. Therefore, parents and children need to spend time together every day, talking and eating meals with each other.

❶ 我覺得父母花時間陪伴孩子無比重要。

❷ 我認為當今很多兒童的情緒和發展問題，都源自於父母的忽視。在許多家庭中，由於父母的工時長，幼童因此必須和祖父母一起生活，等孩子到了學齡才會跟父母同住。這對許多孩子來說可能是一種創傷，因為對他們來說，父母幾乎就像是陌生人一樣。接下來，孩子一整個星期都在上學，而父母都在工作，他們只有週末才會見到彼此。

❸ 親子關係是非常重要的。因此，父母和孩子必須每天花時間交談、用餐。

Analysis

In order to emphasise how important this issue is, the Sample Answer uses the following terms: 'absolutely vital', 'need to', and 'extremely

分析

為了強調此議題的重要性，範例答案使用了 absolutely vital（絕對重要的）、need to（必須）及

important'. Words such as these help add weight to your personal opinion.

extremely important（非常重要的）等字詞，使用這些字詞可以讓你的意見顯得更有份量。

🔊 7-25

Q10 Do you think that elderly people are treated in the same way in all countries?

你認為所有國家的長者都有相同待遇嗎？

Strategy

Compare and contrast what you know about your own culture and other cultures with regard to the treatment of the elderly.

策略

針對長者被對待的方式，從你所知的自身文化及其他文化進行比較。

A

❶ I think that in general, elderly people are respected in most places.

❷ Specifically, the elderly are valued for their past contributions to society, how they raised their families, and the wisdom and experience that they share with the next generation. Within families, grandparents are generally treated with a measure of respect stronger than that afforded to young people. I think it is a rare occurrence to find a society where elderly people are neglected.

❸ I think that the elderly have a very important role to play in every society.

❶ 我認為一般來說，多數地方的長者都會受到尊重。

❷ 尤其是長者過去對社會的貢獻、對家庭的付出，以及他們能夠與下一代分享的智慧和經驗，使他們的價值備受重視。在家庭當中，祖父母通常會比年輕人受到更多尊重。我想很少有社會會忽視長者。

❸ 我認為長者在所有社會當中，都扮演著非常重要的角色。

Analysis

This Sample Answer lists the types of contributions that older people make to society and their families over their lifetime. These are the reasons that generally, in every culture, the elderly are given some measure of respect.

分析

範例答案列舉了長者一生中，為社會和他們的家庭所做的貢獻，一般而言，這些就是每個文化都會給予長者一定程度尊重的原因。

LESSON 8

Health

健康

LESSON 8

Health 健康

Part 1 Questions 第一部分 問題

8-01

Q01 Are you a healthy person?

你是個健康的人嗎？

Strategy

You could describe the general condition of your health or any of your habits regarding diet, sleep, or exercise.

策略

可以描述你的整體健康狀況，或是任何與飲食、睡眠及運動有關的習慣。

A I am a highly health-conscious person, so I am very mindful of my diet. I don't eat fast food, and I go jogging usually three times a week. I would say that compared with most people my age, I am very healthy.

我非常注重健康，所以我很重視我的飲食。我不吃速食，每週大概慢跑三次。我認為跟同齡的多數人相比，我非常健康。

8-02

Q02 How often do you exercise?

你多久運動一次？

Strategy

Similar to the question above, you should describe your personal habits when it comes to exercise.

策略

這題類似於上一個問題，可描述你個人的運動習慣。

A I don't exercise as much as I used to. When I was younger, I played basketball several times a week with my friends, but after I started working, I became too busy and too lazy to work out. I know that I should go bike riding or

我現在不像以前那樣經常運動了。我年輕時每週都會跟朋友打個幾次籃球，但是開始工作之後，我就太過忙碌，也懶得運動了。我知道我應該去騎腳踏車或

join a gym so that I can be healthier.

是上健身房，這樣才比較健康。

🔊 8-03

Q03 How often do you visit a doctor?

你多久看一次醫生？

Strategy

How often you see a doctor, as well as the reasons that you usually go to see a doctor, can be commented on in this answer. Some people are extremely concerned about their health. A person who believes or imagines that they are always sick and thus often goes to the doctor for minor problems is called a 'hypochondriac'.

策略

可以在答案中談論自己看醫生的頻率及原因。有些人會極度擔心自己的健康，一個認為或想像自己總是在生病的人稱為 hypochondriac（慮病症患者），他們常會為了小問題就去看醫生。

I am not a hypochondriac. I go to see a doctor only if I am really sick. If I have a cold or a stomachache, I stay at home and take some medicine. My co-workers are always going to the doctor, even for minor problems. I think that this wastes a lot of time and other resources.

我不是慮病症患者，我只有在真的生病時才會去看醫生。如果我著涼或是胃痛，我會待在家吃藥。我的幾個同事一天到晚去看醫生，即便只是小問題也一樣。我認為這浪費了許多時間和其他資源。

🔊 8-04

Q04 What do you do to keep in shape?

你如何維持健康？

Strategy

This question relates to the condition of your body and physical health. You can answer this question by describing how you maintain your health through diet and exercise. This question could also be asked as follows: 'What do you do to keep fit?'

策略

此問題與你的身體健康狀況有關，可以描述自己如何透過飲食和運動來維持健康。這個問題的另一個問法是：What do you do to keep fit?。

I do both cardio and weight training exercises at the gym. For cardio, I go to a spin class,

我會上健身房做有氧運動和重訓。在有氧運動方面，我會去飛

where I ride a stationary bike. In addition, I cook all my meals at home. I eat a lot of fresh vegetables and have protein, such as eggs or chicken, with every meal.

輪課教室上健身飛輪課。此外，我每一餐都會自己在家做飯，我都吃大量的新鮮蔬菜，每餐都會有雞蛋或雞肉等蛋白質。

8-05

What types of foods do you think should be included in a healthy diet?

你認為健康的飲食應該要包含哪些食物？

Strategy

There are many different dietary trends nowadays. These include eating organic food (food that is grown and processed without chemicals), vegetarian diets (where the person does not eat meat but may eat eggs, fish, cheese, milk, and other animal products), and vegan diets (where the person does not eat any animal products).

策略

現在有許多不同的飲食趨勢，包括「有機飲食」（種植和加工過程不添加化學物質的食物）、「素食主義飲食」（不吃肉，但可能會吃雞蛋、魚、起司、牛奶和其他動物製品），或是「純素飲食」（不吃任何動物製品）。

A

I think that a balanced diet is the key to staying healthy. I think we should eat fruits and vegetables every day and avoid junk food. In addition, processed foods that are high in sodium and fat should be avoided. However, I don't think that a person needs to go to extremes, such as becoming a vegan, to maintain a healthy diet.

我想均衡飲食是維持健康的關鍵。我認為我們每天都應該吃蔬菜水果，並且避免吃垃圾食物。此外，還要避免高鈉和高脂肪的加工食品。然而，我不認為一個人需要走極端路線才能吃得健康，例如成為純素主義者。

8-06

How do you feel about alternative medicines, such as herbal remedies?

你對於草藥等另類療法有什麼看法？

Strategy

In many Asian countries, what is known as 'Western Medicine' refers to medicines such as pills for a headache or cold. Traditional Chinese medicine, by contrast, uses only natural ingredients.

策略

在許多亞洲國家，「西藥」所指的是頭痛或感冒時所吃的藥錠等，而傳統中藥則只使用天然成分。

A I think that herbal medicines can be helpful in addressing some health conditions, such as skin or digestive problems. However, such medicines may require several days or weeks before they start to have an effect. Therefore, if I have a cold or an upset stomach, I take some pills that can be bought at a pharmacy because I wouldn't want to wait for a herbal medicine to take effect.

我認為草藥可以用來治療某些健康狀況，例如皮膚或消化道問題。然而，這些藥物可能需要幾天、甚至幾週才會開始發揮療效。所以我如果感冒或腸胃不適，我會服用一些藥局購買的藥丸，因為我不想等傳統草藥慢慢發揮效用。

8-07

Have you ever had a massage? Do you think massages are good for human health?

你曾經去按摩過嗎？你認為按摩對身體好嗎？

Strategy

There are various types of massages. Some types are designed for relaxation, while others are used for rehabilitation of an injury. Your personal experience and opinion should be given when answering this question.

策略

有很多不同種類的按摩，有些是為了放鬆，而有些則是用於受傷後的復健。可在答案中提供個人經驗和意見。

A I regularly seek massage treatment for my shoulders and spine because at work, I sit in front of a computer all day, and this is very bad for my posture. I used to experience a lot of tension and discomfort in my neck and shoulders. However, now that I receive

我會定期去做肩膀和脊椎的按摩治療，因為我整天坐在電腦前工作，這造成我的姿勢非常不良。之前我的肩頸都非常緊繃且不適，但定期做按摩治療後，我就不再有這個問題了，我的整體健

regular massage therapy, I no longer have this problem, and my overall health has improved. Therefore, I think massages are very helpful.

康狀況也得到了改善。所以我認為按摩非常有幫助。

8-08

08 Do you have any allergies?

你會過敏嗎？

Strategy

The word 'allergy' is a noun, whereas 'allergic' is an adjective. You can put another word in front of 'allergy' to describe the type of allergy you have. For example: 'I have a peanut allergy'. Alternatively, you can use the grammar structure 'allergic + to + thing', as in the following example sentence: 'I am allergic to peanuts'.

策略

allergy（過敏）一字是名詞，而 allergic（過敏的）則是形容詞。可以在 allergy 前面加上其他單字，描述你的過敏來源，例如 I have a peanut allergy.（我對花生過敏。）或者也可以使用以下文法結構表達相同意思：〈allergic + to + 物〉，例如 I am allergic to peanuts.。

A

I am highly allergic to shellfish. Because this is a very serious allergy, I have to stay away from things like shrimp and crab. If I eat these foods, my skin becomes very red and itchy. A more extreme reaction is that my breathing can also be affected. Therefore, I need to completely avoid these foods.

我對甲殼類高度過敏。這種過敏非常嚴重，所以我必須遠離蝦蟹等海鮮。如果我吃下這些食物，我的皮膚會變得又紅又癢，更極端的反應是，我的呼吸系統可能也會受到影響，所以我必須徹底避開這些食物。

8-09

09 Do a lot of people in your country smoke?

你的國家有很多人抽菸嗎？

Strategy

Your observations regarding this habit should be described. In some countries, certain age groups are more likely to smoke than others, and some people smoke only in certain social settings.

策略

可描述自己對於抽菸習慣的觀察。在某些國家中，特定年齡層的人會比其他人更有抽菸的可能，而有些人可能只會在某些社交場合抽菸。

A Apparently, smoking was far more prevalent decades ago, when my parents were young. In fact, both of my parents started smoking at a very young age and then continued into their adulthood. In recent years, a lot of information has come out regarding the health risks of smoking, and I think this has done much to discourage people from starting to smoke. As a result, nowadays, it is very rare to see someone under the age of 30 smoking in my country.

幾十年前在我父母年輕的時候，那時的抽菸風氣顯然更加普遍。事實上，我父母在很小的時候就開始抽菸，並一直抽到成年後。近年來，有許多資訊顯示抽菸會導致健康問題，我認為這大幅勸阻了人們碰菸。所以現在在我國，很少看到 30 歲以下的人在抽菸。

8-10

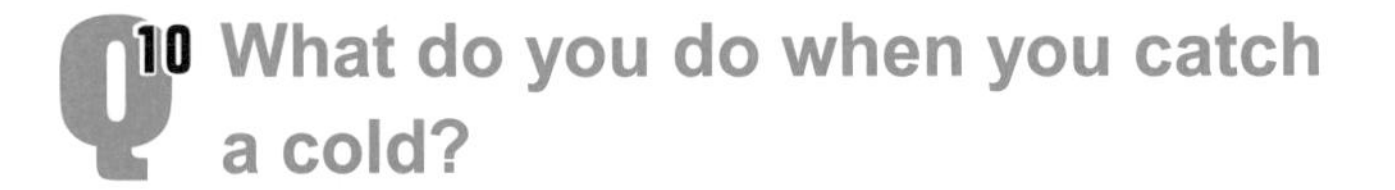

Q10 What do you do when you catch a cold?

你感冒的時候會怎麼做？

Strategy

Your preferred method for dealing with a cold should be described. For example, the types of medicine you use or whether you go to see a doctor can be included in your answer.

策略

可以描述自己感冒時的習慣作法，例如可以講述所服用的藥物或是否會去看醫生等。

A When I start to experience cold symptoms, I immediately take some over-the-counter cold medicine, which helps with symptoms such as fever, headache, and sore throat. What I usually do next is go to bed. I have found that a combination of medicine and several hours of sleep prevents the cold from becoming too severe.

當我開始出現感冒症狀時，我會立即服用一些非處方感冒藥。這種藥物有助於緩解發燒、頭痛和喉嚨痛等症狀。接著我通常會去睡覺。我發現這種藥物再加上幾個小時的睡眠，就可以防止感冒症狀加遽。

Part 2 Questions 第二部分 問題

🔊 8-11

01 Describe an accident you have had.

描述你發生過的一場意外。

You should say:

❶ where it happened
❷ how it happened
❸ in what way you were injured
❹ and explain the treatment you received.

應該提到：

❶ 在哪裡發生
❷ 發生什麼事
❸ 你是怎麼受傷的
❹ 說明你接受了何種治療。

A

❶ I was in a serious motorbike accident not ❷ far from my house about 3 years ago. It was a Monday afternoon, and I was riding home from the grocery store on my bike. I was approaching a red light, so I was slowing down, when all of a sudden, I heard a loud BANG! There was a big hole in the road that I hadn't seen. Riding into it, I lost my balance.

❸ I put my foot down to try to stop my bike, but I went over, and my leg was crushed under the bike. Both bones in my lower leg were shattered, and I had to be taken to hospital for surgery.

❹ The day after the accident, a lot of metal plates and screws were put in my leg to help the bone heal straight. Unfortunately, after a few months, my bones were not healing properly, so I needed to have a

❶ 大約三年前，我曾發生一起嚴 ❷ 重的機車車禍，就在離我家不遠處。那天是星期一下午，我正要從超市騎車回家。前方是紅燈，所以我放慢了車速，突然之間，我聽見很大的「砰」一聲！我沒有看見路面上有一個大洞就騎了過去，因此我失去了平衡。

❸ 我將雙腳放下，試圖要讓機車停下來，但卻摔了出去，結果我的腿被壓在車身底下。我小腿的兩根骨頭都被壓碎，必須送往醫院動手術。

❹ 意外發生後的隔天，我的腿部植入了許多醫療用金屬板和螺絲，幫助骨頭長正。很遺憾，幾個月過後，我的骨頭並沒有完全復原，所以我必須接受第

second operation, and this time, I needed to have a bone graft. First of all, the metal parts had to be taken out of my leg. Next, the doctor took part of my pelvis (hip bone) and grafted it with the broken bones in my leg. After that, new metal plates and screws were put in my leg. This second operation was a success; a few weeks later, my leg started to heal properly. Finally, a year after the accident, I was completely healed and able to walk without crutches.

二次手術，這次我必須植骨。首先要將原本的醫療用金屬從我的腿中取出，接下來，醫生取下我的一部分骨盆（髖骨），並將其移植到我腿內的斷骨。然後又將新的醫療用金屬板和螺絲放入我的腿中。第二次手術很成功，幾週過後，我的腿開始逐漸復原。最後，我在意外一年後徹底痊癒了，不靠拐杖就能走路。

Analysis

In point 4, several sequence words are used to describe step-by-step what was involved in the treatment the speaker received. Sequence words can assist in connecting the major points of your answer and putting them in a logical order. The sequence words used in the Sample Answer above include 'First of all', 'Next', 'After that', and 'Finally'.

分析

第四點使用了很多轉折詞，逐步描述答題者接受的治療涉及了什麼步驟。轉折詞可以串連你答案中的重點，使邏輯順序更清楚。以上範例答案中使用的轉折詞包括 First of all（首先）、Next（接下來）、After that（然後）和 Finally（最後）。

🔊 8-12

Q02 Describe an illness you have had.

描述你曾得過的疾病。

You should say:

❶ what it was
❷ how it affected you
❸ what treatment you received
❹ and explain how you recovered.

應該提到：

❶ 是什麼病
❷ 你如何受到了影響
❸ 你接受了什麼治療
❹ 說明你如何康復。

A

❶ Several years ago, I lived in a developing country for a few months. That country lacks a lot of modern facilities, including

❶ 多年前，我曾在一個發展中國家生活了幾個月。這個國家缺乏許多現代化設施，包括缺乏

access to clean drinking water. I was unaware of how serious this problem was, so I was not careful about the water I was drinking. As a result, I got dysentery.

乾淨的飲用水。我起初不知道這個問題有多嚴重，所以我沒有仔細注意我喝的水，結果我得了痢疾。

❷ Dysentery is a very unpleasant sickness. At first, I had a fever, and my stomach hurt. A short time later, I started vomiting and having diarrhoea. My fever and other symptoms then became progressively worse. I couldn't eat anything, and I could only manage to get out of bed to use the bathroom. I lost 10 kilograms in 1 week. I was in really bad shape.

❷ 痢疾是一種非常難受的疾病，我先是發燒和胃痛，不久之後便開始上吐下瀉。我的發燒和其他症狀也逐漸惡化，什麼都吃不下，僅剩的力氣只能爬下床去洗手間。我在一週內瘦了十公斤，身體狀況真的非常糟糕。

❸ Eventually, my friend took me to a hospital, where I needed an IV drip for nutrition because I hadn't eaten anything for about a week. I was also given very strong antibiotics because I had an infection. I stayed in the hospital for 5 days.

❸ 最後我的朋友帶我去了醫院。我將近一週沒進食，所以我得靠靜脈注射來補充營養。我還需要服用非常強效的抗生素，因為我受到細菌感染。我住院住了五天。

❹ After I got out of the hospital, I needed time to regain my strength. At first, I couldn't eat solid foods; I could only have soup. However, gradually, I became able to eat things like rice and then fruit and finally meat. I think it took almost a month in total before I started to feel like myself again.

❹ 出院後，我需要時間恢復體力。起初我吃不下固體食物，只能喝湯。後來我漸漸能夠吃米飯等食物，然後是水果，最後是肉類。我想前後總共花了將近一個月的時間，我才開始感覺自己恢復正常。

Analysis

- Point 1 gives the backstory of how the speaker became ill.
- Point 2 describes the illness and all the symptoms the speaker had.
- Points 3 and 4 discuss the treatment the speaker received and how they were able to recover.

分析

- 第一點描述了何以染病。
- 第二點描述了該疾病以及出現的所有症狀。
- 第三及第四點談論了所接受的治療以及康復過程。

This answer contains some professional medical terminology. If you know any such terms—for example, if you can recall treatments you have received for illnesses—you should use them in your comment. The Sample Answer above uses the following terms: 'dysentery' (a sickness affecting the stomach, intestines, and digestion), 'IV drip' (a needle and tube inserted into a vein to provide someone with nutrition), and 'antibiotics' (medicine used to kill harmful bacteria).

範例答案中使用了一些專業的醫學術語。如果你知道這些術語，例如回想起某次生病時，所接受的治療，就可以拿出來講。以上答案就提到了 dysentery（痢疾）、IV drip（靜脈注射）以及 antibiotics（抗生素）等字。

8-13

Q03 Describe an operation you have had.

描述你接受過的一場手術。

You should say:

❶ what type of operation it was
❷ why you needed it
❸ what steps were involved
❹ and explain how you recovered.

應該提到：

❶ 是什麼手術
❷ 你為何需要接受手術
❸ 包含了哪些步驟
❹ 說明你如何康復。

A

❶ When I was in my early 20s, I had to have my appendix removed. This was the first time in my life, and the only time to date, that I have needed to have surgery. It was not a very pleasant experience.

❶ 我在 20 多歲時不得不切除闌尾。這是我人生中第一次，也是唯一一次需要動手術的時候。這次經驗不是多愉快。

❷ One day, while at work, I suddenly felt a stabbing pain in my abdomen. At first, I thought it was an upset stomach because I had eaten a lot of ice cream at lunch. However, the pain didn't go away; in fact, it got worse and lasted for several hours. In

❷ 有一天我在工作時，突然感到腹部刺痛。起初我以為只是因為午餐吃了太多冰淇淋而胃不舒服。但後來疼痛感沒有消失，甚至愈來愈痛，而且還持續了數個小時。最後，太劇烈

the end, I almost passed out because the pain was so intense.

的疼痛讓我差點就暈倒了。

❸ My friend rushed me to hospital. There, I was diagnosed with appendicitis. If I had waited much longer, my appendix would have burst, and then the problem would have been far more serious. The surgery took a little more than an hour. The doctor made a small incision in my lower abdomen and took out my appendix.

❸ 我的朋友急忙將我送往醫院。在醫院我被診斷出患了闌尾炎，要是再多拖一下，我的闌尾就會破裂，那麼問題就會更嚴重。手術持續了一個多小時。醫生在我的下腹部切了一小個小開口，並取出了我的闌尾。

❹ Subsequently, I stayed in the hospital for several days, and I had to take antibiotics for a week to clear up an infection. I then had to recover at home for almost a week, and I couldn't go to work. I was so glad that my friend had taken me to the hospital so quickly. This was certainly a very memorable experience.

❹ 接著我在醫院待了幾天，服用了一週的抗生素，以清除感染。之後我在家中待了近一週調養身體，不能去上班。幸好我的朋友那時候立刻帶我去了醫院。這真是一段非常難忘的經歷。

Analysis

The Sample Answer above contains several terms to describe pain and the effects of the illness. For example, the speaker uses terms such as 'intense' and 'stabbing pain'. These terms describe the discomfort experienced by the speaker. In point 3, general terms are used to describe the steps involved in the surgery. You do not need to use complicated medical vocabulary to describe medical procedures in your answer.

分析

以上範例答案中使用了多個用語來描述疼痛和該疾病的影響，例如 intense（劇烈的）和 stabbing pain（刺痛）。這些字詞描述了答題者所經歷的不適感。第三點使用基本用語，描述手術過程中所涉及的步驟。描述醫療流程時，不需要用到複雜的醫學字彙也可以清楚說明。

🔊 8-14

Q04 Describe an unhealthy habit you have.

描述你的一種不良健康習慣。

You should say:

❶ what it is

❷ what is involved in this habit

❸ how it affects you

❹ and explain how you could break this habit.

應該提到：

❶ 是什麼習慣

❷ 此習慣包含哪些事

❸ 如何影響你

❹ 說明可以如何改掉這個習慣。

A

❶ I have very poor eating habits. Specifically, ❷ I never cook for myself; I always eat out, and I eat too late at night. In the morning, I don't feel like getting out of bed. As a result, I am always in a rush to get to work, and I don't have time to eat a healthy breakfast, so I just get bread and coffee at a convenience store. There are a lot of fast food places near my work, so for lunch, I usually eat at one of these. All day long, I snack on chips and cookies and drink soda. I usually eat dinner really late, and I often have something like fried chicken.

❸ These bad habits have really affected my health. I have gained 15 kilograms in the past year. I'm always tired, and my back and knees hurt all the time. Plus, I am always in a bad mood.

❹ I know that this habit can be broken very easily. All I need to do is develop some self-discipline so that I can get out of bed earlier every morning. Then, I need to start cooking for myself. I know this is not

❶ 我的飲食習慣非常糟糕，尤其 ❷ 是我從來不下廚，總是外食，而且都很晚才吃。早上我會賴床，結果就是我總是匆匆忙忙趕去上班，沒有時間吃一頓健康的早餐，只能在便利商店買麵包和咖啡。至於午餐，我公司附近有很多速食店，所以我通常會在其中一間店裡解決午餐。我整天都在吃洋芋片、餅乾，還有喝汽水。我通常都很晚才吃晚飯，而且我都吃炸雞之類的東西。

❸ 這些壞習慣確實影響了我的健康。我在過去的一年內增加了 15 公斤，總是覺得很累，背部和膝蓋也時時刻刻都在痛。此外，我的心情還總是很差。

❹ 我知道這個習慣很容易就能改掉，我所需要做的就是自律一點。我早上可以早點起床。然後我得開始自己下廚，我知道這並不難，煮飯真的很簡單。

difficult; cooking is really easy. Finally, I need to stop making excuses and thinking that convenience is the most important thing in life. Health is more important than convenience.

最後，我必須停止找藉口，也不能再認為方便就是生活中最重要的事情。健康比方便重要多了。

Analysis

- Points 1 and 2 are answered together and are the longest part of the answer. Here, the speaker gives details about their bad habit.
- Point 3 discusses the physical and emotional effects of this bad habit.
- Point 4 outlines the changes the person needs to make to break this habit.

分析

- 一併回答第一及第二點，這是整段答案最長的部分。答題者在此詳細說明自己的壞習慣。
- 第三點談到了這個壞習慣對身體及情緒的影響。
- 第四點概述了需要做出什麼改變，才能改掉此習慣。

The beginning of this Sample Answer shows how the speaker's bad habit began and how it affects all areas of their life. The conclusion shows that the solution is known by the speaker but that a change of mindset is what is needed to take appropriate action. A similar structure can be used in your answer when you describe how a certain bad habit affects your life.

範例答案在一開始講述了答題者的壞習慣是如何產生的，以及如何影響到答題者生活的各個層面。最後的結論則講述答題者自己知道解決辦法，但他需要改變心態，下定決心採取行動。在講述某個壞習慣如何影響到你的生活時，就可以使用類似結構。

8-15

Q05 Describe a healthy habit you have.

描述你的一種良好健康習慣。

You should say:

❶ what it is
❷ what is involved in this habit
❸ how it affects you
❹ and explain how you developed this habit.

應該提到：

❶ 是什麼習慣
❷ 此習慣包含哪些事
❸ 如何影響你
❹ 說明你如何培養此習慣。

A

❶ Many people have harmful addictions, but I am addicted to working out at the gym. I am a real fitness addict.

❷ I start my day at 6 a.m. by going to the local fitness centre near my house. I would go earlier, but the centre only opens at 6, so I'm always there first thing when they unlock the door. My routine includes weight training and cardio, usually four times a week. I train a different muscle group each time I go to the gym, such as chest and triceps one day and then legs and shoulders another day; I make sure that I never skip leg day. In addition to exercising regularly, I also watch my diet; I don't eat fried or greasy foods, and I do not drink sugary beverages.

❸ I think of these choices as part of a lifestyle and not just habits. Since I started watching my diet and exercising regularly, I have seen dramatic changes in my health. I have lost a lot of weight, and I have more energy and am generally in a better mood now.

❹ Several years ago, I noticed that I was putting on weight and was tired all the time. I decided that I needed to take control of my life. I didn't want to look and feel 20 years older than my actual age, so I started this new routine. I think that everyone should exercise regularly. If they did, a lot of health problems could be avoided, and people would generally feel better.

❶ 許多人對有害事物成癮，但使我上癮的是上健身房運動。我算是個健身狂。

❷ 我的一天始於早上六點，我會先去我家附近的健身中心。我是可以更早去，但那裡六點才營業，所以我都在一大早他們開門時就到了。我的日常健身流程包括每週四次的重訓和有氧運動。我每次去健身房都會鍛鍊不同的肌群，比如一天練胸肌和三頭肌，另一天練腿部和肩膀。我會記清楚，以確保自己不跳過練腿部的日子。除了定期鍛煉之外，我也很注重我的飲食。我不吃油炸或油膩的食物，也不喝含糖飲料。

❸ 我將這些選擇視為一種生活方式，而不僅僅只是習慣。自從我開始注意飲食和定期鍛煉以來，我發現自己的健康狀況起了很大變化。我的體重減輕許多，精力更充沛，心情也更好。

❹ 多幾年，我注意到自己的體重增加，而且總是感到疲倦。我決定要掌控好自己的生活，我不想要看起來和感覺起來都比實際年齡老上 20 歲，所以我開始了這個新的例行日程。我認為每個人都應該定期運動，如果做得到，就可以避免許多健康問題，身體感覺起來也會更好。

Analysis

In point 2 of the Sample Answer above, specific details are given regarding the types of exercises performed by the speaker. Including details such as these will lengthen your answer and improve your vocabulary score. Additionally, there are several idiomatic phrases that the speaker uses, including 'watching my diet' and 'take control of my life'. Such phrases can also help to improve your vocabulary score.

分析

以上範例答案在第二點詳細說明了答題者進行的訓練項目。添加這些細節，能加長你的答案，並提高字彙分數。此外，還有幾個慣用詞也能提升字彙分數，包括 watching my diet（注意飲食）和 take control of my life（掌控我的生活）。

Part 3 Questions

第三部分 問題

🔊 8-16

Q01 Is obesity a problem in your country?

你國家的人有肥胖問題嗎？

Strategy

Pay attention to how you use word form in this comment. 'Obesity' is a noun that refers to the medical condition of someone being extremely overweight, and 'obese' is an adjective.

- Obesity is a major problem.
- She was obese as a teenager.

策略

在回答本題時，請注意詞性的使用。obesity（過重，肥胖）是名詞，在醫學上指某人極度超重；而 obese（過重的，肥胖的）是形容詞。

- 肥胖是一個重大問題。
- 她在青少年時期就過重了。

A

❶ Obesity has become a modern-day health epidemic in my country.

❷ A recent news report stated that more than two thirds of the population in my country are now obese. Most people today have a sedentary lifestyle and poor eating habits. These two factors are the main reasons why so many people are becoming obese.

❸ If people became more physically active and didn't eat so much junk food, we could greatly reduce this problem.

❶ 肥胖在我國已經是現代人健康的流行病。

❷ 最近一則新聞報導指出，我國現在有超過三分之二的肥胖人口。現今大多數人的生活型態都習慣久坐，飲食習慣也很差，這兩個因素就是有這麼多肥胖人口的主要原因。

❸ 如果人們能夠多活動，不要吃太多垃圾食物，我們就能大幅降低肥胖問題。

Analysis

In order to emphasise the seriousness of obesity, the Sample Answer above uses the term 'epidemic', which refers to a widespread health crisis. Additionally, a news report is referred to with the statistic of 'two thirds'

分析

為了強調肥胖問題的嚴重性，以上範例答案使用了 epidemic（流行病）一字，指出這是一種相當普遍的健康危機。此外還引用了新聞報導中「三分之二」這個統

to give evidence for how serious a problem obesity is in the speaker's country. Major causes of obesity are also mentioned in this answer.

計數據，以證明肥胖在答題者的國家裡，是多麼嚴重的問題。造成肥胖的原因也在答案中一併提及。

🔊 8-17

What health problems are related to obesity?

有哪些健康問題跟肥胖有關？

Strategy

If you know the names of any health problems that are associated with being extremely overweight, you can use them in your answer. Alternatively, if you are not familiar with any such terms, you can use more general vocabulary to describe the effects of obesity.

策略

如果你知道極度肥胖會造成的其他健康問題，可以提到是哪些健康問題，但如果不熟悉這些術語，則可以使用較一般的字詞來描述肥胖對人的影響。

❶ Obesity has harmful effects on a person's health.

❷ Many obese people are also diabetic, and this can lead to a lot of other health problems. Being extremely overweight affects a person's heart and blood vessels, so heart attacks and strokes are very common in obese people. It is important to note that the majority of these health problems are preventable. Generally speaking, obesity is not the result of an accident or a genetic disorder but rather is the result of poor lifestyle choices.

❸ If an obese person changed their lifestyle, they would not have so many health problems.

❶ 肥胖會對人的健康造成危害。

❷ 許多肥胖的人也是糖尿病患者，這會導致許多其他健康問題。極度肥胖會影響一個人的心血管，因此，心臟病和中風，相當常發生在肥胖的人身上。務必要注意的是，這些健康問題大部分都可以預防。一般來說，肥胖不是因為事故或遺傳疾病所導致，而是因為選擇了不良的生活方式所致的結果。

❸ 如果肥胖的人能改變其生活方式，就不會有這麼多的健康問題。

Analysis

Several health conditions are mentioned in this answer, including 'diabetic' and 'stroke' (damage to blood vessels in a person's brain). The conclusion of the answer discusses how health problems such as these can be prevented, namely through lifestyle changes.

分析

範例答案中提到了幾種健康問題，包括diabetic（糖尿病患者）、stroke（中風）。答案的結論講述了如何預防此類健康問題，也就是靠改善生活方式。

8-18

03 What is your opinion about the amount of health care your government provides for its citizens?

對於你的政府提供給國民的醫療保健，你有什麼看法？

Strategy

The term 'health care' can refer to health insurance. When answering this question, you can compare and contrast the health services your country provides with those provided in other countries.

策略

health care（醫療保健）一詞也可以指健康保險。在回答這個問題時，可以針對你國家提供的該福利與他國的福利進行比較。

❶ I think that the health insurance I have is excellent.

❷ The country I live in has socialised health care, which means that a person can go to any doctor or hospital and get the same treatment. If a person has a job, they qualify for health insurance, and a small amount of money is taken out of everyone's pay cheque every month to support this system. I used to live in the United States, where the healthcare system is very complicated. There, everyone has a different type of insurance, and most people have to pay hundreds of dollars every month just to have

❶ 我認為我現在有的健康保險非常好。

❷ 我居住的國家，有社會醫療健保，這表示每個人不管去看哪位醫生或哪家醫院，都可以獲得相同的治療。如果有工作，就符合這項保險的資格。每人每月的薪水會被扣除少量金額，以維持這個系統。我以前住在美國，那裡的醫療健保系統非常複雜，每個人的保險類型都不同，且大多數人每月必須支付數百美元才能獲得保險。而且並非每位醫生或每間

it. Also, not every doctor or hospital accepts everyone's insurance.

醫院都會接受所有人的保險。

❸ This is why I love the health care I have access to now.

❸ 這就是為什麼我喜歡我目前醫療健保的原因。

Analysis

The Sample Answer above outlines the basics of the speaker's country's health insurance system. Then, to explain why this system is a good system, a contrast is made with the far more complicated healthcare system found in the United States.

分析

以上範例答案概述了答題者國家的基本健康保險制度，接著舉出美國非常複雜的健保系統做為對比，以說明為何該國的制度較好。

8-19

Does having a positive outlook on life affect a person's health?

保持正向的人生觀是否會影響到人的健康？

Strategy

Discuss the relationship between a person's mental and physical health. A positive outlook refers to the emotional state or general mood of a person being good.

策略

談談人的心理與生理健康間的關係。保持正向指的是一個人的情緒或心態維持在良好的狀態。

❶ Yes, definitely.

❷ An optimistic person does not let small problems get to them, and they are not easily excited. A person like this does not often feel stressed out. Additionally, research has shown that laughing regularly can boost a person's immune system. Finally, positive people rarely get depressed and generally have a lot of friends.

❸ I think that if everyone was more optimistic, we would have a happier and healthier society.

❶ 肯定是的。

❷ 一個樂觀的人不會為小問題所苦，他們的情緒比較不容易激動，像這樣的人通常不會有過大的壓力。此外有研究顯示，定期大笑可以增強一個人的免疫系統。最後，正向的人不太會憂鬱，通常也有很多朋友。

❸ 我想如果每個人都樂觀一點，我們的社會會變得更快樂及健康。

Analysis

An optimistic person is the same as a positive person. The Sample Answer above describes this type of person and then briefly refers to research that shows the physical benefits of laughing regularly, which is a characteristic of a positive person.

分析

樂觀的人就等於正向的人，以上範例答案描述了這類人，接著簡要地提到了一則研究，說明定期大笑對身體有益，而正向的人就有這種特質。

8-20

05 Why do you think people smoke?

你認為人們為什麼要抽菸？

Strategy

Comment on the basic reasons why people develop this bad habit. You could use a personal experience or that of someone you know who smokes.

策略

談談人們養成這個壞習慣的基本原因，可以是你的個人經驗，或是某個你認識的吸菸者的經驗。

❶ I think that the number one reason why people start smoking is peer pressure.

❷ In other words, a person usually starts to smoke because another person introduces cigarettes to them. The first person then feels pressure because they want to fit in or 'look cool'. A lot of young people don't want to be different from their friends, so they feel pressure to smoke. Later on, these people continue to smoke because they have become addicted to nicotine.

❸ It's interesting that every smoker knows that this habit is very harmful and that they should quit. They just need the determination to take positive action.

❶ 我想人會開始抽菸的首要原因是因為同儕壓力。

❷ 也就是說，一個人通常是因為別人向他介紹香菸而開始抽。他會開始感到有壓力，因為他想要融入大家，或是想要「看起來很酷」。許多年輕人因為不想跟朋友不一樣，在此壓力下而開始抽菸。最後，他們會因為已經對尼古丁成癮而持續抽菸。

❸ 有意思的是，所有吸菸者都知道這個習慣非常有害，應該戒除。他們只需要下定決心，積極採取行動。

Analysis

Peer pressure is given as the main reason that people start smoking. The remainder of the answer describes how peer pressure affects a person's thinking and actions, leading them to start smoking.

分析

答案先提出同儕壓力是人們開始抽菸的原因，接著開始說明同儕壓力如何影響一個人的思維和行動，從而導致他們開始抽菸。

8-21

06 How can people quit bad habits?

人們要如何改掉壞習慣？

Strategy

To answer this question, you could choose a specific bad habit as your primary example.

策略

回答這個問題時，可以舉出某個壞習慣作為主要例子。

❶ A bad habit becomes a part of a person's routine, so changing one's routine is the key to breaking bad habits.

❷ Take smoking for example. People's smoking habits are usually related to some other activity. For instance, some people smoke right after they finish eating a meal. If the smoker were to go for a walk or brush their teeth immediately after eating, this behaviour could replace having a cigarette. Also, some people smoke only when they are with certain friends, so if they were to change the people they associated with, they may not feel inclined to smoke.

❸ Routine behaviours are difficult and take time to change, so it is important to have reasonable expectations when attempting to quit a bad habit.

❶ 壞習慣會融入一個人的日常習慣中，所以改變日常習慣是戒掉壞習慣的關鍵。

❷ 以抽菸為例，人們的抽菸習慣通常跟其他行為有關。舉例來說，有些人會在吃完飯後馬上抽菸，如果吸菸者在吃飽後立刻去散步或刷牙，那麼這個習慣就能取代抽菸。此外，有些人只會在與某些朋友在一起時才抽菸，所以如果能改變往來對象，他們就比較不會想去抽菸。

❸ 日常習慣很難改變，而且要花上一點時間才改得掉，所以在戒除壞習慣的同時，務必要抱持合理的期待。

Analysis

This Sample Answer uses smoking as a prime

分析

範例答案舉了抽菸作為壞習慣的

example of a bad habit. Possible routines that smokers may have are discussed, and then specific suggestions are given for how a smoker can break this bad habit.

主要例子，並談論了吸菸者可能有的日常習慣，接著就吸菸者可以如何改掉壞習慣，給出具體建議。

8-22

07 Is mental health as important as physical health?

心理健康和生理健康是否同等重要？

Strategy

News reports, personal research, or personal observations can be used to express your opinion on this issue. Mental health and emotional health have increasingly gained attention in recent years, so it should not be hard to find an example to support your answer.

策略

可引用新聞報導、個人研究或觀察來表達你對此問題的看法。近年來，愈來愈多人關注心理和情緒健康，因此舉出一個支持你答案的例子並不困難。

❶ I think that a person's mental health and emotional health are as important as their physical health.

❷ A person's mood or emotional state has a direct effect on their health. I have observed that people who are often in a bad mood or suffer from depression tend to have chronic health problems. At first, these problems might be minor, such as headaches. However, if someone suffers from depression for an extended period of time, they usually develop more serious problems. I have also found the opposite to be true: People who are upbeat and positive usually do not have as many health problems.

❶ 我認為一個人的心理和情緒健康，與生理健康同樣重要。

❷ 一個人的心情或情緒狀態會直接影響健康。據我觀察，常常心情不好的人或憂鬱症患者，往往也會有慢性疾病的問題。起初這些問題可能很輕微，例如可能是頭痛。然而，一個人若長期受憂鬱症所苦，通常會發展出更嚴重的問題。反之亦然；樂觀且積極的人通常沒有那麼多健康問題。

❸ I believe that staying mentally and emotionally healthy is as important as maintaining good physical health.

❸ 我認為保持心理和情緒健康，就和保持生理健康一樣重要。

Analysis

The Sample Answer above states that physical health and mental and emotional health are of equal importance. To support this viewpoint, first, an example related to depression is given. Then, a comparison with people who have a positive outlook is made.

分析

以上範例答案指出，生理健康、心理健康以及情緒健康同等重要。為了支持這個看法，答案先是舉了憂鬱症為例子，接著再跟樂觀的人進行比較。

8-23

08 How has medicine improved over the past few decades?

醫療技術在過去幾年有什麼進步？

Strategy

This question requires a specific example. Your example could be taken from a news story or an experience related to medical care that you or someone you know has been through.

策略

此問題需要以具體例子來回答。可以取材自新聞報導，或是引用你自己或你認識的某個人所接受過的醫療照護經驗作為例子。

❶ I think that understanding of the causes of diseases is an area where medicine has greatly improved over the past few decades.

❶ 在過去幾十年，我認為醫學界在認識病因上大有進步。

❷ Years ago, when someone became seriously ill with something like cancer, often, doctors would only treat the symptoms, such as tumours. This is one of the reasons why many people in history have died from this disease. By contrast, nowadays, doctors can not only treat a cancer patient's tumours but also address the causes of the disease. As a result, survival rates for diseases such as cancer have greatly improved.

❷ 幾年前，每當有人患上癌症等嚴重疾病，醫生往往只會針對症狀治療，像是只治療腫瘤，這正是歷史上這麼多人死於該疾病的原因之一。相較之下，現在的醫生不僅能治療癌症患者的腫瘤，還能夠根治病因。因此癌症等疾病患者的存活率才能大幅提高。

❸ As medical research continues to improve, the greater people's overall health will become.

❸ 隨著醫療研究的進步，人們的整體健康狀況也會愈來愈好。

Analysis

Cancer treatment is used as an example to describe improvements in modern medicine. A contrast is made between how cancer was treated in the past with more recent developments in cancer treatment.

分析

範例答案舉了治療癌症這個例子，說明現代醫學的進步，並對比了以前的癌症療法，以及治療癌症的最新發展。

🔊 8-24

09 How do you think medicine will change in the future?

你認為醫學技術在未來會有什麼改變？

Strategy

This question requires you to speculate or make an educated guess as to how medicine will develop in the future. Your answer could include trends that you have observed in medicine and how you think these trends will continue to progress in the future.

策略

這個問題要求你對醫學在未來的發展走向，進行推測或有根據的猜測。可以在答案中講述在目前的醫學領域中，你所觀察到的趨勢，以及你認為這些趨勢在未來會如何繼續發展。

❶ I think that the way doctors perform surgery will continue to improve.

❷ Many years ago, every surgery required the doctor to make a large incision in the patient in order to operate on them. This usually resulted in the patient losing a lot of blood and having a long recovery time. In recent years, however, the tools that doctors use have become smaller and more precise, and as a result, many surgeries now require only small incisions. I think that this trend of incisions becoming smaller will

❶ 我認為醫生動手術的方式將繼續進步。

❷ 多年前，醫生在動手術時，都要先在患者身上切出大切口才能進行手術，這通常會導致患者大量失血，也需要更長時間復原。然而近年來，醫生使用的器具變得愈來愈小，也愈來愈精確。因此，現在有許多手術只需要切出小切口。我覺得微創手術這樣的趨勢，將在未來持續發展。其實我認為在短

continue into the future. In fact, I think that in just a few years' time, many surgeries won't require doctors to cut into patients at all. If this is true, it could eliminate a lot of risky measures, such as the need for blood transfusions.

短幾年內，許多手術將不再需要醫生切開患者身體，如能成真，這將能排除許多危險狀況，例如輸血。

❸ In summary, I believe that surgery will become a lot safer in the future.

❸ 簡言之，我認為手術在未來會變得更加安全。

Analysis

The aspect of medicine that this Sample Answer focuses on is surgery. The recent trend of incisions (cutting open a patient's body) becoming smaller is contrasted with medical practices from the past. The answer then predicts that this trend will continue and that surgery will become safer as a result.

分析

此範例答案所關注的醫學層面是手術。近期手術切口變得愈來愈小，這項趨勢被提出來與以前的醫療狀況進行對比，接著預測這項趨勢將持續發展，因此手術會變得更安全。

8-25

Q10 How do you feel about genetic research?

你對於基因研究有什麼看法？

Strategy

For this question, you can choose to argue either for or against this controversial issue. Alternatively, you could choose to remain neutral and discuss both sides of the issue in a balanced way.

策略

回答時可以選擇支持或反對這個有爭議的議題。或者也可以選擇保持中立，以對等的立場討論該議題的正反面。

A

❶ As with most controversial issues, I think that there are both benefits and drawbacks to genetic research.

❶ 與大多爭議性議題一樣，我認為基因研究既有好處，也有壞處。

❷ Regarding the positive aspects, genetic research has helped scientists and doctors understand diseases better, and this

❷ 基因研究的好處是，有益於科學家和醫生了解疾病，如此能為長時間存在的疾病提供新的

improvement in understanding has enabled new cures and treatments to be developed for diseases that have been around for a long time. Vaccines are another benefit of genetic research. On the other hand, some people are concerned that this type of research could be abused. For example, some fear that just like in many movies, genetic research could lead to the development of a deadly disease that might result in the deaths of millions.

療法。疫苗也是基因研究的另一個好處。而另一方面，有些人擔心這種研究可能會被濫用。例如有些人害怕像電影演得一樣，有心人士可能會利用基因研究製造出致命疾病，造成數百萬人死亡。

❸ Caution should be exercised so that genetic research will be used only for good and not to harm others.

❸ 我們需要謹慎對待此事，讓基因研究僅用於良好用途，而不得用於傷害他人。

Analysis

The Sample Answer above presents a neutral stance where both the positive and negative aspects of the issue are discussed. A greater understanding of diseases is cited as a benefit, while the development of a deadly disease is used to support the opposite side of the argument. The examples used are taken from the news and popular culture (movies). Popularly held views regarding an issue such as this can be included in your answer.

分析

上述範例答案提出了中立立場，談論此議題的正反兩面。對疾病的深入理解被提出來作為正面例子，而致命疾病可能被製造出來則用以支持反面立場。這些例子取自於新聞和流行文化（電影）。回答此問題時，你也可以說說一般大眾對此類問題普遍所抱持的觀點。

Additional Tips and Resources 補充技巧及資料

British and American English Comparison 英式及美式英文比較

Both British and American vocabulary is accepted for IELTS. The following table contrasts common words and expressions in British and American English that you may encounter when preparing for the test.

在雅思考試中，英式或美式拼法的單字都是可以使用的。以下表格提供常見單字和說法。

Housing/Accommodation/Building/Household Item 房屋 / 住宿 / 建築 / 家居用品

中文	British 英式	American 美式	中文	British 英式	American 美式
公寓	flat	apartment	衣櫃	wardrobe	closet
電梯	lift	elevator	垃圾桶	bin/dustbin	trash can
爐子	cooker	stove	吸塵器	Hoover	vacuum
藥局	chemist	drug store/ pharmacy			

Clothing 服飾

中文	British 英式	American 美式	中文	British 英式	American 美式
長褲	trousers	pants/slacks	毛衣	jumper	sweater
內褲	pants	underwear/ underpants	運動鞋	trainers	sneakers/ sports shoes
背心	vest	undershirt	尿布	nappy	diaper

Transportation 交通運輸

中文	British 英式	American 美式	中文	British 英式	American 美式
石油	petrol	gas/gasoline	人行道	pavement	sidewalk
高速公路	motorway	highway/ freeway	引擎蓋	bonnet	hood

卡車	lorry	truck	後車箱	boot	trunk

Food 食物

中文	British 英式	American 美式	中文	British 英式	American 美式
香腸	banger	sausage	甜點	sweet(s)	dessert/candy
洋芋片	crisps	potato chips/ chips	外帶	takeaway	takeout

LESSON 9

Abstract Concepts

抽象概念

LESSON 9

Abstract Concepts 抽象概念

Some Speaking Test questions do not fit into the categories already discussed in this book. This lesson discusses challenging topics that will require you to use specialised vocabulary and strategies to give complete and academic sounding answers.

有些口說測驗的題目，並不屬於本書先前所探討過的任何類別。本課將會談談較具有挑戰性的主題，考生需要使用到較特殊字詞及策略，才能說出完整且具學術性的答案。

Part 1 Questions 第一部分 問題

Clothes and Fashion 服裝與時尚

🔊 9-01

Q01 Is keeping up with the latest fashion trends important to you?

趕流行對你來說重要嗎？

Strategy

Avoid common grammar mistakes when answering this question. 'Fashion' is a noun in this question. However, 'fashion' also has an adjective form, 'fashionable'.

- I am really into fashion.
- Your clothes are very fashionable.

策略

回答這題時，要避免常見的文法錯誤。問題中使用的 fashion（時尚）是名詞，其形容詞為 fashionable（時尚的）。

- 我很喜歡趕流行。
- 你的衣服很時尚。

A Looking my best is extremely important to me, so I like to keep up to date with what is in fashion. I go shopping every few weeks and

對我來說，好看的外表極為重要，所以我喜歡跟上時下的最新流行。我每隔幾週就會去逛街，

always plan my wardrobe for the next season. I never wear clothes that are out of fashion.

為我下一季的治裝做打算。我從不穿過時的衣服。

9-02

02 Is wearing brand name clothing important to you?

穿著名牌服飾對你來說重要嗎？

Strategy

The term 'brand name clothing' refers to clothing produced by any well-known or famous clothes company, such as Gucci, Nike, or Adidas. Famous brands like these could be specifically mentioned in your answer.

策略

brand name clothing（名牌服飾）這個詞，是指知名大品牌所生產的服飾，例如 Gucci、Nike 或 Adidas。可以在答案中提出這些知名品牌。

A In general, wearing brand name clothing isn't very important to me. However, I have noticed that Nike shoes tend to be of higher quality than most other sports shoe brands. So, if I plan on wearing a pair of shoes for a year or more, I will spend the extra money and buy a pair of Nikes.

一般來說，我不太在意穿不穿名牌。不過我發現 Nike 鞋的品質比其他大多運動品牌要好得多，所以如果一雙鞋我打算要穿一年以上，我就會多花點錢買 Nike 的鞋。

Time Management 時間管理

9-03

01 Do you have a good routine in life?

你的生活作息是否良好？

Strategy

Your personal habits regarding your use of time can be described when answering this question.

策略

回答這題時，可以描述你自己利用時間的習慣。

A I view time as a precious resource, so I never want to waste it. Therefore, every week, I make a schedule listing all the things I need to do that week. This schedule includes not only my appointments but also my daily tasks. I always want to stick to this schedule, so every day, I wake up at the same time, eat my meals at the same time, and go to bed at the same time. I really hate wasting time.

我認為時間是寶貴的資源，所以我從不想浪費時間。因此，我每週都會制定時程表，列出我需要做的所有事情。這個時程表不僅包括我的預定行程，還包括我每天要做的事。我很堅持按表操課，所以我每天都在同一時間起床、同一時間吃飯、同一時間上床睡覺。我非常討厭浪費時間。

9-04

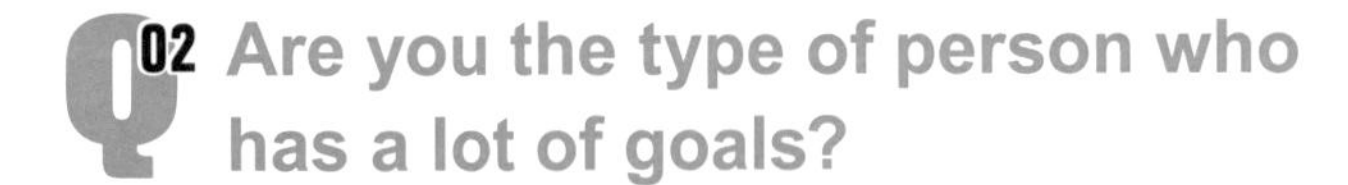

Q02 Are you the type of person who has a lot of goals?

你是會制定很多目標的人嗎？

Strategy

Goals can include personal, educational and professional goals. These can also include the things you want to accomplish as both long and short term goals.

策略

目標可以包括個人、學術和職涯目標，這些目標可以是你長期或短期內想完成的事。

A I have always been a goal-oriented person. Since I was 8 years old, I have known what I wanted to do with my life. Back then, I knew what I wanted to do for work and all the steps that would be involved in accomplishing this goal. When I was 25, I became a lawyer. At age 32, I established my own law firm. If I stick to my goals, I will be able to retire soon. Having goals has allowed me to have a clear direction in my life.

我向來就是個以目標為導向的人。八歲開始，我就知道我的人生規畫。我在那時候就知道自己想從事什麼工作，以及實現此目標需要做的事。我在 25 歲時當上了律師，32 歲時成立了自己的律師事務所。如果我堅持目標，很快就能退休了。擁有目標讓我的人生有了明確的方向。

Art | 藝術

🔈 9-05

01 What is your favourite form of art?

你最喜歡哪一種藝術形式？

Strategy

There are many different forms of art, including painting, sculpture, architecture, music, and clothing design. You may find it easier to describe your favourite type of music or band than to describe a painting or sculpture.

策略

藝術的形式可涵蓋各種類別，包括繪畫、雕塑品、建築、音樂及服裝設計。描述你最喜歡的音樂或樂團，可能會比描述一幅畫或雕塑品來得容易。

A I really enjoy classical music. I find it very soothing and relaxing, especially after a busy week at work. I enjoy going to see performances by the national orchestra, so I try to go to these concerts several times a year. I think that musicians are very talented artists who are generally underappreciated.

我非常喜歡古典音樂，我覺得古典音樂非常舒緩，令人放鬆，尤其是在忙碌了一週的工作之後。我喜歡聽國家管弦樂團的演出，所以我每年都會盡量去聽個幾次音樂會。我認為音樂家是才華洋溢的藝術家，但大家通常都低估了他們的才能。

Generosity | 慷慨

🔈 9-06

01 Do you enjoy giving gifts to others?

你喜歡送禮給他人嗎？

Strategy

In many cultures, gift giving is viewed as very important, so when a guest goes to someone's home, they are expected to take a gift. If your culture has this type of custom or if you know

策略

許多文化都認為送禮非常重要，所以到別人家去作客時，通常會帶上禮物。如果你國家的文化有這種風俗，或者你知道別的國家

of another country that has this custom, you can relate this in your answer.

有這種風俗，就可在答案中談談。

A I really enjoy giving gifts. Whenever I go to someone's home, I always take a gift. I think this is an excellent way to show respect to the host. The host has to spend time and money preparing to have guests over to their home, so giving a gift is a way of showing respect and appreciation for their effort. I usually take something like fruit, wine, or even a homemade gift. Sharing with others gives me a feeling of joy and satisfaction.

我非常喜歡送人禮物。我每次去別人家都會帶上禮物，我認為這是對主人表示尊重的絕佳方式。主人得花時間和金錢來招待客人到家中，所以送禮物能對他們的所作所為表達尊重和讚賞。我通常會帶水果、葡萄酒，甚至是自製禮物。與他人分享讓我感到快樂和滿足。

9-07

Q02 What types of gifts have people given you before?

你曾收過別人送的什麼禮物？

Strategy

When answering this question, you should describe a personal experience. A memorable experience of receiving a gift should be something that you can describe easily.

策略

回答這題時，可描述自己的親身經歷。這是你可以很輕鬆就回答出來的主題。

A When I was in school, my parents always gave me a gift when I got good grades on my report card. These gifts were always appropriate to my age, so they could be anything from a new book to a new computer. I think the best gift they ever gave me was a puppy. That dog became my best friend, and we had him for about 15 years. He really was the best gift my parents ever gave me.

我還是學生時，如果拿到了好成績，我爸媽就會買禮物給我。他們會依我的年齡送我合適的禮物，所以任何東西都有可能，可能是一本新書，或是一台新電腦。我覺得他們送過我最棒的禮物是一隻小狗，那隻狗成了我最好的朋友，我們養了牠大約 15 年，牠真的是我爸媽送過我最棒的禮物。

The News | 新聞

🔊 9-08

01 Is the news a reliable source of information?

新聞是可靠的資訊來源嗎？

Strategy

Because of recent developments in technology, there are now numerous different news sources. However, the news you read may have varying degrees of accuracy depending on where it comes from. For this question, you can relate your personal feelings regarding this issue.

策略

由於近年來的科技發展，我們現在有各種不同的新聞來源。然而，資訊的準確度可能會取決於你是從哪裡讀到的新聞。針對此問題，你可以談談你對這個議題的個人感受。

A Not all news websites are reliable. I think that if a news site has a lot of advertisements, we should regard the information on it with a cautious eye. Usually, news that comes from a government agency is accurate. An example of a government-affiliated website is the website of the Centers for Disease Control.

並非所有新聞網站都值得信賴。我認為一個新聞網站若含有大量廣告，我們就應該謹慎看待其網站內的資訊。政府機構的資訊通常會較準確，例如疾病管制署的網站。

Memory | 回憶

🔊 9-09

01 Do you often think about the past?

你經常回憶過去嗎？

Strategy

Memory is a very abstract concept. In this answer, you can comment on experiences that you had when you were younger. In other

策略

回憶是非常抽象的概念。可以在答案中談談自己年輕時的經歷，也就是說，可以描述自己人生中

words, important memories such as those from your childhood can be described.

重要的回憶，例如童年時期的記憶。

A I feel that it is very important to think about the past and things that I have learned from my experiences. For example, when I need to make a decision, I often recall advice that my parents have given me, and when I start a new project at work, I think about the feedback that my supervisor has given me over the years. I think it is very important to remember important lessons that we have learned throughout our lives.

我覺得思考過去、也反思從過去經驗中學到什麼，是非常重要的。舉例來說，需要進行決策時，我經常想起父母給我的建議。在工作中開始一項新專案時，我會回想主管多年來給過我的意見回饋。我認為記取一生中學到的重要課題，是非常重要的。

🔊 9-10

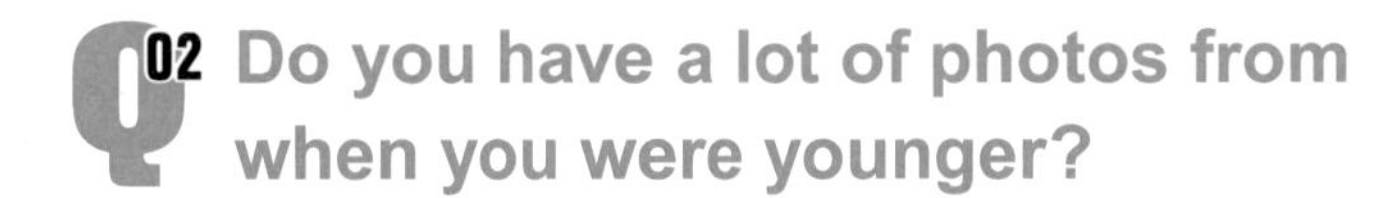

Q02 Do you have a lot of photos from when you were younger?

你有許多年輕時的照片嗎？

Strategy

Such photos can include those taken when you were a child or when you were in school. You may be able to obtain such pictures from your parents.

策略

年輕時的照片可以包括你童年時期，或是在學校時所拍攝的照片。通常可從父母那裡獲得這些照片。

A My mother loved taking pictures of my brothers and me when we were growing up. She chronicled our entire childhood. When I graduated from high school, she gave me a photo album as a gift. This album documented my entire school career, from my first day of kindergarten to my high school graduation. Looking at those old pictures not only helps me to remember what was happening to me at that time but also brings back old feelings. Sometimes, I can actually remember what

在成長過程中，我母親很喜歡幫我和兄弟們拍照，她用照片記錄了我們的整個童年。高中畢業時，她送了我一本相簿當禮物，這本相簿記錄了我從幼稚園第一天，到高中畢業的整個學生生涯。看著那些老照片不僅能讓我想起照片中所發生的事情，還能勾起往日情懷。有時候我真的都還記得拍照那個當下的感受。

I was feeling at the moment that the picture was taken.

Part 2 Questions | 第二部分 問題

Life Event | 人生大事

🔊 9-11

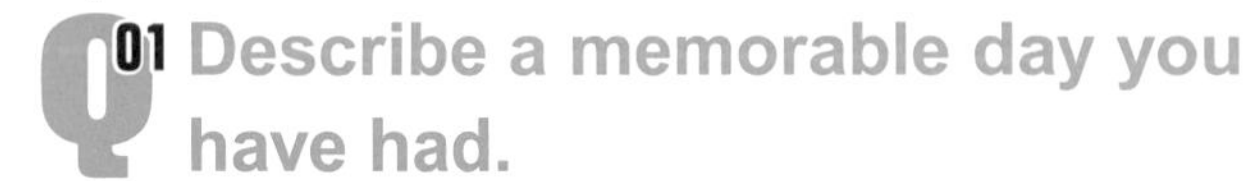
01 Describe a memorable day you have had.

描述一個值得你紀念的日子。

You should say:

❶ how long ago it was
❷ where you were
❸ what happened
❹ and explain why this day was memorable.

應該提到：

❶ 是多久以前的事
❷ 你當時在哪裡
❸ 發生什麼事
❹ 說明此日子為何值得紀念。

❶ I will never forget my first day of work. I ❷ was hired to work at a small store in my hometown. Because it was a small town, this store sold everything. Customers could buy sandwiches, coffee, tools, paint, and even parts to fix cars and other vehicles.

❶ 我永遠不會忘記我工作的第一 ❷ 天。我被家鄉的一間小店錄取，由於這是一座小鎮，所以這家店賣的東西應有盡有。顧客可以買到三明治、咖啡、工具、油漆，甚至是修理小客車和其他各種車輛所需的零件。

❸ On this first day of work, I received a lot of training because I needed to learn how to handle many things. First, I was given a tour of the store to learn the layout and where all the items were located. After that, I spent some time in the kitchen, learning how to make sandwiches and how to keep things clean. Finally, I spent a few hours at the cashier counter so that I could learn

❸ 上工第一天，我接受了很多培訓，因為我要學著如何處理事情。首先，我參觀了店裡，熟悉店內動線和各種商品的位置。接著，我花了一點時間在廚房裡學習製作三明治，以及如何清潔環境。最後，我在收銀櫃台待了幾個小時，學習如何使用收銀機，還有接受顧客

how to use the cash register and take customer orders. It was a very long first day.

點餐。那是非常漫長的第一天。

❹ What enabled this day to have a lasting impression on me was that I was extremely nervous. It was my first job, and there were so many new things to learn. I was afraid of making a mistake, but the store owner who trained me was so kind and patient. He explained things very well. As a result, I still remember the skills that I learned on that first day. The interesting thing is that I ended up working in that store for 5 years, and I really enjoyed my time working there.

❹ 那天之所以讓我印象深刻，是因為我當時非常緊張，這是我的第一份工作，有很多新東西要學習。我很害怕犯錯，但是訓練我的老闆非常友善又有耐心，他把工作內容解釋得非常清楚，因此我至今仍記得第一天學到的技能。有趣的是我最後在那家店工作了五年，我非常享受在那裡工作的時光。

Analysis

When answering this question, you should choose an important event from your life that is easy to remember and speak about at length. Such an event could be your first day at a new school or moving to a new town. The Sample Answer above describes the experience of a first day at a new job. In point 3, details regarding the training the speaker received are given, and sequence words (e.g., 'First', 'After that', 'Finally') are used to help explain the main points in chronological order. Point 4 describes the speaker's emotional state and the impression this experience had on them.

分析

回答這題時，你所講述的人生重要事件，應該要容易回想且足夠你講上一段時間。可以說說第一天到新學校或是搬到新城鎮的回憶。以上範例答案描述了第一天上班的經驗。在第三點使用了轉折詞（First、After that、Finally）說明事件的時間順序，講述自己所接受到的培訓細節。第四點描述了答題者的心情，以及該經驗所留下的印象。

9-12

Q02 Describe an important life event.

描述一件重要的人生大事。

You should say:

❶ what it is

❷ when in a person's life it occurs

❸ what happens during this event

❹ and explain why it is an important event.

應該提到：

❶ 是什麼事

❷ 發生在哪個人生階段

❸ 當中發生什麼事

❹ 說明這件事為何重要。

A

❶ In most developed countries, a person's graduation from formal education, usually high school or college, is seen as a major life event.

❷ After being in school for the majority of their life, a young person, usually aged 18 years, graduates from high school and enters the 'real world'. At this point, they are considered a legal adult.

❸ Graduations do tend to be rather boring. A very dry ceremony takes place at the person's school, and family and friends of the graduates are invited to come and hear speeches or departing advice from teachers and school administrators. All of this is done to wish the students well as they go out into the real world. At the end of the ceremony, the students receive their diplomas.

❹ At this point, the graduate becomes a part of society and is expected to begin to contribute to society in a meaningful way. The following transitional period can be challenging for some people, but it is hoped that the new graduate will be able

❶ 在多數的已開發國家，一個人正式從高中或大學畢業，通常會被視為是重要的人生大事。

❷ 完成了大部分的學業之後，一個 18 歲的年輕人會從高中畢業，並進入「現實社會」。通常他們在此刻就會被正式視為成年人。

❸ 畢業典禮往往相當無聊，畢業生的學校會舉行一場非常枯燥的儀式。畢業生的親朋好友會受邀來參加典禮，聽學校老師和長官的致詞與祝福，這一切都是為了祝福學生在進入現實社會後一切順利。典禮尾聲，學生會拿到他們的畢業證書。

❹ 此時畢業生已經成為社會的一分子，會被期待要對社會做出有意義的貢獻。接下來的這個轉變期，對一些人來說可能頗具挑戰性，但這是希望畢業生能夠將在學校所學付諸實踐。

to put into practice what they have learned in school. The young person is expected to enter the workforce and become a productive member of society and should be able to support themselves without having to rely on their parents or the government to take care of them.

社會期望年輕人進入職場並成為社會上具生產力的一分子，且能夠自給自足，無須依賴父母或政府來照顧他們。

Analysis

Other examples of important life events are getting married, having a baby, and retiring; any of these could be used to answer this question. The Sample Answer above describes the significance of a high school graduation. Point 3 describes how some people feel about attending a graduation ceremony. Point 4 discusses why a graduation is considered a turning point in a person's life and describes what a young person is expected to do after they graduate.

分析

其他重要人生大事還包括結婚、生子或退休，這些大事都可以是這題的答案。以上範例答案講述了高中畢業的重要性，第三點描述了部分人對於出席畢業典禮的感受，第四點則談到畢業為何是人生的一個轉捩點，並描述年輕人在畢業後會接收到什麼社會期待。

Art 藝術

9-13

01 Describe a piece of artwork you like.

描述一件你喜歡的藝術品。

You should say:

1. what it is
2. where you saw it
3. what it looks like
4. and explain why you like it.

應該提到：

1. 是什麼藝術品
2. 在哪裡看見
3. 是什麼樣子
4. 說明你為何喜歡。

A

❶ I really love the painting of the *Mona* ❷ *Lisa*. I even got to see it in person once at a famous museum in Paris. Since I was young, I always wanted to see this painting. Then, about 5 years ago, I was on a long vacation, touring multiple countries in Europe. When I got to France, I made plans to go to Paris so that I could visit this museum. It was a fantastic experience.

❶ 我非常喜歡《蒙娜麗莎》這幅 ❷ 畫。有一次在巴黎一間知名博物館，我還親眼見到了這幅畫。我從年輕時就一直想看看這幅畫，然後大約五年前，我趁著一個長假，到歐洲周遊列國。抵達法國時，我就計畫要前往巴黎，為的就是要去參觀這間博物館。那是一次非常棒的經驗。

❸ At first, I was very surprised by the size of this painting. Because it is so famous, I always imagined it to be very large, but actually, it isn't very big. The colours the artist used to paint this portrait are a little dark; he didn't use many bright colours, maybe because hundreds of years ago, when the painting was made, they didn't have as many colours as we do today. This painting, or portrait, is of a woman, and you can see the upper half of her body and her arms, which are crossed in front of her.

❸ 起初，我對這幅畫的尺寸感到相當驚訝。因為此幅畫相當知名，我一直以為會是非常巨幅的畫作，但實際上尺寸並不是很大。畫家使用較暗的顏色來繪製這幅肖像畫，沒有用太多明亮的顏色。我想這或許是因為幾百年前，畫家在繪製這幅畫時，並不像現今有這麼多顏色可用。這幅畫作，又或者說是肖像畫當中，是一位女性，可以看到她的上半身，和交叉在胸前的雙臂。

❹ I have always really liked the expression on the *Mona Lisa*'s face. Some people say that she is smiling; other people say she is hiding a secret. I also like her eyes. If you stand in front of the picture, it seems as though she is looking right at you. No one knows who the *Mona Lisa* was, and I also enjoy this mystery. I have done a lot of research to find out who she was, but no one knows her true identity for sure. These

❹ 我一直很喜歡《蒙娜麗莎》臉上的神情。有些人說她在微笑，有些人說她隱藏著祕密。我還喜歡她的眼睛，要是站在畫的前方，她彷彿就直視著你。沒有人知道蒙娜麗莎是誰，因此我很喜歡這種神祕感。我做了很多研究想知道她是誰，不過沒有人能肯定她的真實身分。這些是我喜歡這幅

are just some of the reasons why I love this painting.

畫的部分原因。

Analysis

To answer this question, you can describe a well-known painting, statue, or other work of art. Choosing something famous will make answering this question easier. The Sample Answer above describes the *Mona Lisa*, which is a painting that almost everyone has seen either online or in books. The answer describes well-known aspects of the painting and things that many people have commented on before. The answer does not give specific dates, the name of the artist, or the name of the museum where the painting is located. It may be challenging to think of these details and to try to remember them while speaking fluently, so remember that such details do not need to be presented in order to give a complete answer.

分析

回答這題時，可以描述一幅眾所周知的畫作、雕像或其他藝術品，選擇知名作品會比較容易講述。以上範例答案描述了《蒙娜麗莎》這幅畫，這是幾乎每個人都曾在網路上或是書籍中看過的畫。答案描述了這幅畫為人所熟知的層面，以及大多數人對該畫作的看法。答案沒有給出畫作的具體年代、畫家的名字，或是收藏該畫作的博物館名稱。要想到這些細節資訊，並流暢地講出來，可能會有點困難，所以請謹記，並非一定要講出這些細節，答案才會完整。

Time Management | 時間管理

9-14

Q01 Describe a time you had to wait for someone.

描述一次你等待某人的經驗。

You should say:

❶ who the person was
❷ how long you had to wait for this person
❸ what you were going to do together
❹ and describe how waiting made you feel.

應該提到：

❶ 你等的人是誰
❷ 你等了這個人多久
❸ 你們原本打算一起做什麼
❹ 描述你等待時的感受。

A

❶ My sister is such a procrastinator. She always waits until the last minute to get ready for things. She and I have opposite personalities. I am very good at managing my time, but I am not a patient person, so I really hate waiting for other people.

❷ I once had to wait for my sister for 3 hours outside in the boiling heat. She kept calling and texting me, saying that she was 'almost there' and that she would 'be there in 2 minutes'. It was so ridiculous!

❸ The plan was to meet some friends for lunch and then go to see a movie. We had already bought our movie tickets and made a reservation at a really nice restaurant next to the theatre. All of our friends arrived on time, but my sister didn't. After waiting for a long time, my friends were afraid that we would lose our restaurant reservation, so they went ahead and had lunch. I decided that I would be responsible and wait outside for my sister at the subway stop. She had never been to that subway stop or restaurant before, so I was afraid she would get lost. I waited so long for her that our friends finished lunch and went to the movie theatre before she arrived.

❹ When she finally arrived, she had many excuses as to why she was late. I was so annoyed. I was starving and was so hot from being outside that I lost my temper. I was so frustrated with her because I am a punctual person and she is always late.

❶ 我妹是個拖延症患者，她總是等到最後一刻才把事情準備好。她和我的性格完全相反，我很擅長管理時間，但我可不是個有耐心的人，所以我非常討厭等別人。

❷ 有一次，我在酷暑中等了我妹三小時。她不斷打電話和傳訊息給我，說她「快到了」、「再兩分鐘就到了」，真的很荒謬！

❸ 我們的原訂計畫是要和一些朋友見面吃午餐，然後再去看電影。我們都已經買好電影票了，還在電影院旁邊一間不錯的餐廳訂了位。我們所有朋友都準時到了，就我妹還沒到。等了很久之後，我朋友擔心餐廳會取消我們的訂位，所以就先進去吃午餐。我盡責地在地鐵外面等我妹，她之前從沒來過這個地鐵站，或是這間餐廳，我擔心她會迷路。我等她的時間久到朋友們都已經吃完午餐、去看電影了，而她還是沒到。

❹ 等她終於到了之後，她搬出很多藉口，解釋她為什麼遲到，我覺得很煩。我在外面等她等到又餓又熱，所以我大發雷霆。我實在覺得她很討厭，因為我是一個守時的人，而她總

Unfortunately, my sister did not learn from this experience. She still continues to be late for everything.

是遲到。很可惜，我妹並沒有從這次經驗中記取教訓，不管做什麼事她還是都一樣不守時。

Analysis

The Sample Answer above contains a number of vocabularies and phrases that can be used to describe the feelings a person may have when dealing with a less than ideal situation. These terms include 'ridiculous', which can have the same meaning as 'unbelievable'; 'frustrated', which describes how people tend to feel about a situation they wish they could change but cannot; and 'lost one's temper', which means to become angry.

分析

以上範例答案使用了各種字詞，適用於在描述惱人的情況時，包括 ridiculous（荒謬的），等同於 unbelievable（難以置信的）；frustrated（洩氣的），用於表示人們希望改變情況，但又無力改變時的情緒；以及 lost one's temper（大發雷霆）。

9-15

Q02 Describe a time when you were late for an important event.

描述一次你在重要活動上遲到的經驗。

You should say:

❶ what the event was
❷ what made you late
❸ how you dealt with the situation
❹ and explain how you felt about being late.

應該提到：

❶ 是什麼活動
❷ 為什麼遲到
❸ 你如何處理此情況
❹ 說明遲到給你的感受。

A

❶ My best friend's wedding was a few months ago, and I was the maid of honour. I was so excited to be a part of her wedding, but on my way there, something unexpected happened.

❷ I was driving, when all of a sudden, I got a flat tire. I was still several miles from the

❶ 幾個月前，我的摯友辦婚禮，而我是伴娘。能參與朋友的婚禮，讓我非常興奮，然而就在前往婚禮會場的路上，發生了意料之外的事情。

❷ 當時我在開車，突然之間輪胎爆胎了。我距離婚禮會場還有

wedding venue, and I didn't have any signal on my mobile phone, so I couldn't call anyone for help.

好幾哩路，而我的手機沒有訊號，所以無法打給任何人求救。

❸ First, I tried to change the tire myself, but I didn't have the right tools, so I decided to walk to the nearest house to ask if I could use their phone or if they could help me change the tire. As I was walking down the road, looking for a house, it started to rain heavily. I started to run, and soon, I saw an old farmhouse. I knocked on the door, and a big man with a beard answered. At first, I was frightened by the way the man looked, but he turned out to be very friendly. He gave me a towel so that I could dry off from the rain. Then, he drove me back to my car. He had the right tools with him to change my tire very quickly. I wanted to give him money for his help, but he refused.

❸ 起初我試著自己換輪胎，但我沒有適當的工具，於是我決定走到最近的住家去詢問能否借用電話，或是問他們能否幫我換輪胎。我邊走邊尋找住家，卻突然下起了傾盆大雨，所以我開始在路上狂奔，跑著跑著，很快地我看見一棟老舊農家。我上前去敲了敲門，是一名壯碩的蓄鬍男子前來應門。一開始，我被男子的外貌嚇了一跳，但好在他非常友善。他遞給我一條毛巾，讓我把身上的雨水擦乾。接著，他開車載我回到我的車子旁，他還帶上了適當的工具，所以能夠迅速幫我換好輪胎。我想要給他錢感謝他的幫忙，但他拒絕了。

❹ By the time I reached the wedding venue, I was extremely late, and the wedding had already started. At first, I was so embarrassed that I didn't want to show myself, so I hid in the back. I knew that my friend was very disappointed. However, when she saw me, she became relieved and happy because she had been so worried about me. In the end, I was able to put on my bridesmaid dress, and we both had a wonderful time at the wedding.

❹ 抵達婚禮會場時，我已經遲到了非常久，而婚禮早就開始了。一開始我非常尷尬不想現身，所以我躲在後面。我知道我的朋友非常失望。然而我朋友看見我之後，她鬆了一口氣，而且非常高興，原來她一直在擔心我。最後，我得以換上伴娘服，我們在婚禮上度過了一段美好時光。

Analysis

When answering this question, you could describe a memorable event from your life, such as being late for your first day of work or an important exam at school. The Sample Answer above describes arriving late to a wedding. Some of the words used in this answer are more informal than those used in other answers, but in this case, such language will not have a negative effect on your overall score. Point 3 contains a lot of action words that convey the main points of the experience. Point 4 describes the feelings and reactions of both the speaker and her friend.

分析

在回答這題時，可以描述人生中的一個難忘事件，例如上班第一天遲到，或是學校考試遲到。以上範例答案描述了參加婚禮遲到的經驗，本題答案中部分所使用的字，跟其他題的答案相比顯得較不正式，但這不會對整體得分造成負面影響。第三點用到了許多動作動詞，是這段經歷的主要重點。第四點描述了答題者及朋友的感受與反應。

Part 3 Questions 第三部分 問題

Values 價值觀

🔊 9-16

01 What do you think makes a person successful?

你認為，什麼能造就一個人的成功？

Strategy

Success is related to a person's values or what they view as important in life. Personal values are greatly influenced by culture, beliefs, and family background. Therefore, answers to questions related to this topic vary widely.

策略

一個人的價值觀，或他認為生命中重要的事，和成功息息相關。一個人的價值觀會大幅受到文化、信仰及家庭背景所影響。因此類似於這種主題的問題，有非常多樣的答案。

A

❶ I think that a person can measure their success by what they accomplish, how they feel about what they accomplish, and their relationships with others.

❷ A person can lead a normal life with a family and a job and be considered a success. For example, I think that if a person has a good relationship with their marriage partner, raises responsible children, and is financially stable, they are successful. A person doesn't need to have a lot of money or a high-powered career to feel a sense of satisfaction. Contentment can come from simple things in life.

❸ Being content with your accomplishments and doing your best in any endeavour in life

❶ 我認為一個人的成功，可以透過其成就、對自己成就的感受，以及與他人的人際關係來衡量。

❷ 一個擁有家庭和工作，過著平凡生活的人，也可以被視作是成功的人。舉例來說，如果一個人跟配偶關係良好，養育出認真負責的孩子，且有穩定的財務基礎，那我認為這個人就算成功。一個人不必坐擁財富、登上位高權重的職位來獲得滿足。即使只是生活中簡單的小事，也能帶來滿足感。

❸ 對自己的成就感到滿意，並且在生活中凡事都盡力而為，我

is what makes someone truly successful.

們就可以稱他是成功的人。

Analysis

The Sample Answer above mentions accomplishments and feelings of satisfaction and contentment to define success. This answer also uses several forms of the word 'success'. Forms of this word are commonly misused by non-native English speakers, so please note the grammar reminders.

分析

以上範例答案以成就感、滿足感等來定義一個人的成功。答案中使用了 success 一字及其不同形式的變化，非英文母語者常常誤用這個字，請參閱 Note 的文法提示（本課結尾處）。

9-17

02 Which do you think is more important: having a lot of money or enjoying your life?

你認為坐擁財富比較重要，還是享受人生比較重要？

Strategy

To answer this question, you could choose to discuss one side of this issue. Alternatively, if you feel that both sides are equally important, you could discuss them in a balanced way.

策略

回答這題時，可以選擇其中一個立場談論。或者，如果你覺得兩邊立場同樣重要，也可以對等談論兩者。

A

❶ Many people today feel that their main purpose in life is to earn as much money as they possibly can. I, however, do not agree with this viewpoint.

❷ I know a lot of people who prioritise earning money above all other things in their lives. As a result, they sacrifice a lot of more important things, such as their families, their health, and their happiness. If someone is always working or looking for new ways to make money, they likely do not have time for anything else. Living an enjoyable life by having many new experiences and

❶ 現在有很多人覺得，人一生中的主要目標，就是賺愈多錢愈好。然而我不認同這個觀點。

❷ 我認識很多人把賺錢視為生命的首要之務，他們因此犧牲了很多更重要的事，例如家庭、健康和快樂。如果一個人總是在工作，或是想方設法賺錢，可能就沒有時間做其他事了。體驗新事物、與許多人建立互動關係，過上愉快的生活，這比擁有許多錢更令人感到滿足。

cultivating relationships with many people is far more satisfying than having a lot of money.

❸ If someone wants to be truly happy, they need to start living life and not waste their time worrying about money. Money cannot buy happiness.

❸ 如果一個人想要真正感到快樂，就必須要開始認真生活，而不是浪費時間去擔心錢的事，因為金錢買不到快樂。

Analysis

The Sample Answer above uses contrasts to emphasise the personal opinion of the speaker and to add weight to the argument. The opening statement in point 1 first introduces the opposing viewpoint and then states the speaker's opinion. Point 2 begins with extreme examples of individuals making sacrifices to earn money. This is followed by the speaker's opinion of what gives true meaning in life. This answer structure can be used to help emphasize your viewpoint.

分析

以上範例答案透過比較兩邊立場，強調答題者的個人看法，為其論點增加份量。答題者在第一點的開頭句針對相反立場說明，接著闡述自己的看法。第二點以極端例子起頭，表示有人為了賺錢可犧牲一切。接著提出自己認為什麼對人生才是真正有意義。這樣的答題架構可以達到強調自己觀點的效果。

Time Management | 時間管理

🔊 9-18

01 Are you a punctual person?

你是個準時的人嗎？

Strategy

A punctual person is someone who is always on time and has a good grasp of the concept of time. They know how long something is going to take to finish and are aware of how much time is needed to reach a destination.

策略

一個準時的人，代表他總是守時，並且有良好的時間觀念。他們知道一件事要花多久的時間來完成，也明白抵達目的地要花多少時間。

A

❶ From a very young age, I was taught the importance of being on time, and so being punctual has become a part of my daily life.

❶ 我從很小開始就被教育準時的重要性，所以守時已經成為我日常生活中的一部分。

❷ Being punctual is a way of showing respect toward other people. I hate it when I have to wait for other people. On the rare occasions when I am a little late for an appointment, I am most concerned about the reaction of the person I am supposed to be meeting. In life, there are a lot of things that we have no control over, such as traffic and weather. Therefore, I always plan ahead in case of problems in these areas. For example, if I need to go somewhere and the weather looks bad, I leave a few minutes early so that I will not keep others waiting.

❷ 準時能展現出對他人的尊重，我最討厭要等別人。有時候如果我跟人有約，但我卻有點遲到，我會最擔心對方的反應。生活中有很多我們無法掌控的事情，例如交通及天氣，所以我總會提前為其做好準備，以免發生突發狀況。像是我如果要出門，而那天天氣不好，我就會提早幾分鐘出發，這樣才不用讓其他人等。

❸ In summary, I can say that being punctual is extremely important to me.

❸ 簡言之，我會說守時對我而言極為重要。

Analysis

The Sample Answer above discusses showing respect for others as a major reason for being on time. Specific examples are mentioned to show how punctuality has become an integral part of the speaker's daily life.

分析

以上範例答案講述了準時的主要原因，是為了向他人表示尊重，並提供實際例子，說明準時已經成為答題者日常生活中不可或缺的一部分。

Trying New Things | 嘗試新事物

9-19

01 Do you enjoy trying new things?

你喜歡嘗試新事物嗎？

Strategy

When answering this question, you could relate

策略

回答這題時，可以講述一段初次

a personal experience of the first time you tried a new hobby, such as diving or skateboarding. Then, you could discuss how you felt about this activity at the time.

嘗試新嗜好的親身經歷，例如潛水或滑板，並談談你當下嘗試該活動的感受。

A

❶ I am an adventurous person, so I am not afraid of trying new things.

❷ I had always wanted to try surfing, so one day, I watched some YouTube videos about the basics of surfing. After that, I went to the beach and rented a surfboard to give it a try. At first, I found it very challenging to stand up on the board, but after a while, I got better at it, and I had a very enjoyable time. A few weeks later, I tried it again with several friends. This is something of a habit of mine: I usually try something new the first time by myself, and then, if I am any good at it, I do it together with friends the next time.

❸ In summary, I am not afraid of having new experiences. I really enjoy trying new things.

❶ 我是一個熱愛冒險的人，所以我並不會害怕嘗試新事物。

❷ 我一直想要試試看衝浪，所以有一天，我在 YouTube 上面看了幾支基礎衝浪的影片。之後我就到海邊租了一塊衝浪板，並且試著衝浪了一下。起初我覺得很難在衝浪板上站立，但過了一陣子之後，我的狀況愈來愈好，那次經驗非常美好。幾週過後，我又再試了一次，這次我跟好幾個朋友一起去。這是我的一個習慣，我總是先自己試試看一些新事物，然後如果我變厲害了，我就會找朋友一起去。

❸ 簡言之，我不害怕新體驗，我非常享受嘗試新事物。

Analysis

After talking about their personality, the speaker uses surfing as an example of a new activity that they tried. The process of learning how to surf is then described.

分析

答題者先是談到自己的性格，接著以衝浪為例，表示自己喜歡嘗試新活動，再接著描述學習衝浪的過程。

Photographs | 照片

🔊 9-20

01 What do you think is the importance of photographs?

你認為照片的重要性是什麼？

Strategy

When answering this question, you could comment on photos that have had an impact on you. These could be photos that you have taken personally or those that you have seen somewhere.

策略

回答這題時，可以談談對你有影響的照片，可以是你自己拍的照片，也可以是你曾看過的照片。

❶ A photograph has the power to capture a moment in time and record history.

❷ This can be a part of your personal history, such as a vacation with your family. By taking photos, we can record happy memories or interesting things that happened in our lives. Furthermore, we can usually recall how we were feeling in that moment, even years later, when we look at the photo. A photograph can also record important events in the history of a nation. In history books, we can see photos such as those of the moon landing and the Berlin Wall coming down, to name just a couple of historic events that were captured on film.

❸ Having a camera in our phone gives us all the chance to play the role of a historian. We all can use this technology responsibly to teach the next generation about important events in our personal histories.

❶ 一張照片有捕捉瞬間及記錄歷史的力量。

❷ 這可以是你生活紀錄的一部分，例如與家人共度的假期。我們可以藉由拍照，記錄快樂的回憶或生活中的趣事。此外，看著那張照片，我們往往能回憶起照片中當下的感受，即使早已過了很多年。照片也可以記錄一個國家的重要歷史大事。我們在歷史書籍上都看過人類登月、柏林圍牆倒塌等照片，這些都是被底片捕捉下來的歷史事件。

❸ 手機裡的相機功能，讓我們都能有機會當歷史學家。我們可以好好善用這項科技，教育下一代影響我們的重要大事。

Analysis

The Sample Answer above discusses two ways in which photographs can be powerful. The first involves photos that we take of our own lives and their importance to us. The second concerns photos that have recorded important events in history. The answer then concludes with a thought regarding how we can use new camera technology wisely.

分析

以上範例答案以兩個不同層面，探討照片能夠很有力量。首先是我們在生活中會拍下來的照片，及其對我們的重要性；其次是記錄重要歷史事件的照片。最後以我們能如何聰明使用相機技術作結。

9-21

02 Why do you think people enjoy sharing photos on social media?

你覺得現在的人為什麼喜歡在社群媒體上分享照片？

Strategy

Discuss why this new trend is popular in modern society. Give examples to describe why people place great importance on using social media.

策略

談談現代社會的這項新趨勢為何如此受歡迎，舉出例子來說明人們為何會如此重視社群媒體。

A

❶ Unfortunately, for many people today, their online presence has become more important than who they are in the real world.

❷ Through the use of social media, people can give the impression that they live exciting or glamorous lives through photos and other content that they post. Also, on social media platforms, individuals can spread their ideas and influence the thinking of others. There are many young people today who have become so-called social media influencers; every few hours, these people post something for others to see, and as a result, they seem like very interesting and exciting

❶ 很遺憾，對現在的許多人來說，他們在網路上的存在，已經變得比現實世界的形象還要更加重要。

❷ 透過使用社群媒體，人們可以藉由他們所張貼的照片或其他內容，讓他人覺得自己過著精彩或光鮮亮麗的生活；人們還可以透過社群平台分享自己的想法、影響他人的思維。現今有許多年輕人成為了社群媒體上所謂的「網紅」，每隔幾小時就要張貼東西給其他人看，因此，他們看起來就像是很有意思或很有活力的人。然而在

people. However, in real life, they might lead rather ordinary lives or may not have very good social skills.

現實生活中，這些人可能過著相當平凡的生活，或是根本就缺乏良好的社交能力。

❸ I don't think there is anything wrong with using social media to share events in our lives with the people we know. However, we should be balanced so that our online personalities don't overshadow who we are in real life.

❸ 使用社群媒體與熟人分享自己生活的大小事，我不認為有錯。但我們要懂得適可而止，才不會讓網路上的自己，掩蓋掉了我們現實生活中的樣子。

Analysis

The Sample Answer above begins with some of the negative ways in which people overuse social media. The answer then contrasts the online world with the real world. The conclusion expresses the neutral view that there is nothing fundamentally wrong with social media if it is used in a balanced way.

分析

以上範例答案，先是提出了人們過度使用社群媒體的負面例子。接著比較了網路世界和現實世界的生活，最後則以中立論點作結，說明只要懂得適量使用社群媒體，那麼其本質並沒有任何問題。

The Media | 媒體

🔊 9-22

01 Do you think there are certain things that should not be reported on in the news?

你是否認為新聞不該報導某些事件？

Strategy

For this question, you could give examples of violent images or scandals involving celebrities, for example, and explain how such reporting may negatively affect some people.

策略

回答這題時，可以舉暴力畫面及名人醜聞為例，並說明其對某些人所造成的負面影響。

❶ I think that too many news stories focus on the lives of famous people.

❷ Today, there are a lot of very important issues facing society, such as climate change, health, and personal safety, just to mention a few. If the news reported on these things, it would have real educational value. However, so much time during an average news broadcast is taken up with celebrity gossip. This really is a waste of time and distracts people from more important stories. Oftentimes, my co-workers can be overheard talking about movie stars who are getting divorced, but if you were to ask them about a natural disaster somewhere in the world, they wouldn't know what you were talking about.

❸ I don't think we need to hear about every detail of famous people's lives in the news.

❶ 我想有太多新聞聚焦在報導名人的生活。

❷ 現今有許多攸關社會的重要議題，舉幾個例子的話，如氣候變遷、健康及個人安全。新聞若報導這些議題，會具有實質教育意義。然而一般新聞都花很多時間在報導名人八卦上，這真的是浪費時間，也分散了人們對於重要議題的注意力。我常常聽到同事在討論哪位影星離婚了，但你要是問他們世界上某地的自然災害，他們卻不知道你在說什麼。

❸ 我不認為我們有必要在新聞中了解名人生活的枝微末節。

Analysis

The inappropriate news content discussed in this Sample Answer is celebrity news. More important issues are mentioned to show how news reporting could be used more constructively instead of focusing so much on the lives of famous people.

分析

範例答案先提到名人新聞作為不恰當的新聞內容，然後提出更重要的新聞議題，表明新聞報導應該更具建設性，而不是過度聚焦在名人的生活上。

🔊 9-23

02 How do you think negative news reports can affect children?

你認為負面新聞對孩童如何造成影響？

Strategy

This question is similar to the previous one; however, in this answer, you should specifically

策略

此問題與上一題類似，不過在回答這題時，要特別聚焦在新聞對

focus on how children may be negatively affected by the news.

孩童會造成何種負面影響。

A

❶ I think that children can be traumatised by violent or disturbing images seen on the news.

❶ 我想孩童若看見新聞上的暴力或使人不舒服的影像，會受到創傷。

❷ Images of things like dead bodies and blood are inappropriate for young children to view. Very young children may have nightmares or become overly concerned that the things they see in the news may happen to them personally. I think that before a news story shows graphic or disturbing content, the news anchor should give a warning. This way, parents could have the chance to change the channel or prevent their children from seeing such things.

❷ 含有屍體、血跡的畫面並不適合幼童觀看。非常年幼的孩子可能會因此做噩夢，或是極度害怕自己會遇到那些在新聞中所目睹的事件。我認為新聞報導在播放血腥暴力或令人不安的內容之前，主播應該要給予警告。這樣父母就有機會轉台，或是避免他們的孩子看見這些畫面。

❸ Children are highly impressionable, so they need to be protected from exposure to disturbing images.

❸ 孩童格外容易受到影響，所以他們必須受到保護，避免接觸到令人不安的影像。

Analysis

The Sample Answer above uses specific vocabulary to describe the extent to which negative images can affect children. These vocabulary items include 'traumatised', 'disturbing', and 'graphic'. After the potential harmful effects on children are commented on, a suggestion is given regarding how children can be protected from seeing negative images things.

分析

以上範例答案使用了特定字彙，描述有害影像對兒童所造成的影響，這些字彙包括 traumatised（創傷的）、disturbing（令人不安的）和 graphic（血腥暴力的）。談論完這些畫面對兒童的潛在負面影響後，答題者接著提供了保護兒童不看見這些有害影像的建議做法。

Making Decisions | 做決定

🔊 9-24

What types of decisions do you think children should be allowed to make for themselves? What about teenagers?

你認為孩童應該被允許可做哪些決定？那青少年呢？

Strategy

For this question, try to give examples of what you think are appropriate decisions for young children and teenagers to make on their own.

策略

針對這題，試著舉例說明你認為幼童和青少年適合做哪些決定。

A

❶ I think that as a child is growing up, their parents should gradually allow them to make more and more age appropriate decisions.

❶ 我認為孩子在長大的同時，家長應該要漸漸允許孩子做出符合他們年紀的決定。

❷ For instance, a young child could be allowed to pick out a toy or a snack that they would like to eat. Later on, they could be allowed to choose the colour of their clothing. Teenagers should be given the opportunity to make decisions that will affect their short-term or even some long-term goals. For example, they should be permitted to choose school subjects that they want to study, as such decisions are related to their interests. Eventually, older teenagers should be allowed to select their academic major because this is related to what they may do for work in the future.

❷ 舉例來說，可以允許幼童自己挑選玩具或是決定想吃的點心；接下來，可以讓他們選擇想穿的衣服顏色。而青少年，應該要有機會決定短期內會影響到他們的事，甚至是自己決定一些長遠目標。像是選擇想要學習的科目，因為這跟他們的興趣有關。最後，年紀再大點的青少年，應該要可以自己選擇主修科系，因為這關係到他們未來要從事的職涯。

❸ Parents should gradually give their children more freedom. If a child demonstrates that they are responsible and can make good

❸ 家長應該要逐漸給予孩子自由。如果孩子有責任感，且能做出好決定，家長就應該漸漸

decisions, parents should give them more and more opportunities to make choices for themselves.

給他們更多機會為自己做決定。

Analysis

Examples of age-appropriate decisions are given in this Sample Answer. Parents' gradual granting of freedoms to their children is seen in these examples. For a child, choices can start off very simple. Later, they can become more directly related to the child's future, as shown in the examples of decisions that teenagers can make.

分析

範例答案舉出一些符合該年紀小孩可以做的決定，也在例子中表達出父母可逐步給予孩子自由。以小孩來說，可以從最簡單的決定開始，然後才是可能會關係到小孩未來的決定，例如答案中提到的青少年可以自己做決定的例子。

9-25

Q02 Why do you think some people are better at making decisions than others?

為何有些人比他人更擅長做決定？

Strategy

We all know people who are good at making decisions and people who are not. You can comment on what you have observed about these two types of individuals and what makes them able to make wise decisions or not.

策略

我們都知道有人擅長做決定，也人有不擅長。你可以談談自己對這兩種人的觀察，以及是什麼讓他們得以或無法做出明智決定。

A

❶ I think that decision-making ability depends a lot on a person's personality and life experience.

❷ Some people are very decisive because they have experienced a lot of things in life. Perhaps they have had many different jobs or have lived in several countries. These types of experiences can enable some people to analyse situations and to be

❶ 我想做決定的能力，跟一個人的個性和生活經驗有很大的關係。

❷ 有些人非常果斷，因為他們的人生經歷過許多事情。他們也許從事過各式各樣的工作，或是在幾個國家住過。這種經驗能讓一些人有能力去分析情況，並果斷做出決定。還有人

very decisive. Other people are very goal oriented, so they are able to determine very quickly how a certain decision may affect their life and what they want to accomplish. They can look at the big picture and determine how a decision they make now will affect them later on in life.

特別以目標為導向，所以他們能夠快速判斷一個決定是否會影響到他們的生活，以及他們想要達成的目標。他們具有遠見，能夠判斷自己現在做的決定，會如何影響之後的人生。

❸ All these traits can make a person very confident when making decisions.

❸ 這些特質，都會讓一個人在做決定時特別有自信。

Analysis

This Sample Answer focuses on 2 important factors that allow individuals to make good decisions. They are personality and life experience. An explanation of these 2 factors is given showing how these affect people's ability to make decisions.

分析

範例答案聚焦在兩個能讓人做出好決定的重要因素，那就是個性和人生經驗，並接著說明這兩個因素如何影響了人們做決定的能力。

Note: Grammar

word 單字	form 詞性	Example 例句
success 成功	noun 名詞	The success of the project earned us a lot of money. 這項計畫的成功讓我們賺進大把鈔票。
succeed 成功	verb 動詞	I hope you succeed in your mission. 希望你的任務能成功。
successful 成功的	adjective 形容詞	Apple is a very successful company. Apple 是一間非常成功的公司。
successfully 成功地	adverb 副詞	The team successfully completed the assignment. 團隊成功完成了任務。

Additional Tips and Resources 補充技巧及資料

Spoken English Versus Written English 口說英文 vs. 寫作英文

One of the biggest differences between spoken and written English is the use of contractions. In IELTS essay writing, we usually do not use contractions because we want to sound more formal. However, in the speaking part of the test, using contractions enables you to sound more natural or conversational.

口說及寫作英文最大的差異在於縮寫形式的使用。在雅思的寫作測驗中，為了讓語氣看起來較正式，通常不用縮寫形式。而在口說測驗中，則可以使用縮寫形式，如此能讓你聽起來更加自然或口語。

Common contractions in English:

常見英文縮寫形式：

縮寫	全寫
aren't	are not
can't	cannot
couldn't	could not
didn't	did not
doesn't	does not
don't	do not
hadn't	had not
hasn't	has not
haven't	have not
isn't	is not
mustn't	must not
weren't	were not
won't	will not

縮寫	全寫
wouldn't	would not
let's	let us
I'm	I am
I've	I have
I'd	I had
	I would
I'll	I will
	I shall
you're	you are
you've	you have
you'd	you had
	you would

縮寫	全寫
you'll	you will you shall
he's	he is he has
he'd	he had he would
he'll	he will he shall
she's	she is she has
she'd	she had she would
she'll	she will she shall
they're	they are
they've	they have
they'll	they will they shall
we're	we are
we've	we have

縮寫	全寫
we'd	we had we would
that's	that is that has
there's	there is there has
what's	what is what has
what're	what are
what've	what have
what'll	what will what shall
who's	who is
who've	who have
who'd	who had who would
who'll	who will who shall
where's	where is

國家圖書館出版品預行編目 (CIP) 資料

IELTS 雅思口說最後 9 堂課／Joshua Morgandale 作；留嘉伶譯.
-- 初版. -- 臺北市：眾文圖書股份有限公司, 2023.08 面；公分
ISBN 978-957-532-636-4（平裝） 1. CST：國際英語語文測試系統 2. CST：考試指南
805.189 112009039

IE011

IELTS 雅思口說最後 9 堂課

定價 580 元
2023 年 8 月 初版一刷

作者 Joshua Morgandale
譯者 留嘉伶
英文校閱 Mark Darvill
責任編輯 蔡若楹

總編輯 陳瑠琍
主編 黃炯睿
資深編輯 顏秀竹
編輯 黃婉瑩・蔡若楹・范榮約
美術設計 嚴國綸
行銷企劃 李皖萍・楊詩韻
發行人 陳淑敏
發行所 眾文圖書股份有限公司
台北市 10088 羅斯福路三段 100 號 12 樓之 2
網路書店 www.jwbooks.com.tw
電話 02-2311-8168
傳真 02-2311-9683
郵政劃撥 01048805

ISBN 978-957-532-636-4
Printed in Taiwan